"YOU DID IT," MARION TOLD HOLLIS. "YOU BLINDED OUR SON!"

Hollis said nothing. He turned away.

"You!" Marion screamed.

Hollis kneeled beside Marion and put his hand over hers. She pulled away. "You're emotionally drained," he said. "You don't know what you're saying."

"I think that she does," Mary said.

Hollis whirled. "Stay out of this, Mary. Stay out of it."

"Why? Why should I? I'm part of this family, I am sorry to say. I have its curse, too."

He stepped to her, drew back his hand, and slapped her sharply on the cheek. Mary gasped, her eyes flaring, and tried to strike back, but he had her hands and held them tightly together. Their eyes met, a mutual blaze of anger, perhaps even of hate, and then he let go. He turned away, sighing.

"You did it," Marion said. "You did it to Andrew with your pushing and your manipulation . . ."

She tried to get up, to lash out at him, to strike him down as he stood there. But she did not have the strength to rise. . . .

THE
KINGMAKERS
A Novel

ARELO
SEDERBERG

BANTAM BOOKS
TORONTO · NEW YORK · LONDON · SYDNEY · AUCKLAND

THE KINGMAKERS
A Bantam Book / December 1984

Dedicated to the memory of Reece Halsey

THE
KINGMAKERS

PROLOGUE

MITCH EVERS OPENED the rear door and entered the dark, fantastic world of the Collingsworth gun room. He stood spellbound. He shook a Camel from a crumpled pack, lit it, gushed smoke from his nostrils, and mumbled, "Well, I'll be go to hell." He thought he'd seen it all in his thirty years as a newspaper reporter, but this beat most of it. He'd heard about the gun room, yet had been unable to fully imagine it as it was. And he felt like a stranger here, an intruder to this space, at once struck by its power and its dementia; this was not his family, but the family that had employed him, used him, and he was here now in partial judgment of its patriarch. Seeking what? Truth? He did not really know. It was almost over now, his obsessive need to know about the Collingsworths, to solve the riddle. What would occur here this morning probably would end it, burn it from his mind and his body, from his soul. So he would not leave. Not just before the end of it. He stood motionless, smoking. Again he said, "I'll be go to hell."

He glanced at his watch. It was just past two A.M. A smell of must, of decay, drifted to his nostrils. He thought he heard the sound of trickling water; from above, from a room in Green Manor, came a faint sound like the hesitant tinkle of piano keys. But, no; it was silent here. His mind was playing tricks. Yet he did sense another presence in the room, ahead of him at its end.

"Anyone here?" he asked.

There was no response. Mitch Evers waited, peering through the semidarkness. He heard the scraping of a chair on the floor in the darkness ahead of him. Then white light flashed throughout, running to full illumination, a fluorescent lightning that at first hurt his eyes. He blinked. The room was about a hundred yards long and fifty yards wide. It had paneled walls and a hardwood floor. It was an extraordinary clutter of weapons. There were pistols, rifles, shotguns,

1

machine guns, lances, bows and crossbows, swords and spears;
there were grenades, cannons, flamethrowers, bazookas, mor-
tars. Some were tagged in compartments and arranged neatly
on green-carpeted tables. Others were scattered carelessly on
the floor. Weapons lined all the walls, displayed on iron pegs,
like the paraphernalia at a museum. It was both splendid and
terrible.

A muffled laugh sounded across the room. "Welcome to the
Inner Sanctum," said a voice. "I am Andrew, your host. How
do you like the place?"

"Not much," Mitch Evers replied, stepping forward. "I
don't think I'm all that comfortable here."

"It might grow on you, down here," the other said. "It
grew on me."

Now Mitch saw him. Andrew Collingsworth. He stood at
the far end of the room, a broad-shouldered figure in a dark
suit, his eyes hidden in shadows. He had been the man who
had it all—looks and drive and brains and bloodline. Now
Mitch felt only pity for him. He walked slowly toward him,
fumbling for another Camel. It was the last of the pack.

"We're all here now," Andrew said.

Mitch lit the Camel. "You're sure you want to go through
with this?"

"There is no other way."

"Then let's get on with it."

"I admit to slight fear."

"Then call it off."

"No," Andrew said. His eyes remained hidden in shadow,
as if he wore a mask that revealed only his jaw and neck. "I'll
bring him down. The king. Will he look at me and say 'Et tu,
Brute?'"

Yes, Mitch thought. *We will now judge a king.* If not king,
certainly a kingmaker. Hollis Collingsworth. At the newspaper he owned, he was still known as the Gray Fox; if he were
king, his son, Andrew, had been prince. It was entirely
possible, Mitch reflected to himself, that Andrew could have
made it all the way to the Oval Office. His father had seen it
that way, and his father was seldom wrong. They were
assembling here in the basement of the king's mansion, his
son and his illegitimate son, his wife and daughter and
mistress, and the enemies he had created, finding in each
other a courage they could not show individually to judge the
man they hated or loved. They were here like ghosts, seeking

truth or satisfaction or vengeance. Mitch recalled a Chinese
saying: *He who seeks vengeance digs two graves*.

Andrew Collingsworth had disappeared into the shadows
behind him, a silent master of the darkness. At the head of
the room a desk had been placed; on both sides of it stood
two rows of austere, hard-backed chairs. It was a courtroom.
Mitch felt the need for another Camel. Had he brought an
extra pack? He fumbled in his jacket pockets and produced
one, sighing with relief. The silence was absolute again, a
silence even more profound against the backdrop of thousands of instruments of noisy destruction. Mitch found himself gazing at two portraits on the wall directly in front of
him, above the desk and the bleak rows of judgment chairs.

One was of a man on a horse. He sat defiantly in the
saddle, his powerful legs in chaps clinging to the black
stallion, bent forward, so much a part of the animal that it
was difficult to imagine man and beast separated. The man's
hat and gloves were black. On his boots were sharp silver
spurs, their rowels glistening like knives. Above him, the sky
seemed to be darkening almost visibly, as if the scene even
now were being created by the strokes of the artist. It was a
portrait of Thomas Collingsworth, Andrew's grandfather and
the founder of the newspaper, television, and motion-picture
empire called Collingsworth Communications. The second
painting was of Hollis Collingsworth. He looked almost be-
nign, seated behind a rolltop desk in his office at the Los
Angeles *Bulletin-News*. Staring at the portraits, Mitch felt the
past creeping into the present. He felt chilled.

Behind him, the door creaked open. Mitch whirled. Hollis
Collingsworth had entered the gun room, flanked by two
men. One was Andrew. Mitch heard other sounds from the
front of the room. He turned slowly. Several persons he
recognized walked toward him. Mitch felt a twinge of amusement, even foolishness. There was no turning back now. The
pawns had come to judge their king. He looked at the
portraits and again the present seemed unreal. The man on
the horse, the first generation Collingsworth, watched them
like a dread deity, as though he were there to judge them all.
But where was the other son, the illegitimate son, the one
among them who sought the truth most relentlessly? For
Peter Russell sought not only to solve the riddle of his
parentage, but also the solution to a murder. Mitch looked
about anxiously. Then Peter Russell appeared, coolly joining

the mock jury. *Morning, Harvard,* Mitch thought, reaching for a Camel. *Now let's finish your quest.* In that moment he knew why he'd come here this morning. It was for Peter, for the illegitimate son, the real seeker of the truth.

Mitch could not take his eyes off the portrait of the man on the horse. It had all started with him, decades ago, when Thomas Collingsworth had arrived in California, a man-child who sought to escape death. This day had begun on that day; all time emanated from then in great successive waves to now. Mitch knew that past. He saw it. It was as real as the white lights that glistened on the array of weapons deep in this gun room under the magnificence of the Collingsworth Green Manor.

PART 1

Thomas Collingsworth

1.

HIS FIRST WORK for pay was at the Los Angeles Santa Fe railway yard, where he unloaded boxcars for ten cents an hour. He was familiar with railroads. He'd listened to the clank-clank of steel wheels on tracks all the way from New Jersey, slung like a slab of meat on the rods or crouched in cars with cattle, sleeping on their scarce straw. He had a serious skin rash, which might have saved his life, since it discouraged those who wanted to get near him. He coughed a lot, too; that also kept them at a distance. Sometimes he coughed up blood.

"You ain't long for the world," said a bum, reeling red-eyed from an empty freight car. "Why bother beatin' it across the country when you know you ain't gonna last?"

The bum threw back his head and laughed, revealing crooked, yellowed teeth. Thomas Collingsworth ignored him. He would not die. He'd come from death, New Jersey, where his family had settled and died. He didn't know his age; he wasn't sure of the year. But he knew he was alive. And he had learned to do things. He could read. He could add figures.

In that rail yard he made his first enemy, a Pole called Dominick, and also his first friend, a big man called Swede. But they were the same to him, friend or enemy.

The cough was painful, yet he was the best worker in the yard; getting paid for work was a delicious and head-spinning experience. Thomas bought shoes and a shirt when he got his first pay. The air out here was warm and clean, and he didn't notice that his cough had lessened until Swede pointed it out to him.

"I come here from Minnesota," Swede said. "In three week, the cough go. I tink it be the air."

"My whole family seemed to cough to death," Thomas said. "Ma coughed up her gut in blood. So I left. Grabbed a freight."

They lived in a flophouse near the tracks. The men brought

in whores, but Swede ignored women. He had a wife i Minnesota who'd join him when he'd saved enough mone and he didn't want to greet her a diseased man. He wanted family. He saved his money in gold sacks carried around h neck.

One day the Pole, Dominick, seized Thomas and pinne him down on the tracks. "Gonna kill you, boy," he said "Gonna kill you now." The Pole's hold was like iron. Me made a circle around them, urging Dominick on. Then th Pole loosened his grip, as Swede literally lifted him from the ground and hurled him against a boxcar. Dominick got up, glared, and ran.

"Why did he want to kill me?" Thomas asked.

"You work too hard. You showed him up."

When Swede got his legacy from his father in the Old Country, he quit his job and moved out of the flophouse. He said he was going to the country.

"But I thought it was all city here," Thomas said.

Swede laughed. He had a new hat. The gold sacks bulged under his coat. "Come with me, I show you."

It became an adventure. They took the Cahuenga Valley stage, a four-wheeled, open-windowed vehicle pulled by six spirited horses. There were ten passengers, including a young woman in a silk dress and a pink, Sunday-outing bonnet. Two Mexicans, both half-drunk, guided the horses, one throwing pebbles, the other snapping them with the reins. They started off on the unpaved road at a gallop, sending thick streams of dust behind them, hitting ruts at breakneck speed, the Mexicans swearing loudly and expertly in Spanish and English. The pink-bonneted woman gasped and hung on, her face turning white. The other passengers sat in tight-knuckled terror.

Swede threw his head back and laughed, and Thomas found himself enjoying it. Roadrunners scattered in front of them and hundreds of ground squirrels darted to their bur rows in the dry open fields on both sides. He had a feeling that if he lived through this trip, something important would come of it. And he knew he would live through it. He had not survived this long only to perish in a stage acciden caused by drunken Mexicans.

There was a small station at the end of the line where was possible to rent bicycles to ride up the Cahuenga Pas but Swede said he preferred to walk. The curved unpav

ath led upward, bordered by barron hills Swede said a few
miles ahead they would come to a point where they could
overlook the entire valley. He had an ad from the *Times* that
proclaimed the sale of land at bargain prices. Swede had a
plan. To be complete, he said, a man had to have a home,
some land, a good wife, and a family.

"Why a family?" asked Thomas.

Swede didn't answer right away. Finally he said: "For
immortality. When you die, the family goes on. This is
especially true of sons."

To Thomas Collingsworth it seemed a meaningless reply.
Yet Swede certainly could be right about the importance of
owning land. The plant and railroad owners, those who
strutted in suits and straw hats with flower-delicate women
on their arms, no doubt were landowners.

When he saw the valley, full with crops and orchards, he
gasped with wonderment. There were no rocky, stubborn
hills here, no forests to clear. The land was ripe and flat and
ready for the taking. Swede said he had a hundred acres, paid
for in cash, in gold.

"How much land will three thousand dollars get?" Thomas
asked.

"I suppose you have three thousand dollars in your pocket?"

"No. But that's my goal."

"You go for a mortgage, three thousand dollars will get very
much."

"Why didn't you take a mortgage?"

"They can foreclose if you have a mortgage," Swede said. "I
deal in cash."

It had been an important day, for it gave Thomas a goal. It
was the start of his plan, a plan unlike Swede's. Before, for
Thomas Collingsworth, it had been merely survival; now it
would be development and growth. He saw the future. He
would not be held back, as Swede no doubt would be, by
concern for family or fear of debt. He would acquire. There
must be ranches in the valley that needed help. He would
find them. The system favored those who owned. He would
own. He would grow. Here, the future was easy to see. The
skin rash had gone away. So had the cough.

2.

THE LANDOWNER IN the valley who was said to be the smartest person there was Colonel William C. Dickerson, a big man in the country as well as the city. He had commanded a division in the Civil War. He spoke Spanish fluently and he was said to be unafraid of debt. Although he was a Methodist, he'd been a factor in the establishment of a Catholic church in the valley. He raised apricots, oranges, tomatoes, and lettuce and held controlling interest in a tomato-processing plant that employed three hundred at harvest times. Actually he lived in the city, where he owned a daily newspaper and was a partner in a bank, coming to the valley in a private stage only on weekends. He stayed in a two-story house under the shadows of oaks. A foreman handled the crops on weekdays. When Thomas Collingsworth applied for a job as a picker, the foreman said:

"Ye look a little pale. Do ye think ye kin keep up?"

"I've been sick, but I'm all right now."

"Well, awright, I'll try ye out."

He was quartered in a dirty shack with several Mexicans. There was one white man there, a picker named Tom Thornton, who had a cracked, dry leather face and a gray beard like tangled wire. He was a news carrier and seemed to know everything, past and present. Speaking in a singsong manner, no doubt picked up from the Mexicans, he liked to tell stories. He told about the Chinese massacre of '71, at a place called Nigger Alley. The warring Tongs had wounded a policeman and killed a rancher who'd gone to the policeman's aid, and the crowd had moved in on the Chinese, catching them one at a time and hanging them from gate beams at a corral. Thornton described it as if he'd been there, capturing in a language of blood and thunder the tramping boots of the mob, the echoing gunshots, and the hapless Chinese dangling from nails like sides of beef. Thomas listened. They passed a bottle of strong, homemade whiskey back and forth.

"It shows ya only one thing," Thornton said. "It don't pa·

to be different. Them Chinas, they was strung up only because they was Chinamen. People are suspicious of somethin' different."

"Tell me about Colonel Dickerson."

"Well, he's a city man, no farmer. That's for sure."

"Have you ever spoken to him?"

Thornton nodded, taking a swig from the bottle. "I'll tell ya somethin'. Never eat with no Mexican."

"Why?"

"Wal, back a-ways a Mexican invited me to a cookout over near Calabasas. He said it was rabbit. It was good. But when I was leavin', I saw a big pile of catskins there."

Thornton threw back his head, laughing.

"Tell me about California," Thomas said.

"Ya want truth or a story?"

"Tell me a true story."

"Wal, here's somethin' ya didn't know about California, about Los Angeles. It was the first city that got electric light, back in '82. Ladies said it would give 'em pimples, electric light."

"But it helped the city grow."

"It made the rich richer. They's a lotta rich in this place, I'll tell ya that."

"How did they get rich?"

"On land, mostly."

"Where do they live?"

"Some of 'em like hotel livin'. The Bellevue Towers or the Belmont. Or the Van Nuys, on Main. McKinley stayed there once. They was white carnations all over. I'll tell ya somethin'. This city's big, but it ain't gonna get much bigger."

"Why?"

"Water. They ain't gonna be enough water."

"Then we must get the water," Thomas said.

Another of his information suppliers was a fat Mexican woman named Mary Jurado, a picker who was available free to almost any man interested in her. The workers said she got pregnant every summer and returned to Mexico to deposit her babies. One night Thomas saw her bathing in an irrigation pond. Later she came to his shack, removed her clothes, and lay beside him in his bed, ignoring the snores of Thornton and the Mexicans. She smelled of musky earth. He had his first climax in her hands and, shortly thereafter, his second deeply within her.

"You never done it before," she said.

"No."

"Good. I show you. Good."

She came to him almost every night. She called him her *criatura de cuna* and, in the next breath, her lover man. He learned more than sex from her. She knew what was going on for miles around and she liked to talk about it. Her English was good.

"There's going to be something happening," she said.

"What do you mean?"

"The weather. It is too hot."

"What is going to happen?"

"Now there is a job for each worker. Soon more workers will come. There will be three workers for each job. The union makes promises—"

"What union?"

"Industrial Workers." She spat. "Communists."

He had heard of the Communists. "Troublemakers," he said.

"I saw them show the body of a boy," Mary said. "The boy had been killed by the police when there was unrest, when there were two thousand pickers for five hundred jobs. The union took the boy's body and made speeches over it."

She seemed affected by the story and wiped a tear from her cheek, a tear for the dead boy used by the Communists. It seemed foolish. The boy was dead. Nothing could change that.

"You said something would happen?" he asked.

"The workers will strike. Soon."

"Are you sure? Find out more. Then tell me."

"You love me? Your Mary?"

"Yes."

"I'll take your baby to Mexico."

"All right," he said.

It was full season for the tomato crop. The heat was dry, yet relentless, causing undulating waves to rise from the earth. In the night Mary came to him, telling him the workers would strike the next day. She would say no more. The smell of her body was like heady wine; she held him with her strong, fleshy legs, writhing under him. Later she wept.

"My man-child," she said. "I would die for him."

It was a new stage for him, important in his life's plan. After Mary left, he walked to Colonel Dickerson's house, deciding upon a bold approach. He knocked loudly on the door. A Negro in a white suit materialized.

"I want to see the colonel," Thomas said.

"Go round back," the Negro said. "Wait there."

"No. I will not go to the back."

"Joseph, who *is* it?" asked a girl's voice. She peered out, a young girl in riding slacks. "Who *is* he?" she said to the Negro.

"Doan know. He say he want to see the colonel."

"Don't do that," the girl told Thomas.

"Do what?"

"Stand with your hands in your back pockets. It's slovenly."

"Just tell me where the colonel is."

"My, you're a dirty little one, aren't you?" the girl said, looking him over. "Perhaps we shall take you in and clean you up. I think I have taken a dislike to you, however."

A pipe-smoking man with a small beard appeared behind the girl. "Who is it you dislike this time, Elizabeth?" he asked.

"He's come for a job. He won't go to the back door."

"I haven't come for a job. I have a job."

"Then why have you come?" the pipe-smoking man asked.

"To talk to you."

"Go around to the back. I will talk to you there."

Swallowing his pride, he did as he was told, hating the snickering Negro. They talked for fifteen minutes. The colonel did not let him in.

He would never again go back to the fields. Mary's information proved accurate and the colonel rewarded Thomas Collingsworth with a job in the canning plant after taking action to abort the strike. He had a bed in the basement. And he'd discovered something else. Colonel Dickerson had a good library, books bound in leather with gold-edged pages, and he was willing to lend them. Thomas did not merely read the books; he absorbed them, memorizing long passages. He read volumes on grammar, mechanics, agricultural procedures, finance and banking, mathematics and science. He ignored history, philosophy, and literature. He did the reading at night under candlelight and on Sundays outside under a big elm. One Sunday he saw Elizabeth, in a sun hat, coming toward him. She had three books for him.

"How can you read them?" she said. "They're so *boring*."

"I don't find them boring."

"How old are you?"

"Twenty."

"You're not that old."

"Then I'm not."

"I've heard about you, you and that Mexican . . . woman." She turned away, adjusting her bonnet. She was a pretty girl, he decided, with maturing hips and breasts, but she was spoiled beyond rescue. A thousand workers slaved for her bonnets, her education, her homes. "I shall go now," she said.

"Thanks for bringing the books."

He had not seen nor thought of Mary for some time; he was now above her and no longer needed her. He was on his own path. One Saturday afternoon Colonel Dickerson asked him about that path.

"What is your ambition?"

Thomas shrugged. He was lying back on his cot, a book on his stomach. "To learn," he said.

"And then?"

"I don't know."

"I suspect you do. I suspect you do not make a move without considering your future." The colonel snorted smoke. "I want to say something to you. You are not to talk to Elizabeth again."

"You came here to tell me that?"

"Yes. Exactly that. You are still a boy, yet you have the experience of a man. She is a child." The colonel walked square-shouldered to the door, a splendid military stride, a tall figure of a proud man. "If you do as I say," he said, turning, "you will prosper. If you do not, I will destroy you."

Mary Jurado came to him that evening, giving him sex with a hot passion that far exceeded his. When they had calmed, she lay clinging wetly to him.

"You are not one of us now," she said.

"No."

"Come to Mexico with me."

"Mexico? Are you a loco woman?"

"There is good land in Mexico."

"This land is better," he said. "It needs only water to be the best."

In the morning he heard a commotion by one of the
irrigation ditches. He pushed through the crowd and could
see the limp hand of a woman floating in the water. Waterbugs
hurried around it. He touched the hand. A red towel covered the head of the dead woman. He removed the towel and
gazed at Mary Jurado's face, serene and unimpassioned in
death.

3.

HE HAD HIS three thousand dollars within four years,
making most of it during the one-month harvest of the third
year. He'd become foreman of the canning plant and had
convinced Colonel Dickerson to set aside a portion of the
profits for investment. Capacity and profits doubled. The
plant's board of directors awarded Thomas Collingsworth a
small percentage of the profits and the colonel allowed him to
sharecrop some of his land. Thomas had grown a great deal
physically. He was now a broad-shouldered six-footer with a
hard body and strong, quick arms that could bend an iron
bar. But he'd grown even more in mind. He knew every lever
and pulley and strap and cog and wheel in the plant, how
they interacted and interconnected to produce results. He
absorbed local and national news from the newspapers the
colonel brought him each weekend. He continued to devour
the books.

He knew the colonel did not quite trust him, due to his
relentless ambition, but he also knew the colonel was vulnerable. Dickerson was paying more attention to his interests in
the city, his newspaper and bank, and less to agriculture. He
needed a good man at the plant. And then there was Elizabeth.
The colonel adored her to the point of distraction and seemed
obsessed with fear that she would someday fall into the arms
of the dirty gypsy boy now transformed into a strong, thinking man with a full mustache and dark wavy hair.

"I think I might live to regret the day I let you in my
house," he said one Saturday afternoon.

"As I remember it, I wasn't exactly let in."

"I may regret that even more."

"Don't worry about it. My only interest is in doing a good job here and getting paid right for it."

Occasionally Elizabeth came to the ranch with her father and Thomas would see her strolling in the walnut tree grove accompanied by two Irish wolfhounds. The sight of her stirred his blood. She had become a woman of ravishing beauty who walked with trained grace, her proud chin up. He avoided contact with her; he was not yet ready. His sexual activities were limited to occasional liaisons with Mexican women who came to pick the crops and with whores in the city, whom he visited frequently, borrowing a horse and buggy from the colonel.

By now he had a life plan and a fully developed view of how the system worked. It was not too different from a slave system. Above were the owners; below were the slaves. He was amazed at how easy it was to acquire property; you could control it with as little as ten percent down. With his three thousand dollars and another three thousand dollars borrowed from the colonel's bank, he already controlled hundreds of acres in the valley. He then used the land as collateral for a loan to buy more land. It could be worked almost to infinity. The crops were continually good and land prices were rising. The more land you owned, the more willing were banks to do business with you. The colonel was a cautious businessman and a bad farmer. He had loans but most of his land was owned in full. That limited his expansion. It showed fear—fear of a crop failure, inadequate water, or labor troubles. Thomas Collingsworth had no such fears. If he lost, he could start over.

Most of the ranch owners, he had discovered, were cautious men. As a result, they would always remain small ranchers. Like the Swede. Thomas saw him during harvests, when the crops were brought to the plant. Swede said his wife had joined him and they'd had the initial issue of the planned family. Swede owned all of his land. His crops were good, but he was not expanding; therefore he was stupid. He did all of his own work. He didn't know how to keep books—nor, apparently, did his yellow-haired wife. They were owners but they acted like the Mexican slaves, those brainless and ambitionless drones who were content with their small pay, their outdoor, firelit dances, their pulpy red wine, their pointless crucifixes, beads, and papal crosses.

Thomas was now keeping the books for the colonel's agri-

ultural operations, working with a young accountant named
Lowenfelt, who had a shrewd, practical mind. Education was
his defense against the prejudices of the city. He'd earned his
accountancy degree at night school and was now studying law.
He had ambitions of going into business for himself, but he
said he couldn't get a loan because he was a Jew.

"I thought Jews were the lenders," Thomas said.

"Not in this city. They've yet to get established here."

"Maybe I could help you establish them." Thomas paused,
thinking. "If you could get a loan, what would you do?"

"Buy a newspaper. I've learned a lot about the business."

"How is the colonel's paper doing?"

"Well, he's got some problems, that I know. That daughter
costs him a mint. He's in a bank that could belly up and a bad
crop here would flatten him. The newspaper has labor troubles and is in a tough circulation war."

"Do you like him?"

"I'm his Jew," Lowenfelt said.

"His Jew who wants a piece of him?"

"I wouldn't do it because I don't have the money, but I
know how somebody could get a piece of him. Buy the
newsstands, then refuse to handle his paper. The unions
would be with you, I'll tell you that. You could dictate terms
to him."

"You surprise me, Lowenfelt."

"Well, I wouldn't do it, you understand."

"I don't think it's a good idea. There's too much risk."

"Well, it's just a thought. I wouldn't do it myself."

"Will you do one thing? Will you bring a message to the
colonel for me?"

"Sure. What?"

"I've accumulated quite a stretch of land out here, as you
know. But it's highly leveraged. I'm mortgaged to the hilt. I
couldn't stand one bad crop. So I'm thinking about pulling up
stakes, trying something else. Would you ask the colonel if
he's interested in buying my land?"

"I would think you'd be the last to want to sell."

"You don't know how squeezed I am."

"Well, I'll pass it on to the colonel, sure," Lowenfelt said.
He was back in two days with a message that the colonel
was interested in making a bid. Thomas smiled. "Tell the
colonel," he said, "that I've changed my mind."

That evening, under a crescent moon, Thomas Collingsworth

walked to the irrigation ditch where the body of Mary Jurac had been found. He kneeled and stirred the water with h fingers. He thought of the progress he'd made since he ha come to this valley. He controlled hundreds of acres of h own land, he had the run of the colonel's land, including th use of his servant Joseph for chauffeuring him around, an now he was quite certain of a new bonanza—water, a perma nent supply. He'd heard rumors of it before—even hints from the accountant Lowenfelt—strengthened by promoters i straw hats and suspenders who'd been sneaking around the valley lately, dickering for land and offering to buy mortgages He figured if anyone knew for sure it would be the newspa per lords, who would keep it quiet in fear of starting a lanc boom. So he'd tossed up a trial balloon, letting the colone know he might be willing to sell, and Dickerson had bitter like a hungry bass. It was additional evidence that water was coming.

Thomas stood up, his fists clenched, excitement running high in his body. In truth he liked Lowenfelt's newsstand idea and he planned to look into it. It could turn out to be the biggest coup he'd pulled. It could get him inside a newspa-per. He stood tall, feeling an overwhelming jubilance. Never again would he labor behind mules clearing impossible land, never again would he cough and sweat unloading potash from a boxcar, never again would he stoop-pick in a hot field. He had risen to the class of the owners. He would rise much higher. He felt strength and power in every fiber of his being.

The colonel had stopped visiting the valley on weekends, apparently satisfied with the profit reports, so Thomas took off some Sunday afternoons to jaunt around, driven by Joseph in a four-wheeled buggy. On one of the trips he saw Swede in the now-paved road ahead, holding up his hand. The buggy stopped. Swede came up to him.

"I see you have another new hat," Thomas said.

"This hat? It is not new."

"How is the family?"

"Still growing."

"Is it going well with you?"

Swede turned away. He turned back. "No, it doesn't go too well. My youngest daughter is sick. And the plant has cut prices paid to independent growers."

"There are other plants."

"They are too far away. Shipping costs make it unprofitable, as you well know."

"Do you want me to recommend we raise prices?"

"If the independents are to survive, that is essential."

"I'm afraid I can't help you. I could lie and say I'll recommend higher prices, but there's no reason to lie to you."

"No," Swede said. "We have never lied."

"How bad off are you?"

"I have medical bills I cannot pay."

"Go to a bank, get a mortgage on your land."

Swede's eyes were pleading. "I have taken a mortgage, against my deepest feelings. What I need is an unsecured loan."

"Well, I'm not a bank that lends money."

Swede gestured, his palms up. "I ask for old time's sake."

"I'm sorry." Thomas drew a thin cigar from his vest, lit it, and slowly blew a perfect smoke ring. Joseph watched in awe. As Swede turned to go, Thomas called out for him to wait.

Swede turned back. "Yah?" he said.

"How much is your mortgage?"

"Six thousand dollars."

"Who holds it?"

"Colonel Dickerson's bank."

"I'll take it off your hands if you give me a discount on it. I'll delay the interest payments until the harvest. But if you get behind when the payments are due, I'll have to treat you just like anyone else. Friendship is all right, but business is business."

"I understand."

"I hope you do. I mean what I say. I'll send a man over tomorrow with a written offer. There'll be a check for you so you can pay off the bank and some of those doctor bills."

Swede didn't seem too happy about the proposition, but he knew there was very little else he could do. "All right," he said.

"My best to the family."

Thomas Collingsworth told Joseph to move on.

He now had enough income from interest payments and crops to make a change in his life. He would quit the plant and move into the city, getting someone to manage his land for a share of the profits. He had been in the valley for more than five years and was one of its largest landowners, although heavily mortgaged, but now was the time to meet the moneychangers and civic leaders of the city. It would be his real start on the path to wealth and power. Vivid in his mind were the stories of the rich told to him by Tom Thornton. Thornton's drinking finally had caught up with him; he died in a hot field, thrashing and flapping on the ground, his stomach distended like the belly of a bloated fish. He died penniless, yet he'd known about the rich. Thomas Collingsworth, too, knew about the rich and knew that he would someday stand among them. He had defeated death in the hell pit of New Jersey. His brain had absorbed and assimilated knowledge from the colonel's books. He had conquered a large portion of the valley. He was ready for the new phase.

His first move was to invest five hundred dollars in clothing—good suits, shoes, and hats. Next he rented a furnished apartment close to downtown Los Angeles and opened a modest office on Temple Street. Then, dressed in a blue cotton suit, he went to see the colonel at the newspaper.

It was a dingy building on Main Street. The elevator was not working and the ink-stained staircase was scrawled with graffiti in crayon and charcoal. He opened a second-story door marked CITY ROOM and found himself in a strange new world that instantly caught and held him spellbound. Coatless men with shirts flecked with sweat and cigarettes hanging crookedly from their mouths battered feverishly on typewriters. Editors stood over them, shouting orders like slave masters. Teletypes clicked out streams of narrow yellow tape. Copyboys rushed past with pastepots. A series of clocks gave the time in various cities around the world. Morose, old copyreaders in green eyeshades sat slump shouldered at a large wooden desk, scribbling on papers handed to them by editors. The atmosphere was electric. He found the colonel's office at the south end of the big room. The colonel put down the phone and shook his hand.

"Sit down," he said. "Do you want a drink?"

Thomas said, "Quite a place you have here."

"Well, it could use some paint, but we get the sheet out every day." He squinted. He looked old and tired. "What brings you into town?"

"I've moved to town."

"What?" The colonel sprang up. "What about the plant?"

"I'm afraid I'm going to have to quit the plant. In fact, to be honest, I'll have to say I have already quit. Miller is replacing me."

"Why didn't you inform me earlier? We could have discussed it."

"Frankly, I was afraid you'd talk me out of it."

"Are you sure Miller can handle your old job?"

"I'm positive of that. I wouldn't have just quit without a replacement. I don't leave people high and dry."

The colonel poured a trickle of whiskey into two glasses. "Cheers," he said, downing his. He coughed, his cheeks turning bright red. "I want to tell you that I think you did a good job. With this blasted union problem around here, I haven't had time to get out to the valley. I'm grateful that you handled it so well. I will miss you. What will you do for a living now?"

"Make money the gentlemen's way," Thomas declared. "Collect interest, play the stock market."

He had no such intentions. If the colonel, who seemed relieved to be rid of the scheming young whelp he'd helped to create, believed him now, he was a fool. Perhaps, indeed, he was a fool. The colonel was a man of accomplishment but clearly he was failing. He'd become a bumbler. He was not the formidable figure of military bearing who several years ago had listened, from his back door, to a young man with news of a pending labor dispute. Or maybe the colonel had remained the same and Thomas had changed. One factor was certain. The colonel was ripe for taking. He had filled out to a pink-pated, aging form with a trembling right hand and a vein-streaked nose. He had begun to die.

The day Lowenfelt passed the bar he brought a mason jar of homemade gin to Thomas Collingsworth's office. They sat drinking until late afternoon, watching gold sun bars spread on the walls and floor. They were young and full with future. After the first cup of liquor, Lowenfelt waxed sentimental, talking about his young wife and newborn son. Thomas put a stop to that.

"Does the colonel have enemies?" he asked.

"Well, there's Hewitt, the union man. He's been trying to organize that paper for years. The colonel hates unions."

"No more than I do." Thomas sprang up and paced. "Lowenfelt, I think I would like to have that paper."

"Oh. Just like that. You would like to have it."

"Tell me, Lowenfelt, are you a wise man?"

"Wiser than most."

"Then tell me, what is important in life? Family? Money?"

"Both."

"Family before money?"

"Yes," Lowenfelt said without hesitation.

"I think I'll tell you what you are. You have a brilliant head for figures. But you are not a hunter, a stalker. You don't know how to move in for the kill. Your newsstand idea was brilliant, but you wouldn't be able to do it, even if you had the money. Because to pull it off, you'd have to face the colonel. It might kill him. Then you'd have to face your family with blood on your hands."

"I was thinking of getting the stands with his blessing."

"Bullshit. Now, Lowenfelt, we've had a few drinks so we can speak honestly. The colonel sent you to see me in the valley because he suspected I was sluicing off the books. Is that right?"

Lowenfelt sat drinking morosely.

"You came up with the circulation scam to gain my confidence, didn't you? To make me think we could be a pair of crooks in conspiracy. Then you could get the goods on me."

"I came here for a friendly drink, not for an inquisition."

"I want you to understand something. Nothing fools me. He sent you to school, Lowenfelt. You're loyal to him. Did he send you in here today?"

"No."

"But what I've just said is close to the truth, isn't it?"

Lowenfelt looked at the floor. "He is very much afraid of you."

"What about the water you hinted at?" Thomas Collingsworth asked.

"I know nothing about water."

"But you hinted at it."

"There is nothing to it. We were spreading false rumors to hold land prices up."

"Why is it that I don't quite believe you?"

Lowenfelt shrugged. "Believe what you want."

"Does the colonel want to sell his land?"

"He might. For the right price. He's hard pressed at the paper, and the paper is his first love."

"Tell him I'll buy the land."

Lowenfelt issued a scornful laugh, almost a sneer. "I thought I was the one who'd been drinking too much. Now I think it's you. You're talking a million-dollar deal. More."

"You get his signature on the deeds and I'll get the money."

"Get the signatures yourself. I assume he invited you to his big party at the Huntington Hotel next Sunday."

"No, he did not. Are you invited?"

"That question tells me you don't know much about the colonel. He hired me and helped train me as an accountant and helped with the law degree, too. For that I'm grateful, yes. But he would never invite me or my family to his social functions, because to him we are not white people."

"And that galls you?"

"On occasion. I'm let to know where I stand with him." Lowenfelt's enormous brown eyes rolled. "Why don't you crash the colonel's party? Show him some chutzpah."

"Lowenfelt, I think I might find a way to hire you and then corrupt you. I think you might be corruptible."

"Understand something." Lowenfelt looked straight at Thomas Collingsworth. "If it ever does come down to your hiring me, I want you to know I'll go only so far."

"The colonel has been telling lies about me again."

"Maybe you might need me to nettle your conscience."

"Conscience is something I'm lucky enough not to have."

He did crash the party in Pasadena, wearing a rented tuxedo and driving a borrowed Rambler. He had driven hardly at all and the car's levers were complex, yet somehow he managed to get to the hotel's parking lot. It was a bright midsummer day, splashed with sunshine, and the mountains were clearly etched on the horizon. Only when he got to the ballroom did he realize the nature of the party he was crashing. Pink streamers proclaimed it to be a salute to Elizabeth Dickerson, a form of a second coming out upon her graduation from college. The sight dazzled him. There was a full band. Champagne corks popped. Other liquor flowed abundantly. A table with dainty cloth napkins, glass plates, and polished silverware groaned under the weight of turkey and ham and shrimp, served by grave Negro waiters in red uniforms. A group of Mexicans in wide-brimmed hats wandered about when the band was not playing, strumming guitars and singing loudly. No one seemed to pay much attention to them. Thin women of various ages strutted in diaphanous silk gowns, dainty and proud and sophisticated, like blue and yellow flowers. Men in formal dress stood mechanically chatting, their mouths twisted in forced smiles, their manicured, uncalloused hands holding highballs in thin glasses. Pasadena's finest families were in attendance, a group scrubbed pink-clean and anointed with deodorants, shaving lotions, and perfumes. Thomas Collingsworth moved among them, circling to avoid a request for his invitation, knowing he was not one of them, knowing he would never really be one of them, feeling in his own way superior to them.

He couldn't avoid the colonel long and soon found himself facing his host. A slim young woman in blue silk with bright red lips clung to the colonel's arm.

"Elizabeth, you remember Mr. Collingsworth," the colonel said.

Elizabeth peered at him. "Yes, I remember a boy who always needed a bath. Daddy, did we invite him?"

"Not exactly," the colonel replied.

"Your man said I could come," Thomas said. "Lowenfelt?"

"Oh, yes," the colonel said.

"Daddy, why don't you start cutting the cake?" Elizabeth asked. "I'll just sort of circulate."

"As you wish."

The colonel moved hesitatingly away. Elizabeth drew in air, pushed out her breasts, and fanned herself with a little blue handkerchief. Her eyes caught and held those of Thomas Collingsworth.

"Do you have a car?" she asked.

"I have a Rambler."

"Well, I can do better than that."

It was a white Pierce-Arrow with the top down. She motioned him in, jumped behind the wheel, and screamed off, accelerator full down. Down the street she braked to a quick stop and began to wriggle her shoulders, her hands behind her back. Slowly she removed a blue brassiere from under her blouse.

"It's too damn sweaty, wearing that thing," she said, depositing it on the seat between them. "My tits like to breathe. Do I shock you?"

"No."

"I meant to shock, I suppose. They taught me how to shock at Smith. Precious little else. This is not an invitation for you to put your hands on me. I'm not a virgin, but I'm not generally available, either."

"All right."

"I suppose it's frightfully bad manners, running out like this. But I've been in there two long hours. I didn't want the party in the first place. Daddy insisted on it. Where do you want to go?"

"I don't care."

"All right. Hang on."

The Pierce-Arrow fled north, aimed at the brown foothills leading to the mountains. The engine howled and the tires squealed as she rounded a curve. She was a skilled driver, blending foot and hand with mechanical apparatus as if she were a part of it. Her hair flowed in the wind behind her, a dark stream unfettered by pins or ribbons. He was caught up in the spirit of it and when she began to laugh, he laughed, too. They were in the foothills and in what seemed like a flash they were curving up a paved mountain road. She missed the fence separating them from the precipice by inches; twice she ticked it.

The sun was going down and the rocks and shrubs had long shadows. Traffic was sparse; they fled upward alone. After fifteen minutes of testing to see how close she could get to the edge without hurtling them over the cliff, she stopped at a roadside overlook. A stream caught the last of the sun's rays five hundred feet below.

"Do you smoke?" she asked.

"Only cigars."

"I hear you have done quite well in the valley."

"I have done very well, I think."

"And you're living in the city now?"

"I see you've kept track of me."

She gazed at him, her eyes shining in the disappearing light. "I have kept track of you. You see, any man Daddy warns me to avoid interests me."

"He warned you to avoid me?"

"Yes. And I'll assume he told you to stay away from me."

"Well, he never quite trusted me."

"I'm over twenty-one and free to do as I like. And it's the twentieth century."

"I think maybe you're just a little too free."

"You interest me, T. Collingsworth. I should like you to call on me. Would you like to kiss me?"

"I believe that I would."

"How formal. 'I believe that I would.' You're not sure?"

"Yes. I'm positive."

"But watch your hands. I'm not ready for much more than kissing. Besides, I'm bleeding. Some girls bleed very little but I'm not one of those. Am I too frank?"

He didn't answer. He leaned toward her, put his hands on her shoulders, and drew her to him. Her lips parted when he touched them with his, pressing hard; she pulled apart, laughing. She brushed back her hair with her hand.

"Not too much now," she warned.

"Why did you bring me up here?"

"To get away. It was an impulse. I'm impulsive."

"So I see."

"And I've had ten glasses of the bubbly. We're lucky to be alive, if you want to know the truth. Let's just stay here and watch the moon come out while I sober up. Tell me, Collingsworth, are you a rich man yet?"

"I couldn't say I'm rich, no. But I will be."

"How rich?"

"As rich as anyone here."

"If you want to feel around a little, it's all right," she said. Her face now had almost disappeared into the gathering night. "But we're not going all the way."

"Will you feel me, too?"

"Yes." She moved into his arms, her breathing suddenly rapid. "Yes," she whispered. "Yes, yes."

When Thomas returned to his apartment about midnight that evening, the ancient landlady intercepted him in the hall. "Phone message," she said, handing him a white slip of paper. Gray cigarette smoke snorted from her nose.

He opened it. Then he took off his coat and flung it into the air, laughing uncontrollably. The note said: "Come in to see me. Colonel Dickerson."

But he did not go to see the colonel. He waited for the colonel to seek him out. Instead, Thomas Collingsworth went back to work. Occasionally he visited the valley, helping out

n the fields, to the amazement of the workhands. It felt good
o get down and dig a stubborn row again, to feel sweat on his
back, to dirty his hands. It got him back in touch with the
earth that had rewarded him so. He was now second only to
the colonel as a landowner in the valley, a very narrow
second; he knew all the valley politicians, contributing what
he could to their campaigns, and he gave liberally to the
newly founded Methodist church. He had no religious con-
victions, a superstition that had afflicted his mother, but
church connections were important. The contributions earned
him the reputation of a beneficent person.

Swede's land lay between two larger parcels owned by
Thomas. It was blocking progress of what was now a com-
bine, but Swede was stubbornly prompt on his principal and
interest payments. One day Thomas drew aside Miller, the
plant manager he'd hired.

"I want you to do something," he said. "When that Swede
brings in his crops next time, I don't want you to buy all of
them. Half maybe, but not all."

"Does the colonel know about this?"

"No. And you'll not tell him."

"Awright," the manager said, spewing a glob of wet brown
tobacco. "You boss, far's I'm concerned. I've never even *seen*
the colonel."

He was seeing Elizabeth on almost a weekly basis, usually
on Sunday afternoons, and he suspected the colonel knew
about it. They did nothing more harmful than drives to the
beach or the mountains. She refused to come into his bed
and he didn't press it, knowing it was only a matter of time.
She seemed to grow more serious, less carefree, and he
realized that he had caught her in an unusual mood the night
of the party.

One day in late April a chauffeur dropped the colonel off at
Thomas's office. The colonel now was walking with a cane.
The lines in his forehead had deepened. He sat down but said
nothing. Thomas took a bottle of whiskey from his drawer and
poured a liberal shot. The colonel pushed it away with the tip
of his cane.

"I can guess why you're here," Thomas said.

"You have come to know Elizabeth well."

"That depends on what you mean by the word know."

"You are not lovers?"

"A gentleman does not discuss such matters."

The colonel rapped his cane on the desk. He spoke rapidly "You promised me in the past that you would stay away from her. You are not a father, so you will not fully understand what I'm about to say." His face softened, his chin fell forward. "Perhaps I have not been the best of fathers. She has had too much. I discharged nurses and tutors at her whim. She was twelve when my break with her mother came. She preferred to live with me. We have been close . . . we are still close. This . . . this wildness in her is not her real character. She will become a fine wife and mother."

"And you think it's best for her that she not fall into my clutches?"

"It is essential. You are not her kind. You have no family, no discernible background."

"What is background?"

"Background is upbringing. Family."

"I'm no one's kind." Thomas stood up. "I'm not her kind, not your kind. I am my own. Perhaps I can't join your clubs or attend your parties, not yet, but I believe I stand out over you and your crowd."

"I'm willing to pay you if you release Elizabeth."

"Are you so sure that I have her?"

"She is infatuated with you. She'll tire of you, as she has of many young men in the past, but right now she has eyes only for you."

"How much do you offer, Colonel?"

"You name a sum."

"I don't want money."

"Then what is it you do want?"

"Two things. I want to know for certain whether or not a permanent supply of water is coming to the valley."

"What is the second matter?"

"I want to hire Lowenfelt from you."

The colonel gazed blankly in surprise. "If you want him, make him an offer. If I cannot match or exceed the offer, he'll work for you."

"No. He will not. He's loyal to you and so you must release him. You've been sending him to me as a spy because you knew you needed me despite your mistrust of me. That mistrust, by the way, was unwarranted. Money is too easy to make in this part of the country to risk jail by stealing it. I even think you tried to get Lowenfelt to fake numbers in the books so you'd have something on me."

"I did nothing of the kind."

"Very well. I'll take your word for that. I'm on my own now, and growing, and I need a good bookkeeper. Do I get him?"

The colonel sighed. "All right. If he wants to go, he may."

"I'm certain he'll work for me. Now, about the water...."

The colonel's voice was low, a conspiratorial whisper. "You will tell no one?"

"No one."

"Water is coming. There are plans for an aqueduct."

Thomas Collingsworth threw his head back and laughed. "Colonel, you are indeed an unholy scoundrel. I salute you. You are keeping the deep dark secret of coming water, a secret no doubt only until the city secures options on the land of the Owens Valley homesteaders."

"How did you know it was the Owens Valley?"

"I didn't, not until this moment." He eyed the colonel. "Then, options secured, we will steal the water from Owens. You will keep your secret, and your land will turn to gold."

"Yours, too, sir."

"Mine, too," Thomas said. "You have your daughter, Colonel. The information is worth six daughters."

She came to him on a Sunday afternoon when he was napping. It was deep autumn. The pungent scent of dry hollyhock and geranium drifted on the breeze through the window screen. The scent was his first awareness. Then he saw Elizabeth seated on the bed, wearing only lace panties.

"Asleep, you don't look so fierce," she said.

"How long have you been there?"

"Long enough."

"How did you get in?"

"You left the door open for me. You left it open because you knew I'd be here."

"Come down here."

He rolled over, seizing her. Her body was slim and firm and athletic and she used it with great skill and passion; it was as if he'd been with her many times before, and she knew the secret movements and touches that pleased him. Especially she used her hands and mouth, caressing his legs, stomach, genitals, his neck and face. He climaxed immediately, one deep thrust; she held him with her thighs, climaxing him again. His every sense was heightened, the sexual smell and feel of her was mixed with the outside odor of a ripening and bursting autumn, and he did not notice that the room had grown dark until they lay close and serene, entangled in damp sheets, drained and on the edge of sleep.

"That was to remember me," she said.

"So the colonel has spoken to you?"

"Yes."

"And like a good daughter, you will obey."

"I'm going to get married," she said. "I love you, Collingsworth, but I'm going to marry someone else."

"I don't understand what love is, but if you say you love me, I guess it's so."

"It's so. I don't understand it, either, but it's so." She turned and he gazed at the outline of her face—the perfect profile, the flowing hair, the thin neck. "I'm enough of a romantic to think that love comes only once. But I'm also enough of a realist to know it can't last."

"I told you that I can't deal with words like 'love.'"

She fell back. "I'm used to getting what I want and I want you. But I'm going to marry a banker with money and connections."

"I also get what I want."

"Do you want me?"

"Yes."

"But you made a deal with the colonel. You'll stick to the deal."

"Yes."

She sat up and fumbled for her clothing. He wanted to call her back—he wanted her, he wanted her—but he did not. He closed his eyes and dozed, aware of her movements in the room and the scent of her on his body. The door clicked and she was gone.

Swede fell three months behind on his payments. Subordinates could have handled the foreclosure, but Thomas did it himself. It was his duty. He drove his new Chevrolet Roadster to Swede's place on a Sunday afternoon in summer. It was a pleasant day with a slight breeze and the smack of rain in the air. He stopped the car by Swede's house. A blond boy sat on the lawn, blowing dust from a dandelion. Thomas knocked loudly on the door.

"I had expected you sooner," Swede said from behind the rusting screen door.

"I won't come in."

"No."

"The papers are all here. I'd like to give you more time, but the law says different."

"Laws must be obeyed."

"You go back to Minnesota. You should have enough to start over there."

"No. I will stay in the area. My daughter is buried here."

"Well, suit yourself. Good luck."

Swede's eyes were steady, a sharp narrow stare. "I know what you have done to me. When my family is grown and on their own, I will find you and give the devil his due. That I promise you."

Thomas shrugged. It had begun to rain, a light patter that heightened the smell of tomato vines. He looked at the boy innocently playing with dandelions as he walked to the Chevrolet. He wondered if the boy, given his genes and parental guidance, would grow up to be a success or a failure. He decided it was almost certain the boy would be a failure.

4.

IT WAS AN era of guarded optimism, of questioning youth, of violent labor conflict, yet also one of determined expansion. The city burst with excited growth in oil, construction, real estate. Immigrants from other states flooded across California's border, seeking the sun and good jobs. They found both. The skies were clear and the mountains rose like a protective force. The Pacific lapped on clean sand beaches. Orange groves encroached on the city. Expansion was all the mood, despite war clouds in Europe. Grown-ups danced the tango and the gavotte, returning home to tune in citrus and cash-crop reports; children played crack the whip on school grounds, dashing home after the final bell to play the streetcar game or build an erector-set tower.

Thomas Collingsworth grew with it. The colonel remained a big man with powerful friends, so he was difficult to conquer. Yet he lived in fear of defeat, a fear sometimes expressed when he had too many drinks at the club. Elizabeth had the effrontery to invite Thomas to her wedding and he had the effrontery to attend, at least the reception, held at the colonel's Pasadena home. He entered behind two women who chattered about Theda Bara. From within came the strains of a familiar melody—and for one of the few times in his life Thomas Collingsworth felt a human pang of loss. He squared his jaw. He would win in the end, win what he wanted. Once as a boy he'd spent a quarter he could ill afford to see the Redpath Chautaqua, a tent meeting featuring bands, magicians, Hawaiian singers, yodelers, American Indians, and always a lecture. He'd heard, spellbound, Joseph "Gatling Gun" Meeker deliver a golden address, "Money Is in Your Backyard." He'd left knowing he could do anything, conquer any adversity. Now, recalling it in detail, he felt a rush of well-being, of confidence. If he wanted Elizabeth, he would have her, despite her marriage to another. The marriage, in fact, made her more challenging to him. He would have her.

He spied the bride cutting the wedding cake. Beside her stood a tall young man, pale and fragile. The groom. He seemed bewildered and unsure, weak as Milquetoast. Thomas scoffed inwardly. This Milquetoast would not last long.

It was toward evening when he faced Elizabeth. "I will have you yet," he said. "It will be soon."

"So long, Collingsworth," she said. Their eyes met and held. "Good-bye, ragtime minstrel man."

Later he watched her go, under a shower of rice, on the arm of the Milquetoast banker. He would get her back. Never in his life had he had more confidence in himself.

Lowenfelt rushed into his office and plunked the papers down on his desk. "It's coming," he announced, gasping for breath.

"What's coming?"

"Read for yourself."

The newspapers announced the coming of water to the San Fernando Valley. It was to flow west from the Owens Valley. The Roughrider in the White House, doing his duty, had given the right of way over government land. The project sprang vividly before Thomas Collingsworth, as if he were looking at a map—233 miles from Owens Lake to the Hawiwee Reservoir to Little Lake and Indian Wells, across the Red Rock summit, across Jawbone Canyon to the Mojave Desert,

across to Antelope Valley, to the reservoir at Fairmont, to
Elizabeth Lake, San Francisquito Canyon, to the San Fernando
Reservoir. It was like a living thing; it brought life through
pump, siphon, flume, and conduit.

"Ragtime minstrel man," he said.

"Huh?" Lowenfelt said.

"Someone once called me that."

"I know the song."

"Lowenfelt, let's open a bottle."

"Good idea."

"Tomorrow, you call up and make an appointment for you
and me to see the colonel."

"What about?"

"Never mind that. You'll find out when we talk to him."

"Why do I have this feeling you're about to spring your
trap?"

"Maybe because I am," Thomas said.

He was in an extremely expansive mood. Drinking with
Lowenfelt, he felt like gloating, but he did not. He had three
reasons for celebration. The first was the coming water. The
second was that he had indeed finally hit upon a scheme that
would topple the colonel. The third reason came from a note
in a pink envelope that had been delivered to him yesterday
afternoon. It read: "Like to see you. Will you meet me at
Freddie's, seven P.M., Thursday? Elizabeth."

He and Lowenfelt drank and talked in the office until
Lowenfelt's wife called, demanding he come home immediately or risk the viability of their marriage. Lowenfelt obeyed.
Thomas sat in the office until midnight, reading each water
report several times, and when he left he walked with a
spring in his step, knowing he was on the threshold of power
and control he could only dream about a few months ago.

They had met at Freddie's several times before Elizabeth
married the banker. It was a quiet, dark bar in Santa Monica
on a hill with a view of the ocean. The bar was perfect for
assignations. There were motor courts and one-night hotels
nearby; no questions were asked about luggage. Freddie
served good German beer and played older tunes on the
Victrola. Regular customers had their own steins, like shaving
mugs in a barbershop. Couples spooned at tables in dark
corners, pledging everlasting faithfulness and devotion to

each other, and left tipsy and holding hands, lusting for a hotel bed. Most of the trysts had an illicit daring and magic—a married executive with his secretary, a housewife with an on-the-road salesman, a professor with one of his students. The beery, smoke-laden atmosphere was sensual, smacking of the permissibility of the new age, of temporary coupling, of freedom and brief escape before having to face the next bleak day and week and month. To Thomas Collingsworth, seated across a table from Elizabeth, it seemed a grotesque charade, shadow figures frightened of the real world who whispered words of affection and love when all they really wanted or needed was the fulfillment of biologic drives. He got to the point immediately.

"What do you want?"

"Just to talk," Elizabeth said, running her finger lightly over the foam of her beer.

"Talk about what?"

"Us, I guess."

"Us? There is no us. You're married, do you remember? How long has it been now?"

"Long. Very long."

"Your tone suggests it is also very boring."

"And your tone suggests anger. Why are you angry?"

"I'm not. I'm on the top of the world. And you're in bed with a Milquetoast banker."

"It's hardly a bed," she said.

"Are you faithful to him?"

"I have been. Up until now."

"Does that mean we're going to one of those hotel rooms?"

"No. You're going to take me to your place."

"I wouldn't count on that."

"But I am," Elizabeth said, holding him with her deep eyes.

"Why did you marry him?"

"If you'll recall, you were the one who made the deal with my father. My father the colonel?"

"I have him now."

"What do you mean by that?"

"Just what I said."

"I want you to promise me one thing. Promise me that you won't hurt him."

"I have no intention of hurting him."

Their hands brushed. He pulled his away. She said: "Shall

we go now?" She was beautiful. He had to admit that. And he wanted her. At social functions. In his bed. As his wife. He felt a stirring deep within him, highlighted by the piquant odor of the place and the presex whisperings of couples invisible to others in their mating rituals. He paid for the beer and went to where she stood by the door, waiting for him.

The colonel greeted them with the air of a man who was willing to sign an armistice. It was as if he knew he'd been defeated and this meeting was only to discuss terms of the surrender. They met in the colonel's office at the *Bulletin-News* after the final edition of the afternoon paper had been completed. The staff lounged in the city room drinking beer. That was allowed after the last edition was put to bed, the colonel explained, and in fact he sometimes joined his staff for a drink at the end of the day.

"Well, we'll put a stop to that," Thomas said.

The colonel's hand trembled. "What is it you wish to discuss?"

"I want to do business with you," Thomas replied. He looked at Lowenfelt, who turned away. "I have investigated your situation, with the help of the accountant-lawyer you allowed me to hire, and I have found that you have struggled now for a number of years in a war for circulation with competitors. You're losing it. I now have the power to win it for you and hurt several competitors at the same time." He paused, enjoying the moment. "I suppose, Colonel, that we have been at each other's throat, although not openly, ever since that day I came to your door. Do you remember you made me go around to the back? You wouldn't let me in."

"What did you expect me to do? You appeared to be a wild-haired gypsy boy."

Thomas began to pace slowly, his hands behind his back. He stopped. "It is not a gypsy boy you see now," he said. "Do you remember when you sent Lowenfelt to check on me? He suggested I attempt to buy up newsstands. It was a stupid tactic on your part, for I do not buy without investigating. Newsstands account for only a small percentage of circulation in this area. Besides, the newsstand sales are controlled by your circulation agents. They buy from you and distribute through routes in the city. It came to me, not long ago, that the way to proceed was to buy out circulation agents. It has been done, Colonel; I own some fifty percent of the agents in this town. I own almost all of the agents for the *Bulletin-News*. That means in effect that I control the paper. If I stop delivery, you have no paper."

The colonel took it calmly. He opened his drawer, took out a flask of whiskey, and poured a trickle into a paper cup. He drank. His cheeks brightened.

"What is to stop me from establishing an internal circulation department?" he asked.

"Money," said Thomas. "Money you do not have. This circulation battle has been costly. Besides, if you attempted to do it internally, I—now your agent with a contract that has four years to run—will sue your fat ass in the courts."

"I am enough of a military man to know when I have been defeated," the colonel said. He poured a liberal shot of whiskey into his cup and before drinking he said: "Salùte. Will you join me in a drink?"

"No."

"What do you propose to do?"

"I don't want to take any action that would hurt the newspaper. In other words, I don't wish to exercise my powers. Not to the disadvantage of the *Bulletin-News* at least. Since I own circulation franchises in other local newspapers, perhaps I might cut back the sales of your competitors. I even have the power to hurt the *Times*."

The colonel waved his hand. "No, don't do that. I have good friends at the *Times*." He had a third shot of whiskey. He seemed calmed. His hand had stopped trembling. "I have asked you, sir, what do you propose to do?"

"I want you to make me your assistant as publisher of the paper. And I want you to sign a contract which Lowenfelt will draw up appointing me as publisher, with an equity interest, when you retire or die."

"I can't do that. I won't."

"I think you can. I think you will."

"It was almost as if I wasn't there," Lowenfelt said as they were driving back to the office. "He didn't look at me."

"Lowenfelt, you have a complex."

"Why did you ask me to come?"

"To show you I am a man who cannot be fooled."

"Do you think I still work for him? Is that it?"

"Lowenfelt, you are a man of pity, and that is somewhat foolish. You're a Jew and the colonel has not quite accepted you, yet you could never have done what I just did. And I think if I had told you of my plans ahead of time, you might have told the colonel."

"Do you want me to resign?"

"Of course not. I need you."

"Will the colonel accept your terms?"

"He has no choice." Thomas chuckled, feeling his strength. "I held back on the news that will sting him the most."

"What news is that?"

"I'm going to marry his daughter."

"I'm under the impression that she already is married."

"Not for long."

"I'll tell you this," Lowenfelt said. "I'll never ask you to come to my back door to talk."

5.

THOMAS COLLINGSWORTH'S POWER and influence took quantum leaps after he moved into the *Bulletin-News*, taking a small office next to the colonel's. Congressmen and civic officials came to him seeking endorsements and contributions. He developed a simple rule—back the Republicans, smear the Democrats. Men whose presence had once awed him now stood awed by him. He dined with the mayor and police chief, discussing the city's future; the chamber of commerce, the Merchants' and Manufacturers' Association, and several private clubs eagerly solicited him to join. He held the circulation franchises and ordered their managers to squeeze the other papers, which resulted in a sharp increase in *Bulletin-News* sales and advertising. One by one the rival publishers came to him, threatening lawsuits when he refused to sell the franchises, even at inflated prices. Finally, in return for industry promises of a strong antiunion stance and an agreement to back political candidates selected by Thomas Collingsworth, the publishers were able to buy some of the franchises at five times his purchase price. He used the money to buy more land in the valley.

Thomas liked the newspaper business, not only for the power it gave him but also for the beehive atmosphere of the city room, the sense of deadline pressures, the smell of melted lead in the Linotype machines, and the howl of the presses. He wrote twice-weekly editorials, signing them "T.C.," in which he praised conservatives, extolled the merits of Los Angeles, attacked labor. The only aspect of the paper that depressed him was, in fact, its continuing labor troubles. If the colonel had taught him anything, it was about the evils of organized labor. The unions were run by Communists and were therefore enemies of America. He resisted all attempts to organize the paper, raising salaries to unheard of levels, yet union demonstrators often appeared in front of the building, marching with homemade signs and handing out leaflets attacking the paper's management.

One evening a scuffle ensued between the demonstrators and some pressmen returning to the overnight shift from a bar across the street. The police quickly appeared, swinging nightsticks, and four demonstrators had to be hospitalized. Thomas Collingsworth had a personal promise from the chief of police that the building would be closely watched on a twenty-four-hour basis. The chief said he would instruct his men to move in aggressively at any sign of disturbance. The day following the incident with the pressmen was particularly tense, with the union doubling its number of demonstrators. No incidents occurred, but the tension continued.

The colonel's surrender was unconditional. He came to the office each morning at ten, sometimes with the smell of liquor on his breath, and puttered with some pet projects he'd long delayed—a museum in Pasadena he hoped would take his name and a plan to create a civic center on ground he owned nearby. He got nowhere on either project; men of power now bypassed him, waiting instead to see the assistant publisher. The colonel's face grew redder, his skin puffier; he could not take a step without the aid of his cane. He didn't even protest when Thomas announced Elizabeth's divorce and his plans to marry her.

"Does she love you?" he mumbled.

"Well, she gave up a bank president for me."

"I pity her," the colonel said.

But Elizabeth neither wanted nor needed her father's pity.

She came to legal union with Thomas Collingsworth with her eyes open, desiring it, knowing she would receive some punishment for teasing him with her sojourn in the soft Pasadena bed of the refined, uncalloused banker. He married her for two reasons. She had matured into one of the most splendid women in the area, one with impeccable taste and manners, and therefore she would be a valuable addition to him in his business progress. And, secondly, it seemed to him that her genes combined with his could produce an almost perfect son.

It was a thought that had been pressing on his mind lately. He wanted a son. Perhaps Swede had been right about that; a son could carry on the Collingsworth name. He would admit it to no one, but in his alone hours, especially on the Sundays he now spent stalking deer in the foothills, he suffered dreadful apprehensions concerning his mortality. He feared an early death would not allow him to complete his grand design. He was not quite sure what the design was, but he was now convinced he'd been put on earth and allowed to survive what others, kin to him, had not survived for a purpose noble and meaningful, a purpose for the greater good. He did not believe in a divinity, but he did believe in a form of power that separated the gifted from the average, like the "chosen" of the Puritans. He had been one of the select. So, accumulation of assets, no matter by what tactics, was a necessity, a duty, an obsession.

Yet he realized above all that he was mortal; death was his greatest fear. Perhaps it was part of his gift, an inner and instinctive sense of warning, like the senses of the animals he stalked and destroyed. By winning over them, he heightened his senses. Yet he could not rid himself of his fear of death. He knew he had made enemies, many of them, and perhaps one or more plotted retribution by violence, but he was confident he could handle that should it occur. Usually he carried a pistol and he had a rifle and a shotgun in his office. Nor did he fear death by sickness. Since he'd come to California he had not been sick. He had a constitution of iron. What he did fear was death by accident, some grotesque, ironic twist of fate simple to avoid. Thus he became meticulously careful, handling weapons with respect, avoiding dark streets and fast cars, inspecting ahead and behind and above before venturing out. He thus challenged fate. But he'd come to the conclusion that the only real way to conquer death was to produce a person in his image.

He married Elizabeth at the small Methodist church that was grateful for his contributions, with only witnesses and the minister in attendance. Already construction had begun on the Wilshire house that would be their home, with Thomas personally supervising the workers. On their wedding night at the Van Nuys Hotel, he told Elizabeth he wanted a son.

"How soon?" she asked.

"As soon as possible."

"You talk as if it can be done merely by the wanting."

"It can."

"Well, let's get started then. I never exactly minded the process by which babies are made."

"Even with him?"

"Who?"

"The banker."

"Oh. Him." She laughed, her head back. "I think he's impotent. Or a latent boy lover."

Their sex was like it had been before, hard and passionate, almost violent, he the aggressor and she responding; it was as if by his intensity he could assure she emerged from it with sperm deep in her to form the fetus of a boy child. Later, during her pregnancy, he would not sleep with her, fearing damage to the perfect form shaping in her womb. He would instead succumb to the beckoning eyes and suggestive leg movements of once unobtainable women whom he took with the pleasure of a conqueror. He thought of Elizabeth also as one he had conquered, just as he had conquered the valley and her father. She was the winner's prize, a spirit once free now broken and tamed, and perhaps she realized it.

The house was finished in time for delivery of the baby there, a midnight birth during a driving January rainstorm. He felt a moment of anxiety when the old white-haired doctor came to him downstairs, looking exhausted and grim. Then the doctor smiled. "It's a perfect baby," he said. "A boy." Thomas opened the curtains and peered out at the white-sheeted downpour, knowing he had accomplished what he'd set out to do. He made a fist at the rain.

He named the boy Hollis, a derivation of the given name of Henry Huntington's uncle, Collis Huntington of railroad fame. When the Owens Lake aqueduct, which would at last bring water to the valley, was dedicated in an elaborate ceremony, the boy was there in his carriage, flanked by his father and mother, an unknowing witness to an event that would strongly influence his future. It was a colorful picnic atmosphere with an audience of hundreds. Horse-drawn buggies and automobiles dotted the area. Civic leaders bored the crowd with speeches that ended with band blurts and applause, granted more as relief that the address had ended than in appreciation of its words. The crowd was smaller by the time William Mulholland, architect of the project, opened the flume and said:

"There it is. Take it."

Thomas Collingsworth was convinced that Wilson could not keep America out of the war, so he backed producers of military ware and filled the *Bulletin-News* with anti-Wilson editorials. When the war did come, he printed letters from doughboys in the trenches and sprinkled the pages with eagles and flags. Solidarity in home-front production and good wages diluted the power of the unions, and business boomed. The war increased his assets almost as much as had the coming of water to the valley. Aside from that, it did not affect him. He fought the Huns at home while others foolishly ran to enlist, returning to display their medals and damaged limbs and bask in short-lived heroic glory.

He usually arrived at the newspaper office at six A.M., which gave him time to read the war dispatches and out-of-town papers before the morning crew arrived. One morning he heard a noise from the colonel's office and peered in to see the old man dressed in his Civil War uniform, staggering around using his cane for balance. The uniform was too small, the shined buttons popping; the spit-and-polish boots looked new, laced in military style; a holstered pistol dangled from his heavy hip.

"Just what in the devil is this all about?" Thomas demanded.

The colonel squared his shoulders. "You will address me as *sir.*"

"Come on. I'll have you taken home. You've been drinking."

"I do not drink on duty."

Thomas looked at the wretched form, not knowing whether to feel amusement or pity. One thing was clear—the colonel had come to his end. As he stepped toward the old man, the colonel pointed with his cane. There were specks of vomit on his beard.

"You are a rapist, a *rapist!*" he said, his words hissing. The pupils stared crookedly in his bloodshot eyes. "You are the devil in man's clothing. You are gangrene and *rot!* It is my mission and my duty to execute you."

He was fumbling for the pistol, but before he could get it out, Thomas sprang across the room and knocked it to the floor. He kicked it under a desk. The colonel, enraged, started to flail about with his cane, trying to shout words that would not fully come out, his face blood red, his gnarled hands unsteady. Thomas caught the cane in his hand, jerked it away, and broke it over his knee. Still the colonel came after him, trying to reach for his throat, but he was too exhausted to squeeze. He sank slowly to the floor and lay in a defeated heap, his knees up to his chest, trembling and sobbing.

They had him hospitalized and he died of kidney failure a month later. Elizabeth visited him every day, refusing to give reports on his condition to her husband. A distance had grown between them after Hollis's birth, one unsuspected by acquaintances who attended their dinners; they still shared a bed, yet she gave him sex without really participating in it, and soon it dwindled to nothing. She seemed interested only in attending teas at the homes of her friends in Pasadena and in furnishing the Wilshire house. He let her have her way. She had already given him what he had most wanted from her, a son.

Elizabeth left Hollis's care to nurses, wisely understanding that the boy was Thomas's, not hers. Instead she took over the house, filling it with Louis XVI tables of delicate tulip-wood, veneered mahogany commodes, lavish and ornate gilt brass and wood end pieces and side tables. She led guests on tours through the maze of Queen Anne, Adam, Hepplewhite, Sheraton, and Chippendale. Rococo and baroque mirrors ornamented the walls, especially upstairs. She scolded maids if a single speck of dust was found. Bed linens were sent to the laundry every day. She ruled the servants like a proud queen, giving precise instructions and flaring if they were disobeyed.

Thomas began to ignore her. He had his son. He had his

job. His wife's importance stemmed from only one fact. Lowenfelt told him the colonel had died without a will, meaning his properties would revert to his daughter under the laws of intestate succession. Thus, after court clearance, she would own the newspaper and the colonel's land in the valley. Thomas had been able to handle the colonel, but he wasn't sure he could handle the colonel's daughter if she chose to exercise her right of control. He no longer owned any of the circulation franchises in the *Bulletin-News*, so that leverage was gone. He would merely have to get along with his wife, control her resentment toward him, the blame she placed on him for her father's downfall. One evening after dinner when she finally voiced her resentment, he reminded her that she had hardly rushed to the colonel's aid, preferring instead to escape in fast cars.

She flared. "That simply is not true. I loved my father. If you could have seen him in those last few days—"

"I saw enough of him in the office."

Elizabeth stiffened. She had cut her hair, against his wishes, and had gained weight, but she still retained the princess beauty that had made her the belle of many forgotten balls.

"What do you propose we do now?" she asked, sharpness in her voice. "Divide the spoils?"

"No. We manage it and make it grow."

"All right. I'll agree. You run the business. But I want my freedom."

"Divorce?"

"No. I just don't want to be your possession. All of that is out of my system now. I want to travel. I want to go to dances. I want to sleep around. And, if I do, I don't want you having me followed or making a scene."

"Do as you please, as long as you use discretion."

"I have already used discretion," she said.

After that she was gone for weeks on end. She had a liberal supply of money in her own account and that was all she seemed to want or need. She had power over him, since she was the colonel's beneficiary, but she did not exercise it. His insight into his wife was his advantage over her. She still sought love, an emotion Thomas Collingsworth did not understand and perceived as a weakness in those who did understand it. She had disobeyed and forsaken the colonel to rush into a passionate union with the colonel's enemy, his conqueror. Now she felt guilt about her father and sought her punishment or even a form of redemption through adulterous promiscuity and frivolous dissipation. He did not care. He had a business to manage and a son to rear. Elizabeth cooperated with him, promptly signing all the business papers Lowenfelt sent to her, including the liquidation of the colonel's interest in the bank. Thomas had formed a holding company, putting all the assets into it. The dividends alone were sufficient to allow Elizabeth to live affluently in Europe six months out of the year. She could do exactly as she pleased.

One night he returned home to find her seated on the edge of Hollis's bed, watching the sleeping boy. She was crying, something he'd never seen her do before. He took her arm firmly and ushered her out of the room.

For years there had been unrest in the Owens Valley, deprived of water by the Los Angeles Aqueduct. Its ranches had grown barren. The city offered to buy the land, with the backing of the federal government, but the ranchers complained they were offered only barren-land prices. A war veteran named Captain McGree, returning to find his land ravished and denuded, led a dynamite attack at Lone Pine, blowing up a section of the aqueduct. Two months later he opened the control gates at the Alabama Hills, diverting thousands of gallons into the desert. The Los Angeles Water Board could do nothing. After a temporary peace, McGree's men struck again, capturing guards, cutting telephone lines, and blasting out the big No Name siphon. Clearly the battle was on.

The city sent hundreds of guards to the Owens Valley, armed with rifles and machine guns, and searchlights played over key areas of the aqueduct at night. Yet the attacks continued. Wells at Big Pine and Bishop were dynamited. The Cottonwood power plant was blasted. The city wanted to take legal action, but nothing could be proved. Thomas saw it as his personal battle. He envisioned his enemy, the soldier McGree, as a man with a stubby beard and athletic frame who, no longer honored for war triumphs, was now leading his men simply for the thrill of battle. Clearly such a man was dangerous.

Thomas met with the chief of police in a Pierce-Arrow at a

spot that had been arranged by telephone. The chief brought with him another person, a young man named Hunter, who chain-smoked cigarettes.

"Officially, in a situation like this one with McGree, I don't have jurisdiction," the chief said. "But Hunter here, who used to be with us on the riot squad, he's in business himself now, so he doesn't have no jurisdictions to worry about."

"I don't like hiring strangers," Thomas replied.

"Then let's not be strangers," Hunter said, blowing smoke.

"Well, the way I see it, we're all in this together," the chief added. "We got to keep that water coming down here or our land won't be worth a plugged nickel. I've always thought you can stop a gang pretty good if you stop its leader."

Hunter flipped his cigarette out the window and drew another from a supply in his pocket. "McGree lives a dangerous life," he said. "Man like that could have an accident."

"What do you charge?" Thomas asked.

Hunter shrugged. "On the house, introductory offer so to speak," he said. He blew smoke from his nostrils, a young dragon with hard eyes. "I'm a land speculator, too."

The bombings stopped two weeks later. Captain McGree was not heard of again.

Late one February night his bedside phone jarred Thomas out of a deep sleep. It was the chief. "I hate to break it to you this way, but I can't see any other way of doing it. We got a D.O.A. here that's been identified as your wife."

He felt nothing. A squad car took him to the coroner's office where the chief greeted him with a concerned look.

"I'm sorry," he said.

"I want to see her."

"Yes. Yes, of course."

She was unmarred in death, except for her neck, twisted at an unnatural angle. Her hair flowed over her white shoulders and he thought of his times with her in full passion. He was reminded of Mary Jurado's body in the ditch. In the lobby outside a young man sat weeping.

"They ran a red light and we gave chase," the chief said. "He cut a left too sharply, bounced over a curb, and slammed into a tree. He came out with scratches, she with a broken neck. We got him on drunk driving. We'll throw the book at him."

Thomas looked at the weeping young man. "No," he said. "No publicity."

"Whatever you say, but I think we should throw the book at him."

"Let him go. Pull the record on this one."

"All right," agreed the chief. "You call the turn here."

The chief drove him home. Thomas felt no emotion except relief. He would tell Hollis that his mother had died in a traffic accident but spare him the details. He could think only that now it would become all his. It was what he'd strived and driven for; it was what he had been born for. It was his destiny—and the destiny of his son. He would call Hollis at the prep school in the morning and tell him what had happened. There would be a solemn and proper funeral. Elizabeth would be entombed at Forest Lawn beside the colonel. The chief said nothing. The headlights pierced a light patter of rain. It was clear ahead.

Alone now in the Wilshire house with only the servants, and Hollis when he visited on weekends, he found another passion—the game of chess. It fascinated him, a game of war strategy, of sacrifice for victory. He accumulated various elaborate sets, many of them from abroad. He had taken the club membership vacated by the colonel's death and quickly became the best player there, one with a growing national reputation. He wagered heavily and seldom lost.

Working at home on his rolltop desk, Thomas had also begun to write down the story of his life and the rationale for his actions. Life was simple, once you understood a basic fact: It was man against man. You gave no quarter if you were to win. The journal would be part of Hollis Collingsworth's legacy; it would be his, and someday it would be his son's. He now understood family. It reminded him again of Swede, and of the colonel. Family, a son, was all. It was future.

PART 2

The Legacy

1.

HE WAS RIDING the snorting mare named Spirit, a mare he had broken himself, a gift from his father which had become his only after he'd broken her. And this time he rode beside, not behind, his father. That had meaning to Hollis Collingsworth. He'd just turned eighteen and he was now an equal. They were approaching the crest of a hill, forging upward through dry chaparral and yucca. Sage and castor beans filled the flatlands below. The sun was at its zenith. Hollis spurred his mare ahead. Spirit hit a bog and almost went down on her forelegs. Hollis jerked the reins and again dug in the spurs. Spirit recovered and continued upward, dust and chaparral smells thick in Hollis's nostrils. His father, dressed in black riding clothes with leather thongs on his shirt, a Colt .45 holstered on his hip, seemed to Hollis not a man but a knight, a god imbued with supernatural powers. He'd known almost since birth he was the only offspring of an important man; now it came to him that he was the son of someone endowed with immortal strength and power and force, a black-clad entity on a huge charging black stallion that had no name, a driving man-horse mechanism whose wrath was to be feared and whose affection was to be cherished.

It was almost a perfect day, with a high, hot sun and a dazzling clear blue sky. It would be an absolutely perfect day if Lois could be there. But he would tell her about it later. That would be some compensation. When he'd asked his father if she could go with them on this ride, he'd received a cold stare and no answer. Now they were at the top of the hill. They stopped, the horses breathing heavily with green foam trickling from their mouths, and the valley lay before them, filled with purple flowers. It was his father's valley and Hollis knew that it would someday be his. Ahead, a hundred yards down the slope, the two horsemen armed with rifles who always rode in advance had also paused, their hats tipped back, their eyes searching in all directions. Hollis had never learned their names. One was a tiny flat-nosed hard man with tobacco-stained lips and beard; the other was a giant colored man who seldom spoke and never smiled.

"What are you looking at?" his father asked.

"The valley. It's beautiful."

His father was named Thomas but Hollis had seldom heard him called by his first name. To his associates, and certainly to all of the house and yard help, he was "Mr. Collingsworth." His mother, when she'd been alive, had even called him "Mr. Collingsworth" on occasion, especially when she'd been angry at him. Now his father stroked the stallion's mane with his gloved hand and said:

"I never saw beauty in land. In a woman, yes, but not in land. Land is for use. It is for building. It is for development. What you see down there is the future. It is my future, but, more importantly, it is your future. Now that the water is here, the future is assured. Remember that only the weak let forces control them. A strong person can control his future— and also control other people."

Thomas wasn't given to long speeches; he was swift and abrupt, and that was about the longest talk he'd ever had with Hollis. Looking at him, again Hollis thought of the man-horse power, a feeling not of fear or pride but one of awe.

"I understand," he said.

He breathed deeply. It was the Cahuenga Valley of southern California and much of it was theirs. He was grateful for the legacy. He was unknown in the East, where he recently finished prep school, but here in the West the Collingsworth name was almost a legend. And his father's importance was extended now to Hollis, the only son. Below, bees feasted on clover near Spirit's right hoof; the horse shied slightly, but Hollis quickly controlled her by twisting the reins. His father nodded approvingly.

"I want to say something else to you," Thomas continued. He did not look at his son. He looked far down the valley. The two horsemen had separated by some thirty yards and remained searching the hills. "This concerns a young lady you've lately been taking out to dances."

"Lois?"

"I do not know her name."

"It's Lois. It's Lois Mullaney."

"She is Irish, and a Catholic."

"Yes."

"How deeply are you involved with her?"

"I—I really don't know."

"I want you to tell her you no longer wish to see her."

He felt a thud in his heart. "But, why?"

"I want you to tell her you no longer wish to see her." All of this time Thomas had been looking at the valley. Now he turned to Hollis. His dark eyes seemed a hawk's eyes. He had a short gray beard and his suntanned, wrinkled face was like the bark of an oak. "You're far too young to limit yourself to one woman. There are hundreds of women who will be only too willing to provide for your needs. Soon you'll be returning to school, and then, after college, you will become a part of the company. You will grow to become an important part of it. It is a path I have set for you."

"B-b-but she is . . . is important to me."

Thomas snorted loudly, causing the stallion to rear its head. "You have no time for such things," he said. "Strong men do not give into women, no matter how dainty and alluring they are. You will later find a companion who will work with you and help you. Meanwhile, go to whores, if you first assure yourself they are not diseased."

A heart-sinking feeling struck Hollis. The enjoyment of the ride had dissipated. A cloud came over the sun and the valley below seemed darker. He had planned to take Lois to a dance tonight and tell her of his feelings toward her. He knew it would do no good to argue his case with his father. The matter, in fact, already was closed. This ride, the one on which his father had indicated to him that he'd become a man, had turned from one of great joy and escape and beauty to one of disappointment and near despair. He now realized something. He did not like the imposing figure on the stallion beside him. In fact, he despised him. And he would disobey him, defy him.

"Do you want to go back through the valley or the way we came?" his father asked.

"I don't care."

"Remember the parade is a week from next Sunday."

He had wanted Lois to join him in the parade, too; he was going to ask her tonight. "I haven't forgotten," he said, sullenly stroking Spirit's warm, wet neck.

"We'll go back through the valley," his father said.

The horsemen who always rode ahead stirred in sudden

excitement. The big colored man whirled his mount, cupped his mouth, and shouted: "Down! Down, Mr. Collingsworth!" He waved at a distant hill. His rifle snapped up; he held it in one hand, pointing it at a sun glint on the hill.

Hollis sat upright in the saddle, stunned. Movement whirled around him. The dark figure that was his father bolted from the stallion, leaping toward Hollis and driving him to the ground. He felt a painful crunch in his ribs and he could not get his breath. He lay gasping and choking, aware that his father lay over him, aware of sweat smells and the pain and the big rolling sky. He did not hear shots; he heard only echoes of them. Three echoes. The horsemen were racing up the hill, using their rifles as whiplike prods on the flanks of their mounts. The stallion stood stoically still, but Spirit reared, stumbled, and fell on her side. She lay thrashing, kicking her front leg. Blood spurted from the leg and only then did Hollis fully realize that the whizzing sounds were the sounds of bullets.

"Are you hurt?" his father asked.

"I . . ." He couldn't get his breath. He lay gasping.

"I think you're all right," Thomas said. He sat up, glanced at the hill, took his pistol from its holster, and went on hands and knees to the writhing mare. "It's a bad hit for her," he said. "She took what was meant for me. She'll have to go." He cocked the pistol. Then he turned and motioned to Hollis. "Come over. Stay down, but come here." Hollis crawled to his father, conscious of pain in his ribs. Thomas turned the pistol around and handed it butt first to his son.

"It's your job," he said.

Hollis was horrified. "B-b-but I *can't!*"

"You can. You will do it."

He took the pistol, holding it in both hands. The butt was warm. Hollis's finger trembled on the trigger. His father indicated where to shoot, just above the eyes. The mare's eyes were frightened, pleading. Hollis closed his eyes and pulled the trigger. The shot echoed. When he opened his eyes, he saw that the ground was red with the mare's blood. Already it had attracted flies and bees.

Thomas took the pistol from his son. He holstered it and mounted the stallion. He stared defiantly at the hill from which the shots had come, his mouth iron tight.

"I'll go have a look and see if I can get that bastard," he said. "You stay here, just stay down. I'll be back."

He jerked the reins and spurred. Dust kicked into Hollis's face. He lay trembling beside the mare, reddened with her blood. It had happened so quickly he hadn't had time to think of fear, but now he knew that he was afraid. Flies swarmed around him. Hollis put his head against the mare's neck. He smelled her sweat and blood and he knew that he'd loved the mare. But he would not cry. He had never cried.

2.

EVER SINCE HOLLIS'S mother had died, an event he hardly now recalled, his father had hosted an almost ritualistic dinner the last Friday of each month at the big house on Wilshire Boulevard. Hollis had never been invited to the dinners, but on the way back from the ranch, Thomas said he could attend that night. He was asked, however, not to enter too much into the discussions, just to listen. From peeking around at former dinners, Hollis had learned something of their nature. Only men attended; even the servants were limited to men. The dress was formal. There was little laughter; the talk was hushed, almost conspiratorial. The men who attended, in groups of six or seven, were among the top leaders of Los Angeles and California. Hollis had recognized both the mayor and the governor on more than one occasion.

The invitation to attend had thrilled Hollis until he remembered that it conflicted with his plans to take Lois to a dance that evening. He wondered if his father had learned of the date and had then invited him to the dinner to frustrate him. But he decided that was not so. He also thought it was very likely that the dinner with the men was much more important than taking Lois to a dance. When they got to the house, Hollis immediately dispatched a servant to her house across town, telling her he was ill and asking her to see him the following Friday.

Not a word was spoken between Hollis and his father concerning the shooting incident. Hollis had learned long ago that if Thomas chose not to talk about something, it did no good to bring up the subject. Upstairs in his room, peering through the curtains of his high windows at the Fords and Franklins and Chevrolets streaming past on Wilshire, he still felt himself trembling inwardly over the incident. Who hated his father enough to try to murder him? Had an attempt been made before? Would another be made? He sat on the bed, on which the bleak, taciturn manservant Trobridge had laid out his black tuxedo, and discovered his heart was beating rapidly and his hands were visibly shaking. A rap sounded on his door; he looked up, startled, to see Hetty Perkins, the head maid, gazing austerely at him.

"What do you want?" he asked.

"I ain't had your room made yet."

"You had all day to get that done."

"I had lots else to do."

"Well, you can skip it now. If you haven't gotten to it by now, you can skip it."

She stood there, staring. He wanted to send her away—he usually felt chilled in her presence and never could understand why his father kept her on—but he did nothing. In her black dress with a small white collar, her age-spotted gray face with a sharp nose and dark eyes cocked forward, her withered hands hanging like dry sticks out of the wrist-length sleeves, she appeared like a witch caricature in Halloween posters.

"What happened out there today?" she asked in her croaking, dry voice.

He whirled. "How do you know something happened?"

"Word gets around."

He felt a flash of exasperation. The busybody old hag, snooping around and discovering things and then having the nerve—she, a mere servant—to confront him with questions. He stood up and met her dark stare.

"I think I shall ask father to remove you from this household," he said.

"Well, he won't do that."

"I think he might."

She stepped toward him and then stopped. Her scrawny finger moved up and pointed at him, and for a short moment, looking at her, Hollis felt not only chilled but also frightened. She was more than eccentric, he realized. She was mad.

"Oh, he'll pay," she said. "They always have to pay it in the end."

"What in the world are you talking about now?"

"There's a curse on this family. You'll find out; oh, you'll find out, if you don't know already."

His fists clenched. "Get out of my room. You have no business in my room." He spoke softly and coolly, but his mind had begun to flare. He usually was polite to servants, in contrast to his father who treated them with indifference and disdain, but this mad witch had gone too far. "You will be dismissed," he said.

"Try it."

"I have told you to get out."

Her lips twisted in a sly smile, revealing her black teeth. She spoke as she backed away. "Once I thought you was better'n 'im, but I don't no more. He's got you in his footsteps and so you'll carry it on, just like him. I don't think you have much choice."

Now his temper was getting the best of him. "Get *out!*"

She was gone, seeming to fade into the dark hall, and Hollis went to draw his bath. He was seething at her impertinence; she had become increasingly bold and haggish each day since he'd returned from school for summer vacation, but this outburst had been too much. She must be removed. He would talk to his father about it soon. What she said meant nothing. She was mad. Yet he could not get it out of his mind. What stuck most were her final words: "I don't think you have much choice."

He sat down on his bed and began to remove his clothing. One of his shoes was stained with Spirit's blood. Hollis felt a stab of hurt. The incident on the hill flooded back to him, and once again left him trembling. His father had told him that fear was foolish and could be eliminated merely by ignoring it, yet Hollis could not conquer these rising pangs. He had visions of violence in the future. Much as he wanted to be fearless like his father, he could not be. Perhaps it would come to him later, the defiance in Thomas Collingsworth's brows. He would work toward that. He went naked to his bathroom and turned on the hot water. Steam clouded his mirror. He ignored the dull pain from his sore ribs. If he could not yet ignore fear, he could ignore pain.

The house in which they lived was now clearly a man's house; the stamp of the woman who'd once also lived there was becoming less defined. It was a huge, two-story structure, made of ivy-covered brick, with eight bedrooms and five fireplaces. When Hollis's mother had been alive, she often ordered the sliding glass doors between the living room and dining room to be removed, and expansive dinner parties had been held. All of them were formal. Hollis merely got peeks. Bankers and businessmen visiting from the East sometimes stayed overnight. Occasionally they brought their wives. Since her death, there had been no big parties, nor had any visitor stayed overnight. To Hollis the house was cold and lonely. He had few friends in Los Angeles. His father dismissed his requests to bring friends in the summer from the prep school he'd attended in New York. So Hollis spent most of his time reading books, most of them on mechanics and business suggested by his father. Occasionally he snuck in the *Golden Book Magazine* and he had a set of Sax Rohmer mysteries he loved.

The house actually was quite plain, fortresslike. It had no extraneous accoutrements such as a swimming pool or tennis courts. It was set back about thirty yards from Wilshire behind a black iron fence with spear points; the lawn, impeccably groomed by a Mexican worker, was always the same shade of bright green. Rose bushes lined the cement walk to the front door. In back was a huge rose garden where women visitors in silks and satins and men in wool and cotton suits had often strolled during the Sunday afternoon parties his mother periodically held. Its maintenance now required the full-time service of another Mexican, who lived in a bunkhouse in back, seldom leaving it, even on weekends. The backyard had a scattering of stately palm trees and gnarled orange and lemon trees. It too was fenced in by iron. The driveway off Wilshire led to a large four-car garage complete with a lube pit. In it was stored Hollis's Mead Ranger bicycle which had represented his only escape when he'd been growing up in the house. Now he had title to a Franklin touring car, a gift from his father upon his prep-school graduation.

His mother had a dual nature to her personality, preferring brightness outside, represented by the roses, and a rather somber inside, represented by square Georgian furniture and huge paintings by Gainsborough and Rubens. Although she had been a staunch Methodist, there were no paintings of a religious nature. Most of the drapes were of a rich velvet, punctually sent out for cleaning each March 1, a ritual initiated by Hollis's mother and maintained by his father after her death. They were maroon upstairs and brown downstairs. Thomas had not changed a thing in the house after his wife's death, and Hollis occasionally sensed her presence there. The Waterford crystal, the sterling silverware from Germany, the fine thin tea sets from China, and the delicate French dining plates and cups—all smacked of her. Thomas had allowed her to do with the house as she pleased, declaring her taste to be sound, with the exception of two rooms that belonged to him—his study with a fireplace and a giant rolltop desk with secret compartments that had always aroused Hollis's curiosity, and a game room upstairs that both intrigued and unnerved him, for among the Winchester rifles and Smith & Wesson and Colt pistols were a Gatling gun and a Civil War cannon, loaded and primed and in perfect condition.

After his wife's death, Thomas had slashed the in-house help to six—two French maids, pretty women in their thirties who chatted incessantly in their native language, Hetty Perkins, kept on despite the fact that she had no real function, a red-cheeked Irish woman named Harriet O'Brien, who cooked and handled the supplies, a handyman called Josh who doubled as a waiter during social functions, and the manservant-butler Trobridge, who, Hollis had discovered, had a hidden, wry humor despite his outward cool snobbery. Hollis seldom spoke to the servants, except to give them instructions, which, with the exception of Hetty, they carried out promptly and obsequiously; his father had taught him that servants, even if they were not colored or Mexican, were inferiors and Hollis genuinely believed that. He did not know Josh's last name nor Trobridge's first name. He liked Harriet O'Brien, a good cook and a pleasant, competent forty-year-old widow, and he secretly felt a strange and disturbing sexual urging toward her. He was a virgin who'd gone no further than kissing, despite opportunities presented to him by classmates at the prep school—girls from a nearby school smuggled past the somnolent houseman.

The servants lived in separate rooms upstairs; Hollis had never been in any of the rooms, but he knew which one Harriet O'Brien occupied. He had no sexual urges toward the French maids, though they were younger and prettier than the plain-looking cook. Sex was still a mystery to Hollis and he lay writhing on warm nights, not daring to touch his erect penis out of fear someone would discover traces of semen on the satin sheets. He was not allowed to make his own bed—one of his father's rules—and the sheets were changed by the maids every day.

Except for sexual experience, he now considered himself almost a man, and apparently Thomas Collingsworth had so ordained him. He was about six feet tall, with black steady eyes like his father's, a fair complexion inherited from his mother, brown wavy hair, and he considered himself handsome. His father was not handsome, but his mother had been beautiful. When she died, all pictures of her had been removed, packed in a box by the maids, but Hollis had a small tinted photo of her hidden in a dresser drawer and he often looked at it. She had been too busy in the social whirl to pay much attention to him; besides, she always told him he was his father's boy. Yet he had loved and admired her. Now, in his tuxedo, prepared to attend the first dinner party to which his father had granted admission, he removed the photo and looked at it. She was the most beautiful woman he had ever seen.

When he heard the guests beginning to arrive, he took one last look at himself in the mirror, brushed down an unruly lock of hair, and descended the staircase. He noticed Hetty Perkins standing down the dark hall, staring at him. He felt a slight chill. This was his first meeting with his father's associates and friends on an equal basis, and he was nervous. Her presence heightened the nervousness. But he must get control of himself. These were equals, not men to fear.

All the guests arrived on time, practically together. They were assembled in the big dining room, which had the largest fireplace Hollis had ever seen—hundreds of red bricks that ran floor to ceiling, twelve feet wide at the base. A Persian rug covered the hardwood floor. Hollis paused. His father had not yet come down. Trobridge was serving highballs, something that surprised Hollis, for liquor was illegal and he'd never seen it in the house. He waited, hesitant to enter before his father appeared. Hollis knew very little of Thomas Collingsworth's business life, for his father had told him he would learn about business only after he finished college. But he knew there was a newspaper, landholdings, and he'd heard a motion-picture studio lately had been acquired. He felt a hand on his shoulder; turning abruptly, he found himself staring into his father's eyes.

"Come ahead," Thomas said. "I'll introduce you."

The evening passed in an excited whirl, and when it was over Hollis knew for certain something he'd only suspected before. He was the son of one of the most important and powerful men in the city and he was heir to power and influence. There were six guests at the dinner. The first man Hollis met was named Henry E. Huntington, a tall, almost shy, distinguished figure who seldom smiled and talked very little. Then Hollis met the mayor of Los Angeles, who smiled at him and reminded Hollis that his father was to serve as grand marshal for a city parade to be held the following Sunday. Hollis did not need to be reminded, for he had delayed his entry into Harvard to attend it beside Thomas Collingsworth. Next he was introduced to a curious-looking man with a long white beard and a full head of white hair. His name was H. Gaylord Wilshire. There was a twinkle in his old blue eyes and his handshake was firm.

"Hear you're going to Harvard, lad," he said. "It's my school and I'll say there's no better school."

Hollis knew something about Wilshire. He'd staked a claim to some property years ago, named it Wilshire Boulevard after himself, and later sold it. He'd become a Socialist and an admirer of George Bernard Shaw, so much an admirer that he'd groomed himself to resemble Shaw. Wilshire had spent some time in England and had picked up an affected English accent. Why a Socialist would be invited to his father's home was a question to ponder, but perhaps it was because the Socialist Wilshire had made and lost millions several times over.

The next man Hollis met was the Los Angeles police chief, an austere, dark figure who talked and acted more like a banker than a policeman. His name seemed well fitted to his personality—Gray. It quickly became clear to Hollis from Gray's snide, behind-the-back comments that he held no affection for Wilshire. Hollis then met a senator from Washington named Horace Lewiston, and, last—a person he later concluded was the most imposing of them all—William Mulholland, head of the Los Angeles Water Department, who, Hollis knew, had supervised the building of the marvelous Los Angeles–Owens River Aqueduct, which had turned the San Fernando Valley from a rain-dependent, unpredictable farming area into a lush and booming mecca. Mulholland was the huskiest of them all, an outdoorsman with a hard red face and a large, bushy mustache. He often used colorful metaphors in his speech.

Hollis moved among the powerful six—seven, including his father—quietly and respectfully, feeling not quite one of them but realizing he could reach that status someday, absorbing with fascination their talk of acquisitions, the stock market, moneymaking. These men called his father by his first name, Tom. But, although they called him Hollis in their brief conversations with him, he used their surnames, preceded by "mister," in response, a respectfulness he knew his father appreciated.

"I admire that Gainsborough. I say admire," Huntington told Thomas. "But I say also I am not envious of you for the rest of your art. Not envious."

"My taste runs to land, not art," Thomas responded. "And, since we are among friends here, I can say this. I suspect your art taste is guided more by Arabella than you, and your philanthropy to this city, although appreciated, is dictated by guilt and a desire for immortality."

Huntington took no umbrage at the remark. "I don't want to die with my name hated." He looked directly at Hollis. "I say hated," he said.

Hollis had read about Huntington's mansion in San Marino. It was filled with famous works of eighteenth-century art, Shakespeare folios, original manuscripts by Ben Franklin, Tennyson, Poe, Thoreau. It also contained the largest collection of Lincoln letters and writings in existence. The words "name hated" had surprised Hollis, for he was under the impression the city had deep respect for the Huntington name. Henry and his uncle, Collis, had been behind the Southern Pacific Railroad, and, later, Henry Huntington had created the Red Car transportation system in Los Angeles. Some of Hollis's finest days had been spent on Red Car outings. He recalled one particularly joyful day last summer, a wiener roast at Redondo Beach with his Sunday-school class; he remembered vividly the frolicking and laughing by the sea, the taste of the burned wieners and hot marshmallows, the poppies along the track, the tall oil derricks, truck farms of celery and lettuce, the pepper and eucalyptus trees. And, riding back, they sang "After the Ball." Lois had been there and their hands had secretly brushed. It had been the best day in his life.

But this day, despite the incident in the valley, might be

turning out to be an even better one. They filed into the dining room and took their places in high-backed chairs beside the huge table. It was a plain meal—leg of lamb and vegetables preceded by a salad and a thick pea soup—but Harriet O'Brien's skill in the kitchen had made it tasty. Trobridge served gravely while the men ate prodigiously. They talked of their vision of the Los Angeles of the future, of the thousands pouring weekly into the area, of the real estate and oil boom, construction and trade. Hollis drank it in.

Thomas, seated at the head of the table in a chair with the highest back of all, turned to Mulholland. "Bill, d'you remember the time when we all tried to get you to run for mayor?"

"I remember it well. I was touched."

"But you turned us down. D'you recall what you said when you turned us down?"

"No."

"You said, and I quote, 'I would rather give birth to a porcupine backwards than be mayor of Los Angeles.'"

Wilshire issued a cackling laugh. The real mayor smiled tolerantly. Mulholland said: "I deny that I said that."

"It might even be recorded in my paper," Thomas said.

"As I remember, both you and the *Times* supported me, or at least tried to push me into it," Mulholland responded.

The current mayor, seated between the senator and the police chief, decided he'd better enter into the conversation. "Bill is correct," he said. "It isn't an easy job."

"Well, we try to help you as much as we can," added Thomas. "And we know we get your help in return. We appreciate it. With the unions pushing like elephants, we need a strong city hall and a strong police department."

The police chief, who seemed uncomfortable and out of place, said slowly: "When you need that help, Tom, you sing out."

"We need a clean city," Thomas affirmed. "We don't need bums and drifters. We need investors."

"Hear, hear," Wilshire spoke up. "And speaking of investors . . ." He paused, but got no reaction. "I'm up to something that's worth millions."

Thomas eyed the ancient Shavian. "I figured you'd come back to town to push some scheme," he said. "I'll tell you what I'll do, Wilshire. I'll buy into your idea, whatever it is, if you join the chamber, and the Merchants and Manufacturers."

The remarks drew unanimous laughter from the group. Both the Chamber of Commerce and the Merchants and Manufacturers Association were known as stubbornly antiliberal and antilabor, and Wilshire, the self-proclaimed Socialist, had attacked them for years in his newspaper, *The Challenge*. Hollis had learned about Wilshire from an article he'd read in the *Daily News*. Wilshire once had challenged the constitutionality of a city ban on speaking in public parks by inviting a policeman to one of his tirades. Naturally, he'd been arrested; later, a judge exonerated him, declaring that the constitution trumps an old city ordinance. Wilshire, who'd once run for Congress, loved publicity. Once he'd offered ten thousand dollars to debate socialism with William Jennings Bryan. Hollis saw him now as an insincere quack, the butt of jokes. He realized Wilshire had been invited to the dinner only as an object of ridicule. There were only six men of power in the room, not seven.

Hollis had pondered much about wealth and power. His father, he knew, had both, and Hollis had accepted it as a way of life. It made them superior, above the crowd. They would never carry lunch pails, they bathed at least once a day, they never had dirt under their fingernails, they were advanced in education and social graces. The eastern boys at the prep school seemed the most superior of all, scorning Hollis, a Californian, sometimes taunting and ostracizing him. Some were trained to use their fists, in a gentlemanly way, and Hollis had lost many a scrap before he'd taken matters into his own hands, attending the Jimmy DeForest Boxing Course in New York one summer and then returning to defeat the school's best boxer. After that, they had accepted him, drawing him into their political debates, inviting him to their homes on weekends. Politics fascinated Hollis. His father had once told him: "Anybody can be president; you just have to be in the right place at the right time." That seemed true. And it was also true that the best government was that which let businessmen exercise their vision and strength without interference. America was the most powerful nation in the world and it had been created and shaped by its merchants and industrialists.

Thomas Collingsworth pushed back his dessert plate, a signal for Trobridge to bring cigars. They were the finest Havanas. Each man, including Hollis, took one; soon the air was filled with smoke, men's smoke. Hollis puffed, choked, and immediately felt a little ill. He felt the throbbing pain return to his ribs. Huntington awarded him a concerned gaze.

"If it's too strong for you, I say if the cigar is too strong, don't feel compelled to smoke it," he said.

"It's all right, sir," Hollis responded weakly.

They went into the living room, Hollis trailing. His head was swimming and his stomach felt queasy, but he would stick this one out. It was too valuable to abandon.

"The Democrats went out with Wilson," said his father, relaxed in the depth of his favorite easy chair. "I liked Coolidge and I didn't mind Harding. Hoover seems solid. But we're going to wait a long, long time before another Teddy Roosevelt comes galloping by. Most of these new politicians have wild hares up their asses."

"Hear, hear," chanted the mayor.

Thomas paused to gaze at the long ash on his cigar. "You open your purse to send a man to Sacramento or Washington and when he gets there he forgets you, even votes against your interest," he said, tapping the ash into a silver ashtray. "So you have to call him back, tell him that when a man owes you money, you own him. You warn him, remind him he's got some skeletons in his closet."

The senator seemed uneasy. The police chief twitched his mouth and pulled on his mustache. Mulholland cleared his throat and sat stiffly, his eyes squinting, as if deeply lost in thought.

Wilshire stood up and brushed his beard. "I should like to challenge you, sir, but you are my host," he said.

"Challenge," Thomas declared. "I shouldn't mind five minutes of your bullshit."

"I'd rather demonstrate something to this group."

"I grant you the floor for five minutes."

Wilshire had his small blue satchel brought to him by a signal to Trobridge. Hollis, stubbornly unwilling to surrender this pleasure of smoking with men despite his dizziness, saw that the satchel contained a coil resembling insulated wire. Wilshire, looking very serious, placed the coil around his neck. The coil had an electric socket cord, which Wilshire plugged in. Immediately, two small flashlight bulbs came on at the ends of the coil. Wilshire leaned back, his eyes closed.

"Just what in the devil's hell is that?" Thomas inquired.

Wilshire's eyes opened. "I will explain. As you gentlemen

perhaps have heard, I have formed a new company, I-on-a-co. I am a socialist by nature and philosophy but a capitalist by necessity, for one must live."

"Quickly," Thomas said, his voice showing exasperation.

"This small device, gentlemen—" He paused, as if to challenge the order for brevity, and then continued slowly: "This small device has been known to cure many ailments, and I have testimonials to prove it. Cancer, diabetes, heart disease, paralysis, dropsy, varicose veins, gallstones. Your own Bill Sisk has testified that the device cured his dog of Saint Vitus' dance."

The men were laughing, laughter Hollis heard through an increasing unsteadiness in his stomach.

"I want in," Mulholland said.

"Sorry, closed company," Wilshire retorted. "But you can buy one for fifty-eight dollars and fifty cents cash. Good for prostate troubles, Bill."

"My name, to quacks, is William Mulholland."

"I resent that. I am no quack."

"All right now," Thomas said. "Put your toy away, Wilshire."

"I plan a substantial advertising program for this toy, as you call it. Perhaps, sir, I shall use the *Times* instead of your paper."

"Do it. They could use the revenue."

There was a long moment of silence, punctuated by throat clearings. Smoke filled the air. Finally the mayor said:

"I hear you've become a moviemaker, Tom."

"I have a studio, yes, but I think it's of more value as a landholding than as a motion-picture company."

"I understand that you did not buy it. You *won* it."

"In a manner of speaking."

The mayor looked around. "If anyone here wishes to challenge our host to a game of chess, I should be delighted to officiate the massacre."

No one challenged. Hollis had heard his father's skill at chess was legendary, but he had never seen him play. Chess sets, however, were scattered all over the house.

"I should think motion pictures have a good future," the senator said. "They line up to see the talkies."

"Perhaps they do," Thomas agreed. "That chap from Boston, Joe Kennedy, thinks so."

"Kennedy? I don't know the name."

"You will. He's a doer."

Hollis coughed. He gagged. "Father," he said. "Please excuse me."

He turned and dashed up the stairs, making it just in time to regurgitate his undigested dinner into the toilet bowl. He washed his face, brushed vomit from the lapel of his tuxedo, brushed his teeth, pulled off his clothes, and flung himself into bed. The room was going around in circles but finally he slept. A sharp rap on the door awakened him in what seemed only minutes later, but his clock said midnight. It was his father.

"You're all right?" asked Thomas.

"I—I think so."

"Did you learn anything at the dinner?"

"I did, yes. Thank you."

"Do you know why I invited Wilshire?"

"I'm not sure."

"What did you think of him?"

"Like Mr. Mulholland said, a quack."

"I hope you learned something. That man—yes, a quack—has used our system of government to make millions, yet declares himself party to a political philosophy alien to us, one that would destroy us if it had the power. You see him for what he is. A fraud."

"Yes, sir."

Hollis's stomach had settled down. His head was clear. This was the first time in his life his father had visited him in his room and he decided to take advantage of the vulnerability that fact seemed to create by asking a question he probably would not have dared ask under any other circumstances.

"Father?"

"Yes."

"Do you know why we were fired at in the valley today?"

"Are you frightened?"

"No. No longer. I was, but not any more."

"You showed a cool head." Thomas paused. Then he said: "You will grow to discover that those who earn a lot of money of necessity create enemies."

"Do you know who it was?"

"I do."

"Will he try again?"

"The matter will be handled," Thomas said.

He backed away, saying no more.

3.

HIS BODY SCRUBBED pink with Palmolive soap, his hair washed with Packer shampoo and slicked down with Wildroot tonic, his teeth brushed with Ipana paste, his mouth Listerine-doused and his nerves Sal Hepatica-calmed, a maturity-symbol package of Fatima cigarettes in the inside pocket of his gray cotton suit, a Studebaker watch ticking on his wrist, Hollis Collingsworth threaded his new Franklin through heavy traffic, his heart beating with a young lover's desire. He did not know what he would do or say when he saw Lois. He was a different person than he'd been when he'd last seen her; he'd been initiated into the power realm of his father. An anguished conflict raged in his breast. For a while Lois had faded from his memory, but she had returned warmly to his consciousness when he'd been dressing for the dance that evening. He looked forward to touching her and dancing with her, the prettiest girl at the dance. Perhaps there would be a kiss or two, full kisses, the way she kissed with her lips slightly parted, holding him lightly. He wanted to hear her laugh. She was great fun, a free spirit who was extremely popular with boys but had an intelligent serious side.

He'd felt jealous rage more than once when someone had tapped his shoulder to break in on their dance. But he knew his father was right. Lois was not the girl for him, not on a serious, long-term basis; tonight, he would break it off, explaining that Harvard had accepted him and he had at least four years of hard study ahead. It was not the real reason, of course. He was breaking with her because he had decided to obey his father. It was necessary if he was to accept the legacy of Thomas Collingsworth. Their union simply was not right. She was Catholic. He was Methodist. He was from a wealthy family. She was not. Her father owned a radio dealership, providing a modest income for his large family. Hollis believed it was a Crosley dealership. He had a Crosley, a Bandbox six-tube receiver with a power converter. He'd talked with Lois's father only once and he remembered they had discussed Crosleys. Hollis saw him as a provider, but a man of small talk and little vision.

The Mullaneys lived in Hollywood in a Spanish bungalow with a red tile roof. Hollis parked the Franklin across the street, turned off the lights, and sat pondering. Perhaps it would be best to act cool to her from the onset, or maybe even skip the dance, just get it over with. He steeled himself for the task, trying to think of things he did not like about her, but he could think of none. He approached her door full of resolve, but when she opened it and stood smiling before him, the resolve melted and he felt his heartbeat pick up. In the background he heard noises of children playing and Al Jolson on the radio singing "Swanee River." Crickets shrilled around him and he smelled lilacs in the full warm burst of a summer night. He stood gaping at her.

"Want to come in first?" she asked. "Or, shall we just go?"

"Let's go," he said.

"I'll get my purse."

She was wearing an olive-green flannel suit with pleats in the skirt and a white blouse with small pockets just above her hips. The skirt was slightly more than knee length. In a second he drank her in—the thin boylike body, the white neck, the red full mouth and large blue eyes offset by long lashes—and the old stirrings returned. He felt miserable, waiting for her, hearing the sounds of her family in the house, and for a moment he fought deep anxiety, fearing that she would not come out, that her father suddenly had forbidden it. But she returned, a hat over her brown curls, holding a small night purse. He took her hand and they moved across the street in a running skip, lovers escaping, and at that moment he knew he was the luckiest and happiest person in the state. In the Franklin he moved to kiss her.

"You'll get mussed," she said.

"I don't care."

"How long have I known you? Have I known you long enough to allow you a kiss?"

"Yes."

"Well, I won't. I think my mother is watching."

He started the engine, whirled the Franklin around the corner, and stopped it with the emergency brake. The engine coughed and died. When he leaned toward her, she moved her face to meet him and then their lips met, softly at first, then harder, and he felt the tickling edge of her tongue on his.

She pulled away. "We're late for the dance."

"Let's not go to the dance."

"Why not?"

"Let's get something to eat and then go to the movies. *Camille* is playing, with Norma Talmadge. You know how you like the movies."

"No. We're going to the dance. This was to be a dance date and we're going to the dance."

He sighed, knowing she again had him captured. "All right. But you won't dance with everybody."

"I'll dance only with you."

"Is that a promise?"

"It's a promise."

"I like your outfit."

"Thank you. I ordered it through *Photoplay*."

"The movie magazine?"

"I don't like buying like that, but this one seemed so cute I had to try it."

The Franklin rolled onto Hollywood Boulevard, zipping through traffic, cutting in front of the Red Car. He liked to drive at breakneck speeds, braking sharply to stop, swerving around corners, snapping to jackrabbit starts. If the cops stopped him, all he did was show them identification and, seeing who he was, the cops let him go with slight warnings. The car was his and he could do with it as he wanted; it represented freedom and power. He was a good driver who'd never had a serious accident, despite some close calls. Lois had first admonished him for his driving habits, but she'd soon learned it was hopeless to try to cure him. Now she seemed to enjoy the thrill of it. She laughed, said mock prayers, and hung on.

She was a girl with a mind of her own and one who could handle him. She seemed at once close and distant, something he suspected was a deliberate ploy. Once she'd confessed shyly that her ambition was to become a movie star. When Hollis had discovered his father had acquired a motion-picture studio, he'd told her in a burst of excitement that maybe he could get her "in." She'd thrust out her chin and declared she would make it by merit, not by pull, or not make it at all. That seemed to Hollis a rather foolish position, but he accepted it, knowing the fact that his father owned a studio wouldn't hurt their relationship.

"Well," she said over the screech of braking. "We made it here alive."

"Was there any doubt?"

"You should be driving for the Keystone Kops."

He had put on an unusually stunning performance, even for him. It was not to entice her by playing the Fitzgerald role of the careless rich boy; it was a way of ridding himself of the deep frustration and conflict raging within. He cared for her, loved her—yes, loved her with a depth he'd previously thought beyond his capabilities—yet he must tell her to go away from him.

The evening passed in a whirl. Dancing cheek to cheek to the mellow strains of "The Man I Love," he felt as if they were the only ones on the crowded floor. It was the Ambassador Ballroom and the Lewis Carroll band played only popular, sentimental tunes; it wasn't the heated jazz and the Charleston at the Venice Pier dance hall where they sometimes went. He gazed deeply into her eyes, a love look, and he thought she responded in kind.

I'll see you in my dreams ...
Lips that once were mine, tender eyes that shine....

She kept her promise. Every dance was his, despite the fact she received invitations from others. They danced slowly in a linked magic spell, enchanted and spellbound, wanting the evening to go on forever.

Just Mollie and me,
And baby makes three.
We're happy in my blue heaven....

Their table was far from the floor, in a quiet dark space. It had cost him a twenty-dollar bribe to get it, something he knew impressed her. During intermissions they sipped Cokes through straws and held hands. He lit a Fatima.

"Hollis, when did you start smoking?" she scolded.

"Just lately."

"Can I have one?"

"No. It will stunt your growth."

"If I smoked and my mother saw it, she'd skin me."

"What time do you have to be home?"

"Midnight. You know that. Midnight, or I get skinned."

"Let's drive up the canyon and park."

"The last time we did that it was a close call."

"I won't try anything. I just want to talk."

"Well, I don't know."

The band had returned, starting with "Tea for Two." An old couple at the next table was smiling at them. Hollis released her hand and stood up.

"At least let's get out of here," he said.

"I'll go up there with you," she said.

He drove slowly, one arm around her, steering with the other. The scent of her perfume overwhelmed him. The headlights caught the outline of a deer. They wound slowly upward and the city sparkled below like a gigantic swarm of fireflies.

"When I was a little girl, I wanted to be a nun," she told him, snuggling close.

"Whatever for?"

"Oh, nuns seemed so content, so holy." She hummed slowly: "'Who...stole my heart away? Who/...makes me dream all day?'" Then she said: "What do you want to be, Hollis?"

"Well, that's pretty well laid out. I'll be in my father's business."

"Didn't you ever think about being something else? I mean, like a painter or writer or actor?"

"No. That's dabbling."

Perhaps he'd said the wrong thing. She moved away. "Not for me it's not dabbling. I think the idea of performing, especially on the stage, is a wonderful thing. You're not yourself but the character you portray. I've felt it in little theater."

"You're really set on that, aren't you?"

"I think I am," she said.

"What do your parents think?"

"Well, I haven't told them, of course. But if I did, they'd skin me. They want me to find a good Catholic boy and raise a big Catholic family."

"What do they think of me?"

"Daddy likes you. He's awed by your name."

"How about your mother?"

"She looks worried before we go out together. I'm being honest now."

"And how about you? What do you think about me?"

"I'm not going to hold back anything, Hollis. Not tonight. I'm going to tell you what I feel. I've held back before, but I'm not going to hold back anymore. The truth is I'm nuts about you, head over heels. It scares me."

"Why does it scare you?"

"Are we old enough to talk this way?"

"Don't answer questions with questions. Why does it scare you?"

"I don't know. It just *does*. Oh, I guess I do know. I haven't dated another boy for almost two years now. I want you to know that."

"Good. I'd skin you if you did."

They were nearing the top. Now she was humming "Three O'Clock in the Morning." A million stars glistened and the moon was full; they were at a silver height between massive, twinkling blankets below and above. He stopped at the side of the road and turned off the engine and lights. *I'm crazy about you, head over heels*. She had never admitted that before. She'd been coy with him, even taunting him by flirting with other boys, but now he knew she could be his. And he wanted her, this Irish girl with freckles and long thin legs; he wanted to touch and kiss and possess her, to join with her in a long waltz up to mountaintops. *Head over heels*. Looking at her, Hollis felt in a new world, a soft world of love; it was not his father's hard real world, a loveless world. And tonight he would break from and disobey his father.

"Is head over heels the same as love?" he asked.

"I guess so. I'm not sure what love is. But I'm sure a person knows when it's there."

"And you think it's there? For me?"

She paused, thinking very seriously. Then she said: "Yes."

Hollis felt a joyful thud in his heart. Looking at her lovely profile etched in the moonlight, breathing in the scent of her mixed with the ivy and peppertree smells of the night, he realized emotions of both lust and love. He reached out and held her, held her for a long time, looking at the stars and feeling great wanting stabs. A vision of his father on the powerful stallion came to him. He drove it away, holding her even tighter. Her hands caressed his back. When he moved to kiss her, she came to him with a small gasp, her lips parted. His heart hammered and his blood flow quickened. He tasted her mouth, exploring her tongue with his. He felt and heard her breathing rise excitedly. It was a long kiss, one he did not want to end, one he sensed she did not want to end. He touched her blouse, feeling for her breast. She put her hand tightly over his, pressing it down. But when he tried to unbutton her blouse, she broke the kiss and moved away.

"We shouldn't go on," she said.

"Why?" He felt slight anger. "You came up here with me."

"I know I did."

"Then why?"

"It's not right."

"It's not right? What kind of answer is that?"

They sat silently for a long time. Then he said: "You said you were scared of loving me. Why are you?"

"Oh, Hollis, you know the answer to that."

"I don't think I do."

"All right. I'll go over it. We've hinted at it in the past. You live in a big house I've never been in, live with maids and butlers and all those things. I live in a small house that still has diaper smells. It's like in the movies you see."

"That doesn't matter to me."

"And I'm Catholic. Irish Catholic."

"That doesn't matter, either."

"Well, it matters to my parents. That you're not, I mean."

"That's silly."

"Maybe it is. But it's there nevertheless."

Again he reached out and held her, gently this time, and she responded warmly, pressing her cheek against his, and when he looked at her he realized she was crying.

"I want you to marry me," he said, blurting it out. "I'm going away to college, but I want you to marry me and go with me. I wasn't prepared to say that, but I am saying it and I mean it. I *do* mean it."

She spoke between sobs. "Maybe you do now."

"What does that mean? I will forever. I love you."

She moved away, fumbling in her purse for a handkerchief, and sat tightly, her hands clenched. "It wouldn't work," she said. "Besides, I'm serious about wanting to become an actress."

"I can help you."

"But you don't under*stand*! I want to do it on my own."

Again anger flared in him, coming with pain in his forehead. "So you're turning me down?"

"No. I'm not turning you down." She paused. She looked at him. "Oh, I suppose I am. At least for now."

"But you just said that you love me."

"I do. I *do*. But we're not being practical."

"If we wait it won't happen. I know that for sure."

"But we have to take that chance."

"Do you know what you're throwing away?"

"Hollis, I'm not throwing you away. I don't want to do that. I just think we should wait."

"You want your cake and eat it too."

"No. I want you. I'm just perceptive enough to realize I wouldn't be accepted. Not now."

"You'd be accepted if I want you to be accepted."

"Somehow I just don't believe that."

"Now I'm getting angry."

"I'm sorry. I don't want that. I've seen you angry, and I can't stand it."

"Well, maybe he was right," Hollis mumbled.

"Who was right?"

"Never mind. I'll take you home."

"All right."

"It's close to midnight."

"All right," she said.

4.

IT SEEMED AS if the entire city turned out for the parade, held on a glorious summer Sunday that rained sunshine from a giant clear sky. The parade moved along Main Street, assembling at Thirty-sixth Street and ending at Second Street. To Hollis, riding at its head in an open Cadillac beside his father, it was an event to breathe in and to remember forever. The Cadillac bore a yellow streamer: "PARADE MARSHAL: Thomas Collingsworth, Publisher Los Angeles *Bulletin-News*." Main Street was lined ten rows deep with spectators, cheering children and women in bright bonnets, men in suits and straw hats. Vendors sold Cokes and peanuts and ice-cream bars. Behind the Collingsworth car came cars with the mayor, the governor of California, senators from Sacramento and Washington, Los Angeles City Council members, and business leaders. Army biplanes circled in formation above and the Goodyear "Pony" blimp nosed over the buildings like a fat, lazy bubble.

Hollis had watched the assembly of the parade and, as it moved, he knew its exact composition and order. There were high-school and university bands in bright braided uniforms, clowns and jugglers, peanut-eating elephants and pacing caged lions, bicycles and unicycles, baton twirlers and military-school drill teams, and elaborate floats such as that of the Chinese Consolidated Benevolent Association, which featured pagodas, dragon-painted paper lanterns, and Chinese women in native dress. There were Mexican riders in ruffled white shirts and black sombreros with silver braid. They sat square-shouldered on heaving horses with elaborate leather saddles and silver-trimmed bridles. Will Rogers spun rope tricks from the back of a spirited pony. Mary Pickford and Douglas Fairbanks rode waving and smiling in an open coach drawn by six white horses. Tom Mix drove his racing car, *The Speed Machine*. Firemen and policemen marched in uniform and after them came the veterans—sailors in white, marines in full parade dress, army doughboys with rifles over their shoulders and ammunition pouches buckled on their waists, proudly displaying ribbons and medals on their chests. The marchers moved in precise unison, not like individual men but like a coordinated machine.

Riding beside his father, hearing the cheers of the spectators and the boom of the bands, Hollis devoured the spectacle, proud to be at the head of it, so thrilled he felt prickles on his skin and shivers up his spine. Thomas wore a dark wool suit and a broad-brimmed Mexican hat. He neither waved nor smiled, but sat erect and still, as if contemplating an important matter. Hollis was dressed similarly to his father, except for the hat. Also he knew his father carried the Colt .45 under his coat and in an electric moment details of the shooting in the hills and the destruction of his mare flooded in vivid scenes before his consciousness. He shook it away. He did not want to think about that or anything else unpleasant, such as the hours of anger and hurt pride that had followed Lois's rejection of him. These moments of the parade, a blaring human-animal city salute he co-led, were too precious to lose in dark and hurt remembrances of the past.

We are Collingsworths, he thought, *and we lead.* It was something he'd heard his father say many times. *We lead.*

They were nearing the end, passing the Citizens National Bank building, when the driver braked sharply and stopped. Hollis felt a flash of fear. He did not know why. The driver, the giant colored man who had ridden ahead with the small flat-nosed man the day of their ride in the valley, sprang open the front door. He looked at Hollis, his eyes wide and his mouth open. Hollis saw that a man in overalls stood in front of the Cadillac. The man darted to the side of the car and faced Thomas. He was smiling. There was something in his hand and only when he raised it did Hollis realize it was a pistol. The scene then began to shift around Hollis in a quickening pace—his father's hand reaching for the Colt, the black giant rising from the front to spring toward the gunman, the explosion of a shot, his father's head jerking backward, blood spurting from his forehead, the Colt rattling to the floor. He tried to say something—to shout, to scream—but his throat was suddenly too dry to utter a sound. Blood covered his shirt. A red chunk of bone from his father's skull lay in his lap. He brushed it down, snapping at it with the back of his hand. The driver was wrestling the gunman to the ground. Then the pandemonium of the crowd rushed in and Hollis closed his eyes and moaned in the shivering crimson-tinged darkness.

5.

HE'D GONE TO the parade a man-boy but he returned from it fully a man. The day that had begun in the dazzle of sunlight and the clang and color of the parade disintegrated into a dazed, surrealistic nightmare—ambulance screams, the crush of people, police inquisitions, persistent reporters in stained suits and hats pushed back on their heads, patronizing, strained sympathetic smiles, and hesitant comments by a steady stream of men of wealth and power. One man identified himself to Hollis and led him out of the city hall to a Chevrolet parked by the curb.

"You don't have to hold my elbow," Hollis said. "I'm all right."

"As you say."

He was a short man of about fifty, wearing a gray wool suit and wide red suspenders. His face was gray like the suit and he had deep, penetrating eyes. He did not smile. He was not patronizing like the rest. His name was Timothy Helman; Hollis had never met him, but knew Helman was editor of the *Bulletin-News*.

"Where do you want to go?" he asked, moving the car into traffic.

"I'm not sure. Home, I guess."

"Would you like to come down to the newspaper?"

"No."

"My thought is that perhaps you'd want to approve the proofs on the stories about your father's death."

"No. I don't think I want to read about it."

"All right."

"I assume he left things up to you. I'll leave them up to you now."

"Well, he didn't exactly do that. Your father was a perfectionist. Besides, he liked the newsroom. He wrote many of the editorials himself and often approved the layout."

"I don't know anything about newspapers. I'll leave it up to you."

Helman drove very slowly, heading south on Broadway. The traffic had dispersed; the street was nearly empty. It was as if there had been no great parade that day but instead a normal Sunday downtown—loitering men and some ragged winos seeking treasures in trash cans. It was now striking Hollis. He discovered his body was trembling.

"Maybe you could use a shot of gin," Helman said, handing him a silver flask. "Best bathtub stuff around."

"Do you drink a lot?"

"Yes."

"At least you're honest."

Helman took a swig, coughed, and replaced the flask in the inside pocket of his suit. "You'll find I don't hide things," he said.

"Do you know who killed my father?"

"Well, they got 'im, you know. They're looking into his background. All he'll say is that his name is Swede."

Hollis looked at his clothes. The bloodstains had dried. He went through it again in his mind—the sudden appearance of the man with the pistol, his father reaching for his own weapon, the shot, the exposure of red skull bone and the blood gushing from Thomas Collingsworth's forehead. He could not recall seeing the attacker's face; he remembered only that he wore overalls and he remembered the black round barrel of the pistol, pointing like an accusing finger. It reminded him now of the scrawny pointing finger of Hetty Perkins, the household witch, and he recalled her words: "There's a curse on this family." It was almost as if she'd divined this happening. He hated her. Yet now he also feared her, wondering if she had mystical powers.

"You knew my father well?" he asked Helman.

The reply came after a pause. "I knew him, yes. Nobody knew him well, I'd say."

"Why was that?"

"He sort of kept in his own world as far as personal things were concerned."

"You say you're honest about things. Be honest now. I have some questions."

"Let's have them."

"Did you like him?"

"I respected him. Good newspaperman, good businessman."

"Was he a good man?"

"I don't know quite how to answer that. I don't separate men as good or bad."

"He treated you fairly?"

"He gave a dollar's pay for a dollar's work."

Hollis felt slightly amused. "Maybe that should be on his gravestone."

"Maybe so," the editor said.

He recalled that when his mother died he'd felt some sorrow, especially at the funeral, but he felt nothing but emptiness now that his father was dead. He did not know for sure what lay ahead of him, but he knew somehow he would be competent to handle it. His father had imbued him with feelings of self-reliance, and Hollis was grateful for that.

When Helman dropped him off at the big house on Wilshire, he hesitated outside for a few minutes, not wanting to enter. He knew he had been suddenly and violently thrust into a new phase of his life, and the immediate transition confused and worried him. Then, squaring his shoulders, he went in, entering for the first time as a man.

"I can only say I'm sorry," said the stern Trobridge, leading Hollis to a chair in the vast living room. "Is there anything I can get for you?"

"No. Not right now."

"In the future, how do you wish to be addressed?"

"What do you mean?"

"We had addressed you as 'Mr. Hollis.'"

"How had you addressed my father?"

"As 'Mr. Collingsworth,' of course."

"Then that will do for me in the future."

"I will inform the staff."

"Thank you, Trobridge. Trobridge?"

"Yes, sir?"

"I can't say for certain what will happen here, but you may tell everyone, with the exception of Mrs. Perkins, that I wish them to stay on."

"Thank you. I will tell them. I believe, however, that Mrs. Perkins already has resigned. There are some letters and phone messages for you on the table."

Trobridge turned and disappeared, a manner he had of being there one second and gone the next. Hollis opened the first envelope and read Hetty Perkins's exaggerated scrawl: "I have left for service in a S. Pasadena house. Mister once said I had some pension coming, so pls. look into that if you would pls. I been with him near 10 odd yrs. You do like he did, you will end up like him. Mrs. Perkins." He crumbled up the note in a flash of anger and then reopened it and pressed out the crinkles. It would no doubt be wise, for legal purposes, to keep it. Most of the other messages were telegrams of condolence from persons he'd never met but whose names he knew. Trobridge reappeared.

"It's Mr. Lowenfelt, sir."

"Who?"

"Mr. Lowenfelt is here to see you. He handled accountancy work for your father."

"Oh, all right. Have him come in."

Lowenfelt was a slight bald man in an undertaker-black suit. He offered Hollis a cold hand, took a chair uninvited, and opened a leather briefcase.

"Don't sit there," Hollis said. "That was my father's chair."

Lowenfelt shifted to another chair without comment, slipping on reading glasses as he moved. He was all efficiency, all business. He said sternly, hard eyed: "I apologize for bothering you so soon after your tragedy, but I felt I must see you over important matters. I must explain that I was both a lawyer and accountant for your father."

"Did you work only for him?"

"Yes."

"At the paper?"

"I do not go to the paper, Mr. Collingsworth, not anymore. I work out of an office at his headquarters."

"He never told me much about his business."

"He told few about his business. His businesses, that is."

"But he told you?"

"Yes. I kept his books." He regarded Hollis with a hawk's stare. "Tell me, Mr. Collingsworth. Did your father ever mention a will to you?"

"No. I said he told me very little."

"There is a will. That I know. It was a holographic will with a holographic codicil."

"Holographic?"

"Handwritten. I have an unsigned copy of both the will and its codicil. But I do not have the signed original."

"What did the will say?"

"Well, there should be a legal reading, with witnesses."

"There is nothing illegal about your telling me, is there?"

"I suppose not, Mr. Collingsworth. What is important is that we must find the signed document."

"You haven't told me what it said."

"Why—" The lawyer-accountant paused, as if for effect. Again he looked at Hollis. "Mr. Collingsworth left his entire estate to his son. You, Mr. Collingsworth."

Hollis stood up. He turned his back to Lowenfelt. He felt a powerful surge of absolute pleasure, a physical surge that tingled in his loins and warmed his body. He was the heir to wealth and to power, to control, favored with the Collingsworth legacy. And he would carry it on in the name of his father.

"Tell me," Hollis said, turning, "how much is it?"

"I am not really sure, Mr. Collingsworth."

"Is it over a million?"

"Much over that."

"Is it ten million?"

"I would judge it is well over ten million."

"You're his accountant. You must know precisely."

"I don't. Not precisely. Some of the properties have not been evaluated for years."

"Then you evaluate them, or have them evaluated."

"But finding that signed will is of the first order of importance."

"I will work on that. I have an idea where it might be, or know someone who might know. Meanwhile, this is what I want you to do. I want you to take a complete inventory of all of the assets, including personal assets, of the estate. I want the report, in detail."

"That may take some time."

"You have a week."

For the first time Lowenfelt issued a shadow of a smile. "You are your father's son."

As Hollis descended the staircase, planning to enter the mystery room, Thomas Collingsworth's study, for the first time in his life, he found himself yet unable to imagine his father dead, a force so vital and striking that its demise seemed as improbable as the last cataclysmic thunderclap of the world's end. And indeed he saw now that the father perhaps had not totally died, for something of him survived in the son. In fact, much of him survived in the son. He had his father's genes and his blood and he had been trained, guided, and forced to accept the ideas and assume the mannerisms of his father. Thus Thomas Collingsworth had created a form of immortality for himself. He had died before the image had been fully formed, but enough of it had been shaped to judge his plan a success. And it was good.

The French maids had been watching his ascent from the head of the stairs and now they scattered, seeming to suppress giggles. Hollis went to the study and opened the door. He hesitated. He seemed to detect the presence of his father in the dark room. But that was foolish. He found the push-button light switch and turned it on. The room was small and uncarpeted, containing chairs, a cot, files, and the rolltop desk. Hollis knew of the desk only because his father had mentioned it several times, saying many men of means squirrel away important papers in secret compartments of their desks, believing them to be more secure there than entrusted to subordinates or safe-deposit boxes. Hollis rolled up the top slowly, revealing an L. C. Smith typewriter, a pen and pencil set, and scattered blank papers. The desk was made of oak and looked solid as stone. He felt the wood in back. There seemed no evidence of secret compartments. The panel was not of oak, he noticed, but of plywood; at the end to his left, he saw a small groove, deep enough to accommodate his fingertips. Hollis tried it and to his delight it moved, sliding a foot to the right and revealing an inner drawer with a knob. He slid the drawer out. It contained a handwritten manuscript of some hundred pages, seeming to be a hastily written diary of his father's activities in California. He thumbed through it. The paper was old and the ink was blurred in many places. There was no evidence of a will within the pages. Hollis pulled the drawer all the way out and peered into the space it left. Behind it he saw another, smaller, drawer. Cautiously he removed it. He drew out a three-page holographic will, signed on each page by Thomas Collingsworth. Hollis read it rapidly, then again, slowly this time. He backed away, holding it in both hands, turned off the light, and closed the door. When he turned, he saw Harriet O'Brien standing behind him.

"What are you doing there?" he snapped. "Are you spying on me?"

"I wasn't spying. Lord forgive you if you think that."

"Well, you act like it, standing there."

"I knew you were home," she said. "I just wanted to tell you how sorry I am."

He didn't say anything, but he found himself thinking: *I'm not sorry. If I'm honest with myself, I have to say that I'm not sorry.* Harriet O'Brien glanced at the bloodstains on his clothing and when she looked into his eyes it was with a motherly pity that she could not stand. His feelings for her, he knew for certain now, were not filial. She had full hips and full breasts and a face that, although plain, he regarded as sensual and sometimes even wanton. He felt the old stirring for her in his loins.

"Will you be having supper at home?" she asked.

"Yes, I believe so."

"I had planned something simple. Perhaps a stew."

"That would be fine."

"Usually he made out the menu every morning, tellin' a week in advance if there'd be a group and how many."

"All right. I'll do that too, then."

"I am sorry," she said, and went away.

Hollis walked rapidly to his room. He threw off his coat and flung himself down on the bed. Again he read the three-page document, chuckling as he did.

He ordered a small, gravesite-only funeral, attended by the undertaker, a Methodist minister, himself, and the house servants. It was a blustery day and one of the maids giggled when her hat flew off. His father was buried beside his mother in a large family plot at Forest Lawn and Hollis kept looking at the hills beyond. The minister said some foolish words, "We brought nothing into this world, and it is certain we can carry nothing out," and the party moved slowly away to waiting cars. There were no flowers, a request printed in boldface type on the front page of the *Bulletin-News*. Hollis hurried. He had an appointment at the house with Lowenfelt.

Lowenfelt was nobody's yes-man and Hollis respected him for it. "No, no *no!*" the lawyer said, pacing as if for emphasis. "It can't be done."

"I think it can."

"You're only eighteen! The law says you must be twenty-one to take over as administrator."

"Let's change the law."

Lowenfelt's face showed pain. "For twenty years I've been working with your father. For twenty years he's been saying do the impossible, do the impossible. Now I've got him back again, saying do the impossible."

"You said something like that the last time we talked."

"It's true."

"I know it's true," Hollis said. "Tell me. You worked for him twenty years. Why did you stay? Doing the impossible, why did you stay?"

"You ask me why. It's not because I like ulcers."

"That's not answering the question."

Lowenfelt sniffed, drawing in some of the dark hairs in his nose. "Maybe I was a little obsessed with him. He was driven. It wasn't his fault. He missed much in life, but a tiger cannot shed his stripes."

"You've seen the will I found. It names me as sole beneficiary. Does that disappoint you?"

"No. He said that always. That you'd get it if it appeared you were levelheaded enough. Apparently he judged you were levelheaded enough."

"How much do you make a year?"

"Enough."

"I want you to double your salary."

"Why?"

"Why? Because it's what I want. How are you coming along with the asset evaluation?"

"Almost half done, I'd say."

"Good. I'll need it when we go to court. One other matter. Has this man named Swede got a lawyer?"

"Public defender."

"Go out and hire a lawyer for him, a good defense lawyer. But I want to see the lawyer before the trial. I want to see Swede getting all the law allows, but I have a feeling they might try to muddy the Collingsworth name in court and I want to stop that at all costs."

"You think like he did," Lowenfelt said. "You think ahead."

"Tell me, Lowenfelt. It's all profitable, isn't it?"

"All except the raw land, which we should hold for appreciation. We're way ahead on the stocks we own."

"We own?"

"You own." Lowenfelt didn't hesitate. "I think you should sell off most of the stocks."

"Why? It's a bull market, isn't it?"

"That's when it's best to sell."

"Well, I'll think about it." Hollis waved Lowenfelt away. He'd seen his father end meetings with abrupt hand gestures. "Finish the asset evaluation."

"I will," Lowenfelt said.

He had returned to his father's house and his father's possessions, all of which were now his. As he came to the top of the stairs, he saw a light under one of the doors. It was Harriet O'Brien's room. Hollis paused. The light seemed to beckon. He moved toward it, aware of dryness in his mouth and a flutter in his heart. He stood before the door, hesitating, and then tapped lightly on it. He waited. The door opened first a crack and then halfway. Harriet O'Brien stood before him in a blue robe, her hair down, shadowed in the light of the nightstand lamp behind her, the outline of her hip and shoulder showed under the robe.

"What is it?" she asked, her voice low.

"It's—it's about the menu."

"No," she said. "It isn't."

"No," he conceded.

"Come in. They'll hear us."

She closed the door quietly and turned to face him. He found it difficult to control the trembling in his hands. He had always regarded her as a plain woman, but looking at her now he realized she was attractive as well as desirable. He felt a warm flow of blood alive in his veins. She stepped toward him and squeezed him between his legs.

"Ah!" he said. "Do that. *Do* that!"

She touched him with hands surprisingly soft for one who'd scrubbed thousands of dishes over years in the houses of the wealthy, kneading and stroking him until he pushed away her hand in breathless pleasure, fearing he would climax. She stepped back and removed the robe. He gazed almost in awe; she was the first woman he'd seen naked and the sight left him speechless.

"Get in the bed," she said. She smiled. Her eyes were bright. "And it helps to take your clothes off."

She took him, not he her. She left the light on. She lay back, her legs up and spread, and helped him on top of her. She guided him with her hand, thrust him inside of her, and began to rotate her hips, moaning softly. The feeling was so exquisite, so excruciatingly tormenting, that he thought he might faint. He buried his face in her neck and experienced his first climax with a woman.

"No," she said. "Don't take it out. Young fellow like you, you can come again on the same boner."

He couldn't answer. He couldn't get his breath. A half hour later, after three climaxes that seemed to exceed each other in intensity, he lay spent by her side. Only then did she turn off the light.

"It was the first time, wasn't it?" she asked.

"Yes."

"Well, now you're initiated."

"Why did you let me in?"

"I knew you had an eye for me. You'd have done it anyway, just with somebody else. Maybe one of those maids. I thought it might be all right if you were initiated right."

He turned on the bed. "You have a wicked second side."

"I have a second side, but it's not wicked. We all have second sides."

"Have you done this since your husband died?"

"I lost my husband in the war. That was a long time ago."

"So you have."

"It isn't your business but, yes, I have."

"Did you ever do it with my father?"

"No."

"Did he do it with anyone else in the household?"

"I won't talk about your father."

"I want to know."

"What he did wasn't any of my business."

"But did he?"

"Yes. If you want to know, yes. He did it with the maids."

"Both of them?"

"Yes."

"How do you know?"

"Because they told me."

"And I suppose Hetty Perkins knew, too. Is that why she was kept on, because she knew?"

"Yes."

"Then I guess tonight you've earned yourself a lifetime job."

She turned on the light and sat up. "You go now."

"What did I say wrong?"

"I did this for you as a favor, not to earn a job. I'm leaving this house for another job, starting next Saturday."

"So suddenly?"

"It might be sudden to you. Not to me. I decided to leave the day he died. Do you think I would have had you in here if I intended to continue to work for you? Do you think I'm like one of those maids?"

"I'm sorry. I didn't mean it the way it sounded."

"Get on your clothes," she said.

Later, lying in sweat in his room, he realized he'd made a mistake. She had dominated him, trapped and embraced him in her woman's power, and he had been subservient to a servant. For a while he'd reverted from man to boy; she had given him great pleasure, which he knew he would relive in dreams, but she also had extracted from him a measure of his control and manliness. It could not happen again. In the future he would control the women, not be controlled. He realized that sex, perhaps even lust, was one of his weaknesses, just as it had no doubt been a weakness of his father, who had cavorted with the brainless, giggling French maids. But it could be a form of dominance and power if he controlled it. The pleasure then would be much greater. Smelling his sweat in the hot bed, he knew that in his lifetime he would have many, many women. Lust, too, was a part of the legacy. That was just fine. He was glad for it. It was a sign of strength. But he would remain in control. He would have the women, not the other way around.

A week later Hollis Collingsworth's case to become an estate administrator was heard before a probate judge in the courthouse on Spring Street despite the fact he hadn't reached his majority. Lowenfelt presented a forceful argument and then put Hollis on the stand. The judge yawned. Perhaps the case had already been decided.

"Tell me, Mr. Collingsworth," Lowenfelt said. "You are eighteen. Do you think you are mature enough for the responsibilities you face?"

"I think I am."

"You *think*? You are not certain?"

"Yes. I am certain."

"How much schooling do you have?"

"High school. A prep school in the East."

"Do you plan to go on to college?"

"Eventually, yes. Perhaps in a year."

"What will you study?"

"Management and economics."

Lowenfelt turned to the old judge, catching him in the act of scratching his behind. "Do you wish Mr. Collingsworth to present his case personally?" he asked.

"Eh?"

"Should Mr. Collingsworth speak?"

The judge tapped his gavel, as if in answer. "Permission

asked by the appealing party is granted," he said. "I'll sign the papers in chambers."

"That was quick," Hollis told Lowenfelt over lunch.

"Well, he knew your father."

"I'm beginning to think everyone did."

"You may not be too far from the truth."

"What are the total assets?"

"Just over fifteen million dollars." Lowenfelt was going through some papers. "That includes the newspaper and the surrounding land, the landholdings at the beach and the valley, the stocks, and the movie studio. It doesn't include the ranch and house."

"I'd almost forgotten about the studio. I'll want to see that. And the newspaper, too."

"The newspaper is doing all right. But the studio is in bad shape. I still think you should liquidate the stocks."

"All right. If you think so, we'll sell."

"This crazy market scares me. RCA was up almost fifty points the other day. I'm looking for a setback, maybe even a bust."

"Then sell."

Lowenfelt made a note with his fountain pen. "When do you want to go up to the paper?"

"I want to go to the studio first."

"When?"

"Don't tell them. I'll just drop in, surprise them."

"There's something else. The political contributions. Do you want to continue them?"

"Are they necessary?"

"I'm afraid so."

"Then continue them. I like politics."

"So did he, on the money side. Trouble with politicians is you get them elected and then they don't do you any good."

"You have a cynical side."

"I'm mostly cynical. You should know that."

"I think I see now that some cynicism is wise."

"What I see is that you've changed already, since he died."

He found himself thinking of Lois, and the haunting strains of a tune went through his mind.

I'll see you in my dreams . . .
Lips that once were mine, tender eyes that shine. . . .

He shook the memory away. It meant nothing. He had a duplicate set of his father's books and he'd noticed one small outgo entry last night—a five-thousand-dollar payment to Neil Mullaney, Lois's father. It undoubtedly had been a payment to Mullancy to get him to convince his daughter no longer to see Hollis. Now Hollis smiled. The payment had been unnecessary. He was free now. He could see anyone he liked. And Lois Mullaney was the last female he wanted to see. His father had been right.

"Lowenfelt," Hollis said, leaning forward. "I want you to know I'm going to depend on you. Can I?"

"You can," Lowenfelt said.

"By the way, have you heard of a man named Hunter?"

"Hunter? I've heard the name. I've never met him. I think he did some work for your father."

"He called me today, with condolences. He said he was available for work. What kind of work did he do?"

"I think it was rough work."

"Like what?"

"Well, maybe like strikebreaking. It was tough in those days. You had to fight fire with fire."

"I didn't like Hunter's voice."

"Forget Hunter. He's old school."

"I hope I can," Hollis said.

PART 3

Deborah and Marion

1.

HE WENT TO see his father's killer, wanting to know. The guard squeaked open the door to Swede's cell and stood close by, his hands on his pistol belt. Swede lay faceup on a naked stained cot. Deep wrinkles ran across his forehead. He had rejected the defense lawyer Lowenfelt had found. The public defender was pleading temporary insanity and losing to an ambitious new district attorney who demanded the death penalty.

"I'm Hollis Collingsworth."

"I know who you are. You look like him."

"So everyone tells me. I don't believe it's true."

Swede did not move. "Why have you come?"

"To ask why you did it."

"He cheated me once. But that was not the reason."

"Then what was the reason?"

"To protest against his kind, his way." Swede's head turned. A ray of light caught and held in his serene, unafraid eyes. "But I see I accomplished little, for his way will survive in you. Perhaps you will come to his end, also."

Hollis felt a chill. "What do you mean, *his way?*"

"What is sad is that you will follow in his way and not know it is wrong. I don't think you have a choice."

"I don't understand you. You talk in circles."

"It does not matter," Swede said.

"Does it matter to you that you probably will die soon?"

"Nothing matters. My family is gone. Nothing matters."

"How did he cheat you?"

"That also matters little now."

"How long ago was it?"

"A long time ago."

"Then why did you wait all this time?"

"Because I had a family to care for."

*   *   *

The D.A. got his conviction, murder in the first degree, and Swede was executed two months after the shooting. The execution was noted in a four-paragraph box on page 16 of the *Bulletin-News*. Swede's last name was misspelled, an error the copy desk slotman failed to catch, so it ran wrong in all editions.

Swede's words, "I don't think you have a choice," rang in Hollis's mind. He looked and talked and walked like his father, but he believed he had choices in his life. Yet he felt a presence in him, a parasitic being-force, a thing that called to him, guiding and directing. To escape it, he buried himself in the businesses he now owned. First he learned the newspaper business. He served a month's anonymous apprenticeship in the pressroom, emerging each night with ink-stained overalls and wearing the hat made of newsprint the pressmen had taught him to fold. He learned how to operate a Linotype machine and make up the lead type into pages in the composing room. He served two weeks each in stereotype, circulation, display advertising, and worked almost six months in editorial, writing routine headlines, covering minor political events, trying his hand at editorials. He drank with the police reporters and joked with the rewrite men. All of his fellow workers now knew who he was and were sure that when he thought he was ready, he would name himself to the unfilled position of publisher. He did not make friends with them, for he knew that if he did so he would only have to abandon the friendship later; he was headed for a position far above that of workingmen. He gained respect for the workers but refused to enter into their discussions about unions, working conditions, or pay and benefits. Once a pimple-scarred young pressman asked him:

"You gettin' any lately?"

"What d'you mean?"

"Oh, you know what I mean. I can fix you up, you want."

"No. I don't need that."

He didn't. For he was indeed "getting" some. By now both the French maids that had belonged to his father had come to his bed many times, playing expertly with him. Often he had them both at once. They came to him naked like plump uninhibited nymphs and he would lie on his side sandwiched between them, feeling their hands and mouths run tickling over his body, rubbing and stroking his sensitive parts. He experienced tremendous climaxes inside them, in their mouths, on their breasts. Daringly, the older, Marie, called him jeunesse dorée, translating roughly to "rich youth," and both Marie and Janet called him *mon chèr*. He did not worry about being placed in a compromising position, for they understood they would be dismissed if they tried to blackmail him; besides, they believed it to be a part of the job, pleasing an unmarried master of a big house in every way. Yet Hollis played the game secretly, looping a red tie around his doorknob to summon one or both of them rather than risk Trobridge's overhearing a verbal summons. One night he expressed his dislike of the house to Marie.

"It's too big, too cold, and sometimes I sense his presence here."

"Yes," she said.

It was true. Some nights and even days he thought he saw his father in the house—his father in a hunting coat spattered with animal blood and smelling of shotgun powder, his father in a tuxedo snorting cigar smoke from his nostrils, his father eating venison washed down with red wine at the head of the dining-room table, his father open mouthed with red gore pouring from a bullet hole in his forehead.

"I'm thinking of getting out, building a new place," he told Marie.

"Where?"

"Maybe in Hollywood. We have a studio there."

"Oh! Take me with you?"

"To tell you the truth, this place gives me the creeps. His ghost is here."

"But ghosts move, too," Marie said wisely.

Lowenfelt invited him to dinner, and after stalling, Hollis accepted. He didn't like socializing with subordinates, at least on their home turf, but when he arrived at Lowenfelt's home in the Los Feliz area, he was ushered into a warm place filled with the aromas of cooking and the tinkling laughter of children. It was not like his cold house on Wilshire, which was still the house of his father. He was reminded, with a small pang, of the family of Lois Mullaney. (He had not seen Lois; he had merely dropped her.) Lowenfelt's wife was a slim, attractive woman with soft brown eyes. She told Hollis he could use some fattening up.

"How many kids do you have, for God's sake?" Hollis asked, looking at the family photographs on the wall.

"Oh, ten or twelve," Lowenfelt said, handing Hollis a now-legal highball. "I forget."

"What ages?"

"I have no idea."

"He knows exactly," his wife said. "He has a bald spot for each one."

Their youngest daughter, Sue, padded in for good-night kisses, and Lowenfelt said: "How about a song?"

She pouted. "Can't. No mothbox."

"And just what is a mothbox?"

"Piano. Any alligator knows that."

"So just what is an alligator?"

"A person who likes swing is an alligator. It's jive talk. Jerry talks it all the time."

"Your big brother is a bad influence. Avoid him."

Lowenfelt kissed his daughter and sent her up to bed. Hollis had noticed how different the Lowenfelt at home was from the all-business Lowenfelt at the office, and he felt a strange mixture of envy and cynicism. Perhaps it was just as well that a life of close family would never be his. Love was an entrapment, a way inferiors gained control over superiors, and it limited accomplishments. Lowenfelt would never build and create, for that was an all-consuming task and left little time for family. He would always have a job, but he would never make jobs for others. He would be in this house and watch his children leave one by one, like chickadees venturing from the nest, and he would watch his wife grow gray and perhaps domineering. He would only have memories of the daughter who kissed him good night. It was not enough.

After dinner Lowenfelt's wife faded into the anonymity of her sewing basket and the two men sat in soft chairs on the porch, listening to crickets and watching moths self-destruct on the hot open bulb near the screen door. They lit cigars.

"I'm finished with the apprenticeship," Hollis announced. "I'm moving into the publisher's office tomorrow."

"Are you sure you're ready?"

"Positive."

"Then do it."

"Thank you for your permission."

Lowenfelt gazed at the moths for a long moment. "I'd like to ask you something," he said.

"I can anticipate you. You want a promotion, too. Well, I'd like you to take over as general manager of the paper."

"What I had in mind, really, was asking you if I could run the movie studio. I think there's a great future in motion pictures."

"You're too valuable to be fiddling at a run-down studio."

"I think you thought of a nice way to say no," Lowenfelt replied.

The moths struck the hot bulb with sizzling cracks.

The depression clung stubbornly, with "Brother, Can You Spare a Dime?" a favorite song, with soup kitchens and discouraged job seekers, with the New Deal destroying the free-enterprise system under the guidance of a power-lusting dictator in the White House. It was H. V. Kaltenborn and *Collier's* and *Life* reporting on unrest in Europe, it was Charlie McCarthy and *One Man's Family* on radio, it was big-band swing and sentimental tunes like "The Way You Look Tonight" and "That Old Feeling." But none of it affected or deterred Hollis Collingsworth, who plunged into his task, his duty, with a possessed fervor, unchained from the bondage of an apprenticeship and seeking expansion of his legacy. He knew he was fated for a place in history, but that place would not come without effort.

The announcement of his appointment as publisher of the *Bulletin-News* and Lowenfelt's appointment as general manager appeared with pictures on page 1 of the Sunday paper. As he entered the building from a side door, he noticed a group of male pickets walking like gaunt specters in the chilled fog of dawn. Hollis went in, strolled past the dozing guard, pushed the elevator button, and then returned and awakened the guard.

"I went past you just now. You were sleeping."

The guard rubbed his eyes. "Who you wanna see?" He drew out a silver pocket watch. "I don't think there's anybody in this time of morning."

"I'm Hollis Collingsworth. I *own* the damn place, for Christ's sake."

The guard squinted. "Oh, sure. I see. I mean, you look like he did, I shoulda known."

"I want you to understand something. If I catch you napping again, you're discharged. And if you let *anyone* in, including me, without seeing a pass, you also will be discharged."

"I—I understand."

"I hope that you do."

He paused before his father's old office, peering at the shadows within. For the first time since Thomas Collingsworth's death, doubt assailed Hollis; he did not know for certain if he could successfully negotiate the journey he was about to start. His ambition was boundless, his energy was massive, and he was a quick learner. He had, for example, learned to speak fluent French after practicing with the maids, Marie and Janet, for only two weeks. French was spoken around the big house on Wilshire; Janet giggled that it was "the language of the court." He had read widely in finance, economics, and political science during his apprenticeship. Yet he knew he lacked some basics and could be fooled, and he did not know for sure which men he could trust. And there was something else, something he would admit to no one. He suffered an inner fear and a deep loneliness. Sometimes at night he would lie in bed with his knees curled up to his chest, unable to sleep, a wretched, lost feeling sweeping through him. But he must, for now, put that aside. He entered the office.

After the last edition had been put to bed, he called in Helman, the editor. Hollis offered him whiskey from a bottle he'd found in his father's old desk.

"No, I'm a drinking man but I do not drink on the job," Helman said.

"The day is over."

"Not correct. I've got to get out memos for the graveyard shift. We publish every day, you know."

"Do you work every day?"

"I try to take Sundays off." Helman sat down. He looked very tired, with deep dark circles under his eyes, and Hollis realized the editor soon would have to be replaced. With the realization came a slight pang of regret, for he trusted Helman.

"Tell me, Helman. I saw pickets out front this morning. Tell me what that is all about."

"Well, technically, there's a strike on, pressman's strike. There's a union there, but it's open shop and not very strong. These are tough times. Men need work. So we have enough pressmen crossing the picket line to get the paper out."

"Who do I talk with about ending this thing?"

"Hewitt. He's the union boss."

"Have him come in to see me."

"I'm the editor, Mr. Collingsworth. I hardly think such matters as that are my job."

"All right. I'll put Lowenfelt on it. Lowenfelt is my handy-man, my jack of all trades."

"Is there anything else you want to discuss?"

"One very important matter. I don't like the paper."

Helman showed no emotion. "All right. Let's talk about it then."

"It doesn't stand for anything anymore. I want to take a position on important matters and stick with it. Here's what I want. Are you ready?"

Helman had taken out a pencil and notebook, a habit no doubt formed in his reporting days. "Go ahead."

"Write this down. Industrial freedom. Economies of scale. Union abuse. Economic recovery. Excessive power of government. Growth of the city. Helman, I want you to pound on those themes, hit them every day. I want this paper to be a factor in getting that bastard out of the White House. Him and his goddamn woman and dog."

"You mean, of course, in editorials."

"I mean all over the paper. Get a slogan. Put a fucking eagle on the masthead."

For the first time Helman smiled. "A fucking eagle, Mr. Collingsworth?"

"Yes. Not an eagle fucking, you understand."

When he left the building about seven P.M., Hollis noticed that the number of pickets had increased. He stopped, looking at them. He recognized some of them from his days in the pressroom, but he did not remember their names. He crossed through the picket line and headed toward his car, satisfied that his first day as publisher of the Los Angeles *Bulletin-News* had been a success.

The meeting with Hewitt was short and unproductive. Hewitt was a heavyset man with a bulldog face, who wore a double-breasted blue pinstripe suit. He reminded Hollis of a heavy in a gangster film. He cleared his throat before every sentence, and when he grew even slightly agitated, he spoke in showers of spittle. For support, Hollis had Lowenfelt attend.

"As Mr. Lowenfelt will tell you, I dealt with your father on many an occasion, and—"

"You dealt with him or did he deal with you?"

Throat clearing. Spittle. "I did not come here, sir, to be insulted."

"I want you to tell your men to go back to work. If they are not back within a week, there will be no jobs for them."

"That is illegal."

"I know very little about labor relations, Hewitt, and that gives me an advantage because I don't know what is legal or illegal. I only know that I will bring in substitute pressmen unless these men come back within a week."

More throat clearing, more spittle. "I have a case against this institution, one that goes way back, back to his bringing in police strikebreakers with the sanction of the city hall. This newspaper has made a mockery of labor relations."

"You have no strike benefits. You've run out."

"That is not true."

"Lowenfelt," Hollis said. "Speak, Lowenfelt."

"The local, in effect, is bankrupt," Lowenfelt said.

Hewitt cleared his thick throat. "Those men realize they've been exploited, and they are angry. Their pay is inadequate, the fringe benefits are almost nonexistent, and their safety is open to question."

"I'm going to suggest something," Hollis declared, leaning back. "I think you deliberately caused this strike—a strike that, I might add, is not working—because the newspaper has a new publisher, one you're testing to see if he's weaker than the one he replaced. If that is so, you will see how wrong you are. I'm not offering one red cent more. I can get hundreds happy to work for what I pay. End this strike, Hewitt. You're losing."

Hewitt twisted his bulldog's face into a damp contortion. "The strike will continue."

"All right. Continue it. But if there is any resistance when my men cross the picket line, I will have every cop in the city out there. You can't last long. You're cheating those men out of their jobs, using them to enhance your reputation as an organizer in the union, and in the end they will turn on you. Your arguments aren't worth a rat's ass, and you know it."

Hewitt stared at him. He stood up, wiped his mouth with a handkerchief, and stormed out, his face scarlet.

"You might have made a mistake," Lowenfelt said.

"What would you have done?"

"Offered a little something so he could have told them at least you're willing to negotiate."

"But I'm not willing to negotiate. Remember, I worked in that pressroom. I know those men want to work."

"You came on too brassy. You got him mad. That man may seem absurd, but he's got a lot of clout in this town."

"So have we."

"Well, it will be interesting to watch," Lowenfelt said morosely. "I warn you, watch out. Labor is angry."

Hollis did feel concern about the safety problem. There was almost one accident per day in the plant, far above the industry's average. The presses were efficient, but old; installation of protective shields would be costly and would temporarily impair production. Working in the mailroom during his self-imposed apprenticeship, Hollis had witnessed an accident. It had been about a year ago. The newspapers were transported from the pressroom to the mailroom by conveyer belt, then bound in stacks of fifty by a wire bailing machine and dropped down a circular chute to the trucks waiting to take them to the circulation franchises. The machinery was so loud some of the men wore earplugs. A worker named Al, noticing a clog up, stooped to hand stack some papers. At the same time the foreman, miffed at the delay and not seeing Al, pushed the red button that activated the mechanism. The wire coiled over Al's hand and tightened, cutting off his hand at the wrist like a descending meat cleaver. Al looked at the stump, gushing blood, and turned to Hollis. "Be a son of a bitch," he said. "I'll be a son of a bitch." He slumped down, his back to the machine, swearing creatively. His severed hand was wired to the bundle, which went down the shute that way—a calloused worker's hand with dirt under the fingernails.

Hollis, over Lowenfelt's protests, decided not to spend the money for safety equipment, ruling the company simply could not afford the expenditure in the current shaky economy. Lowenfelt was protesting a lot lately, apparently taking his position as general manager seriously, but he knew he had no real power. The editor, Helman, also protested much of Hollis's make-over of the *Bulletin-News*, particularly the impassioned attacks on the man in the White House and the political endorsements, but it did him no good. Finally he shrugged and said, "Well, it's your paper. I just work here." That was right. It was his paper. All of them merely worked there. If they did not wish to do his bidding, they should resign and he would get people who would do as he said without protest. Before, he had welcomed challenges and had admired men who stood up to him. But that was when he'd been a novice, a learner. He had now learned. He was an entirely different person from the young man who'd apprenticed himself for knowledge. He had grown. Men of power came to him for advice and encouragement, hoping for some praise in his editorial page. He had moved quickly into the sphere of the city's influential; already, judges and state senators and county councilmen owed their positions to him. He filed favors mentally, knowing he would someday ask for repayment. The newspaper was his power base and he reveled in it.

Lowenfelt, who seemed suddenly imbued with a streak of righteousness and conscience, told him it was wrong, that a newspaper belonged to the community and should reflect all views. That was silly. This newspaper belonged to Hollis Collingsworth. When the pressmen went back to their jobs, Hollis strutted around the office, giving Lowenfelt "I-told-you-so" looks. Lowenfelt merely shrugged, regarded his boss with a sad gaze in his large dark eyes, mumbled something like "it might not be over yet," and went away.

If he used the newspaper openly to extend his power, he used the motion-picture studio just as openly as a toy. His father had not allowed him to have toys when he'd been a child but had acquired a big one for him just before his death, a real and vibrant game board of thirty acres in Burbank, equipped with sets, vehicles, stages, cameras, animals, and ambitious, yearning performers. He saw it like that, as a game, himself above it maneuvering and manipulating its rolling stock and humans. It was called B. T. Productions, and although big as a plaything, it was not big in its industry. It produced short subjects and B movies, most of them westerns, mysteries, and horror films, the latter a strange rage in gloomy times. In an era of Garbo and Dietrich, Colman and Gable, Davis and Hepburn, and Goldwyn, de Mille, and Selznick, B. T. was a poor neighbor in a rich area. Actually Thomas Collingsworth had not bought it; he'd won it. The studio's manager, a former talent agent named Victor Levin, liked to tell the story. Hollis heard it in detail on his first visit to the studio, choked by smoke from Levin's big cigar.

"B. T. Sackerville owned it," he said, his feet propped up on his desk. "B. T. was a showman, but he had good business sense. He made quite a bundle as an on-the-road advance man for a vaudeville show. I don't know when he came out here, but he got his hands on it during the silents era and made two, three flicks the crowd went for. He was big in chess, played the game like the devil, cleaned up on everybody out on the road. You find some good players out in the sticks, but none was a match for him. Maybe he made more money hustling chess than hustling his show. Anyhow, your old man had a rep as a chess player. Did you know that?"

"I knew he played, yes. I also know this. He wasn't my old man. He was my father."

"Sure," Levin said. Nothing phased him. "Anyhow—"

"And take your feet down."

"Sure," Levin said. "At any rate, B. T. and your... your father, they were members of the same club downtown and everybody there knew it was building up to a showdown between them, like the sheriff and the gunslinger in the movies we make out here. When it came, those who saw it said they shoulda charged admission. They went after each other like war, blood in their eyes. I think they played like thirty games. Your father, he lost the first four, drew three or four, and then he won all the rest. B. T. went into those matches young and full of pep and came out a ruined old man. He'd lost his studio. He left town and the last I heard, honest to shit, was that he was running a whorehouse in Texas. D'you want to go to a party tonight?"

"A party? Why?"

"At my house. We're showing a new flick I got high hopes for. A B budget but it could be a sleeper. It's Deborah Reading's second effort and I think she's found it."

"Who is Deborah Reading?"

"Contract player here. A knockout. But that's not all. She can act. I'll bet my boots you're going to know who she is when this flick hits the circuit."

"Tell me. How is the studio doing financially?"

"Well, it's on its ass. You know that. Lowenfelt musta showed you the books."

"By the way, Lowenfelt once asked me for your job."

"Good. Welcome to it."

"Maybe I'll give it to him."

"Sure," Levin said. "You're the boss. Whatever you say."

"What's your background?"

"My background? Well, I used to work in a rope factory in

Jersey when I was a kid. The only thing I looked forward to was seeing the flicks at night. When I got enough money, I came out here and set up a talent agency, pushing off dumb blondes with tits on dumb directors. That got me in the studios and I learned how they worked from the ground up. I'll tell you something. Where you learn this business is in the film-editing departments."

"I'd like to spend a couple of weeks there."

"Sure," Levin said. "It's your show."

He did attend the party, staged at Levin's rather modest house in North Hollywood on a Saturday afternoon. It was an outdoor party centered around the swimming pool until darkness, when it shifted indoors to be highlighted by the showing of the new movie, *Hope Is Not Enough*. Pretty young girls in daring bathing suits tiptoed around the pool, tinkling childlike laughter as they bent to test the water, bringing leers to the faces of two old men who probably couldn't get it up on a bet. Hollis found himself the center of attention. He was the biggest man there. The girls turned out to be bit or contract players at the studio; he waited for them, lounged in a chair, and they came to him one at a time to introduce themselves, ignoring the old men studio executives and even Levin, who didn't seem to care.

Hollis loved it. It was a new world for him, a new extension of control and power, one not filled with gouty men in eyeshades but one filled with thin, lovely young bodies and flawless faces, with eyes that yearned for recognition and brains sufficiently cunning to realize that cuddling up to power was certainly not a deterrent to success. He knew he could take to bed, perhaps tonight, almost any of the soft-fleshed sex objects that strutted around him, thrusting out their breasts and wriggling their behinds. They were, he realized, his play girls; he could place them in his bedroom, fondle and undress them like dolls, and expend his energy into the warm tight holes between their writhing legs. If he cast off one, another would come to take her place. He was ready for it. He had held off during his learning period, limiting his sexual activity to Marie and Janet, but now he had earned bigger and more diverse game. He was building a house in Beverly Hills. When it was done, it would be the scene of revel and release, a palace he would rule.

"Oh," said a starlet. "There she is."

He looked across the pool to see a dark-haired young woman in a yellow silk dress enter the area. She walked with a sense of dignity beyond her age, as if her entrance should be rewarded with applause. It almost was. The two old studio executives rose in unison and advanced to greet her. Levin kissed her hand, like a fawning knight. The starlets stood hushed. Obviously this was the Deborah Reading that Levin had raved about, but Hollis could not see what was so extraordinary about her. She was tall and thin, taller than Levin by a foot, with legs and arms that seemed disproportionately long. But her face, he had to admit, was almost perfect; perhaps close-ups would make her a star. The high, chiseled cheekbones were offset by dazzling dark eyes with natural lashes and brows. She wore no makeup and sunlight exposure did not harm her. It was a face at once sensual and sophisticated, at once girlish and mature. He found himself disturbingly fascinated.

"Mr. Collingsworth," Levin said, "meet Deborah Reading."

Their eyes met, locked in a gaze that seemed even to disturb the unflappable Levin. He felt some of the old stirrings of his youth, when he had stammered in awe before a graceful female, when he had known temporary surges of what his foolish boy's heart had thought to be love. The feelings had been honorable, good, and soft. But they had gone away, replaced by energy expended to manage and increase his legacy. Now, again, a lost feeling swept over him; he thought, *I can't allow this;* he thought, *I have too much to do.* The evening was closing in. Mockingbirds across the street greeted the appearance of stars with shrill cries. When they went inside, she held his arm.

"I hope of course you do like the picture, Mr. Collingsworth," she said. "But if you do not, I want you to be honest with me."

"It's Hollis," he said.

"Hollis."

"I'll be honest. I always am."

He didn't like it, at least not the tired Cinderella story line, but he found Deborah Reading's performance to be extraordinary. She played not one role but several—first the naive farm girl, then the emerging half-girl, half-woman, and finally the confident full woman who wins her Prince Charming by showing a merit greater than her superficial competitors. The scene where she said good-bye to her honest, hardworking

farm boy ex-lover stirred even Hollis, stirred him with dis-
quieting memories. The director made good use of Deborah
Reading close-ups, taking full advantage of her face.

When "The End" flashed on the screen, the starlets were
weeping. Applause and whistling rewarded the effort. The
lights came on. Hollis had liked everything about the movie
except its implausible story line—a handsome young indus-
trialist would have to be out of his mind to exchange marriage
vows with a poor farm girl, no matter how refreshing her
face—and he judged that it would be a fair commercial
success, perhaps even a hit. But he had decided he would not
give an appraisal of it now. It was an impishness and perversi-
ty his influence allowed him to exhibit, and he chose to do so.

"We should make a sequel," he told Levin. "It would show
her as his wife in the wealthy Pittsburgh home. In-laws would
be tormenting her. The social crowd would spurn her. Finally
the prince himself would turn against her. Imagine the tears
in the audience as she rushes back to the young Minnesota
hick. But by that time—guess what?—he's married to his
sister."

"Aside from that," Levin said, "what did you think of it?"

"Start on the sequel."

"That sounds like a message picture," Levin said sourly. "If
I want to send a message, I use the telegraph."

Hollis Collingsworth turned to Deborah Reading. "Where
do you live?"

"Why, I live in the Hollywood area."

"I would like to take you home."

"Why—" She looked at Levin. Levin turned away. The
only resistance she could mount was a statement that her car
was here. Hollis parried that easily:

"Levin can drive it to the studio tomorrow."

He had acquired a chauffeur, promoting the flat-nosed
horseman who'd ridden ahead of them that day in the valley.
He also had a new Cadillac. With his maturity had come the
knowledge that he was mortal, and since a steering wheel at
his hand and a gas pedal below his foot was a danger to his
compulsive nature, he resorted to the driver (whose name he
finally learned to be Shelton).

"The Beverly Hills place, Shelton," Hollis said.

Deborah Reading asked, "What Beverly Hills place?"

"I'd like to show you something."

"But I really should get home. We're up very early."

"This won't take long. Besides, it's still early."

"I really would like your honest opinion of the movie."

"My opinion is that it's much too small a vehicle for your talents."

She let out a rush of air. "Thank you," she said, smiling. "Back there I was thinking to myself that you'd shelve it."

"I'm not so sure that I won't."

"But you said just now you liked it."

"No, I didn't. I said I liked *you* in it. We may shelve it and look around for a better script for you."

"Oh. Well—"

He touched her arm. "I want to ask you something. Would you come home with me tonight, sleep with me, if I promised to release that film?"

"Somehow I don't think you're the type of man who uses tactics like that."

"Would Levin?"

"No. Levin is a remarkable person. With a remarkable wife and five remarkable children."

Hollis said, "We will go to bed someday, you know."

"I'm not sure of that at all."

"Tell me this. Is Deborah Reading your real name?"

"Yes."

"Perhaps we should change it."

"No. I like my name."

"Are your parents alive?"

"My mother is. She's coming out here now—or, at least, she *was*, before this conversation with you. I'm not at all sure that I like you, Mr. Collingsworth."

"Do you live alone?"

"I live with my sister."

"Well, you may not like me, but I like you," he said. "I think you have backbone. Spunk. I like that."

She was silent. The car streaked onto Wilshire, fleeing under streetlights that hosted wisps of fog. Shelton stopped outside the half-finished house in Beverly Hills. The frame lay before them, bathed in moonlight; it would be a solid house, built to his specifications on a half-acre plot. He planned to live in it the rest of his life. He led Deborah Reading all around it, explaining where every room and closet would go.

"Take the furniture from the living room and you can open it up to a ballroom," he said. "I'm going to have an all-night party to initiate it. You're invited."

"Thank you. And thanks for the preview of it."

"I think you want to go home now."

"Well, the alarm goes off at four."

The evening was warm, with a slight breeze full with the scent of ivy and mown lawn grasses. Insects chirped around them. The scents and sounds were heady to him as he stood close to her, feeling the stirring of sexuality in his loins. He wanted to touch her.

"All right, then. We're on our way." He stopped, looking at the outline of her face in the moonlight. He felt soft and at the same time he felt his strength. He would have this woman, he knew. "Look up there. See the big star up near the moon?"

"Yes?"

"I'm going to put you there."

His eyes opened wide when he met her sister at the small house in Hollywood. "Why, there's *two* of you!"

Deborah Reading smiled. "Forgot to tell you. We're twins."

"Maybe we have another Gish act here," Hollis said.

"You're late," the sister said, pouting. "I was worried."

"Oh, poof, you always worry." Deborah turned to Hollis. "Would you like something?"

"Coffee."

"We have only Sanka," said the stern sister.

They talked for three hours, long after the sister, whose name was Sarah, had retired. He forgot about Shelton, waiting outside; Shelton assumed, no doubt, that the boss had taken the yellow-dressed starlet to bed. But Hollis didn't even try. He relaxed in her presence, saying things he'd never before revealed to anyone; he spoke of his father, the responsibilities he'd assumed, even of his occasional fears. At her doorstep, finally leaving, he kissed her lightly on the lips, then harder. She pulled away.

"I'm missing my sleep," she said.

"I apologize to you. I should have left long ago."

"I'm glad you stayed."

He looked at her, wanting her more than any other woman he'd met. It was not mere sex; it was beyond that. She was not made up, unnatural like so many of the others. She was a dark beauty with full hips and breasts, and he knew without having yet tested it, capable of deep passion. He left, wanting her even more, and disturbed by his wanting.

He had taken up chess, learning it in what little leisure time he had. His favorite of the many sets Thomas Collingsworth had accumulated was a huge board of green onyx with pawns six inches tall and a king and queen almost nine inches tall. Chess became a life symbol for him. The rooks, or castles, represented solidarity and protection. The knights were for war, the bishops for advice. The queen was a lure to the king of the enemy. And the pawns, although limited in range, were the most useful of all. The loss of one or two or three, if surrendered for the greater gain, was not missed. In the chess game of his life, Hollis already had many pawns and several knights and bishops. He was building his castle. What he needed most, he decided, was a queen.

He felt the presence of his father very strongly in the game room of the Wilshire house and often in his off-work hours Hollis sat here at a table under a light, moving his chess pieces back and forth. He played with the ghost of his father, who sat at the other end of the table, his opponent. He no longer feared the presence; he knew when he moved to the Beverly Hills house it would stay here, perhaps in this very room. His move was a symbolic break. It would be the real start of Hollis Collingsworth as his own man. He leaned over the board, chuckling, gloating at his successful assault on the black rook. Finally he was beating his father at something.

His bedside phone jangled at midnight, jarring him from a deep sleep. It was Helman. His voice was urgent.

"I'm afraid I have bad news, Mr. Collingsworth. There's been a fire, an explosion."

"What are you talking about? A fire where?"

"At the *Bulletin-News*."

He took the news with a calm that amazed him; he moved as if in a dream, arousing Shelton and sending him to the garage for the car. He'd just finished dressing when the telephone blurted again. It was the man who called himself Hunter.

"Sorry to bother you so late," the voice said, punctuated by small coughs, "but I heard there could be some trouble at your paper. I wanted to warn you."

"You're too late. There's been an explosion." Hollis paused, suspicious. "How did you know?"

"Connections," Hunter said, coughing. "It may not be too late for something else. You'd better check your car."

Hollis ran to the garage, intercepting Shelton. They raised

the car's hood and looked down at six sticks of dynamite tied to the back of the engine.

The area was blockaded by police. A thick acetic odor filled the air. Fire trucks screamed; men shouted; flame and smoke jumped into the sky. Hollis ran toward the burning building, shielding his face. A fireman waved him back. A wall crashed down in a shower of bricks, exposing twisted innards of wire and pipe. Helman had his arm.

"Who did it?" Hollis asked.

"Somebody said it might have been a gas main that erupted."

"A gas main, shit! It was that fucking goddamn union." He shook away from Helman's grasp. "Can we get out a paper?"

"I don't know. I *think* the presses are okay."

"I want to try and print a story about it."

"We can try, but I have my doubts."

"Don't doubt. Do it."

The chief of police was there, personally in charge. "Whoever did this, Mr. Collingsworth, whoever did it, let me tell you we'll find them. We'll find and fry them, just like they fried those men inside."

"Are there many dead?"

"Ten. So far."

"It was the fucking union," Hollis said.

Lowenfelt came up to him, his head down, and when he looked up Hollis realized he was crying. "I told you it wasn't over," he said, tears gushing down his cheeks. "I *told* you! But you didn't listen. You never listen. I could pound it into you, but you'd never listen."

"Pull yourself together. We're going to have to start over again from here."

Ambulance attendants rushed by, carrying a blood-streaked man on a stretcher. Blood bubbled from a hole in his chest. Lowenfelt walked a few steps away. Then he turned.

"I can't take you anymore," he said.

"Go home. Get some rest. You're no good here."

The scream of the ambulance drowned out their voices.

2.

DEBORAH READING HAD played one of the standout
scenes in *Hope Is Not Enough*—the scene that so moved
Hollis—from the heart. It was as if the scriptwriter had
known her past; at eighteen, she had said good-bye to the
sunburned boy who always walked her to school, carrying her
books. And she, too, had cried that day, cried deep into the
night. But she had no desire to become the wife of an Ohio
farmer; she had seen too much of that as a farmer's daughter.
Her brothers had left one at a time, seeing the uselessness of
the land, following the ads for radio engineers and aircraft
mechanics in the G-8 Flying Aces pulp magazines. She had
her own dream, her own star to follow. It was heightened by
her visits on Saturday afternoons to the theater in Lindstrom.
She wanted to become a movie actress, something that
shocked her father and frightened her mother. Nevertheless
the mother somehow scraped up dimes each week for Deborah
and Sarah, and they set off for the town early in the morning,
wearing sun hats. She would linger around the theater for
hours before it opened, studying the movie posters and still
photographs of the scenes. Sometimes she acted before them,
which often embarrassed her sister. Sarah would turn away
and pretend she did not know the show-off emoting before
the posters, a pretense that didn't work, for they looked more
alike than sister kittens. Deborah practiced everywhere, playing
imaginary scenes she made up as she went along. In the
pasture she performed before an audience of uncaring cattle
as they munched grass and sucked salt bars, often substitut-
ing defecation for applause. Once, her mother took her on a
train to the city to see a play and she wept at the curtain call
as the leading lady in an evening dress received applause and
roses. That was what Deborah Reading wanted. Applause and
roses. It was all she wanted. The sisters had had six dollars
between them when they arrived at Union Station in Los
Angeles. Deborah followed the typical path of the hundreds
who poured into the city seeking fame—working behind the

counter at Schwab's drugstore, bluffing her way into parties, taking drama classes, getting unnecessary facial massages and hairdos. She had yet to realize that her principal merit was in her natural look. After six months in the town, broke and discouraged, nagged by Sarah to return home, she had met only one member of "The Industry" who seemed to take to her, a technician in the film-editing room of a small studio named B. T. Productions. He said he could get her a screen test.

"I've heard that before," she said.

"No. Honest."

"What will it cost?"

"Nothing. I'll fix it up for you."

He did, claiming his reward after it landed her several bit parts. It was a night in a Hollywood auto court. It hadn't been the first time for her. She'd gone too far on several occasions with the sunburned farm boy. That had been different, however; she had loved the farm boy, or at least thought she had. The technician had an incredible sexual appetite, which she accommodated; she had learned if you are to get somewhere you must pay.

Levin gave the young actress her first real break, a supporting role in a B western. She was the young pioneer wife who got killed by Indians at midpoint in the movie. Levin encouraged her to keep her natural look because the others, her competitors, always seemed to come on with makeup an inch thick and conspicious false eyelashes. He told her to act natural, also; this was the talkies now and exaggerated emoting wasn't necessary. He treated her well. One night he made a pass at her, but after she stopped it, he didn't try anything again and she was grateful for that. She made several more B pictures, twice as the leading lady, but after a year there seemed to be no more parts and Sarah was even more discouraged than before. But Deborah saw no future in returning to Ohio to perform before cows. Visions of applause and roses still danced before her.

Finally she got a break. Levin offered her the lead in *The Touch of Your Hand*, opposite an unknown stage actor named Michael Parry. It was a wartime story of young love, hyped by publicists' whispers to gossip columnists that the stars were actual lovers. They did it without consulting her. When she complained to Levin, he sat her down and explained the facts of Hollywood to her.

"There's no basis of reality in this town. It's all flackery. You accept that or you'll flop."

"I'll tell you what. I'll spend a night with him in the window display of the bedroom at a Hollywood Boulevard department store."

"I'll consider that," Levin said. "It might not be a bad idea."

Michael took her to the premiere, where a publicity man told her that the film's "cry index" was three times average. It was a full premiere—searchlights, formal dress, big cars. At the ensuing dinner Levin toasted his two young hopefuls with Mumm's, forecasting *Touch* would be a hit. It was her first premiere; she found herself both thrilled and disappointed. Sarah, home with the flue, worried her. Michael got drunk and made a scene when she turned down his invitation to test his skill in bed. She went home by taxi, exhausted.

Levin was right. The film proved to have what he called "legs." Within two months it had grossed more than all other films produced by B. T. that year. Deborah found herself in a whirl of press interviews, nightclub parties, and popping flashbulbs. She had an agent, the guards recognized her at the studio gate, elderly Iowan couples asked for her autograph at the Farmer's Market. Levin signed her to a five-hundred-dollar-a-week contract. It was, she knew, a tinsel whirl, but she loved it. Days and nights sped past in a delicious revel. She tried to bring Sarah into it and sometimes they played pranks, like seeming to be in the same place at the same time, but Sarah really hadn't taken to Hollywood. She retained too much of the gloom of Ohio.

"Let's take what we have and open a dress shop," Sarah said.

"You open the shop. I want the champagne and roses."

"Just promise we won't be separated."

She took Sarah's hand. "I promise. I couldn't function without you around. You know that."

She waited for another role, but Levin said no script in the house was right for her. She trusted his judgment, so she waited, noting how quickly fame flees. The public seemed to have forgotten her, although the starlets and executives at the studio treated her with leading-lady respect. Finally came the lead in *Hope Is Not Enough*. Levin said she was a natural for it.

That was her word now. *Natural*. It was her advantage, at

least at this stage of her career. And career was all. She forced herself to believe that, despite some doubting moments deep in the night when she found herself yearning for romantic attachment and even children, conventions inbred in her by her mother. But she had no time for such entanglements, not now. She dismissed Michael Parry when he suggested they turn the publicity scam into reality. She dated occasionally, but discouraged groping hands and deep kisses.

One day a freckle-faced mail boy, who imitated Mickey Rooney in voice and mannerism, brought her an invitation to attend a party hosted by Gilbert Jason, who rivaled Gable as the era's leading man. With the invitation was a single red rose and a note: "Belated congrats on your smashing job in *Touch*.—Gil Jason." Her heart jumped. It took her ten seconds to accept. She bought a new outfit for the occasion, a chiffon evening dress with a ruffled skirt, hoping she wasn't overdressing. She didn't drive, so she took a taxi to the Hollywood Hills address, fashionably arriving an hour late. But it was obvious from the loud swing music emanating from the sprawling, ranch-type structure that the party was already in motion. The street was filled with big cars, some double-parked. Deborah followed lawn lights up a rosebush-lined path to the front door, rang the bell, and waited. Laughter and a babble of voices came from within. No one answered her ring. She tried the door, pushed it open, and stepped from a sedate, firefly-sparked night into a pit of writhing human forms linked in a blatantly sexual revel.

She stared, at once horrified and fascinated. Slowly she descended the stairs, as if drawn by a magnetic force. Music blared around her. The room was lighted in pale red from overhead bulbs. The air was filled with the blended odor of cigarette smoke, gin, and marijuana. Figures snapped at fruit taken from huge bowls and tore at ribs served in large, flat warming pans, gnawing and throwing the cores and bones on the floor; couples danced as though molded, caressing each other's body; others petted heavily on couches and chairs. It swayed before Deborah Reading like a dream sequence. There were young girls in skimpy bathing suits with beauty-contest ribbons across their bodies. Some of the men wore tuxedos, others were dressed like hoboes. All of the bodies were young and most of them were trim. When a girl got pinched, she reacted either by slapping the hand away or pinching back, a symbol of acceptance. The couple then either started to dance or made a place for themselves on a couch.

"Oh, clever, you came dressed as a socialite, how clever!" gushed a big-breasted bathing-suit blond.

"I didn't know it was a masquerade party," Deborah said.

"But it isn't. It's a pillow party. A come-as-you-like pillow party. Come as *much* as you like, if you know what I mean." She snapped her fingers. "Aren't you, aren't you?—oh, you know who I mean."

"Yes, I am," Deborah said.

"I saw your flick. I *liked* that flick."

"Where is Gilbert Jason?"

"Oh. Well, he's performing right now. Upstairs, first bedroom to your right. He said he'll have every girl here if it takes until dawn. Go get in line. It's worth waiting for, let me tell you."

A man she recognized as an MGM star tapped her shoulder. "Buy you a drink," he said, his voice slurred.

He had been one of those she'd waited in line to see, her heart jumping at his love scenes. Now she was repelled. "I don't drink," she said.

"Next you'll tell me you don't put out."

She sighed. "Tell me something. Why am I here? Why are *you* here?"

"It's an occasion. We're celebrating his Oscar nomination. If he gets it, we'll have a real party."

"Is there a telephone here?"

"Twenty of them."

"I want to call a taxi," she said.

"What's the matter? You a dyke or somethin'?"

"Yes," she said.

Deborah Reading was hardly a dyke. She was in fact now concerned that she was in danger of entering into an enervating heterosexual relationship. Hollis Collingsworth haunted her after their first talk and she knew he'd been similarly drawn to her. His strength both attracted and frightened her. Would-be leading ladies who slept with producers and directors—not to mention studio owners—were only being used. She didn't want that reputation. She wanted to make it on ability. Yet she sensed something genuine in this relationship. She called him after the explosion at the newspaper. A secretary took her number and Hollis returned the call that evening. "I was worried," she said.

"Well, the presses are working. We're printing. Look, I've been too busy to think about much except the paper, but I want to tell you I've decided to release that picture of yours."

"I hope you understand that isn't why I called."

"I want to see you," he said. "Is Friday night all right? Maybe we can go to the Ambassador Ballroom."

She was ready by six-thirty, nervously awaiting him, changing her dress several times until deciding upon a two-piece frock in crepe de chine. When a man called at seven to say Mr. Collingsworth would be late, she began to puff cigarettes and guzzle brandy. The doorbell rang at eight. He apologized for being late. He looked tired, exhausted. His presence in the room seemed to fill it, a stalking man with narrowed eyebrows and a hard mouth, a face strained with worry and perhaps even fear.

"Would you like a brandy here before we go?" she asked.

"Where is Sarah?"

"Sarah is home, visiting mother."

"I will have a brandy. In fact I'd like to send Shelton out to get us something to eat. Frankly, I'm bushed."

"I thought you wanted to go dancing."

"I've been to the Ambassador before," he said.

Their eyes met. She could not escape his gaze. "I'll make something here," she said. "Don't ask that poor Shelton to wait. Let him go home. You can take a cab."

Still he gazed at her. "When?" he asked.

"Whenever you like."

"I don't want you to think I'm rushing things. But I want to be frank. I would like to spend the night with you here."

"All right," she said. The words were out before she could think. "All right."

Now that she had consented to make love with him, there seemed to be no hurry to go about it. She prepared a simple dinner of salad, soup, and steaks, and they ate seated across from each other at the dining-room table, candles burning between them. He did seem tired and sometimes his conversation ebbed to listlessness. He would not discuss the explosion at the newspaper. He said he had plans for expansion of the studio but would not be specific. He seemed more subdued than the man with whom she'd talked before, when he'd alternated between braggadocio and despair. She wondered if she would ever get to the heart of this man, to understand his complexities and his drive, but she knew she wanted to try. She was falling in love. Despite herself, she was falling in love.

"I'll do the dishes in the morning," she said.

"Why don't you have a maid for that?"

"I'll get one. After this picture, I'll get one."

"After this picture, you'll be in a mansion in Beverly Hills."

"Do you think so?"

"I know so."

She was suddenly very happy. This man seemed to need her, despite his occasional far away lapses, and she found herself overwhelmed with the wanting of him. To hell with the gossips. To hell with the horrible trade magazines. She wanted him. She wanted to get to his soul, to know him, to discover his deepest and most secret thoughts and dreads. She felt softly romantic, caught in his power.

Slow, girl, she thought. *Slow.* But she didn't go slow. Almost against her will she found herself the aggressor. She curled up next to him on the couch as he listened to the news reports and when the news was over she lifted her chin and moved close for a kiss. He put his hand on her cheek, holding her back.

"I want to be straight up," he said. "We're not going to church tomorrow because of tonight."

"Did I suggest that?"

"No. But I want to be straight up. I have a lot to do. I must do it. I don't have much time."

"I don't want to talk about the future. I don't want to be in the future. I just want it to be now."

Their kiss was long and hard, open mouthed, and she felt passion rising quickly within her, encouraging his hands, wanting the strength of him deeply in her. When he began to tear at her blouse, she pushed apart from him and took his hands.

"We'll be more comfortable in the bed," she said.

It had begun to rain, a homey patter that made it even better. She opened the bedroom window, letting in the breeze, and let her clothing drop as she went to him on the bed. Her nipples were aroused and she felt moisture between her legs. Every sensation in her body was awake. She slipped under him, feeling his hard sex on her stomach; she began to rotate her hips in the motion of the act, not wanting preliminaries, wanting him inside.

"Put it *in!*" she moaned. "Do it, *do* it!"

When he thrust deeply in her, she felt an immediate high-soaring climax. He held her to him, his face buried in her neck, thrusting in and out. He withdrew, groaning, and squirted thick semen on her hips and legs.

"Come inside," she said. "You can come inside of me."

"All right."

"Next time, leave it in. Don't be afraid."

"All right."

"Ah," she sighed, holding him. She listened to the rain. "My God."

"I'm not afraid," he said.

3.

THE BOMBING OF the newspaper turned out to be a blessing in disguise. Fifteen workers had died but they had not died in vain, for the incident brought sympathy to Hollis Collingsworth's antilabor stance. Leaders of the city rallied around him; those who had been friends of his father but who had been waiting for Hollis to emerge in his own right saw that he had done so. He handled the situation firmly, using the sympathy for all it was worth. He accepted all invitations to speak before the Chamber of Commerce and the Merchants and Manufacturers, deriding labor in impassioned harangues for its clumsiness and evils, suggesting much of it was a tool of the Communists. He lunched regularly with the mayor and city-council members, gaining information and favors for promises of support. He was not yet thirty, but he found himself one of the leaders of the city, a behind-the-scenes man of power, and he enjoyed it. The plant had been fully insured, thanks to Lowenfelt's meticulous efforts, allowing Hollis to install new equipment in the composing room and pressrooms which gave him an advantage over competitors. When the new building was dedicated, Hollis unveiled busts of Colonel Dickerson and Thomas Collingsworth in the lobby. They were a reminder of his heritage.

The dynamite found in Hollis's car was traced to a plant in San Francisco, and from there quite quickly to two radical union supporters, the brothers A. M. and D. R. Sheehan. They were accused of hiring a dynamiter in the employ of the Iron Workers, one Leonard McCracken, to do the dirty work. Evidence mounted. McCracken, promised a lighter sentence by the district attorney (who wanted to be governor), confessed, even bragging about his skills with dynamite. Labor shouted foul, claiming it was all a setup, and rallied the workingman to its cause in fighting the pervasive Collingsworth evil. Meanwhile, businessmen of the city had raised $100,000 to investigate the bombing and see that its perpetrators were brought to justice. Labor suggested it had not been a bombing at all, instead a faulty gas main; thus, the explosion was the result of inadequate plant safety. They even suggested that Hollis Collingsworth himself had arranged the explosion and planted the dynamite sticks found in his car.

It was a glorious battle, a war, and Hollis reveled in it. Now he fully knew his power. He was in the center of a cause that had spread nationwide and he knew he would win. Labor would lose, a setback from which it would take years to recover. His name was praised across the country, even in the newspapers of his competitors.

He admitted privately that the incident had unnerved him, but he fought that with physical action. Silent Shelton, the nickname he'd bestowed upon his chauffeur, now carried a Colt .45 under his uniform, and a 16-gauge Smith & Wesson shotgun was standard equipment on the floor of the Cadillac's backseat. Hollis moved some of the weapons from his father's game room to his office, including two rifles and several handguns. He placed the cannon at the far end of the office where it would be in clear view of anyone who entered. Looking at it each morning, he rubbed his hands and chuckled. They wanted war. They would get war. Deftly he plotted behind the scenes, moving his troops for action and defense. He sent identical letters to the bereaved family members of the workers who had been killed.

I feel great personal regret and sorrow that this horrible tragedy occurred, but I have resolved that these men shall not have died in vain, that their deaths will bring greater freedom to all of America's proud workingmen.

> *I knew your husband [son, father] personally and
> worked side by side with him for several months. He
> was a person of dedication and accomplishment, a
> provider who placed the health and happiness of his
> family above all else.*
>
> *His death is a great loss, not only to his loved ones
> but also to the city and the nation. Resolve with me that
> he has not died in vain.*

He enclosed a five-thousand-dollar company check with all
of the letters, which were hand delivered by a messenger.
None of the checks was returned. Lowenfelt had told him the
funds were tax deductible.

He had more than mere sympathy. He had the newspaper,
an effective tool to rally his cause. The elite who ran the city
and county from their power posts in the civic center were
men who writhed with personal ambition; this case was
bringing them statewide and national attention, much to their
delight. A man's ambition was also his vulnerability. His
father had once told him that if you find out a person's
greatest need and help him fulfill it, you own him forever.

He'd asked Lowenfelt to prepare a full report on the
company's downtown landholdings and when Lowenfelt brought
a map with Collingsworth-owned parcels filled in with blue
crayon to his office, Hollis beamed.

"You have the colonel to thank for much of it, but your
father certainly added to it," Lowenfelt said. "They made a
deal to sell the city the land under the city hall, but they kept
most of the property around it."

"Lowenfelt, we own this fucking city. And the people in it.
To build downtown, they've got to dicker with us."

"I fear thee, O master. Is that cannon loaded?"

"Of course it's loaded. Cut your sarcasm and answer a
question. Who is the most ambitious man downtown?"

"That's an easy question. Demming. The D.A."

"Not the mayor?"

"The mayor is burned out."

"I agree. On both accounts. Yet I need that mayor."

"Am I excused, O master?"

"Can that shit, Lowenfelt, or I'll can you. You're excused.
Send Helman in."

Helman brought proofs of the latest edition. He sat down,
reading the proofs. Hollis snatched them from him, threw

them on the floor, and stomped on them. He left the door open so the staff could hear.

"We're not hitting this hard enough, Helman! This is our backyard story, for Christ's sake, and some of the other papers are hitting it harder. Did you see the *Times* today?" Helman tried to answer, but Hollis cut him off. "How is the Hewitt investigation coming?"

"There is no direct evidence he knew of it."

"Well, find something. Find it quick. That sonovabitch *did* know and I want his ass. I want all these fuckers. Do you hear me? Helman?"

Helman gazed at him with bloodshot eyes. "I think you're wrong. I do not think Hewitt knew of it. Our investigation—"

"Investigation? What investigation? You just told me you've come up with nothing."

"That, to me, shows Hewitt innocent of it."

Hollis smiled. "Helman, I once thought you a fairly capable editor. I no longer do. You are discharged."

Helman took it with a blank stare, as if he had expected it. "May I say something?"

"You may."

"You have already exceeded your father—"

"Good. Thank you."

"—exceeded him, sir, in corrupt use of this newspaper for your own gain, in attacks on labor for your own gain, and general misuse of power."

"It is not for me. It is for the greater good of the city, the state, and the nation."

Helman stood up. He caught Hollis's eyes with a steady stare. "When a man of power is corrupt, that is bad enough. But when a corrupt man of power thinks he is right, that is terrifying."

Hollis snorted. "All right. I'm corrupt. Evil. Why did you stay with us as long as you did?"

"I have a family to support."

"I suggest a different reason. You stayed because you couldn't find another job."

"I'll leave after the last edition," Helman said.

"No. Leave now. Go get a drink."

He had an unexpected visitor that afternoon. His secretary brought him the card of F. Montrose Lukens, head of the

Iron Workers. Hollis made him wait for twenty minutes and then let him in. Lukens was a wounded war veteran who walked with a cane. He was a tall, imposing figure in a double-breasted suit. Hollis greeted him with a disarming smile and a firm handshake. Lukens sat down and crooked his cane over his knee. They looked at each other, sizing up.

"You are even younger than I was told," Lukens said.

"I'm older than I appear to be."

"I am told you are a very able and wary young man."

Hollis leaned back in his chair. If this would become a negotiating session he had the advantage, for it was on his home ground. "I want to say I do not wish to antagonize you nor the sensible aspects of labor in general. There is plenty out there for both of us."

"You are too young to be so cynical."

"I'm not cynical. I'm practical. I was taught to be practical. What are you?"

"Me? Somewhat of an idealist, I suppose."

"Now that we've revealed what we are, may I ask to what do I owe the honor of this visit?"

Lukens paused a full minute before answering. Then he said: "This matter has gone far enough. To continue it does neither of us any good. I propose a compromise."

"All right. Propose."

"We will ask the Sheehans to plead guilty if the prosecutor does not ask for the death penalty."

"It seems to me that your proposal should go to the district attorney's office."

"It's my understanding that you, Mr. Collingsworth, are the commanding officer in this affair."

Hollis began to pace. "Suppose I contact the D.A. and say I'll compromise. What do I get out of it?"

"Labor peace."

"I have labor peace."

"But perhaps not forever."

"How can you guarantee it?"

"I don't think you realize who I am."

Hollis paused, his mind turning. This limping veteran before him was a powerful and shrewd man whose endorsement had furthered countless political careers. Hollis felt slightly outmatched. Yet Lukens had come to him for compromise, indicating the Sheehan defense lawyers were insecure. He had come to sign a peace treaty.

"I can't see I have much to gain by it," he said.

"Then you do not see much, Mr. Collingsworth."

He fought to control his temper. "I don't profess to see everything. I know only what is in my good and what is good for my organization. Fifteen of my men were killed in a night sneak attack. An attempt was made on my life. There must be retribution for this."

"If you change your mind," Lukens said, standing up and leaning on his cane, "my number is on my card."

He went to see the district attorney.

Myron James Demming wasn't born in a log cabin, but he thought he could become president of the United States despite that. He was born in a modest house in Pasadena, a house his father had built. At twenty-five, he was the youngest man in the history of the county to be elected district attorney. He had campaigned vigorously on a platform that bringing criminals to quick justice was a deterrent to crime. The *Bulletin-News* and most of the other newspapers had supported him. He had a law degree from the University of California, a young wife named Sandra, two infant daughters, and a dog named Chipper. He dressed impeccably in grays and blues and never was there a strand of his dark hair out of place. He was driven, confident, and open.

"From here, it's the governorship, then the Senate, then the presidency," he told Hollis. "I don't want to be the goddamn vice-president. It's a spit job."

"You might become governor with that mustache," Hollis said, "but if you want the White House you'll have to shave it off."

"I may shave it for this trial."

"Has Monty Lukens contacted you?"

"Lukens? That asshole? No."

"He was in my office yesterday. He wants to work a compromise."

"Well, you can bet your ass the fucker's up to no good."

"He wants you to cut a deal with the defense attorneys. The Sheehans confess they plotted the bombing and you reduce the charges so they can get nothing worse than life."

Demming sprang up and walked excitedly around the

office. He threw legal briefs on the carpet. His face turned red. "Shit, Hollis! What kind of payoff could that be for you?"

"Labor peace. He says."

"How in hell can he guarantee that? That man has connections with gangsters, for Christ's sake. Organized crime."

"Organized crime? Are you sure?"

"Labor and crime run as entries in the same race. You know that. They want to overthrow the system so they can boss people around. They're eating at our way of life, just like the Communists."

"Well, I certainly didn't indicate to Lukens I'd go along with him."

Demming smiled. He touched Hollis's shoulder. "We have a good case. We don't have to offer a fucking thing. It was enough that we let McCracken cop a plea."

"What will McCracken get?"

"He thinks he'll get off in fifteen, twenty years. But I think I can work it so he gets life. Look." Again he smiled, a short, forced smile. "They'll fry. We have public sentiment with us. Darrow and Giesler together couldn't save them. I'll be up front with you. Their frying will be a feather in my political hat."

"I want to meet that judge. Can you arrange that?"

"Carmichael? I'm afraid not. He's straight as a rod of iron. Harvard, you know." Demming tried to pronounce Harvard with a Boston accent. He laughed. "If you see him before the trial, he could be compromised. Besides, he's a loner. He grew old before his time. Did you know the governor went to school with Carmichael's daddy? Harvard, of course."

"I didn't know that, no."

"Well, don't tamper with him."

"I hadn't intended tampering with him. I just wanted to meet him."

"I'll just warn you that he's a hard man to see."

"Did you get anything on Hewitt?"

"No. I don't think he's clean, but I can't prove it."

"By the way, we're getting a new editor at the paper."

"Good," Demming said. "I never liked that bastard you had. I think, down deep, he's a left-winger."

Demming was right. Judge Nathan Carmichael was not an easy man to see. He replied in a handwritten note to Hollis's request:

I feel since you are involved in a case I am about to hear that it would be improper for me to meet with you until the trial is over and the jury has rendered its decision. I would be delighted to meet with you after this matter has been resolved.

Hollis filed the note in his Carmichael dossier. Then he called the governor in Sacramento.

Two days later he received a second note from the judge.

I will meet you at the University Club, Friday at 7 P.M. I cannot, however, discuss anything about the upcoming trial.

Judge Carmichael was under forty but he looked over fifty. His hair was gray and he squinted behind thick glasses. He chewed on the stem of an unlit pipe and sometimes he paused in the middle of a sentence and looked far off, as if lost in personal thought. They met in a private room at the club, lined with ancient high-backed chairs and decorated with paintings of austere landscapes. A grave waiter in black served them salads and briskly departed.

"I was aware you knew the governor, but unaware you knew that my father and he were roommates at college," the judge said.

"Actually I didn't know that when I called the governor. I asked him to plead my case with you only because you seemed so stubbornly bent on avoiding me."

"One cannot be too careful."

"I merely wanted to meet you. We like to meet and find out about the people we may endorse. Your record is excellent."

"Thank you. At least I've not been reversed—so far."

"You're known as a pretty firm fellow on the bench. If I were a defendant in your court, I'd want a good lawyer."

"Laws were passed to be enforced."

Hollis had a complete file on Carmichael, information assembled by staff members at the newspaper. Carmichael came from a prominent New York family and had been slated for law almost since birth. He'd followed the pattern set for him—Phi Beta Kappa in political science at Columbia, graduate of Harvard Law School, a law professor there for two years, marriage into a good family, then a member of a law firm in which his father was a senior partner. His life was patterned and orderly until tragedy struck. His four-year-old son was killed by a speeding auto. Carmichael never recovered. He divorced his wife and wandered in Paris for a year, joining the would-be artists on the Left Bank to drink wine, play chess, and debate over how many angels could dance on the head of a pin. He'd come to California for a new start and was doing probate work at a law firm when the governor appointed him to complete the term of a judge who had died. Carmichael quickly gained a well-deserved reputation as a hanging judge— perhaps, Hollis reasoned, because the reckless driver who had struck down his son escaped severe punishment on a technicality.

Now he sat at a table with Hollis Collingsworth, exhibiting the morose bearing of a man who has suffered and been plagued by guilt, alternately picking at his salad and drawing on the stem of his cold pipe. Hollis put on a modest face, believing that most judges, like most priests and doctors and bankers, expected and indeed demanded respect, especially if they had been educated in the Ivy League. He admitted that the role into which he'd been thrust sometimes gave him feelings of inadequacy. Perhaps he should have gone on to school. But—no—there hadn't been time.

"Sometimes it's frightening," said Hollis. "Unions are out for blood these days. They simply do not fight fair."

"I detect no fear in your eyes."

"My father had a motto, Judge Carmichael. 'I fear to be afraid; therefore, I am unafraid.' He had a phobia against fear."

"Remarkable."

"And perhaps somewhat foolish. Sometimes I think he placed bravery and defiance above life. He allowed his killer two cracks at him that I know of, perhaps more I don't know of. It was almost as if he considered himself immortal, impossible to bring down. But I'll say this about him. He could see the future. I think I inherited that vision."

"And what does your vision tell you of the future?"

"I see war, for one thing."

"And for yourself?"

Hollis leaned back. "I see myself as a political backer."

The waiter served a bland meal of pot roast and potatoes. They ate in silence. Now that he'd met the judge, Hollis felt confident Carmichael would not shirk his duty. The Sheehans would go to their death not as martyrs but as conspiratorial murderers, a warning to all labor agitators; McCracken would spend the rest of his life behind bars, suffering Judas taunts from fellow inmates.

"Speaking of futures," Hollis said, "how do you view yours?"

"I do not often ponder the future."

"I have a general manager named Lowenfelt. He might make a good general counsel, but he's not exactly a member of the family. If I'm out of line here, say so. But I'd like to know if you'd consider the job after this is all over."

The judge drew carefully on his pipe stem. "I believe I will not respond to that, Mr. Collingsworth."

"It was just a thought. Frankly, I'm impressed with you."

"My plans, if you must know," Judge Carmichael said, "are to return to Harvard when this judgeship is over."

"To teach?"

"I rather enjoy teaching."

"Well, to each his own."

Nathan Carmichael knew he was a man of contrasts. He had lost all drive and ambition, but he secretly yearned for a return to life. This trial could bring him national recognition, arouse him from his dismal waste, clotted with scar tissue of hurt and guilt over the death of his son. He had promised to take the boy to Central Park, but, lost in legal briefs, had sent him out with the governess. The boy did not return. He did not blame the governess; he blamed himself. He abandoned his work and his wife. His life had ended when the life of his son had ended.

Yet Judge Carmichael had not surrendered all hope for revival and redemption. He was not old. He was in good health. He had an excellent background. There were moments of excitement when he felt his brain expand, usually over new enlightenment on a point of law. Despite his questioning of the ways people ascended to political power, Nathan Carmichael retained a consuming interest in government. Some of his most enjoyable years had been spent teaching constitutional law at Harvard. Even now he dissected and mentally filed every Supreme Court decision. He believed court decisions were, in effect, lawmaking, for the law was flexible until interpreted. These interests gave Nathan

Carmichael, the professor and the judge, some small measure of hope.

He also had strong beliefs—formed at Columbia only after agony and vacillation and long debates with fellow intellectuals. Once, he had embraced the teachings of Karl Marx; he'd absorbed the philosophy of dialectical materialism with the full energies of a seeking mind. He'd attended Communist meetings, discussing them into the wee hours of the morning as he drank beer with gifted classmates. Had his father received only the slightest hint of the aberration, he would have stopped all financial support; a parent who prepares briefs in defense of capitalists does not pay good money for a son's lessons in communism. In the end Nathan Carmichael abandoned his Communistic leanings, studied and also abandoned socialism, and came around to embracing the free-enterprise stance of his family. He considered his sojourn into political philosophies alien to his nature to be a small and unsuccessful revolt against the pattern his upbringing had established for him. He was now a conservative Republican.

Carmichael had accepted his appointment to the bench with hesitation, not because he was selected by a friend of his father's but because he feared that a man who could not manage his own life was hardly competent to judge others. Yet he did take it, feeling somewhat disturbed that a man of his age remained under the fine guiding hand of a parent but thinking it might restore some vitality to his collapsed psyche. But it hadn't helped much. Neither had living in Los Angeles. He had been hoping for a miracle, a task so engrossing he could think of nothing else.

The trial before him now might prove to be sufficiently consuming to do that, and he looked forward to it. His one meeting with Hollis Collingsworth had left the judge both intrigued and concerned. Obviously Collingsworth had something to gain—an absolute victory over labor and a personal revenge—if the defendants were found guilty and given the maximum sentence. If the defense learned of the meeting and blew it out of proportion and context, it could ask for disqualification of the judge. That blow might send him reeling back into his previous bleak depression. But he would not think about it. He would hear the evidence and judge according to that evidence. In a way he'd been tricked and deceived by a man younger and less educated than he, but that served only to heighten Judge Carmichael's interest in

Hollis Collingsworth. This man of cunning, native intelligence, and shrewdness was extremely formidable. He had the confidence and bearing of someone much older.

On the surface the judge and Hollis Collingsworth were remarkable opposites; yet, he realized, there were similarities between them. One was western, the other eastern; one throbbed with energy and ambition, the other had become enervated; Carmichael had been educated in the best of schools, Collingsworth had learned by experience and hard work. Yet they shared the same political philosophies, were mutually concerned about an entrenched administration that seemed unaware of the threat of war, and they had been formed by the guidance of strong fathers. Nathan Carmichael believed in the value of firm guidance. It was in fact one hope for his rebirth, a return to the path of promise hewn for him by his father. Perhaps it could be true that some alliance, no matter how minor, with this man Hollis Collingsworth could return him to that path.

4.

HOLLIS TOLD LEVIN to go all out on the premiere of Deborah Reading's second big film, *Hope Is Not Enough*. Levin was personally a miser, but he loved to spend company money, so he rose gleefully to the task. He hired an unscrupulous, hard-sell Hollywood publicity agency, a shop of heavyweight flacks called Ravely & Casey, which arranged for junkets for newspaper and radio reviewers and columnists all over the nation and some parts of the world. Heater and Winchell marked affirmatives on their R.S.V.P. cards; Hedda Hopper said she'd buy a new hat for it. Rumors again were circulated of a real-life romance between Reading and her costar, the Prince Charming part played by Douglas Masters, an unknown whom studio flacks ranked with John Gilbert in his prime. It was a four-searchlight premiere—held, of course, at Grauman's Chinese. It was to be followed later that evening by a second premiere: Hollis Collingsworth's new Beverly Hills home would be shown to about a hundred carefully selected guests. Hollis had discovered that owning a studio had a secondary advantage. The inroad to Hollywood allowed him to invite *Bulletin-News* advertisers to exciting film events, such as premieres or the Academy Awards. Many of his advertisers, and civil leaders as well, had been invited to the dinner party at his house following the *Hope* premiere. No one from Hollywood, except Deborah Reading, had been invited. Levin protested.

"Look," Hollis said, "for a businessman, everything is business. This party is business. The premiere is business. Make up your own party for the movie types. My party is for others."

It rained the night of the premiere, but that didn't discourage hundreds of onlookers from huddling under umbrellas, hoping to catch a glimpse of an idol who had made them feel emotions such as joy or sorrow, fear or pity, love or hate, sheltering them from the cold reality of their small, striving lives. The searchlights peered high into the sky, turning the rain to a dancing yellow, bathing the area in an electric shower of colors, dazzling and unreal.

As he escorted Deborah from the Cadillac to the theater, Hollis heard his name being called. He turned. Lois Mullaney, a child about three years old clinging to her leg, stood gazing deeply at him. He took Deborah's arm and pushed her inside.

"What was that all about?" Deborah asked.

"What?"

"The woman with the child. Her eyes sought only you."

"You're imagining things. Relax."

It wasn't just the woman in the crowd. She was miffed at him for another reason, over a spat concerning Sarah. He had said it would be all right to invite Sarah to the premiere but not to the house party; hearing that, Sarah had fled to her room complaining of a stomach ache. It was a childish act, but Deborah blamed Hollis more than Sarah. But perhaps that was wrong. Sarah often retreated, complaining of sudden ailments, when disappointed or hurt. Once Deborah had thought Sarah and she were alike, as inseparable as Siamese twins. When they had been younger, it seemed as if they could almost read each other's minds and one always knew where the other was. They were allied, with identical emotions. It seemed, however, that Sarah was the stronger, the leader. She watched hog slaughtering and cock fights with wide-eyed interest while Deborah turned away in revulsion.

When they walked to school, carrying their lunches in syrup pails, Sarah often walked slightly ahead, in winter taking the brunt of the cold winds. But as they grew, they developed differences. Deborah now was by far the stronger and more motivated, with Sarah often breaking down in tears for no reason or sinking into spells of depression. The differences had become more pronounced since Deborah had met Hollis Collingsworth.

"I hate him," Sarah said one evening.

"Why? You don't know him."

"I think he's an evil man."

"Don't you say that. It's simply not true. You take that back."

"He has you blinded. Not me."

"Maybe you are somewhat right," Deborah said. "All I know is that I can't get him out of my mind. I can't help myself."

She enjoyed seeing herself on the screen and although she had seen *Hope Is Not Enough* several times in rushes and studio previews, this showing was the one that counted. Before it had been in-house; now it was public. Her studio regarded her as still a novice in acting, but she did not. This film, she was certain, would prove her right. She was more than an actress, at least in *Hope*, for she'd given suggestions to the director which he'd taken and had even enraged the excitable film editor by questioning his judgment in front of Levin. She had won her most important points. The picture was hers; from it, she would step to stardom.

The select group at the premiere seemed impressed, applauding and cheering several of her dominant scenes. "And that bastard with his wild scissors wanted to cut that one," she whispered to Hollis as the crowd sat in hushed involvement during the farm-boy scene. Hollis ignored the comment. He seemed bored. Perhaps he was thinking about his party tonight or the upcoming trial for the plant dynamiters. Or maybe about the young woman in the crowd, the woman with the child who had gazed so deeply at him. She did not know. Often in her presence, even in her bed, he disappeared mentally from her, slipping into a deep reverie. At these times she realized she did not know him and feared she never would. He had come to her a full-formed force, an iron that could not be reshaped nor even penetrated; she had accepted that, holding him for as long a time as he'd permit, wishing for more but knowing she would not get more.

She knew he loved her, at least as much as he could love, although he never articulated it. His lovemaking was intense, powerful, leaving her spent and sleepy, helpless in his spell. When he left her bed she felt alone. She then had only her career. It was a lot, but not enough. Perhaps someday it would be, would have to be, but now it was not. On occasion, staring at her silent telephone, she hated him and hated herself, a person who could be independent and universally admired caught and emotionally imprisoned by a being unfathomable and often blunt and even crude, but when the phone rang and he said hello, the hatred dissipated and she found herself canceling appointments to accommodate his schedule.

When *Hope Is Not Enough* moved through its final fade-out and "The End" flashed on the screen, the audience sat in silence, and for a moment Deborah feared they had not liked its finish. She looked around as the house lights went up and realized that the silence did not register disapproval but instead a stunned acceptance. Then the applause started, quietly at first, quickly breaking into a unanimous thunder. The audience was on its feet. Hollis sat quietly, as if he were someplace else. Deborah found herself being escorted to the stage by her costar and Levin. The applause and cheering roared in her ears. A uniformed theater usher brought her two dozen red roses. She bowed gracefully, her eyes filled with tears, and when the applause died down and she was asked to speak, she was too choked to find her voice. Again the applause started. She held the roses.

Trobridge, as efficient a machine as man or God had ever devised, was put in charge of the catering and entertainment for the opening of the Beverly Hills house, while Hollis and his secretary at the *Bulletin-News* handled the logistics of the invitations. He had promoted Trobridge to housekeeper, increasing his salary and putting him in command of hiring, and had been pleasantly startled when Trobridge's first act was the drawing up and presentation of a household budget. It outlined a plan to hire a cook, two gardeners, two maids, and an apprentice butler to train for the day when Trobridge would retire. It contained no provision to keep Marie and

Janet, as if the observant manservant had divined his employer's wishes. In fact, Trobridge himself dismissed the French maids and took it upon himself to find new positions for them. Hollis was thankful he had no one in his business endeavors who understood him as deeply as this servant; it was difficult to keep a person off guard if he knew you well. Trobridge knew him, he reasoned, because he'd known his father.

The house was an impenetrably solid structure of brick exterior and oaken interior. It had five bedrooms upstairs, each with a separate bath and three with fireplaces. There was a smaller house in the back, behind the four-car garage, with cooking facilities and bedrooms for the servants; only Trobridge slept in the main facility, occupying one of the bedrooms with a fireplace. The fireplace in the living room downstairs resembled that in the other house on Wilshire, but there the resemblance stopped. All of the downstairs, except the kitchen, was partitioned by collapsible oak dividers, which, when opened, gave the area the appearance of one giant room, differentiated only by the furnishings. The floors were bare stained oak scattered with Persian rugs. All of the windows had oak louver boards, which could be snapped shut and locked. The kitchen had a dumbwaiter to Hollis's room upstairs and a window to the dining room. Trobridge had ordered hundreds of books for the downstairs library; they were arranged in neat, even rows on glassed-in floor-to-ceiling shelves, their bindings uncracked.

Hollis had brought over most of the furnishings from the Wilshire house, crating and storing the surplus, and all of his mother's dishes and linens. He had taken almost all the chess sets, arranging three of the best on tables in the upstairs game room, but he'd crated most of the weapons. Though not all of them. He had a 30-30 rifle hung on pegs above the fireplace in the library and made sure there was a pistol hidden somewhere in every room. He kept a pearl-handled .32 automatic in a nightstand beside his bed, the bed in which his father had slept.

Trobridge had limited the entertainment to a strolling accordionist and violinist. The guests milled or stood in circles, sipping drinks delivered by roving waiters and nibbling Perino's catered food from a long buffet table. The invited were the anointed. If one not sure he belonged to this power clique was invited, he knew then he'd been initiated; if one who thought he belonged was not invited, he knew he'd been displaced. Deborah Reading did not belong, but she was there for show. Guests gushed around her. The mayor captured Hollis's attention.

"The election is a month away," he said, "and we might be in trouble. This labor thing. Abrams is gaining on me."

"Abrams? He's left of Lincoln Steffens."

"Sure, and now he's allied himself with the Sheehans. Have you seen those political buttons? Abrams/Sheehan. You see them all over where there's lunch pails. They hero-worship the Sheehans, think they're being railroaded. And you know who's going to defend them? No less than Timothy S. Lockwood."

"Lockwood? How in hell can they afford him?"

"Union members are chipping in. A buck here, a few bucks there. Oh, they're guilty, all right, but that Lockwood is an artist in court. If this trial comes off, we're dead ducks. You'd have Abrams to do business with at city hall."

"What do you suggest?"

The major shrugged. "You might suggest the Sheehans cop a plea. Demming has enough to fry them, that's for sure, but we're going to lose city hall, like I say, if we waste enough time for that trial to start. If you get them to plead guilty, those buttons will come off."

"We went through that before. No dice."

"What would you rather have? Those boys to fry or a Commie in the city hall?"

"No. No compromises."

"All of life is a compromise, Hollis."

"All right. I'll think about it. But I don't want to discuss it here."

It bothered him. He knew the mayor was right; he'd thought about it before. If the left-winger Abrams was elected, he couldn't get anything out of city hall even if he still owned the land under it. He stood filled with thought, his mind turning. Perhaps he'd been wrong when he'd turned down Lukens's offer for a compromise. After all, he would score just as important a victory over labor if the Sheehans pleaded guilty. Demming, deprived of his prey, would be disappointed, but he'd have to take it. Also, Hollis would have to work on Timothy S. Lockwood, the impassioned supporter of the closed shop, convincing him he had no case and that a guilty plea for a reduced sentence was his best course. Lockwood was the best known and most successful criminal lawyer in the country. His very presence would rally labor.

"Damn!" Hollis said, slamming his fist into his palm.

"And who are you damning now?" asked a deep male voice.

Hollis found himself looking into the handsome, suntanned face of Clarence Jordan, the supermarket-department store king, and his most important advertiser. The frown disappeared, replaced by a smile.

"Nothing," he said. "It's nothing."

"I saw you talking with our mayor. I think that man is in trouble."

"I don't agree, Clarence. He's going to win again."

"If you can get that man back to city hall, I'll present you with a year's free groceries."

A young woman with long blond hair slipped to Jordan's side and put her hand on his arm. "Father, do I get a proper introduction to our host?" she asked

"Meet Hollis Collingsworth. My daughter, Marion."

Hollis held her hand, peering into her eyes. "Would you like to see the house?"

"I'd love to see the house."

"I'll circulate," the father said, edging toward the forlorn-looking mayor.

The guests had all left by ten, the time set on their invitations. Deborah Reading left at nine-thirty, amid hand clapping, but came back by taxi at eleven, holding an overnight bag. Hollis was waiting for her in the library.

"Let's go right upstairs," he said. He held her arm, hard, guiding her up the staircase and into his bedroom. "Get undressed."

"My, we're in a hurry tonight, aren't we?"

"Just take your clothes off."

"Who bit you? You act like you'd had another bombing."

He drew back his hand and struck her sharply on the cheek. She snapped her hand to her jaw and backed away, her eyes blazing. "Don't ever mention that bombing to me again," he said.

"All right. You're big and strong, I know that."

"Just don't mention it."

"I think I'll go home."

"You're not going home and you damn well know it. Get your clothes off. I'll wash up."

"You son of a bitch," she said. "You bastard, son of a bitch." She came at him, her fists drumming his chest; he caught her wrists and bent them behind her body. He held them locked in one hand and tipped back her chin with the other. He kissed her long and hard, open mouthed, hungrily seeking, and she found herself breathing deeply. When he let her go, she said, "You bastard," flinging herself on the bed, weeping, "bastard, bastard, bastard."

While he shaved, she slowly removed her clothing and lay back naked on the bed, waiting for him. Why had she come to do his bidding? Why didn't she go home? Was she indeed the whore of the studio owner? No. It wasn't that. She didn't need him, for she would be a star in her own right. It was that she somehow needed his strength; the very domination she loathed drew her to his bed. "Foolish girl," she mumbled. It would be easy to leave. He would not stop her. Yet she did not. She could not. She lay back in anguish, hating herself. She was trapped, but it was a trap of her own creation. She loved this driven, complex man whose sex often was so furious it seemed an explosion of anger. But she did not like him. Nor did she know him. She wanted to strip away the exterior hardness and get to the soul of him, to fulfill a need in him beyond sex, but she had concluded that was almost impossible. One thing she knew for sure. At this point in her life, she could not get along without him. She needed him. It was far more than sex. It was something she did not understand, could not articulate. It frightened her, because she was not in control of herself.

She stretched out under the glow of the red bulb he usually used during sex and her hand brushed the open nightstand, touching the barrel of a pistol in the drawer. She took it out and held it lightly. The bathroom door flew open and Hollis stood naked above her, the red light dancing on his body like electricity. He reached down and snatched the pistol.

"Don't fool with that, for Christ's sake, it's loaded! I'll show you how to use it sometime in case you're alone here some night and need it, but remember it's not a toy."

He replaced it and closed the drawer. Deborah moved over.

"I saw you with that woman tonight," she said.

"What woman?"

"You know what one. You spent half the evening with her."

"Oh. Her."

"Who is she?"

"Marion Jordan."

"Of the Jordan stores?"

"Yes. I have to keep him happy. He supports the paper."

"I'm not going to pretend I'm not a jealous woman. I am."

"You have nothing to worry about. You have the best ass in town and you know it." He lay down beside her and began to fondle her breast, running his thumb over her nipple. "You're cold tonight. Is anything wrong?"

"I'm just not ready, that's all. Let's lie here for a minute."

"Tell me what's wrong. Get it out."

She sighed. "Hollis Collingsworth, Collingsworth, Collingsworth, whatever ticks inside you? Has anyone ever affected you?"

"You do."

"Sure. I have the best ass in town."

"And talent. And brains."

"And I sleep with the studio owner. That doesn't hurt."

"Now you're putting yourself down. Stop it. You'd be going where you are if you slept with the office boy. Come over here now."

"It's been an exhausting day. Can't we wait until morning?"

"There isn't time then. Come on over here."

"Hollis, I don't want to keep this a secret anymore."

"What a secret?"

"Us."

"No, we have to keep it a secret."

"Why?"

"I have reasons."

"We can't keep it secret forever."

"Who knows now? I mean, that we sleep together."

"Well, my sister, of course. And Levin."

"Levin? How in hell does he know?"

"You can't keep any secrets from Levin. I can't, at least. Levin is the kind of man who seems to know."

"Then keep away from him." He moved against her. "Keep

away from all of them. You're mine and don't you forget it. When the time comes, we'll tell the world."

Levin spoke rapidly. "There's no doubt the flick's got legs. It's big on both coasts and it's real big in the midwest. Chi. Pitt. Cincy. When they're a hit in the armpit towns, you got real legs. Big legs."

Joseph Simon said, "Then you're ready to talk business?" He was Deborah's agent, a small gray man with hunched shoulders and beady eyes, a legendary ten percenter who once handled both Gilbert and Garbo. "What's the first bid?"

Hollis rose from his seat on the couch beside Deborah and walked over to Simon. "Get out," he said. "We'll settle this with her alone. This isn't some fucking auction."

Simon bristled. He shrank back, snorting. "She's my client, my signed up client." He kicked his heel on the carpet. "I will be here during these negotiations."

"I don't like flesh peddlers in general and I don't like you in particular," Hollis told him. "Levin, you have to start being more selective about who you let into your office."

Levin shrugged. "What am I? I'm only the studio manager, that's all. I don't have anything to say about the stars, the pictures, or the budgets; I'm just the studio manager."

The agent stood his ground. "Shall we begin again?"

"Simon," Hollis said, "you have exactly sixty seconds to remove your ass from this office."

Simon looked at his client. "Where do you stand in this?"

"Maybe you had better wait outside," Deborah answered. "I'll talk to them alone for a while."

"Don't sign anything."

"I won't."

The agent sniffed the air, glared at Hollis, and stomped out, snapping on his hat. Hollis went to Deborah.

"You don't need a parasite," he said. "Get rid of him."

"I needed him once."

"You don't anymore."

Levin jumped up, his arms waving. "I don't see the agent as an issue here. The issue is simple. He drew up a contract paying her five thousand dollars a week for two years. If she flops the next time out, we're out a half mill. Is she worth the chance?" He addressed Hollis. He slumped down on the couch and put his hands over his forehead.

"It's the terms, not the money," Hollis said. "I want a longer term. And I do not want a clause saying we have to loan her out to another studio if they top the five thousand."

"Oh, *Christ!*" Deborah screamed, her cheeks flaming. "You two talk with each other as if I weren't here. I'm *here*, don't you see? For the sake of Christ, can't you *see* that? I'm not the mop that walked into this place a century ago looking for bit parts, but I am here and I am still loyal. So will you two for the sake of sweet Jesus recognize I'm here?"

Levin groaned. He buried his face in his elbow. "Jesus, I hate contract talks," he said. "Christ, how I hate them."

Hollis drew Deborah aside. She was not this moment a woman who shared his bed and one to whom he'd revealed as much of his inner self as he dared; she was instead a product of his, one he'd helped to create, a product whose value could decline if not properly used.

"I don't care about the leech," he explained. "You can keep the leech if you want."

"I intend to keep him. He helped me through hell."

"But you must understand we can't give you a contract that would allow other studios to borrow you. I'm putting a lot of money into this studio now and it's going to be one of the majors in two, three years. I want you to grow with it. Are you listening?"

"I'm listening. You're bullshitting, but I'm listening."

"I want you to sign a five-year contract. No loan outs."

"How much?"

"Six thou a week."

"Do I get script approval?"

"As long as you make at least two pictures a year."

"All right," she said. "I'll tell Joe to come back in."

"No. The contract's here. You sign first."

"He gets his percentage?"

"Give him whatever he wants. He's your burden, not mine."

It took Timothy S. Lockwood only one session with his clients Arthur and Donald Sheehan to determine he was defending guilty parties. The evidence against them was in fact so overwhelming that he'd taken the case already believing them guilty. After his initial session with the older brother, Arthur, who would be tried first, the man had

broken down in tears and confessed to Lockwood that he and
Donald had masterminded the scheme. McCracken had set
the dynamite in an alley, where tubs of ink had exploded,
spreading throughout the building.

"We hadn't intended it go that far," the tearful Sheehan
said.

"What had you intended?"

"To frighten them. Do you realize what those people have
done to labor?"

Lockwood did. He'd once been counsel to a union in New
York; he'd always likened union disputes to war. He remembered going to the struck freight yard one night in New
Jersey and watching torched railcars burn a brilliant red in
the cold night. The workers stood and watched the fire,
cheering, like Indians victorious over a fort. He did not
condone such actions, but he was a friend of the workingman
and he thought he understood him. Even now he understood
and felt pity for Sheehan, a man, bred in poverty and
prejudice, turning to the union after helplessly suffering
countless injustices in his youth. He'd been formed before his
birth, like so many others Lockwood had known and defended.
It was a path that led inevitably to this.

Lockwood was much more than a lawyer. He was an
impassioned participant in life. He was a philosopher, a
writer, a political activist. He believed the accident of life was
a great gift not to be wasted, and yet he also believed a man's
path was determined almost fatalistically by biological and
environmental blessings or constraints. The system took a
man and held him down, and when he raged violently against
his chains, the system put him behind bars where he became
an even more violent animal, or, worst of all, took from him
his only gift—life. Man had little choice. How then could
man be guilty?

Outside the jail a small group paraded, wearing buttons
that read:

SHEEHANS INNOCENT!
ABRAMS FOR MAYOR!

They cheered him as he got into the car, driven by Henry
Mann, the lawyer who would argue the case under Lockwood's
guidance if they went to trial. But Lockwood wasn't at all sure
they would go to trial. He would defend, of course, if

Demming, the driven, ambitious local prosecutor, refused to compromise. Yet he knew his case was weak. He realized a lengthy trial would hurt organized labor. Labor had condemned violent practices, yet one of its own, Arthur Sheehan, who was the secretary of a local in San Francisco, had resorted to violence. The opposition would make the most of that, particularly the Collingsworth newspaper. Lockwood sighed. He slumped down in his rumpled gray tweed suit and slowly began to roll a cigarette. His wife had urged him never to take another labor case; perhaps she had been right. He had come to this alien, raw western city, leaving his loved and orderly New York only to answer the pleading stare of his client with a helpless shrug, like a doctor whose patient has terminal cancer.

"It didn't go well?" Mann asked.

Lockwood lit the cigarette and inhaled deeply. "They're guilty," he said.

"How about second degree?"

"That won't work. There are fifteen dead men. We could argue they had no intent to kill, but it would be very weak."

"Then what can we do?"

"The best we can do is save their lives. I'm not sure we can do that, even."

"Have them confess for a lighter sentence? Would Demming stand still for that?"

"I don't know. We can ask."

"Don't ask Demming. Ask Collingsworth. We're all players in this game. He's the conductor."

"All right. I'll try to see him."

"A meeting's already been arranged," Mann said. "He called Lukens the other day. He's meeting us at the hotel this afternoon."

It turned out to be a summit meeting. Demming and Lukens were there. A line was kept open to Judge Carmichael's chambers. And Mann had been right. Hollis Collingsworth was the conductor. He paced excitedly, waving his hands to drive home a point; he was a confident young man not awed by his elders, in fact a cunning manipulator of his elders. He did not speak to Lockwood. He did not look at him. It was as if Hollis Collingsworth knew by instinct the only man in the room who understood him was Timothy Lockwood. Direct communication was not necessary; Collingsworth spoke to the others, but he addressed Lockwood. It seemed additional evidence that Lockwood's theory of fate was correct. Hollis Collingsworth was not unlike the Sheehans. He was merely on a different level. He had been formed to lead, to carry out missions prescribed for him before his birth. The Sheehans had been created to walk a path to disaster, zigzag as they may. They were absolutely different from Collingsworth, yet they were alike.

Hollis Collingsworth paused in the center of the room. "I will lay my cards on the table," he said. "I was taught to do that. It seems to me that the situation is simple. We all want something here. It should be possible for intelligent, grown men to work that out. What is it that I want? It may not be what you think. I have been accused of trying to sink labor, but that is unfair. I am opposed only to that aspect of labor that advocates violence."

"So are we, sir," Lukens said, tapping his cane.

"I understand that. But I am sure the court will look at it differently, since one of your members will be tried for an act of violence. It will smear labor. That is only one aspect of this. The other is that the Sheehans are guilty. If this case goes to trial, they will be executed."

He paused, as if for effect. He looked at Demming. "I said I would be frank. I will. Except for one factor, I would continue to advocate that the trial proceed and the guilty receive the maximum punishment the law of this state allows. As I see it, there are two forces here. One is organized labor, represented by Mr. Lukens, the other is the rank and file, whose individual contributions of money have brought a noted lawyer to our city for defense." He did not look at Lockwood; he looked away, out the window. "That same rank and file is demonstrating all over the country, declaring these murderers to be innocent, rallying men to their cause. In this city they are supporting a candidate for mayor who has few credentials yet has rallied backing for his irresponsible liberal demagoguery based on this issue alone. The election is soon. This man must be defeated. I have come to the conclusion that responsible management in this city and in the nation has as much to gain if the Sheehans were to *plead* guilty as it would gain if they were *proved* guilty. So I suggest we consider a guilty plea in return for a lighter sentence, as Mr. Lukens once suggested to me."

Demming jumped up. "What's happening here? Hollis, you've switched decks on me. You're letting me down."

"Then I'll help you back up, later."

"Why didn't you discuss this with me before?"

"There wasn't time."

Demming stuttered. His face was pale. "You're letting me down. I'm—I'm not going to take it."

"Do you want a goddamn Commie in the city hall?"

"We should have talked privately."

"We'll talk later."

"It's my office. It's my decision. I have a perfect case. I'm not going to go along with this."

"I think you will," Hollis said.

Lockwood methodically rolled a cigarette. He ignited a match with his thumbnail and held the flame up. "Mr. Collingsworth, there is one other factor we haven't considered. How will Judge Carmichael react to a guilty plea?"

"Talk to him." Hollis looked down. "Lawyers talk to judges, don't they?"

Demming flung an angry snarl at Hollis and headed toward the door. Then he paused, reconsidering, and joined the group. Hollis Collingsworth addressed Lukens:

"One other matter. A slight matter."

"Yeah?" Lukens asked.

"I want Hewitt removed. I still think he had something to do with this, and I want him removed."

"We will consider it," Lukens said.

As the meeting broke up, Lockwood delayed Hollis, trapping him momentarily in a corner. "You missed your calling," he said. "You should have been a lawyer. Where did you attend college?"

"I'm sure your file on me shows I did not attend college."

"It does. And that is good. College only delays us for several years. What it teaches, we must unlearn."

"If you'll excuse me, I have to get back to the paper."

"We will accept your compromise. But you knew that."

"Yes."

"Most of my life I have fought for the workingman. Now the workingman will think me his enemy."

"But you will prevent much grief for labor."

"And save two lives."

"Useless lives."

"No life is useless, Mr. Collingsworth."

*   *   *

Two days later the Sheehans pushed through a crowd, handcuffed and guarded, wearing "INNOCENT" buttons, and entered a courtroom filled with buzzing spectators. Demming approached Nathan Carmichael on the bench. He whispered some words. Lockwood nodded at Mann, who stood up. The silence in the court was absolute.

"If it please the court..." Mann began, then paused. He cleared his throat. "If it please the court, we wish to change our plea. We wish to change the plea to guilty."

A murmur went through the court. Reporters leaped up.

Long after the courtroom had emptied, Lockwood sat in silence, chain-smoking his hand-rolled cigarettes. Mann came in with an extra edition of the *Bulletin-News*. The headline cried:

SHEEHANS PLEAD GUILTY

"It's quite a crowd outside," Mann said. "Let's go out the back."

"No. No, I'll face them."

"I wouldn't advise it, Tim."

Lockwood stood up. "I'm not a brave man, but this is one I'll face."

They came outside to be greeted by a hundred men, who hissed and hooted at them. "SHEEHANS INNOCENT" buttons littered the sidewalk, flattened by the heels of angry men. They made a path and Lockwood walked through it. A man spat at him. He wiped the spittle off his cheek with a handkerchief and went to the car. Mann drove. The crowd closed in, jostling the car, but they let it through.

"I saved two lives," Lockwood said.

"You might in fact have saved organized labor. That trial would have been murder."

Lockwood drew out his tobacco. "I wasn't going to take any more labor cases," he said. "But a man never should be so foolish to say he isn't going to do this or he isn't going to do that. Especially if it's against his nature."

*   *   *

The mayor was reelected by a slim margin. He called Hollis at home the moment his aides told him he'd won.

"Thanks," he said. "I owe this one to you."

"Has Demming calmed down?"

"He's calmed. But he still thinks you sold him out."

"Well, he'll come back to the camp."

"I'm having dinner at home Saturday. A celebration. I'd like you to come."

Hollis hung up and dialed Deborah. "I won't be able to make it Saturday," he told her. "Something has come up." Then he dialed another number.

"Oh," said Marion Jordan. "I'm surprised you called so soon."

"I have an invitation from the mayor for dinner Saturday," he explained. "I was wondering if you'd like to go with me."

"I have an engagement for Saturday."

"Break it."

"That would be difficult."

"Break it."

"All right," she said. "I will."

Judge Nathan Carmichael sentenced the Sheehan brothers to twenty-five years in prison; the tobacco-stained, toothless McCracken, who had actually done the deed, ironically received only fifteen years. On the train to New York, beside his wife, Timothy Lockwood rolled a cigarette, heaved his huge head backward, and said: "Perhaps that is just."

"What, dear?" his wife asked.

"McCracken got less than the Sheehans. You see, McCracken was merely a robot. He had no real brain. He could merely follow orders. I hate his crime, but I can't hate him."

"Yet he is guilty."

"Look at it this way. If a father tells his small son to burn a haystack, isn't the father more guilty than the son?"

"That is a quite different matter."

"Is it? Let's examine it. Suppose the son continues to burn haystacks and finally burns up two hoboes. He may be of age by this time; he is a haystack burner by trade. His plea, when caught, is: 'My father told me to do it, taught me.' It is too esoteric a plea for a jury to understand, somewhat like devil possession, yet it is an illustration of something. We can have laws and still not have justice." His wife didn't respond.

Lockwood peered out the window. Snow swirled around the casing. He turned and sighed, leaning back. "Suppose, as the labor side in this case had once wanted to show, Hollis Collingsworth had indeed planted that bomb. Would he have been punished?"

"I should hope so," his wife said, knitting.

"I submit not. No jury would have believed it, despite the evidence. But McCracken, if he had not squirmed out of the ultimate punishment by confessing, would have gone to court already convicted. So, again, law is not necessarily just."

"I think you're brooding too much about this case."

"Well, it will go down as a defeat for me. But I don't feel as if I've been defeated."

"You did your best, considering the circumstances."

"Hollis Collingsworth's father was murdered. Assassinated, you might say. I should have liked to defend that assassin. In many cases of murder where money or jealousy are not factors, the victim has brought it upon himself, as if he were his own assassin."

"I think you are well rid of that town and well rid of the Collingsworths of the world."

"I find them fascinating. They control, yet they are controlled. These people have no conscience, no real sense of right and wrong. Therefore they believe they can do no wrong. They are gods. Yet retribution often is in their fates."

Lockwood fumbled in the pocket of his rumpled coat and brought out cigarette makings. The train rushed on through the blanket of soft snow.

5.

WORLD WAR II brought a prosperity to Hollis Collingsworth that not even he dreamed could be achieved in his lifetime. Workers flooded west for time-and-a-half in southern California war plants. The circulation of the *Bulletin-News* almost doubled, fed by war extras. He leased his valley land to the government for the duration; it became an army basic training and replacement depot called Camp Collingsworth. The studio, renamed Collingsworth Productions, was kept busy turning out war propaganda movies and newsreels. He established a printing and bindery shop in east Los Angeles, where itinerant Mexican workers turned out government manuals and reports. While some others of his age and status enlisted in the service, promised commissions and cushy jobs, Hollis obtained an exempt ranking due to his civilian war efforts. He served on the draft board and headed war-bond drives. He accepted invitations to join the boards of directors of an aircraft company and a ship-building firm. He sponsored USOs, entertained soldiers and sailors at his home, and willingly lent stars, including Deborah Reading, to entertain at military posts around the nation. Never had the country seemed more united or prosperous.

"I never thought I'd hear myself saying this, but I'm going to support that man in the White House until this is over," he told Nathan Carmichael over dinner at the Beverly Hills house one evening. "It may take a decade or two to undo the damage he's inflicted, but he has my vote and support until we've killed every last Nip and Nazi."

Carmichael didn't respond. His eyes seemed far off. They sat across from each other at the ends of the big dining-room table, served turtle soup, French endive salad, veal piccata, and poached pears for dessert. Wars produced shortages, but one of the glories of war was the amazingly elastic black market, and one of the marvels of Trobridge was his ability to acquire almost anything if armed with sufficient cash. Trobridge could find tires, gasoline, tobacco, chewing gum, and food with the efficiency of a veteran scavenger hunter. Now he paused and scowled because Carmichael seemed to be rejecting much of his meal.

Carmichael was no longer a judge. He'd decided not to stand for reelection when his term expired, explaining to Hollis, with whom he now lunched or dined often, that he would soon be returning to Harvard. But he didn't go. He remained in his three-room, book-lined apartment on Western Avenue, sometimes seen playing checkers in Westlake Park with much older men who somehow didn't seem older. Hollis had given up trying to lure him into the company, now doubting that Carmichael would have much value there. His relationship with the ex-judge had developed into something he'd had with no one before. He now regarded Carmichael as a friend, someone he could trust and depend upon. He also thought he could cut to the truth of the man; later, having a cigar in the living room, he did so.

"I rather think you play a part. A part of a defeated old codger. But, down deep, you feel neither defeated nor old."

"You may be correct. I am endlessly analyzing, endlessly analyzing." He looked up. "But I am returning to Harvard, this time for sure."

Hollis's cigar had formed a long ash. He held it up the way his father had smoked. "I have a proposition for you. I would like to put you on my payroll."

"I really *am* returning to Harvard."

"I understand that. Hear me out." Hollis put the cigar down in a silver ashtray and leaned back, folding his arms. "I want to keep in touch with you. There are services you can do for me in the East for which I will pay. I need to know the brightest brains in the Ivy League, in the whole East. I want to know who is planning what for the future. I was serious when I said I'll go along with F.D.R. but only until the war is over. I think then there will be such a pent-up demand in this country that we'll see unprecedented prosperity. I have this city now. I have the county. I'm strong in the state. My next move is national. I want to be in a position to put men into Congress, even the White House."

"Do you have a candidate in mind?"

"I think my candidate will be Myron Demming."

A small spark came into Carmichael's eyes. "He has the cunning, the ambition, and the drive, perhaps even the brain for it, but I don't think he could be elected."

"Why?"

"Because he is insincere and untrustworthy."

"We can change that. When the time comes, he may be the right man for that time. Do you accept my proposition?"

"I will think it over."

"I would prefer to have your answer now."

"If you insist on an answer now, it will have to be no."

"All right. Take your time, then." Hollis picked up the cigar. He looked at the long ash. "By the way," he said, "did I tell you that I'm getting married?"

Myron Demming, like Hollis Collingsworth, could have wrangled an exemption from the service, but he'd decided, in consultation with his wife, that some military experience on his record would be good for the political career he planned to launch vigorously after the war. So he accepted an appointment as a captain in the army, with the stipulation he would be based at the Pentagon. The experience proved to be invaluable. He gained insight into how America's war machine worked—a slow, ponderous gearing up for production while existing forces barely held the enemy at bay, then a marvelous outburst of planes and tanks and guns that gave Pentagon insiders early assurance that the war eventually would be won. He gained clearance for top-secret information, was privy to FBI activities, and met top members of the Armed Forces Committees of the House and Senate. He and his wife moved in Washington social circles and they entertained at lawn parties at their Maryland home. The rationing restraints that applied to others did not handicap Demming; for the ranked and the privileged, there was plenty.

"Stop," he told the taxi driver one afternoon as they passed the White House. He got out. "Will you wait?" he asked the driver.

"You goin' ta see the president?" the driver inquired.

Demming gave him his best smile. "No. Just a minute or two."

He went up to the gate and put his hands on the bars, gazing in at the magnificent house. His eyes began to mist. He'd yearned for it since grade school when, asked to do a report on a president of his choice, he'd received a letter of commendation from the principal himself for his initiative of doing reports on every one of the presidents.

He returned to the taxi, his loins tingling.

Myron Demming did not try to fool himself. He knew he could not will his way to the White House. But he was certain he could plan his way there. He had the brains and the desire and the presence. He had taken all the right courses, and read all the right books. Political gain depended upon a strong financial backing, a cadre of loyal volunteer workers, skilled advisers, a willingness to compromise, and an understanding of the nation's mood. He had all that. He kept a log of his daily activities, noting the strengths and weaknesses of those he met, studying how they had achieved, dissecting reasons for their failures. His notebook was filled with data on competitors. The political animal was a fox, skillfully stalking prey, granting and collecting favors, avoiding traps. Each job was a stepping-stone to the next higher one.

Each represented progress. Even wars were not setbacks, if used correctly.

He had already made valuable contacts in this Washington duty. He'd let his views be known to the right people—mistrust of the Russians, strength through continuing defense, concern over some of F.D.R.'s maneuvers, especially his appointments to the High Court, admiration for Eisenhower, and a lack of confidence in the autocratic Douglas MacArthur. He played the Washington game with finesse, making no enemies and gaining friends; he let all know he was conservative but expressed opinions on personalities only to those known to be in sympathy with his views. Although he was only a captain, his advice was sought after by southern California war contractors. He lobbied effectively on their behalf on the Hill and at the Pentagon. Demming had a remarkable versatility and resilience; he was smooth and smiling before Washington ladies in pink flowing gowns at receptions, bawdy and coarse before men's club groups titillated by a good dirty joke. He knew when to pray and he knew when to cuss. Once, a wise old codger, considered a Washington sage, a midwest Republican on the House Ways and Means Committee, cornered Demming after a couple of Jack Daniel's, and said:

"M'boy, I don't think you'll make it."

"Make it where?"

"To the White House."

It was at their place in Bethesda, at a Sunday lawn party. Demming managed a smile. "I wasn't aware I was running."

"You will, someday."

"Then why won't I make it?"

"Because you stand for too much. You stand for both sides. It depends on who you're with. To catch a wind in this country, you got to stand for somethin' and stay with it, pound it. Hoover had prosperity, F.D.R. had the Depression and war. You . . . you stand for everything."

Demming fidgeted. Finally he said, "Have another drink?"

"Two's my limit. To victory."

"To victory," Demming said weakly, raising his glass.

Usually he didn't pay too much attention to Washington old-timers, knowing they'd be out after the war, with new faces and new ideas in, but the aged congressman's remarks bothered him. He admitted it to Sandra in their bed that night.

"The bastard thinks he has my number," he said.

Sandra, her glasses on, was reading from the printed pages of the *Congressional Record*. "I'd ignore him. Read some of his speeches here. They're meaningless dribble."

"But he might be right. I must have an issue."

"There's a lot of time, dear," Sandra said. "We'll find an issue."

"I thought it went well today."

"Yes, I thought so, too."

At one time Demming had had a terrible temper, lashing out wide-eyed and redfaced when matters did not go his way, but he'd learned to control it. His last display, in fact, had been when Hollis Collingsworth had pulled the rug out from under him in the Sheehan case. He brooded for a while and then decided to apologize. He apologized, in fact, almost every time he called Hollis.

"I want you to know," he'd say, "that I think you did the right thing."

"I know I did the right thing."

"Look, we're all interrupted by the war. But when this is over, I want to see you."

"I insist on it," Hollis said.

"I have plans. But you know that."

"I know, yes, and I intend to help you. And while you're in Washington, you can do some things for me."

"Name them."

"Just keep your eye on things for me, keep me informed what's going on. I need eastern connections. I have a man in Boston watching the scene there."

"Who is that?"

"Nathan Carmichael."

"The judge? I'll be damned."

"He's back at Harvard."

"I hear you're getting married, Hollis."

"News travels."

"You could do worse. I'm a Deborah Reading fan."

"But it's not Deborah Reading," he said.

If any career had been delayed by the war, it had been that of Deborah Reading's. Her salary remained constant at six thousand dollars a week, but she made no major pictures. She spent half the year on tour entertaining troops. Most of her movies had war backgrounds; she played the nurse raped by Japanese in the Philippines, the home-front wife, Rosie the Riveter, a test-pilot's lover. She and Sarah had moved to a large house in the Hollywood Hills, one with a front embankment covered by ivy and a thirty-step stairway to the front door. They had a full-time maid and gardener. Deborah found herself impatient and bored; she had grown and developed in Hollywood, but not fast enough. Levin bore the brunt of most of her complaints.

"Just take it all in stride," he said, shrugging. "This war can't last forever. Meanwhile, you're not starving."

"Artistically I am."

"All right. Blame me. I'm here for that, for blaming, God knows little else. But did I create Hitler? Am I the father of Tojo?"

She opened her bedroom to Hollis when he wanted, but she no longer visited him at the Beverly Hills house. He came to her, ate, made love to her, and left. Usually he had very little to say. He seemed wearied by the war; they were all weary. She was tired of travel, tired of playing the same role, perhaps even tired of him. But when he told her, tactlessly in her bed, that he was going to marry Marion Jordan, she flew into a rage. She struck at him with her fists and elbows, writhing and kicking, a rage not of a woman scorned but that of a woman fooled, misled, and hurt. He held her down, his naked body over hers, one hand holding her wrists together while the other stroked her breasts.

"You pick a nice place to tell me," she said, calming.

"I could have taken you to Perino's to tell you. I could have brought you flowers and taken you to Perino's. Would that have been any better?"

"You are a son of a bitch and a bastard," she hissed, the anger rising again. "Get your hands off me."

He held her tighter, hurting her. "You knew something like this would happen."

"I did, did I?"

"Yes. There were no promises from me. You knew that."

"I suppose I did. Well, go to it. Go to the nice rich lily-livered society woman. I'll bet she's a lousy lay."

"I wouldn't know."

"You're going to marry her without testing her pussy? Pig in bag?"

"Yes."

"And daddy will give the bride away? And the virgin bride

will blush. And all of Beverly Hills will be there. And the bride will throw rich rice. Will there be tin cans tied to the ass end of the Cadillac? Will you bust her cherry at Niagara?"

"Are you finished?"

"I'm finished, you bastard. I'm finished."

He released her wrists. He held her, his lips next to her ear. "I don't know how to say this and I don't think you'll understand no matter how I do say it. You think what I'm doing hurts only you. But it hurts me as much. Maybe more."

"Somehow I have difficulty in believing that. I know you."

"Maybe you don't. I have feelings, too. Maybe I don't often express them, but I have feelings, too."

Her arms slipped around his shoulders and she found her hands moving lightly on his back, rubbing and massaging and holding. In all the times they had been together, this is what she had wanted to hear from him, some expression of feeling, an unlocking of emotion he kept hidden in secret depths, lost sentiments now cloaked with mistrust and cynicism. It was the iron of his mind and body that attracted her to him physically, but it was the unexpressed, only hinted at, depth of loneliness and unadmitted need of intimate outpouring that held her to him emotionally. She had wanted to break through to him. Now perhaps she had.

"I don't use words like love or caring, yet I feel them," he said slowly. "I have too much to do to spend much time worrying about someone else. I have big jobs to do. It's the way things were set up for me. I don't know if I'll live long enough to get them done. But I do know this: No matter what I do or where I go, you're always going to be the woman I want."

"Then let them throw rice at us."

"No. That's not right for me. Or you."

"That lily is? She's about as strong as a pussy willow."

"You don't know her."

"I know her type."

His hands started to run over her body, her breasts and stomach and thighs, and she felt a quickening of her heartbeat and breath. She wanted him. For now. For all time. She fought tears and anger; she loved him, she hated him.

"I won't let you go," she said. "I won't."

"But I'm going. It just has to be."

"I won't let you go."

"You're going to the top of the top. When this war is over, it won't take you a year to be on top."

"Stay in this bed," Deborah pleaded. She was sobbing, holding him. Outside came the tentative creep of dawn, a whiteness breaking up the gray, and she heard the cry of a lone bird. She held him. He was still. "Stay," she said. "Don't leave."

Marion Jordan descended the staircase at the Beverly Hills Jordan house on Whittier Drive, her creamy body comfortable and warm and trim in a blue silk cocktail dress, the right touch of rouge on her cheeks, her hair brought to a golden sheen by maid Clara's one hundred brush strokes, her chin high and proud and sophisticated. A faint whisp of French perfume drifted from her as she moved. She was young, she was beautiful, and she was in love. It had struck her so rapidly that it sometimes frightened her. Men in college and after had petted her, touched her, come close with her, but none before Hollis Collingsworth had so quickly and absolutely swept her away. *He* was the one who had stopped it before it had gone too far. It had been there that first day at his housewarming, it had developed at dinner dates on the Sunset Strip, it had deepened with kisses and fondling and sighs at her place while her parents attended theater, and it had become a promise during a walk on the Malibu beach a week ago. She had said yes without thinking about it; after thinking, she had said yes once more. Now Hollis was coming to dinner for a talk with her father, a strange formality for the modern age, but he'd insisted on it.

Her father, waiting at the foot of the stairs, a martini in his hand, greeted her with a bow. "A princess," he said, taking her arm. "One who will someday rule the city."

She kissed him on the cheek. He was a man so distinguished and handsome that even her girlfriends batted their eyes and swooned in his presence. He had silver-gray hair, high red-spotted cheeks, and blue twinkling eyes. He wore a gray suit and a black tie. Marion's eyes met his. Rule the city? Well, hardly. But she did yearn to be instrumental in the city's improvement. Yet, so far, she'd done nothing; she could not do it alone. Also, she could not do it until she made up her mind to do it. Perhaps it would come in a sudden revelation, a resolve to act. She thought of herself as beautiful—a woman with fine facial bone structure, thin hipped and narrow shouldered, adept at tennis and golf—but she also knew she had a brain. She had hidden her brain from men. One day she would reveal it; the city then, and the nation, would know who Marion Jordan was.

Hollis was in the living room talking with her mother. Marion entered on the arm of her father. Her mother, Audrey, was aging faster than her father. She erased lines with thick makeup and dressed in dark clothing to hide extra pounds. Now she advanced, puffing smoke from a cigarette in a long holder, and took Marion's hands. The trio strolled, linked, toward Hollis, who had not moved from his spot.

"You know what they're discussing, don't you?" Marion said to her mother after dinner.

"Of course I do, dear. I saw the way you looked at him."

"I think he would be a magnificent partner."

"Well, he is most certainly handsome. And you two do most certainly make a handsome couple."

"Then why are you moping?"

"I'm not moping, dear." Her mother sipped brandy and inserted a cigarette into a holder. "I suppose we have to face the fact we're going to lose you."

"You're not going to lose me. We'll be living less than a mile away."

"Marion, have you discussed children with him? Does he want children?"

"We've discussed it, yes. And he wants children. Mother, you still have reservations. I can see reservations in your eyes. What is it?"

"It's the way he looks," her mother said. "I mean by that it's the way his eyes seem to look right into you, right down to your soul."

"So you noticed that."

"Noticed it? How could you avoid it?"

"I guess that's what struck me the minute I met him."

"With you, his look undresses."

"I want him to undress me."

"Marion, you know your mother is easily shocked."

"Mother, I've saved myself for someone like him. Maybe I shouldn't have. Maybe I should have gone out and gained some experience."

"Well, you can be sure he has experience."

"That certainly doesn't bother me."

"And there's talk about him and that actress, that Deborah Reading."

"How do you know about that?"

"Dear, Beverly Hills is a very small town."

"Well, whatever it was, it's over."

Her father came in to the patio, beaming. Hollis trailed him, smoking a cigar. "Mother," her father said, "we're going to have another member in this family."

"How nice," her mother said.

Marion Jordan lay in bed in her soft cotton nightgown, unable to sleep, feeling alternate pangs of apprehension and happiness. She had never really been able to talk heart-to-heart with her mother; it had been her father who'd been her inspiration and guiding light. Tonight her mother had expressed her feelings perhaps as deeply as at any time in the past. It was clear she did not like Hollis Collingsworth, nor did she trust him. Perhaps she feared him. Or maybe it was that she wanted to select a groom for her daughter; Hollis's sudden appearance and whirlwind courtship had spoiled her plan. She was always having young men over to tea or tennis, beginning doctors or lawyers in blue cotton blazers or wool turtleneck sweaters who smacked of the Ivy League and bragged about how easy it was to avoid the draft. Marion had scorned them all. She did have a mind of her own. And she did know her worth. She'd had all the very best things since childhood; she did not understand anything else. She drove her own Jaguar to private high schools, her Mercedes to USC, where she'd majored in music and art history. She knew instantly the quality of crystal and silverware, pearls and diamonds, furs and shoes, furniture and carpets; these things she'd learned from her mother, but they were the only things she'd learned from her—a woman who was always on the telephone, at luncheons, or entertaining.

Her father taught her that she was too important to give herself to anyone who didn't measure up to her stature, that each day was a precious experience, that home and children were sacred, and that civilization could not exist without culture. Perhaps she had been spoiled. She had never been spanked; she had never been scolded. When the dentist hurt her, she bit his finger, offering the defense that he'd said it wouldn't hurt; her father, laughing, had backed her up, telling the wounded dentist to double the bill. Perhaps, she thought now, her mother was jealous, because she was indeed closer to her father. If that was so, then it was so; there was precious little she could do about it at this stage in her life. She considered herself special; a glow of light followed where she walked. She had found a special man. She would marry him and bear his children. She would help him make a home.

Yet her mother's worried eyes haunted her.

Deborah Reading came awake at midnight and snapped upright in her bed, issuing a cry. In a minute Sarah was there, turning on the light.

"What is it?" she said, concern wrinkling her features.

"N-n-nothing. A dream, that's all."

Sarah sat down on the bed. She stroked her sister's wet face. "I don't believe it was a dream. It was him. Again, him."

"No. He's gone now."

"I don't believe it. I'd like to believe it, but I don't."

Deborah ran her fingertips lightly over her forehead, which was beginning to throb. "I need an aspirin," she said.

"I'll get it."

When Sarah returned with pills and a glass of water on a tray, Deborah said: "You will have to stop taking care of me like a nursemaid."

"I always have."

"You were always the bravest one. I was the foolish one. Do you want me to tell you the truth about something? Do you know the real reason why I didn't go to mother's funeral?"

"Because it would have made you too sad."

"No," Deborah said. "It was because I couldn't feel anything for her. It was because I didn't care."

"Oh, Deb, I don't believe that."

"I remember on the farm when Pa drowned some kittens we made a funeral for them. Do you recall that?"

"I think so."

"I felt so sorry for the dead kittens that I cried. Now I can't even cry for my mother. It's what this damn town does to you."

"Maybe it's the war. We're all changed by the war."

"I hate the war, but I can't blame it for my moods. It's this town. And maybe people like Hollis Collingsworth. They get into a person's soul, people like him."

"Forget about him. He's not worth your worrying."

"I intend to forget," she said.

But she wasn't sure. On lonely nights, studying scripts, she looked at the private line he'd had installed in her bedroom, wanting it to ring. She had told herself to have the phone torn out, yet had done nothing about it. She did not know how much she could hate until she discovered how much she could love.

Lowenfelt sulked in anguish. It had been building for years, back even to the time of the colonel, but recently it had intensified. It was not one thing; it was many things. When he sat down to think them all out, he discovered he could not quite articulate his grievances to himself. If he forced a confrontation with Hollis, perhaps he would be unable to express himself. So he sulked, holding it in. His mood certainly wasn't helped by the fact that he had two sons on a battleship in the Pacific—just recently, it seemed, they were laughing children opening Hanukkah presents, now suddenly they had become six-footers in white uniforms—but that was certainly not all. He was sick of it. Maybe that was it. And the old guilt gnawed at him. He had betrayed the colonel, who had taken him in, for Thomas Collingsworth, reaching for the lure in a trap. Now, with Hollis, the son, it was the same.

Lowenfelt had observed pronounced changes in Hollis since the death of Thomas Collingsworth; the son had metamorphosed from an uncertain adolescent into a confident, unstoppable force in which the spirit of his father lived. *The child is father to the man,* Lowenfelt thought. *The child is—* He paused, his head snapping up. He, too, had changed. Once, he had been open and challenging and opposing; now he existed in passive obedience, like a dog that had been whipped too much. Once, he'd prized the human spirit highly. Now he'd come to consider the human animal rather absurd, a struggler for small goals, a chemical factory imprisoned by biological limitations, a protoplasm that belched and broke wind and sweated and gasped for life through its nose and mouth. His family had grown and left. His wife had turned sullen. And Lowenfelt, reflecting severely on his sins, felt that perhaps he deserved his fate. He had done nothing. He had let things ride. He had seen one generation of abuse, even corruption, and he had not tried to do much to stop it. He had in fact been a part of it. Now he was seeing the rise of another generation, the creation of the other, and he merely sat in silence, observing and finding the idealism of his youth shredded to the cynicism of an old man.

"I'm general manager of the paper, but he won't let me think for myself," he told Levin at the studio. "He consults me on the hiring of an editor and then he goes out and hires a weak 4-F yes-man who serves as his puppet. I really don't have anything to do."

"So? I run the studio but I only follow orders. So what's new? Take the money and roll with the punches."

"I can't do that."

"Well, learn."

"He's his father."

"Sure. We all know that."

"You and I are in the same boat. You know the truth of that, don't you?"

"Enlighten me."

"Have you ever been invited to his house?"

"Hell, he didn't even invite me to his wedding next week."

"You know why, don't you?"

"Sure. It's a gentile company. Learn to roll with it."

"I don't think I can."

"Look," Levin said. "You've been with him and his father for a lot of years. You saved him tons of money. Now just take your paycheck and lean back."

"I can't. That's not my nature."

"Then get out."

Lowenfelt twitched, his jaw unsteady. "I've been around so long I'd be lost on the outside. I was ambitious in the twenties and I thought I was into something good. Then in the thirties I hung in because I needed work. Now in the forties I guess I'm just an old, scared guy."

"Just roll with it," Levin said.

"We're Lowenfelt and Levin," Lowenfelt said. "L and L. We should do an act, L and L."

"Roll with it," Levin said.

Lowenfelt decided to see Hollis, to get it out. He fortified himself with four martinis at the Red House, took the shaky elevator to the second floor, crossed unsteadily through the city room, and pushed open Hollis's door. Hollis, signing papers behind his desk, didn't look up.

"Don't stand there, Lowenfelt," he said. "Come in."

Lowenfelt crossed to the chair by Hollis's desk and sat down. It was a deep, velvet-covered high back that had been around the building since the colonel's days. It was known as the electric chair, for if a person were called in and asked to sit in it, he knew he was in for a severe reprimand and perhaps dismissal. Lowenfelt went to it voluntarily. He looked at the cannon Hollis still kept in his office. It seemed to be pointing directly at him.

"What is it?" Hollis hadn't looked up. His desk was a mess, cluttered with newspapers, clippings, and letters. Hollis gazed at Lowenfelt. "I can guess you want a showdown. You've been sulking for a month. Well, get it out."

"I want to know what makes you tick," Lowenfelt said.

"Tick? What makes anybody tick? What makes you tick?"

"I don't like what's happening here."

"I do. Circulation is up. Advertising is way up."

"I don't like what's in the paper."

"What's in it is my business. It's your business to sell it."

Lowenfelt leaned forward, intending to speak a man's speech from the chair. He jumped right to his point, knowing that Hollis's attention span wasn't very long, aided by the four ounces of gin still swimming in his bloodstream.

"My selling of it will be obstructed if we don't change. It's too one-sided. It recognizes only one political party in America, so members of the other party do not read it. It is so violently antilabor that union members spit on it. It—"

"Union members don't read it?"

"No."

Hollis grinned. "Why, I can't understand that. We carry 'Dick Tracy' just for them."

"Shall I continue?"

"No," Hollis said, "not with that line of shit. Tell me what really bothers you."

"What bothers me is what has been bothering me for a long time. I have a position but no real duties."

"That's not really it, Lowenfelt. It goes deeper."

"All right. It goes deeper. Tell me something. Do you know my first name?"

"Of course I know your first name."

"Then why don't you use it?"

"I like your last name. It has a nice ring to it."

Lowenfelt stood up. If he were to be executed, he would be executed on his feet. "I've seen too much," he said. "I watched your father and the colonel rape a valley to get water here. I helped. I watched as your father killed the colonel. I did nothing. Now I watch you twist the news and break labor and run city hall for your own benefit."

"And the county. And Sacramento. And Washington. And, after this war, the world."

"Don't be absurd."

"Why not? Anything is possible. Stay on and watch."

"I thought maybe I could temper you. But I can't. No more than I could temper your father."

"That's right, Lowenfelt. You can't change me. Now let me tell you what it is that really bothers you. It is you that bothers you, not me. You may think I'm an evil, possessed sinner, the devil incarnate. I have no doubt you do." Hollis had risen; he began to pace, his voice louder. "But the problem with you is that you know you've been a part of the act, even longer than I. You think it's wrong. It's not, but you think so. So you grieve. You grieve because you feel guilt. Am I close to correct?"

"Perhaps you are."

Hollis went up to him. "Look," he said. "You're burned out. Take a couple of weeks off. I'll even give you a leave of absence if that will help."

"I think I shall resign."

"If you think that will solve your problem, then resign. Come back and tell me—when you're sober."

It had been a bad day, but the worst was yet to come. When Lowenfelt got home that evening, he found his wife seated, unmoving, in her living-room rocker. There was a telegram on the floor. His wife did not speak; she stared straight ahead, as if mesmerized. Lowenfelt picked up the telegram, already knowing what it would say. He was right. His sons were missing in action in the Pacific.

"Both of them?" he said to his wife.

She nodded. Lowenfelt fell to his knees and put his head in her lap. He began to sob bitterly, holding her. She ran her fingers through his hair, comforting him like a child.

Hollis Collingsworth got married where his father had been married, in the San Fernando Valley Methodist Church.

It was a full, formal wedding, with bridesmaids and a flower girl. Myron Demming flew in to be best man. Mrs. Jordan wept on cue when her husband gave away the bride; later, at a reception at the Jordans in Beverly Hills, she drank too much Mumm's and had to lie down. The reception brought out a Who's Who of Los Angeles business and civic leaders. Hollis stumbled through the unnecessarily long ceremony and patiently bore congratulations.

"You picked a beauty," Demming said. "Where did you find her?"

"Her father arranged it."

"Well, you got a beauty."

"When will this war be over?"

"Soon," Demming said.

"It's been a blessing for business, but I'm sick of it now."

"We're all sick of it."

"I'm only starting," Hollis said.

"You're only starting?"

"I'm really only starting on the things I'm going to do. As soon as you're out of uniform, you come see me. But not in uniform. I don't want any soldiers in my office."

"I'll be there," Demming said. "With bells on."

They left the reception early, sneaking to the Cadillac. Shelton waited with their luggage. They planned to honeymoon on Cape Cod, where Hollis hoped to see Nathan Carmichael. About halfway to the airport, he asked Shelton to stop.

"I have to make a call," he explained to Marion.

"Use the telephone in here."

"It's not working."

He went to the booth in the darkness and dialed Deborah Reading's number.

6.

THE FIRST OFFSPRING of the union between Marion Jordan and Hollis Collingsworth was a girl. Marion wanted to name her Audrey after her mother, but Hollis, who didn't try to hide the disdain he felt for his mother-in-law, opted for a more universal and simple name, and thus his daughter was christened Mary. Marion protested only slightly. She was married, she knew, to a man who usually got his way. He'd awakened her several times on their first night in bed to inflict his will on her, an act at first painful but one she soon learned to accept. The birth had been difficult for her— Marion did not have the ideal physiological makeup for childbearing—and to drive that point home to Hollis, she spent two weeks in bed after coming home from the hospital, seeing the baby only when the nurse brought it for breast-feeding. Her mother visited every day.

"Now that I'm a grandmother," said Audrey Jordan, "I suppose that I ought to take up knitting."

"Mother, please don't smoke in here. Hollis—"

"It's Hollis this, Hollis that. Are you a wife or a slave?"

"If you're going to be unpleasant, please don't come."

"Oh. Testy daughter. Already you're taking on his characteristics. Serves you right, marrying a Capricorn."

"My marriage is quite happy, thank you."

"Then I'm happy for you, dear. I am."

"Learn to accept him."

"Oh, I accept him, all right. He can be gracious and charming. Your father likes him, but your father also is easily fooled. Well, time will tell."

Marion did admit she had married a man she did not know. She had realized during his courtship of her that Hollis had little interest in anything except his business enterprises, but she hadn't discovered until they had been married several months that this aspect of his life possessed and dominated him. Also, even worse, he would not discuss his office life with her. And Marion wanted to become a full part of her husband's life, wanted to help him, share his victories and setbacks, explore his views on what he thought significant. Yet he froze her out. He usually came home with a briefcase, ate dinner with her in preoccupied silence, retired to his study for an hour or two, and then came to their bed, almost every night arousing her to participate in passionate sex with him. His lovemaking, it seemed, was not alone for pleasure but for a higher purpose—to rid his frustrations, to vent his energy or anger, or, as she had promised him on their wedding night, to produce a son, something that had become a deep yearning in him. Often his male secretary called from the studio or newspaper—an efficient, polite young man named Thomas Featherington—to say Mr. Collingsworth would not be home for dinner or that Mr. Collingsworth had unexpectedly been called out of town. Marion sighed, putting up with it, promising herself she would rectify it in the future. But that future never seemed to come.

She liked the house, although she thought some of the furnishings and artworks hideous; she had the run of it, but she knew she was unwelcome in his study. Lying in bed after Mary's birth, she planned changes, calling in a decorator from her parents' department store, the exclusive Jordan's in Brentwood. She wanted to lighten their home, to brighten it. She wanted it to reflect more of her, her precise tastes meticulously acquired by years of study; if the business offices belonged to him, then at least the house could be hers, or theirs. Hollis, when she showed him the redecorating plans, objected.

"I like the house the way it is," he said.

"You may, but I do not. I don't look forward to prospects of entertaining in a mausoleum."

"A mausoleum? Is that what you call it? Do you know who my designer was on this place?"

"Yes, I know who it was. It was you."

"Well, I happen to like it."

"Hollis, one thing you're going to discover about me is that I know the temper of the times and have the taste for it."

"I don't like workers around, tearing things up."

"They will only be here when you are gone."

He waved his hand in surrender. "All right, Marion. Go to it."

She lay back, satisfied if not smug. She had won her point, based on his knowledge of the business value of entertaining, and she felt she was learning how to handle him. Perhaps he considered it a small matter, but she did not. She was sure that this victory, won with such ease that it surprised her, would force her later to surrender some future disputes to him, but she would handle that when the time came. It was the initial step in a goal she had developed during her years in college. She had realized then that her life at home, a debutante in a pink bonnet who stood fluttering and glowing at lawn parties, the irresistible attraction for handsome young men with croquet mallets over their shoulders and cocktail glasses in their hands, was superficial and meaningless. She wanted more, much more. She wanted union with a man who would bring her into contact with the city's elite. Thus, Marion Jordan had set her hat for Hollis Collingsworth before she had even met him. Now that she had him, she told herself that she was happy. It was a good marriage, a power union that enhanced her position socially and economically. She had not known Hollis when she had come to him that first time in their honeymoon bed, letting him do his will with her, enjoying it as much as possible. She did not know him yet, but she would try her best to understand him and help him. And help herself. He had not yet allowed her even to visit his companies, but that would come with time, after the baby-making function ended.

One matter concerned her. Despite the fact she accommodated his enormous sexual appetite, never complaining or resisting even though she often had to fake her passion, she suspected he was maintaining his affair with the actress, Deborah Reading. And, if he played with her outside of wedlock, he probably played with others. She discussed it with her father, the only person she'd known in her life to whom she could speak with absolute candor.

"You're sure he plays around?" Clarence Jordan asked. They were at a trapshooting range in Encino; she'd found it was usually easier to talk to him while he was occupied. "Pull," he said, raising the gun to his shoulder and firing from the standing position. The clay pellet disintegrated in flight. Clarence Jordan lowered the barrel. "Sometimes wives have fears that aren't justified," he said.

"No, I'm quite sure."

"Have you asked him, had it out with him?"

"No."

"Well, maybe you should."

"Pull," Marion said, snapping up the gun and blasting her target. She fired almost in anger.

"Good shot," her father said. Then he asked, "Why did you marry him? Do you love him?"

"Oh, I suppose that I love him. He's not an easy man to love, or to know."

"You will have to learn to handle him."

"Does mother handle you?"

"Most of the time."

"We're always honest with each other, Father. So I will say I think you haven't always been faithful to her."

"Men's needs differ from the needs of women."

"I'm not sure that's true but, at least for now, I'll go along with it. I know this. I don't want to end up like mother, martini-logged and surrounded by birdbrain friends."

"What do you want to do, then?"

"Pull," Marion said, and fired. "Pull," she said. "Pull." She made three perfect hits. She turned to her father. "Don't laugh at me when I tell you."

"I won't laugh, of course not."

"I want to help this city. It's sprawling and alive and I've lived here all my life and I love it. Yet when it comes to culture and sophistication, it's an arid desert. I want to be instrumental in doing something about that."

"Why would I laugh? I think that's splendid."

"I only hope I'm strong enough."

"I rather think that you are."

"Now you know one reason why I married Hollis, a Collingsworth."

He smiled his handsome, even-toothed smile. "I think you married him for many reasons. And I think it will work out just fine."

"Pull," she said. "Pull, pull, *pull!*" She missed the last, jerking the trigger. She seldom missed.

Next it was a boy.

After viewing the baby, Hollis raced down the corridor at Hollywood Presbyterian Hospital, seeking the obstetrician. He dodged an orderly, jostling his cart. Ahead of him the corridor weaved in a white, uncertain, undulating pattern; it was as if he moved on a treadmill, unable to make real progress, struggling and sweating and breathing rapidly. Finally he caught the obstetrician, about to enter Marion's room. He took the man by the lapels of his white coat and pushed him against a wall.

"You made a mistake," he said. "That is not my son."

"Mr. Collingsworth, we do not make mistakes," the doctor answered coolly, trying to escape.

"You did this time. That is not my son."

"No, no," the obstetrician said to some orderlies who were rushing to his rescue. He dropped his clipboard and shook away from Hollis's grasp. He was a tall gray man with thin glasses. A half hour ago he'd given the news to Hollis, his voice mechanical and precise, as if this happened in many of his births. He said, "Are you calmer now?"

"Yes," Hollis said. "I'm all right now."

"Has there been any history of this in your family?"

"No. Of course not."

"To your knowledge has there been any history of it in your wife's family?"

"I know very little about her family."

"Her parents? Grandparents?"

"I don't know her grandparents."

The doctor straightened his glasses. He retrieved his fallen clipboard. "Obviously it's a recessive character, a recessive gene," he mumbled.

"What can be done about it?"

"Nothing, Mr. Collingsworth."

"There must be *something.*"

"I'm sorry."

"If there is another child, could it be affected, too?"

"You would take that chance, Mr. Collingsworth. Also— and this is even a greater risk than the risk to your children— if your son were to have children, the chances are they would be affected."

"Have you told my wife yet?"

"No. I was thinking that perhaps you would want to do that."

"I don't want to see her. Not now."

"Very well, Mr. Collingsworth. I'll tell her."

"No," Hollis said. "I guess it's my job to tell her."

When they brought the boy to Marion, she held him against her breast, feeling his warmth and wetness. She did not cry. She held him tightly, knowing she would love this one the most.

Hollis dismissed Shelton and took the Cadillac himself, driving wildly in the night, cutting lefts in front of oncoming traffic, running yellow and red lights. A motorcycle cop picked up his trail and stopped him near Sunset and Vine.

"Oh, Mr. Collingsworth," the cop said, looking at his license. "I'm afraid you were driving rather recklessly."

"Just write the ticket."

"I'll just issue a warning. Please slow down. If this is an emergency, I'll be happy to escort you."

"No, I had my emergency," Hollis said.

An hour later, close to midnight, he found himself in front of Deborah Reading's house. A wind-driven rain had appeared suddenly, causing instant rivulets of water to rush downhill along the curb. He sat slumped over the wheel, his hands opening and closing, staring out at the rushing rain. Then he got out, leaving the door open, and hurried up the walk to the house, his coat collar turned up. He tried the bell. When there was no immediate answer, he banged loudly on the door. Finally it opened.

"Deborah—" he said.

"No. It's Sarah. What do you want?"

"Where is Deborah?"

"Deborah is sleeping."

"Wake her up."

"No. No, I won't do that. Now go away. You're drunk."

He stepped toward her. Sarah flinched and shied backward. "You *get* her!" he shouted. "You tell her to come out or I'll break down her door and drag her out. Now you tell her now. Do you under*stand*?"

"Oh, all right, come in then," Sarah said. "You're soaked."

When Deborah came out, dressed in a blouse and slacks, he put his raincoat over her shoulders and led her to the car. He drove slowly up Laurel Canyon to Mulholland Drive, through the now-lessening rain. He parked in a dark side street at the top of the hill, turning off the engine and sitting silently. Deborah had not spoken a word.

"Are you cold?" he asked.

"No. But you must be."

"I'm all right."

"Are you ready to tell me what's happened to you?"

He stared straight ahead. Now the rain had stopped and the sky was clearing; below, he could see faint twinkling lights of the city. In the past he had sometimes come here alone at night, recalling his youth, looking down at the lights of the place where he would lead, own, and conquer. He now felt only emptiness, disbelief, and despair.

"My son was born," he said. "It is malformed."

He heard her quick intake of air. "Oh, Hollis," she said, genuine concern in her voice.

"The baby has a shrunken arm. There is nothing that can be done about it. If you wonder why I got you out of bed to tell you, I can't answer that. I just wanted to tell you."

"I understand."

"I don't know sometimes why I do what I do. I wish that I had married you."

"We won't talk about that. It's far too late to talk about that."

"I'll take you home. I shouldn't have bothered you."

"I'm glad you did," Deborah said. "I'm seeing a human side of you."

Hollis got drunk for the first and last time in his life the evening the city exploded in celebration of victory over Japan. He took Deborah to Hollywood and there they moved anonymously among the revelers, caught in a writhing mass of delirious humanity, at last freed from years of frustration and uncertainty and deprivation. The street exploded. Bonfires burned on corners. Sailors danced with marines. Horns bleated from cars frozen bumper to bumper. Couples smooched on streetcar benches. Bottles of wine and gin were passed from hand to hand; the old and the young, the ugly and the beautiful, the wealthy and the poor, mingled as one, drinking and shouting. Streamers and water-filled balloons rained down from windows and rooftops. Two army privates held up an army colonel who'd had too much to drink, forcing him to drink more. Bars did land-rush business, pouring free drinks for anyone in uniform. Women squealed with delight and swooned into the arms of unknown G.I.'s who pinched their behinds.

An era had ended; another was beginning. The loved and hated but undefeated man who had occupied the White House for almost a generation had been ousted only by death. The nation had an awesome new weapon that could destroy cities in a single attack. This was a dance not only of victory but also a celebration of power, a revel to show world supremacy. No nation would ever again even consider challenging such might. Drums rolled and horns rang out, saluting America's strength.

It was almost dawn when Deborah and Hollis emerged

from the crowd, wet and torn and exhausted, deliciously
intoxicated. They held each other up.

"How many times have I kissed you?" he asked. "Have I
kissed you a hundred times?"

"At least. Others, too."

"But you didn't kiss anyone, did you?"

"No one. Cross my heart."

"I shall kiss you a hundred more times."

"Wars should end more often."

"Are we drunk?"

"I'm what they call looped. Feeling no pain. You're drunk."

"I have a car around here somewhere. I shall find my car
and drive you home, where I shall show you I am not drunk
by inflicting repeated sexual assaults upon your body."

"No driving. For once you listen to me. I've taken care of
the matter ahead of time. I've rented a motel room."

"How perceptive of you! How far is it?"

"We can stagger there in a matter of minutes."

"I'll carry you."

"You might have to. I broke my heel. I hope to Christ I can
find my goddamn key."

She did, opening the door and falling on the bed. He
kicked off his shoes and fell on top of her. They held each
other, not moving. Faint noises from the diminishing revel
drifted in from the street. He got up and looked out the
window at the pink dawn beginning in the sky. He felt a
renewal of spirit and purpose. Closing the drapes, he went to
the bed and removed his shirt and trousers. He heard
Deborah giggle.

"What's so funny?"

"Those boxer shorts you're wearing."

"Then I'll take them off."

"In shorts, you're not a bear. You're human."

"I am human."

"You have two sides, a dark side and a light side. I think
they're always fighting each other."

He lay down beside her and held her. Her body was fuller
and more perfectly formed than Marion's tall, gracious, milky
body; also, Deborah liked foreplay adventures with her hands
and mouth that proper Marion found repelling. Since the
birth of their son, named Andrew by Marion, she had not
seemed interested in sex at all, submitting to him only if he
forced the issue. Now, running his tongue over Deborah's

arm, he felt his sexual need rise through a liquor-fogged brain. He realized something. This was the woman he really wanted. And she would forever be his, yet not his.

"I think the dark side of you is losing tonight," she said. "I like it."

"I would like you to give me a baby," he said. "A son."

"Don't joke."

"I'm not."

"Oh, God, Hollis. God, oh, God."

7.

MYRON DEMMING CAME marching home with his wife, children, and doggie, convinced that he'd done much to win the war even though he'd never visited a military installation nor as much as thought about approaching a battlefield in Europe or the Pacific. There were squads of rowdy servicemen, newly mustered out, on the train from Washington to Los Angeles. He drank and played cards with them, praised each one as his son or his brother, detailing his political plans and enlisting their support. They called him "major" at the first clicking of glasses with him, "senator" after the third or fourth, and "Mr. President" as they approached the sixth or seventh. They showed him their war scars and he blessed them, weeping with them in memory of their slain comrades after drink nine or ten. He took a nap in the afternoons, lulled to sleep by the liquor and the clicking of the wheels on rails, awakening refreshed to begin another bout.

"You really gonna be president?" asked a half-smashed sergeant.

"It is my goal, yes."

"I'm betting on Ike. I served with Ike. My money's on Ike."

"I couldn't agree more. I'm thinking down the road."

"Oh. Luck to you. Here's to you."

Sandra, holding down the unruly kids in the dining car, commented: "You'd better take it easy. You'll be a wreck before you get off this train."

"I enjoy it," he said. "It's good practice."

"Practice for what?"

"As if you didn't know."

"Then you really are going to go all out for political office?"

"Yes. I am. You know that. Why do you doubt it?"

"I don't doubt it. I just want to know, for sure, what is ahead."

"I want you to be with me. That's very important to me."

She smiled and took his hand. "I'll be with you. No matter what you do, I'll be there. I don't have to say that."

"If there is anything that bothers you about it, let's get it out of the way now, Sandra."

"Well, the man you'll go to for backing, Hollis Collingsworth . . . well, I don't know how to say it, but he sort of spooks me."

"Don't worry about him. I can handle him. What else?"

"I want to know for sure if you're sincere about it."

"Of course I'm sincere. I've pointed to this. I've known what I wanted ever since I became student-body president in high school. I thought I could do anything then, and in college I thought I could do anything. I still do. I want you to know that. I still do. I matured in this Washington experience, and so did you. We're ready now. I listened, I read, I met people. We made friends. And I sized things up, Sandra, I sized them up. There is no one in that Congress, in that cabinet, or in the White House complex itself, who is any smarter or more able than I. Most are less able. So my hat belongs in the ring. Sincere? Of course I'm sincere. And I have an issue. This is the greatest nation in the world and we're now at peace, but we must not lose that peace, as we did after the last great war. And we're threatened by another great power, Russia, leading to a possible conflict simply because their system differs from ours."

"I think I have heard your first political speech."

"And what is your opinion?"

"My opinion is that I believe I'm married to a great man."

"A concerned man, darling. A very concerned man."

Hollis Collingsworth plunged into his work with a new dedication and fervor that amazed even those who had known him for years. He considered his learning years to be over and now was the time to apply what he had learned. He established a central office at the *Bulletin-News* for all of his enterprises, moving the publisher's suite to the fourth floor of the building. He merged everything into a single corporate entity, Collingsworth Communications, Inc., wholly owned by himself. He induced leading bankers and industrialists to join his board of directors and he joined some of theirs in return. He began to limit his public appearances, becoming an intensely private individual almost inaccessible to anyone except the higher-ups in his organization and outside business and city leaders. He enjoyed his new role, spinning webs and planning behind the scene while others carried out his wishes. The night guard saw him arriving at dawn and the same guard, on the next day's shift, often saw him leaving at midnight.

Hollis did not consider himself bound by the limitations of other mortals; he needed only work, a few hour's sleep, and sex. Marion alone was not enough; no one woman was. So he went to Deborah Reading, or, lately, a host of willing and discreet women, some of them married, who would meet him in motel rooms or satisfy his needs in the backseat of the Cadillac, which had windows tinted to obstruct the view of someone outside. He enjoyed the risk of such meetings; it seemed to strengthen him for the tasks ahead. Marion no doubt knew, but she did not complain. She suffered periodic depression but always seemed to emerge with a shopping spree or by staging a party at the newly redecorated house. He allowed her the parties only if he had authority over the guest list.

What he had learned more than anything else was how to hire and how to subordinate responsibility. He had finally judged Levin to be sufficiently capable of moving the studio out of its wartime doldrums and he put him in full charge. The studio promptly responded with a Deborah Reading hit, *Caring*, which was nominated for an Academy Award and raised her box-office appeal to the top ten in America. He hired a general manager for the newspaper and profits quickly improved. Much of his real estate was subdivided and turned into single-family homes, quickly snapped up as the city burst into a middle-class suburbia. His assets had quadrupled since Lowenfelt had made the evaluation after the death of Thomas Collingsworth.

Lowenfelt had not appeared at the office nor called since the day of their confrontation, a day that to Hollis now seemed to have been a decade ago. Regular retirement checks went out to him from the company. Hollis did not think about him. That was past. He'd been helpful in his time, but his time was over. Hollis did not care for his own past, particularly the fumblings of his youth, and if he was grateful for anything it was that his father had steered him on the right path. Yet he did feel a slight stirring one day when his secretary, the indispensable Thomas Featherington, brought him a message that Lois Mullaney had phoned. On impulse he dialed her number.

"Oh," she said, "I really didn't think you'd call back."

"Then why did you phone me?"

"I was just thinking back. It was foolish, I suppose."

"How have you been?"

"I've been fine. I married a policeman, who was the first to enlist when the war started. He didn't come back."

"Have you remarried?"

"No."

"Do you have children?"

"I have three kids. Well, I suppose they're not exactly kids anymore."

"Would you like to see me?"

She hesitated. "W-w-why, I—I don't know."

"Isn't that why you called?"

"I guess it was."

"I have a driver who'll pick you up. I'll meet you at the Ambassador tomorrow night. No, make it Thursday. I haven't been to the Ambassador for years."

He took a table in the downstairs lounge, and when the waiter brought her to him, he thought at first she couldn't possibly be the same girl he'd courted and even loved in his youth. She had put on weight and there were some premature streaks of gray in her hair. She wore an inexpensive blue cotton dress. He had deliberately selected a table under a harsh light so that she could not camouflage the physical changes he suspected had taken place in her. How long ago had it been? It seemed ages; it seemed another life. She sat down, nervously moving her hands.

"What will you have?" he asked.

"To drink? Oh, I don't know. A crème de menthe, I guess."

"A crème de menthe," Hollis told the waiter.

He looked at her. She turned away. Finally she said, "I guess I shouldn't have called you."

"I'm glad you did. Tell me about yourself. You have three children. Are you working?"

"I work as a waitress in a drive-in restaurant."

"Good tips?"

"So-so."

"What happened to the acting ambitions?"

"Well, you know, a handsome young policeman, Irish and all that, comes along and the first thing I know I'm married and pregnant. Bill was going to take over my father's business after the war. Instead he got killed."

"I'm sorry."

She sipped the crème de menthe, her once pretty, youthful face now chubby and lifeless. Only her eyes remained the same, bright and seeking, the sole girlish feature she retained. He stirred restlessly, looking at his watch. He wished he had not made the appointment. He had a memory he was proud of, and now he recalled in detail the dances with her at this very place that evening so long ago, and the ride in his Franklin to the peak of the mountain, the stars so bright and silver. It was lost, long gone; now, again thinking of the wisdom of his father, Hollis Collingsworth also reflected upon the foolishness of youth. That night, enchanted by false emotions, he would have risked giving it all up to escape with her. He needed no further evidence than this to realize fully what he had long suspected. The fluttering of heart, especially in youth, was a trap and a delusion.

"You seem anxious to leave," she said. Now even the brightness of her eyes seemed diminished. "Please don't let me hold you."

"Well, as a matter of fact I do have an appointment tonight," he said, again looking at his watch.

For reasons she herself could not understand, Marion found it difficult to show affection to her daughter, Mary, but her heart went out fully to her handicapped son, Andrew. She refused to allow the nurses to have much to do with him, bathing and changing him herself, and when his slightest whimper came from the nursery, she rushed from her bed to attend to him. Hollis sometimes returned home as late as midnight to find Marion in the nursery, seated in the semidarkness watching the boy sleep. She had taken the burden on herself; it affected her and depressed her, yet she would not ignore it. Hollis, lost in his work, found it easy to escape. His daughter had never mattered to him and the son he had wanted had been born not only imperfect but monstrously deformed. He considered it the cruelest trick fate had ever perpetrated on him. The withered limb haunted him in dreams, jarring him awake deep in the night to clutch at his pounding heart. He would not even look at the boy.

"It's not right," Marion said one night in their bed. "You will have to learn to accept him."

"It's not as easy as that. I'll try, but it's not easy."

"And you blame me."

"Why in hell do you keep saying that?"

"Because you do. And that is why you come to bed and turn away on your side."

"It's just that I'm tired."

"No. It's not that you're tired. You're not too tired to sack in with twenty other women."

"Oh, for the sake of Christ, Marion! Just because I can't get it up in bed with you, you think I'm sleeping all over town."

"Aren't you?"

"No."

"Aren't you?"

"All right, Marion," he said, sighing. "Have it your way. I'm sleeping all over town."

"I thought you were crude when I married you. Now I know you're also cruel. I should have listened to my parents."

"Just go to sleep. Go to sleep. You won't have to worry about my coming here for a while. I'm taking a trip."

"Oh? That's news. Where?"

"Paris," he said.

It had come about when Levin had arrived at his office some weeks ago, and had plopped a movie script down on Hollis's desk.

"It's what we've been waiting for, Reading's next flick," he said. "It's got it all. Love. Conflict. Postwar Paris setting. Separation of lovers by war. They'll laugh and they'll cry. Believe me, this one will fly. In glorious Technicolor yet. It'll fly."

"Levin, why are you underselling it?"

"Oh. Humor. All right."

"Has she read it?"

"She'll love it."

"What's the budget?"

"About two mill production, half mill marketing. If we can borrow Gable for the part of the captain, we could bring back six to ten mill domestic alone."

"Gable?"

"I'm working on it."

"I think what you're working on is a free trip to Paris."

"Not so. I get nervous two miles outside of Hollywood."

"Well, maybe I'll take this one myself," Hollis said.

He did, partly to escape Marion and the wrenching taunts of his son's eyes, partly because he wanted some time alone with Deborah, but most of all because he wanted to get away and see parts of Europe in reconstruction. He told his editor he would be filing some Sunday columns. He bought a new wardrobe of tailored suits and two big steamer trunks. It had been years since he'd looked forward to something so eagerly. Perhaps he'd stretch it into a month or two, meeting with some heads of state. It was a semi-vacation, and he deserved it. But before he left he had one more matter to take care of. Myron Demming had phoned several times for an appointment; Hollis granted it for a Friday in March, the day he and Deborah planned to catch a train for New York. Demming greeted Hollis with a hearty handshake and a wide smile. He was wearing a gray cotton suit, a sincere tie, and black shoes with military spit shine.

"We'll have a drink in my office, then I'll take you to the conference room to meet some people," Hollis said. "I may have to leave you with them on your own because I have a train to catch tonight."

"What sort of people are they?"

"Oh, you know. An assortment. The state Republican committeeman. Some local party bosses. A community mayor or two."

"You anticipate me."

"I always have."

"I knew I could count on you, Hollis."

"I ask only that when you get where I'm going to put you that then I can count on you."

"You know that you can."

"I'm never too sure. When a politician feels the power of his office, he sometimes is tempted to forget his friends."

"There is no way in hell that is going to happen with me, and I think you know that."

Hollis shrugged. "Bring your drink," he said. "Let's go in."

Heavy cigar smoke filled the conference room. Hollis introduced Demming to the six men there and they sat down by the long table, Hollis at the end, Demming in the middle. The men wore suits with vests and most of them had pocket watches with dangling gold chains. Californians seldom wore hats, but these men did, leaving them on a rack by the door. They seemed sincere and businesslike. Hollis knew them as doers, vote getters; frustrated by inactivity due to the war, they were chomping for action. They knew what they wanted. They could not be fooled, they knew what they expected in return for creating and pushing a candidate, they were vicious and vengeful if double-crossed, they thought alike in party unity. And, right now, they were looking for a U.S. senator. They grilled Demming for an hour.

"Christ," he told Hollis at a break. "It's like the fucking Inquisition."

"You did fine," Hollis said. "I see you've found an issue."

"The Reds."

"They liked that. I like it, too."

Hollis interrupted midway in the session following the break. "Gentlemen, I'm sorry, but I have to leave. If you want to go on into the evening here with Myron, I'll arrange to have meals sent up."

"One matter," said the state committeeman. "Your paper supports him."

"That goes without saying."

"And other support, financial support?"

"I will handle that."

Hollis shook hands with Demming, who was beaming. The committeeman walked with Hollis to the elevator. "I don't know," he said. "He's awful green. I don't know that we have a chance jumping him right to the Senate. We might try to get a seat in the House for him."

"I thought you were after a senator."

"We are. But he's green, Hollis."

"I think he's learned a lot. I think you shouldn't dismiss him that easily."

"Well, I'll take it up," the committeman said. "Have a good trip."

The Cadillac, Shelton behind the wheel, waited for him in front of the *Bulletin-News* building. Hollis hurried into the backseat, not waiting for Shelton to open the door. Deborah came into his arms. She was wearing sunglasses and a big hat. She had cut her hair.

"Recognize me?" she asked, after a long kiss.

"Barely."

"Well, I hope no one else does. I'm at a stage in my life where I don't want to be recognized."

"Thank God little Sarah isn't tagging along on this one."

"You really do dislike her, don't you?"

"I dislike her exactly as much as she dislikes me. Which means I dislike her very much."

"I have something to tell you. But I'm not going to tell you right now because you're tired and in a bad mood. I'll tell you on the train."

She did, over drinks in the club car streaking out of the city. He took the news without showing any emotion.

They had first-class tickets on the liner *Amsterdam*, leaving New York for London on Wednesday morning. Hollis put Deborah up at the Waldorf early Tuesday and caught a noon train at Grand Central for Boston. He was alone and now he had time to think. It was coming to him, all of it was coming together, and he knew in a flash revelation, that the experiment now hatching in his fertile brain was indeed a clever and noble one, and it would work. It would work. The wheels of the train went click, click, click beneath him, like the workings of his mind.

Professor Nathan Carmichael looked years younger.

"You have found a youth fountain here in Boston," Hollis said. "I would like to buy a share of the franchise."

"I've found a job that pleases me, that's all," the professor said.

They met at a café on the Common, in sight of Freedom Trail. It was a blustery day, with some of the wind of winter still in the air, and people exhaling frost breaths hurried past on the sidewalk, intent on their missions. Carmichael tapped his pipe while Hollis eagerly attacked a fresh New England lobster. If Marion had taught him anything, it was to temper his eating manners, but Marion was not here now so he ate with the zest that was his nature, washing the food down with great swigs of beer.

"Do you think this man Truman will be elected?" he asked.

"Yes. I do."

"Then you're certainly in the minority camp."

Carmichael smiled. Hollis had not seen him smile very much. "This is Boston. Here the Democrats rule."

"Next you'll tell me you've defected."

"I have not defected, that is for certain. But I will tell you this. We're going to hear from these Kennedys over the next few years. Of that I'm certain."

"We're launching Demming. Would you care to help with the campaign?"

"No, I fear I'm too entrenched here right now."

"The information you've provided me with has not been spectacular, but it has been useful. It has been worth its cost. Now I would like you to consider doing something further for me."

"I think I've been overpaid for what I have done for you."

"You haven't. You may think so, perhaps, because you don't realize the value of your information to me. I have only a few outposts on the East Coast, as I've told you, and the newspapers are absolutely unreliable."

"What is it you want me to do now?"

"I have a son and a daughter," Hollis said, leaning forward. "Parents may plan for their offspring only to have the gods laugh in their faces."

"I don't understand."

Hollis waved his fork. "Hear me out." He paused, eating. Then he said: "I need your help. I want to adopt a son. I want you to be his caretaker. Until I can get him."

They had separate cabins on the *Amsterdam* and did not sleep together, although they did dine together, usually at the captain's table. Deborah got sick the third day out and when Hollis opened her door that evening, he saw her lying on the bed, a wet towel over her forehead.

"Feeling any better?" he asked.

"I'm feeling even worse. I wish I could die and get it over with."

"Would you like to try dinner?"

"Oh, good God, no."

"You should eat."

"Why don't you get sick? Everybody else is sick."

"I don't get sick," he said. He sat down beside her and ran his hand over her stomach. "Are you sure it's seasickness? Not the other thing? I mean, the morning sickness?"

"No, I'm sure it's not the other thing, as you put it."

"You rest," he said. "Then give me a perfect son."

"How do you know it will be a son?"

"I know, that's all."

"You're always sure of things, aren't you?"

"Only of some things."

"All I want to do is have this baby so I can get on with my work."

"You will. I have it all arranged now."

"What do you mean 'all arranged'?"

"You'll see," Hollis replied. "Now you get some sleep."

With a last groan of agony, Deborah thrust the new life into the world. She lay back in a dazzle of light and pain, looking at the baby as it hung above her in the doctor's hands like a bloody, quartered animal, and she thought, *ugly. Ugly*. The baby cried. Later Deborah slept. When the nurse brought the infant to her, she held it warmly.

"*Doux yeux*," the nurse said, smiling.

"Thank God it's a boy," Deborah said.

Hollis visited her an hour later. "The doctor says it's a perfect boy," he said. "That birthmark on its forehead will go away."

"I didn't even notice it."

"It will go away. I'm returning home now, but I have Nathan Carmichael here to handle everything for you. The boy will be taken care of, so don't concern yourself. You get your strength back. The crew arrives next week and you begin shooting in a month. Will you be ready?"

"Yes."

"We've picked a name for the boy. Peter Russell."

"I had thought of Henri as a first name."

"It's Peter Russell," Hollis said. "That's been decided."

Again she slept, awakening to the creep of evening shadows. Deborah felt a rare contentment. The boy was not ugly; he was beautiful. Too soon, the nurse came in to take the child from her. A chill of loneliness swept through Deborah, a mounting apprehension that never again would she be allowed to see her son.

8.

MARION JORDAN COLLINGSWORTH woke one morning with a headache and a sickness in her soul. She struggled from the big bed, fighting tiredness and dizziness, dragged herself across the floor, and studied her face in the mirror. It was horrible, as if she had aged overnight. Desperately she smeared on makeup, driving away the lines, but when she had finished, her face seemed artificial, rouged like the savage reds and oranges and blues concealing the ravaged faces of old women attending parties in gold and silver ankle-length gowns, puffing cigarettes and chattering nonsense ad infinitum to anyone they could corner. Like her mother; yes, like her. It was a role Marion had sought to escape, yet she seemed drawn into it. She had no real friends, persons with whom she could talk, reveal secrets, share triumphs or frustrations. Her parties were for his friends, dry men of distinction with wives of leisure, often shallow and even catty women who worried about insubordinate servants, declining service at restaurants, and the rise of the black man.

With a small sob, Marion filled the basin with warm water and scrubbed off the makeup. Her face peered at her, cruelly revealed in light that did not hide. Her skin was tight. She wanted to get back to bed, under covers, to escape from a life that each day seemed to become less meaningful.

Some days she thought she knew what afflicted her, others she wandered around in confusion, unable to sort out her thoughts. It was not one thing; it was many. She felt not a part of the house, but a prisoner in it. The servants, except her personal maid, were his. They were polite to her but loyal to him. She could not confide in them for fear of their telling her husband. When she gave them instructions, they waited to consult with their master before carrying them out. Somehow, she could not implement her lingering determination to do something on her own. He was in the way. The small victory she had won over him in redecorating the place had been her last. He granted minor matters, but denied her larger expression. Even now, while he was in Europe, she dared not institute major changes in the house, fearful of his wrath when he returned. That was not all; it was only a tiny part of it. She feared she was being used. At social events he introduced her to his friends as "my wife," or "Mrs. Collingsworth," relegating her immediately to a secondary position, an object of possession. His friends accepted her, treating her with polite respect, admiring her grace and beauty, but discussed only superficial matters with her, banalities such as the weather, their golf handicap, or the quality of the food they were eating. They were important men in formal dress whose decisions set the course for the city and the state, even the nation, but they regarded her as merely a woman, if a striking and splendid one.

But now, suddenly, she seemed to herself neither striking nor splendid. She was washed out, burned out. Golf and tennis, sports she had loved and played well, no longer intrigued her. Most of her friends had left after her marriage. Her father, busy with his retailing enterprises, didn't seem to have time to listen to her sometimes inarticulate and ambiguous complaints; her mother had grown even more flighty and eccentric, spending her days in a dazzle of meaningless luncheons and dinner parties.

She flung herself on the bed and lay writhing, thinking *Mrs. Collingsworth*. It was their room, this giant bedroom, the only one in the house they shared privately, but it too had become a prison cell to her. Often he came in late at night, arousing her to perform a ritual of sex, then turned over to issue an immediate series of grunts and snores, a master ogre of a big house who had again inflicted his will upon his captive bride. She did not love him anymore—if she ever had; in fact, she realized that she hated him, already wishing that he would die, waiting for it. Yet divorce was out of the question. Divorce, to Marion, was an admittance of failure and she would not admit that. She held out faint hopes, in her most optimistic moments, that she could someday emerge fulfilled and even triumphant over him. It was the hope that kept her going.

She sat up on the bed and flung back her hair. Her hand reached down and opened the nightstand. She took out the pearl-handled .32 automatic pistol and examined it. This had become an almost daily routine with her and she did not really know why. Perhaps it was because the pistol seemed to give her some measure of comfort, of safety. She was not afraid of weapons. Her father had schooled her in their use and she had become a better shot than he. Now she put the .32 back, assured it was loaded. The maid Clara tapped on her door and entered.

"Go away," Marion said. "I'm not ready yet."

Clara retreated. Marion lay back, waiting for the headache to subside. She did not believe in aspirin or painkilling pills of any kind. She believed most sicknesses to be psychosomatic, curable by rest and concentration. Marion had a high threshold for pain; besides, she feared even minor pain remedies could lead to addiction. But perhaps the reason went even deeper. When she felt pain, she knew that she was alive, that she could fight. She tightened her fists and gritted her teeth, driving away this pain, and forced herself to think of the most important reasons for her unhappiness and agony.

She had a daughter she could not love, for reasons that totally perplexed her, and a son to whom her heart went out but whose deformity she secretly detested. She was ashamed of Andrew, agonizing over thoughts of his future. Hollis had solved the problem by merely ignoring both children, making them Marion's burden, even blaming Marion's ancestry for the son's deformity. And that led to the other real reason for Marion Collingsworth's agony. Her husband. Willingly she had left the society world that had begun to bore and disgust her to join in wedlock with the area's most eligible and illustrative bachelor, but what had come of it was even more boring, even more disgusting. He did not hide his infidelities, flaunting them in her face, declaring they were due to her inadequacy in bed. Even now he was flouncing about Europe with a fluffy movie star he had created. And if it were not Deborah Reading it would be someone else. Marion realized she'd married a man who had unusual sexual powers, a man who showed his strength by the deep thrusts of a long, hard penis, but she had found herself unable to keep up with him.

And now, on this bed, she thought, *It is his*, wondering how many women had lain there before her, giving him the satisfaction she was now unable to provide. It seemed crude to her that a marriage should succeed on conjugal harmony alone. She had attempted to talk to some of her married women friends about it but they refused to talk sex, saying it was too private. Her father, usually open in any discussion, always turned away when she brought up specifics. And it was the only subject in the world that embarrassed her mother.

"You look pale, dear," Audrey Jordan said to her daughter at the Polo Lounge of the Beverly Hills Hotel, sipping her second luncheon martini and inserting her fourth cigarette into the stem of a new silver holder. "Have you been well?"

"I'm just fine, Mother. Now let's not talk about that."

"No, I insist. You are, after all, my only daughter."

"I tell you that I am all right. There is nothing wrong with me. Now let's order."

"We will order soon enough. Oh, there's Abigale. Abigale, you look *stunning*!" Audrey and a woman who wore bright red lipstick kissed on the cheeks. "Have you met my daughter? But surely you've met Marion."

The woman named Abigale acknowledged Marion with an, "Oh, but of course," chatted rapidly with Audrey, ending with a mechanical, "But I fear I shan't be able to make it, a birthday, you know," and flitted to another table. Audrey puffed smoke and wrinkled her brow.

"If you only knew how much I detest that woman," she told her daughter.

"Then why do you speak to her?"

"Why do I speak to her? Well, dear, I *must*. It wouldn't do not to speak to her. She is part of it."

"Part of what?"

Audrey gestured around. "Of this, of course."

"Mother, have you ever thought that you might live an empty life?"

"Empty? With all this? Don't be foolish, dear."

Marion sighed. "All right, Mother." She had been looking at the menu and now she threw it down. "I don't think I'm very hungry."

"I know something is bothering you, but whatever it is, it's not that serious. And I think I have a solution for you."

"Which is?"

"A woman I've been seeing. She is absolutely marvelous."

"No. I'm not quite ready for psychoanalysis."

"Mrs. Sandborn is not a psychiatrist, dear. But she is a woman of unusual powers. She sees that which is there but which others do not see."

"Mother, if I didn't know you better, I'd be thinking right now that you've been consulting a spiritualist."

"Yes. Mrs. Sandborn is a medium. Why does that surprise you so?"

Marion suppressed a laugh. "Oh, I suppose that it doesn't. I suppose that nothing does, not anymore. And I'll tell you what, Mother. I'll see this woman. In fact, I'm looking forward to seeing this woman."

"Another martini, Henry," Audrey told the lurking, attentive waiter.

Mrs. Sandborn was no ordinary medium. She operated out of a Beverly Hills house that had a Mercedes in the garage, turned down half her prospective clients, was available by referral only, and charged enough so that those who had to ask her fee were considered unworthy of an audience. She didn't use crystal balls or star charts and accoutrements such as swami hats and robes were not part of her equipment. She was a large, plain middle-aged woman with gray hair heaped in a bun, wearing a dark dress with an apron like a maid's. She had huge brown piercing eyes—the one asset, Marion thought as she entered behind her mother's lead, that perhaps had led her to assume a seer's role.

She had an unusual act. Clients were conducted to a stiff, high-backed chair under a bright overhead light and asked to extend their hands, palms up. Then Mrs. Sandborn grasped the hands tightly, her fingers pressuring the wrists, and drilled her owl's stare into the eyes of her visitor, straining her brown flat face, her eyes widening and moistening as she fought to receive a message. She quickly dropped Marion's hands and turned to Audrey.

"I can do nothing with her. She is resisting me. She does not believe in me."

"Please don't resist," Audrey said. "We're trying to help you, dear."

Marion felt foolish and amused, but she submitted to another attempt. Mrs. Sandborn held her tightly, so tightly that it hurt. Her eyes pierced into Marion's.

"Ah," she said, about a minute later. "You have a daughter. And a son." She paused. Her eyes seemed to soften. "I am sorry for the son."

"Why do you say that?" Marion asked.

"I am sorry for his future."

"Let go. I think I want to leave now."

"There is another one," Mrs. Sandborn said. "A boy."

"No. There is no other one."

"There is."

Marion wrestled her hands away. Mrs. Sandborn's chin fell, as if in exhaustion, as if she had expended her powers. Outside the house, Marion said to her mother:

"How much do you pay her?"

"Oh, she's very expensive."

"I'll bet she is. And a total fake. How long have you been going to her?"

"Oh, several years."

"Has she helped you? No, don't answer. I think I know. She's helped you get over living your life."

"You resisted her," Audrey chided.

It got worse. Some mornings she could not get out of bed, lying in a sleepless exhaustion until evening. She couldn't eat. Nothing seemed to interest her. Sometimes Clara sat with her all night, stroking her hair.

"I love you," she said one night. "You are perhaps the only person in the world I love. My dear Clara."

"There, there," Clara said. "Try to sleep."

It was not quite true; she still loved her father. She sought him out at the Bel Air Country Club, where he usually spent mornings on the putting green. "Perhaps you should see a doctor," he told her. He was a lonely figure on the green, if striking in his white slacks and blue blazer. "I know a good one. Shall I make an appointment?"

"No. No shrinks. I'm going to whip this by myself."

"Marion, you may not think of me as one qualified to give advice. I'm *totally* leisure class, you know. What I have was inherited, her side. So, in her way, she runs things. Yet I am not exactly a mush head. Or wet brained—yet."

"Of course you're not, Clarence."

"I never really approved of your marriage to Hollis Collingsworth. He is a man who grinds people up." He tapped the ball into a hole, a perfect curving putt from thirty feet. "But that is done. Now the question is what to do about it. You could divorce him. But I don't think you want that. You're not a person who gives up."

"I want him. But I also want to . . . well, *tame* him."

"You're never going to be content with very little, you know. You've had too much for that. And you've pretty well had your way, up until now." He turned to her, his handsome face serious. "I've done *nothing* with my life. But you could. With him, you could. Don't try to control him, because you can't. But don't lose your identity to him. Remember you're a Jordan. You can let him run you—God knows I've done enough of that—or you can take hold of your life and use him, work with him, to accomplish what you want to accomplish. Remember the queen is the strongest piece on the chessboard."

"But this is not a game of chess."

"He thinks it is."

She kissed him and caught a taxi to the beach, riding for hours. She thought, *I am Marion Jordan*. Perhaps it was that simple. She *was* losing her identity to a man who wanted to dominate her, to force her to meld her identity into his, so that she became him. She had no desire to dissolve her union with him. That would be foolish. It also would be surrender. There in the taxi, breathing the warm sea air, she made a resolution. She would change. She didn't need a psychiatrist; the thought of therapy terrorized her. She would do it by herself. He would see some change, but he would not see the total change. She would start immediately.

She reentered the Beverly Hills house with resolve. The first tactic in her assault was to make friends with the old manservant Trobridge, who treated her politely yet tersely, letting her know he was responsible only to his master. After he served her tea in the dining room one afternoon, she said:

"We'll have a party when my husband returns from Paris."

"Very well, madam."

"And stop that *madam* reference. I suppose you should call me Mrs. Collingsworth." She sipped the tea, a bitter Keemun she drank because Hollis liked it. "Do we have Darjeeling tea? I would prefer that in the future."

"If we do not have it in the household, I will locate some."

"You've been with the family for a long time, haven't you?"

"I was with his father before him," Trobridge said.

"There is a French saying. *La propriéte c'est le vol*. Property is robbery. Do you think there is any truth to that?"

"I speak French, Mrs. Collingsworth. You need not translate."

"I've often wondered why you stay here beyond your retirement."

"Where is there to go?"

"Yes, I suppose so." She leaned forward, almost conspiratorially. "Tell me, Mr. Trobridge, do you like him? My husband?"

Trobridge considered. Then he said: *"Nul n'est un hero valet à son."*

"Then why have you stayed?"

"Tout comprendre est tout pardonner."

"I like you, sage Mr. Trobridge. We shall plan a party together. We will conspire on the guest list. It will be a humdinger of a party."

It was, right down to the streamers and balloons. She hired Perino's to cater it but drew up the menu herself; if Perino's didn't have it, they were asked to find it. She had veal cordon bleu, green beans Caesar, Philadelphia cabbage, raspberry top hats, anchovy open-faced sandwiches, and fruit salad with pomegranate, persimmon, papaya, and mango. It was an outdoor-indoor party, mostly outdoors, starting at three P.M. and ending when everybody had left. She sent out exactly one hundred invitations, mostly to younger people she'd known in college, yet carefully included some of Hollis's friends and business acquaintances; all but four accepted and the four who couldn't make it had legitimate excuses. Two bars and a serving table were set up on the big lawn in back of the house. She invited some artists and musicians she knew, but only those properly schooled in dress. Two days before the event, which was a surprise for Hollis, she went to her hairdresser.

"Off with it," she said.

"Off with it, Mrs. Collingsworth?"

"I want to try a curly poodle."

In recent months Hollis had developed an ability to hide showing his surprise, and when he returned home on a Saturday, true to his telegram, he did not seem to notice that

Marion had cut her hair. When she told him of the party to be held the next afternoon—a complete surprise perhaps would have angered him—he merely shrugged and said all right. He seemed slightly more subdued than when he'd left for Paris.

The party *was* a success, with no one drinking too much and everyone having a good time. It moved in a swish of silk dresses, a babble of voices expressing optimism for the future, well-mannered young men who wore sincere ties, elderly city statesmen in dark suits, their cheeks sun-pinked, tufts of white hair edging their bald pates. There were no show-business types. The artists she'd invited had currency and success. Hollis seemed pleased; she'd selected well. He circulated politely. He'd spent an hour studying the guest list, at her suggestion, so that those he did not know would not have unfamiliar names to him. Marion moved among the group, the hostess and mistress of her party, congenial and pleased. Everyone complimented her on her weight loss and new hairdo. Myron Demming and his wife Sandra gushed all over her, almost to the point of embarrassing her.

"You can't fool me," Demming said. "You've had a face lift."

"No. No, I've just been resting, that's all."

"You look stunning, Marion. You're truly a beautiful woman."

"Thank you. I hear you're running for the Senate."

"Yes. I'm taking votes now."

"I wish you luck."

"I just love Washington," Sandra Demming said. "It's my second favorite city, behind only Los Angeles."

It was a true Los Angeles party, with even the piano player on the patio outside. If men wished to cement a contact with someone they had just met, there were chairs, an open bar, and cigars in the living room, but no one left to do that. Everyone mixed well. It was a triumph. Marion decided she would have more parties; an invitation to the Collingsworths would become a status symbol in the city. She glowed in her own newfound success.

Her daughter Mary, allowed for the first time to participate in a party, pulled at her dress. "Andrew's sick," she said.

"Sick? Why, he was just fine this morning."

"He's sick now," Mary insisted.

She took her daughter's hand and went into the house. Andrew lay stomach down on his bed. She had promised the boy that he too could make an appearance at the party, a promise that he'd reacted to at first with apprehension but later with enthusiasm. He'd been fitted with his first trouser-length suit for the occasion. When Marion touched his back, she realized her son was sobbing bitterly.

"What's wrong, Andrew?" she asked. "Why are you crying?"

He didn't turn. Finally he said, "Ain't crying."

She sat down on the bed. He hid his shrunken hand under his body, a habit he'd acquired. At meals he kept it on his lap under the napkin. Marion said, "Mary thinks you're sick."

"Ain't sick."

"We don't say ain't, young man."

"Ain't, ain't, *ain't!*"

"All right, you can lie here and cry if you want, but I think you'd have more fun outside with the party."

"Can't go," he told his mother.

"What do you mean, you can't go? I invited you."

He hesitated, his face buried in the covers. "Can't go."

"Father told him he couldn't go," Mary said, standing primly, fire in her eyes.

"Andrew, did your father say that?" Andrew didn't respond. His small shoulders trembled. Slowly Marion turned him over. The deformed arm came into full view. She reached down and touched it, held it. "Well, you're going," she said. "You dry up your tears, because you're going."

She walked between them, holding their hands, guiding them to the light and revel.

Marion took a long bath in bubbly warm water, arousing the nipples on her breasts with gentle, slippery-wet strokes. She ran her thumbs over the hair between her legs, her hands warm on her thighs. She felt her breath quicken. She rose from the tub, dried herself with a towel, and dabbed perfume on her arms and breasts. It was from one of the bottles of perfume Hollis had brought her from Paris. She slipped on a pink silk negligee and went into the bedroom. Hollis lay on the bed, reading, his glasses on. She lay down quietly beside him, slipped off the glasses, and put her leg between his. He reached to turn off the light.

"No," she said. "I want the light on."

He sprang to a quick erection under her stroking hand, and when she bent down to run her mouth and tongue over the head of his penis, he began to rotate his hips in the motion of the act. He entered her with a rapid thrust and she had an almost immediate high-soaring climax. For a moment it was dark. Then she felt his spurts deep within her. She smiled.

"*Le petit mort*," she said, opening her eyes.

He lay quietly spent for a few minutes. Then he said: "Where have you been taking lessons?"

"Well, it's been a while, Hollis."

"You cut your hair."

"Oh, then you *did* notice."

"Of course I noticed."

"Do you like it?"

"I think I might get used to it."

"Did you like the party?"

"I think you mean *your* party."

"Ours."

"Who was that Ira Brambly?"

"Friend of a friend. He's in television. He says the future in television is great."

"I believe him. I asked him to come see me. I'm thinking about going into television myself."

"Instead of the newspaper?"

"Oh, Christ, no. The newspaper is bread and butter. I'd never get rid of the newspaper. I'm thinking about starting a morning paper in fact, going head to head with the *Times*. I met a man on the boat coming back, an editor for the Associated Press in Europe who I might hire to get that project going. The television would be a part of the studio, you see."

"Yes, that would fit in." She lay still, secretly excited. He had never talked at this length to her before. She said, "I've only been to the newspaper once. I'd like to spend the day there soon."

"If you like."

"You seem changed, Hollis."

"You're the one who's changed."

"Perhaps so. You noticed my parents weren't invited?"

"I most certainly noticed."

"Father would have been all right, but mother wouldn't have fit in, I'm afraid. I've only lately come to see what a cross that man bears with her."

"I think you've grown up."

"I don't know how to explain it. I feel that I'm part of

something now. Before I didn't know what my role was, or even if I had a role. But now I see quite clearly that I do."

"And it is what?"

"To help you," she explained. "To help you achieve what you want. I'll even get in back of Myron Demming for that."

"You don't like Myron Demming?"

"He has a weak chin," Marion said.

"Well, we're stuck with him. As sure as shooting, he's going to the Senate."

"What movie did you make in Paris?"

"We haven't started making it yet. I just got things rolling over there. The working title is *Paris Interlude*."

"Starring Deborah Reading?"

"Starring Deborah Reading."

"I want you to stop seeing her," Marion said. "Sleeping with her."

A new era jumped instantly out, an era of mambo dancers, drive-in restaurants and theaters, Monroe and Willie Mays, 3-D movies, and the miracle of chlorophyll. The quiz shows, Lucy, Arthur Godfrey, and Edward R. Murrow dominated the growing television industry. Elvis Presley shot to stardom. Teenagers answered, "Hey, crazy, man," to almost any greeting. Flying saucers were sighted in the skies, amateur uranium prospectors used rent money for a grubstake, someone named Bridey Murphy tempted the most cynical to believe in reincarnation. Ike went to the White House on a promise to end the Korean War; the land was properous and sedate, despite the Russian threat. The leading female star of the age was one Deborah Reading, transformed from her girlish, heartthrob parts to the image of a woman of understanding and dignity. Myron Demming, Republican from California, became a national figure with impassioned defenses of free enterprise against the progress of government control in other nations; he steered skillfully away from the extremism of McCarthy, yet did not take the middle road on the issue of communism, publicly praising the studios for expelling those who refused to sign loyalty oaths. In an age where grown men began to wear pink shirts, Demming preferred white.

Collingsworth Communications started a morning newspaper, the *Light*, and became a diversified media giant, acquir-

ing several television stations and newspapers in Arizona,
Texas, and New York. The *Hit Parade* proclaimed "Tennessee
Waltz" and "Oh, My Papa" as the top songs. TV viewers liked
the innocent *Life of Riley* and *Our Miss Brooks*. It was an age
of tranquility and tranquilizers, of peace in suburbia despite
mounting sales of bomb shelters, of wrought iron and the
Iron Curtain. When Myron Demming's tireless investigation
in the Senate resulted in an indictment of Francis Morris and
his wife for passing on military secrets to the Russians, the
nation cheered. So did Hollis Collingsworth. He held a party
for Demming at the fifth-floor executive dining room of the
Bulletin-News. Hearst and Chandler from the rival newspapers were invited, and, to Hollis's surprise, they attended.

"When will you remove the eagle from your masthead?"
Chandler asked, sipping brandy.

"When you do," Hollis said.

An invitation to one of Hollis's periodic Friday afternoon
cocktail parties in the executive dining room of the *Bulletin-
News* was considered a signal honor. The parties were limited
to no more than twenty-five guests and seldom did anyone
have more than two drinks. There always was a guest of
honor, usually a person of distinction from another town.
Name tags were unnecessary, for most of those invited knew
each other. If a person did not accept twice in succession, his
name invariably was stricken from the list; one regularly
invited who failed to receive a summons twice in a row had
reason for concern about his diminishing importance in the
area. Together the twenty-five ruled and owned the city.
They were of one political mind, of one economic status, and
of one ethnic group. They were bankers, politicians, industrialists, financiers, and university professors. They dressed,
acted, thought, and even looked alike. Most of them, like
Hollis, had been shaped to care for second-generation wealth
and power. All of them, since they were westerners, were
considered to be in the forefront of new thinking. None of the
twenty-five, except the politicians and university presidents,
had a net worth under a million. They had achieved this
inner circle, however, not by wealth but through their leadership qualities and their economic contributions to the city.
They provided the jobs and money that made the city grow.
Although they were new thinkers, they were not mavericks;
they were growth minded, yet restrained in risk taking; they

were accomplishers and go-getters, yet fiscally conservative and bland in personality. Hollis, founder of the group, was perhaps its most outlandish member, since a portion of his assets was in the entertainment industry. Also, he was the single member of the group who did not have a college degree.

The guest of honor, if he was foolish enough to do so, could shatter the unwritten two-drink rule, and Myron Demming was either foolish enough or ebullient enough to do so. He downed five stiff martinis in an hour and would have launched into a speech if an unexpected incident hadn't occurred. A heavyset, gray-haired man, his face red as a tomato and his hands trembling, pushed his way through the group and stood shoulder-to-shoulder with Hollis, his bloodshot eyes blazing. A quiet descended. He wore a rumpled tweed suit and wide suspenders. Hollis eyed him evenly.

"Helman," he said.

The man threw back his head and spat into Hollis's face. There were murmurs and gasps and then the silence was absolute. Hollis stared at his former editor. Calmly he withdrew his handkerchief and wiped the spittle from his cheek. Two of the younger men in the group pressed forward and took Helman's arms. Helman shook them angrily away.

Hollis squared his shoulders. He grinned. "No, let him have his say. The man obviously has something to say. Are you, sir, a dissatisfied subscriber?"

A smattering of nervous laughter ensued, breaking the tension. Hollis stood calmly. "Go on, talk," he said to Helman. "Or would you like to have another drink first?"

Helman surveyed the circle of gray-suited power around him, eyeing each man for long seconds. Again there was silence, interrupted only by an occasional musical tinkle of ice in a cocktail glass. Shelton had appeared, but Hollis waved him away. Hollis felt a tension, electric and invisible; he struggled inwardly not to show it. He laughed quietly, more of a sneer than a laugh. The former editor in his scruffy suit, a day's growth of tough whiskers on his chin, seemed a ludicrous apparition from another age, a Victorian with a removable celluloid collar, an absurd pantaloon the butt of clown antics. Yet Hollis felt no pity; he felt only disdain. And fear. Unaccountably, fear.

Helman's lips moved. His red eyes rolled in their dark puffy sockets. He turned slowly and pushed his way back through the group, walking head held high with a stiff-kneed dignity.

Anger mounted in Hollis's brain as Shelton drove him home that evening. The old editor had embarrassed him before his peers, an attack worse than a physical assault, reminding him of something he had tried for years to drive from his consciousness. It was that he still lived with fear. In the darkness on a street he often sensed that a figure stalked behind him, waiting to strike. He occasionally woke at night in a sweat, the vivid memory of shifting dreams, nightmares, swimming darkly before him. He saw the skinny, pointing finger of the witch Hetty Perkins; he saw skull fragments explode from his father's head. He feared death more than any other fear. He had so much more to accomplish before he died. He was nearing the age at which his father had died, and he lived in dread that the pattern would be repeated. He told himself that there was no reason to fear. Men of power had enemies, of course, but his enemies, disgruntled former employees such as Helman and perhaps Lowenfelt, were vanquished and weak. Yet he feared. He could ask the police for special protection, but he did not want to admit he was afraid. He considered Shelton too old to be effective as a guard and now, trembling both in anger and in fear, he placed the acquisition of an efficient and loyal bodyguard high on his list of priorities, and he vowed to tighten security at the newspaper and studio. He telephoned Levin from home that evening.

"I think security is sufficient, but anything you want done I'll certainly see to it," Levin said.

"I think we're going to have some labor troubles there. Those goddamn Commie writers at the studios are going to stir things up."

"No signs of that yet."

"Do something before you see signs. I want any guard who lets anyone in without a pass fired. You put that in writing to the guards and receptionists."

"All right. Consider it done. When are you coming out here?"

"Pretty soon."

"There are a number of matters I'd like to discuss with you."

"Give me a memo," Hollis said, hanging up sharply.

He rang the buzzer for Trobridge, intending to set the

butler immediately to work on improving house security and
searching for a successor to Shelton, and when there was no
immediate response he pushed the buzzer time and time
again. Hollis fought anger. The bastard Helman had unnerved him; he was experiencing a delayed reaction that sent
shivers down his spine. The son of a bitch had staggered into
the cocktail party as if he owned the place, and for all anyone
knew he could have been carrying a pistol. Hollis stormed
out of his study into the upstairs hall. Marion was there.

"Where in hell is Trobridge?" he asked.

"I've been meaning to talk to you about him. But you
hardly seemed in a mood to talk tonight."

"What about him?"

"He's locked himself into his room. He won't come out."

"Oh, good Christ. Is everybody going crazy around here?"

"He says he wants to die," Marion said.

That night Hollis had another dream—he was back in the
Wilshire house with his father, playing chess in the game
room. It was dark and he could not see his father's face. He
could see only his thick hands moving the chess pieces,
moving each time immediately after Hollis moved. Hollis felt
comfortable. He was winning. He had captured most of his
father's pawns, taking them with quick movements of the
knight, and now he planned a bold assault upon the black
queen, which had not been moved. He liked to strike with
his knights. He had a strategy firm in his mind, planning five
moves ahead, and it was working—until his father moved his
queen, striking down a knight, leaving the queen prey to a
white rook. Hollis took the queen, only to see his king
vulnerable to the black rook. He heard his father's laughter.
Light seemed to creep into the room, at first slowly like the
light of a dawn, and then rapidly, exaggerated, almost blinding. He looked into his father's face and saw not a face but a
grinning skull, black holes in the eyeless sockets. Hollis
screamed.

"What is it?" Marion said, turning over.

"N-n-nothing. Just a dream."

"You've been having bad dreams lately."

"They're nothing. I've been working too hard, that's all."

His mouth was dry. His body ached. He went to the
bathroom for water and then to his study. He picked up the

telephone and dailed Deborah Reading's number, the line
he'd had installed years ago. He fully expected a message that
it had been disconnected, and it was with rising elation that
he heard it ring. Then she answered sleepily and he felt a
sudden warm calm flowing in his veins.

They met the following afternoon at a place where they had
met before, an inconspicuous fish shanty where Sunset joined
the Pacific Coast Highway. He had not seen her for months.
He could not articulate his feelings toward her, not even to
himself, but he knew that he could not get her out of his
mind. That frightened him, for he was now secure with
Marion, gaining respect for her after discovering she had a
mind of her own. Through crafty female maneuverings, which
Hollis watched with amusement, Marion had managed to get
her way in several matters that he would have stubbornly
rejected before. Modern art now decorated the house, and to
Hollis's surprise, guests found it more interesting than the
old canvases of Reynolds and Gainsborough and Ramsay—all
now on loan to museums. Marion had assumed command of
the servants, invited guests to parties without consulting him,
and had extended their sphere of influence by bringing
educators and scientists into their social circle. She had
proved a valuable asset to him.

Her latest effort was to urge him to pay more attention to
the children. He agreed to spend more time with Andrew,
but he found it almost impossible to pay much attention to
Mary. She was a distant, aloof child, a dreamer who spattered
paint on canvas and read poetry. Hollis did not really care.
She was a daughter. But Andrew was a son, and, despite the
cruel burden of his birth, he had possibilities. He was
extremely bright, constantly amazing his tutors at home and
his instructors at the private school he attended. Yet he was
shy and unaggressive, physically awkward, fearful of public
contact. He had no close friends. He was advanced beyond
his age, yet, by allowing his handicap to limit his activities,
he was multiplying the disadvantage it gave him. He was
afraid of crowds, unaware that persons in crowds were too
concerned with themselves to notice or care about the pecu-
liarities of others. To succeed, Andrew would have to rid
himself of the shyness and find a way to compensate for his
handicap. Each day he seemed to be slipping deeper into his

cocoon; the deeper in, the more difficulty he would have in emerging.

"Hey," Deborah Reading said. "Are you here? You seem a thousand miles out on that ocean."

"I'm here."

"You called this party. So become a part of it."

"I was pleased you didn't take out the phone line."

"I'm tempted to do it. It doesn't ring very often."

"I've been busy."

"So have I," she said.

She was indeed, averaging two pictures a year, selecting her own scripts and costars, challenging for the top spot as the country's leading female box-office attraction. She had metamorphosized from an unsure girl into a stately woman. Her face had changed from pretty to beautiful. In a big hat and sunglasses, she seemed to him the rose of all-woman. A lost feeling that had not inflicted him since his youth surged through him. He fought it.

"I'm going to see Peter in Paris," she said.

"I asked you not to see him."

"Have you seen him?"

"No."

"Don't you want to know how he is?"

"I get reports from Carmichael about that."

They lapsed into silence. This time he broke it. "I want to tell you I've made up my mind about something. After today, I won't be seeing you anymore, except professionally."

She stiffened. "Did you take the day off just to tell me that?"

A young girl in shorts approached timidly. "Excuse me," she said, "but you're Deborah Reading, aren't you?"

Deborah sighed. "I am," she replied, looking up.

The girl laughed, a short, embarrassed tinkle. She had clear skin and bright blue eyes. "I saw you in *Monsoon* just yesterday," she said. "In fact, I've seen it three times. I just *loved* it, you know. I've seen all of your pictures and I just loved them all. Could I have your autograph?"

Deborah took the pen and notebook. "What is your name, dear?"

"Lois," the girl said.

"Very well. I'll write, 'To Lois, with love.'"

"That's just super."

"Where are you from?"

"Ohio."

"And, I assume, you want to get into pictures."

"I want to be an actress, yes. Like you, Miss Reading."

"Well, I have some advice for you. Go back to Ohio. Marry a lawyer there."

The girl's face fell. She walked away, her behind wriggling. Hollis watched her go. Deborah lit another cigarette, snubbed it out after two puffs, and lit a second.

"I'm sick of it," she said. "Girls from Ohio, stage mothers, casting couches, asshole producers with hard-ons, little Hitler directors. I think I'll take Sarah and go back to the farm."

"You can't quit now. You're on top."

"The top is for the birds. They can be on the wire without burning."

"I don't think you really believe that. I think it's just your mood today."

"Because you told me you're walking off? Don't kid yourself, Buster Brown. I don't know why I've let you in my bed this long. Because, of all the pricks in this town, you're among the biggest."

He whirled to face her, his nostrils snorting. "All right, call me a prick. And tell me you live a shitty life. But don't expect me to believe it. You live like a queen. And remember that you're where you are because I put you there. I put my money on you."

"I'm flattered," she said, lifting her head and returning his snort. "Is there a drink in this dump? Order me one."

He reached for her hand. She pulled it away. "I want to say something," he began. "I'm not doing this because I don't have feelings for you. I do. I haven't felt this way for somebody but once, and I was just a green kid then. I'm never going to get over you. But it has to end."

Deborah glared silently at him. He glanced past her, out at the sails on the ocean like white dots against the blue of the horizon. He turned urgently, seizing her hand and squeezing it. He felt her heel digging into his instep, hurting him, but he did not care. They sat glaring, trying to hurt each other, like schoolchildren in a territory dispute. Then he let go. The tension broke. His words tumbled out.

"You think you understand me, but you don't. You understand very little about me. What I want is to take you and run off. All of me wants that. But it's no good. I was given a job to do. It was set up for me that way. I've got to do it."

"No, you don't. You want to do it. You enjoy what you are, pushing people around, being in control."

"If so, it's only because that's the way it was spelled out."

Deborah sighed. "All right, Hollis. Let's go to work."

"Would you like that drink?"

"No. I have a picture to finish. Little Hitler is pissed off enough at me now."

"Tell him you were with the studio owner."

"I'll tell him I broke it off with the studio owner."

"All right. Tell him anything."

"Don't walk out with me, Hollis. I want to walk out by myself."

"All right."

"Good-bye," she said.

"Good-bye."

He didn't watch her go. He sat for ten minutes, staring into his cup of cold coffee and looking at the ocean. When he did leave, the girl in shorts named Lois stopped him.

"Deborah Reading," she cooed. "I honestly couldn't hardly believe it. Isn't she beautiful?"

"Yes," Hollis said. "She is beautiful."

Trobridge, true to his pledge, died without leaving his room. Marion summoned doctors but the old butler refused to see them. Finally she took the matter into her own hands, asking Shelton to force open the door. The room smelled of must and decay. Trobridge was in a much greater state of deterioration than she had imagined. He lay on the bed like a shrunken corpse, his face white, his breathing ragged. She had hesitated to force her way in earlier because she had wanted to honor his request that he remain undisturbed. Now she felt both guilt and anxiety. She sat down beside him. Trobridge winced, his thin hand moving.

"An ambulance is coming," she said. "We're taking you to a hospital."

His eyes had a death glaze and there were sores on his dry lips. "*Se jeter dans l'eau de peur de la pluie,*" he mumbled.

"What?" Marion asked, leaning closer. She said to Shelton, who lurked nearby in silence: "He's delirious. Where *is* that ambulance?"

"On the way, mum."

With great effort, Trobridge lifted his gnarled hand and touched her arm. His lips moved. "I die in . . ."

"Yes?"

". . . in no fear . . . in dignity . . . because . . ."

The doorbell was ringing downstairs. "Shelton, show the ambulance attendants *in*!"

"Yes, mum." Shelton seemed unconcerned.

". . . because I die . . . of my own choice."

His eyes closed. Marion held his hand and gazed into his face. It seemed serene. Marion had never before been in the presence of death and now she felt humbled before it, reminded of her own mortality. She realized she knew very little about Trobridge, perhaps nothing. He had no apparent family or friends. He spent his time-off reading. He moved about the house a shadow figure, part of its fixtures, a keeper of secrets who performed his duties with uncomplaining efficiency. In a sense his stiff dignity bespoke, invisibly, of superiority over those he served. Marion heard a stirring behind her and she turned to see Mary and Andrew peeking in the door. Mary held her nose. The ambulance attendants pushed noisily in, bringing with them smells of the crisp outside air.

Trobridge had arranged everything before his death, including a private cremation and a scattering of his ashes at sea. He left a neatly typed will that instructed his executor, a man named Lowenfelt, to see that all of his meager assets were converted into cash and donated to the United Jewish Welfare Fund. He left a gift-wrapped book for Marion, a first edition of Carlyle's *The History of the French Revolution*, which she treasured but did not read. Andrew got a well-thumbed edition of *Walden* and *Morte d' Arthur*; Mary got *Pride and Prejudice* and *Little Women*. When the hospital told Marion that Trobridge had died of cancer, she felt a renewed burst of guilt, punishing herself for not acting faster to make his last days more comfortable. Hollis didn't see it that way.

"It was what he wanted," he said.

"But he must have been in frightful pain."

Hollis shrugged. "Maybe he had needles."

"No. There was nothing like that in his room."

"You liked old Trobridge, didn't you?"

"I liked him very much."

"Well, he'll be hard to replace."

"He was reserved, even cool, but he had an extraordinary dignity about him. You couldn't find a speck of dust in his room, not even toward the end."

"I'll take care of the will. Lowenfelt once worked for me. He's been to the house, but I'd swear not a word passed between those two. It goes to show that you can be around people a long time and never know what's in their heads."

"Yes," she said.

On Saturday the *Bulletin-News* carried a four-paragraph item on page 18 stating that Timothy Helman, former editor of the newspaper, had died on Main Street of a gunshot wound, apparently self-inflicted. Helman's death was noted in the obituary columns of the other local papers, and the Associated Press moved two paragraphs on it over the state wire.

The deaths of two persons associated with him had an exhilarating effect on Hollis Collingsworth. Both had dictated to something most men did not control, death; both had hurried to that dark, unknowing limbo to cheat the inevitable call. They had not known how precious even one day more could be to a man who had a constructive and accomplishing attitude about life. Even as he'd died the butler had suffered pain in stoic exile, a foolish gesture to demonstrate his priestly superiority over the master he served. And the former editor—after an act he no doubt thought courageous but which in reality proved him to be a fool—had put a gun to his head in a futile attempt to show he had final mastery over a life he'd never been able to control. Contrary to their beliefs, death had been the master of them both, tricking them into surrender before the last second alloted to them by nature had expired. It was not death in dignity; it was death in defeat. Death had no dignity, for dignity was a property of life. And life Hollis Collingsworth possessed, ringing like a bell on a clear morning through his body and mind. His fear of death, he decided, was a great asset, since it aided longevity. The past was gone, building a base for the future. He was in a new phase.

Andrew always obeyed the stern servants and his mother, but his sister Mary had more spunk, delighting in defying and tricking them. It was strictly against the rules to visit each other after bedtime. Yet Mary crept to his room many times for whispered conversations. Once she'd found him crying.

"What's wrong?"

He lay stiffly, ashamed of his tears. Then he managed: "Some boys at school, they've been picking on me. They want to fight me."

"Well, fight back."

"How can I?"

"Fight with anything. Fight with your knees and feet. Hit them with sticks and rocks and baseball bats."

"They'd catch me later and beat me up."

"I don't think so. Show them you can fight and I don't think they'll pick on you. Grandma's coming Sunday. She's starting to smell like an old schoolteacher. What book did you get? I got that romantic crap *Little Women*."

"He gave me *Morte d'Arthur*."

"Did you like him?"

"He never spoke to me."

"I liked him," Mary said. "Do you want me to read to you from *Morte d' Arthur*?"

"Would you?"

"Sure," she said, adding, "fight them back."

9.

PRIVATE TUTORS, GRAVE stern men in dark suits and white shirts, came to the house to teach Andrew science and mathematics, but he received most of his grade and prep-school training at the Stuart Institution in Pacific Palisades. Mary, given piano lessons and tutored in art at home, attended a girl's school in Pasadena. Every morning a bus from the school picked her up, returning her in the afternoon. Stuart also had bus service, but Andrew hated public vehicles and protested so vigorously that he won the point with his mother. The older of the two full-time maids, Agnes Quirt, drove him to and from the school in one of the cars. She was a maid, so she considered chauffeuring an unfair extension of her duties, punishing Andrew with silent scowls and a sharp word jab or two every trip. But Andrew didn't care. He enjoyed his power to order the hag to deliver him at precisely eight A.M. and pick him up at four P.M. It was in fact about the only power he had.

One morning he came bouncing to the car full of spirit, thrusting an invisible sword at a mythical pack of attacking knights.

"Now what is *this*?" Agnes inquired, freezing her features into her favorite scowl.

"I'm Sir Lancelot, rescuing the maiden in distress. I have a singing sword."

"Oh, you couldn't use a sword."

"I could *too* use one. And ride, too."

"Get in. We'll be late."

"I can ride," he said as she awkwardly backed the car into the street. "Shelton took me riding. Father says he'll take me soon."

"Well, that'll be the day," Agnes said.

Morte d'Arthur had thrilled him, putting him in a world of imagination and excitement where good defeated bad and gallantry and comradeship ruled. It was so unlike his own strictured life. He loved learning, but he hated the school. He hated the bleak uniforms, the all-male instructors, the proud and spoiled rich boy students. They knew who he was, but since he was the smartest one in any class, capable of showing them up at any time, he had no friends. His shrunken arm, which forced him to learn to write with his left hand, made him the butt of jokes and occasionally the object of torment at recess.

He had one particularly malevolent enemy, a thick-headed home-builder's son named Bo-Bo Yardley. Bo-Bo, a six-footer with huge shoulders and powerful arms, ruled the playground with the swagger and authority of a commanding general. He was never called out at first base and he was given a clear path to the goal with the soccer ball. He was uncoordinated and awkward, often tripping over the ball as he moved down the field, but no one challenged him to prove his abilities in a fight; he ruled through fear and threat, untested, a bully as unmatched outside the school as he was outclassed inside. Since the school graded on the curve system, Bo-Bo tried to bully intelligent students into making deliberate errors on tests. Andrew feared Bo-Bo, but he refused to cooperate, which turned him into a particular target. And he had to face his problem alone. There was an unwritten rule at the school that you did not appeal to the headmaster or instructors when you had a problem with another student. The rule had no doubt been authored by Bo-Bo Yardley; certainly he enforced it. It was Andrew Collingsworth's introduction to power politics.

One day, after Andrew had dazzled Bo-Bo to an ignominious defeat in a political-science debate, Bo-Bo came up to him at recess on the playground, hate blazing in his piglike eyes. Students closed in, making a circle around them.

Bo-Bo pushed Andrew's chest with both his hands. "Queer!" he snorted. "I'm gonna make you suck my cock, queer."

Andrew trembled. He thought, *Fight them back. With sticks and rocks.* But he did nothing. Bo-Bo stood an inch from him, his fat red face streamed with sweat, his lips twisted in a cruel snarl, his eyes rock hard. "Take a shot at me, queer," he taunted. "Take your best shot. But remember it'll be your last. It'll be your *last!*"

"Take it, take it," the audience chanted. "Hit him, hit him."

Andrew found he was fighting tears. But he would not cry. He was too old to cry. Bo-Bo sniffed the air. His thumb brushed rapid strokes across his nose. The crowd snickered. No one tried to interfere—another unwritten rule. Andrew quivered in humiliated fear, hating Bo-Bo, hating himself.

"Hey, queer, c'mon queer," Bo-Bo taunted. "Take a shot, queer. Crippled queer, I give you a couple free shots."

Andrew turned and pushed through the crowd, his head down. Driving him home that day, even Agnes noticed his mood. She asked what was wrong. He didn't respond. He fought angry tears, knowing he would face school each new day with sick apprehension.

Hollis spent some Sundays with Andrew, riding in the Cahuenga Valley hills, where he kept a ten-acre ranch that quartered six horses. An old Indian named T. T. maintained it. It had a telephone which confused T. T. and a television set which frightened him. Shelton usually accompanied Hollis, riding some yards ahead. Andrew's horse always trailed his father's. On almost every ride, Hollis went to the place where the rifle shots had echoed those many years ago; he went there in defiance, to prove that by facing fear he could defeat it.

"I used to come here, long ago, with my father," he told Andrew. "We owned all the land down there then."

"Where the houses are now?"

"That's right. They called it Collingsworth Valley."

It was a hot day, full with sun, and the horses smelled of sweat. Hollis thought of how far he'd come since the death of his father and he knew, seated here on the warm saddle, drinking in the sun, feeling fully alive with a clear head and a healthy body, that he would go much further. The legacy he had doubled would go to his son doubled, at least, once again. It would go to his son, that was, if his son proved worthy of it, as he himself had proved worthy. He turned to Andrew.

"Your mother tells me you're doing well at school. She says you're ready to go to college now, despite your tender years. What do you think?"

"I like that idea. I hate the school I'm in now."

"Why do you hate it?"

"Father, I don't want you to think I'm being impertinent, because I'm not. But I simply cannot answer your question."

"Why?"

"Because if I answer it, you'll think I'm asking for your help."

Hollis smiled. "I think I might be seeing that you have some spunk in you, boy. I also think I know what's bothering you. I'm pretty good at cutting to the truth." He eyed Andrew evenly; Andrew met his father's gaze without flinching. Hollis's eyes fell to the boy's shrunken arm. "I'd guess you're being picked on at that school. Is that right?"

"Yes," Andrew said, his head dropping.

"And you want to transfer right into college because of that?"

"It's one reason, yes."

"What do you want to study? What do you want to become?"

"I—I really don't know yet."

"If I could start over again, I'd go into politics."

"Politics *does* interest me," Andrew said. "Government is my favorite class."

Hollis took out a cigar, bit off the end, and lit it. "You're not going on to college, not quite yet," he said, blowing smoke. "You see, you must go back to that school and face up to it. You let things slide, they'll haunt you to your grave."

"Yes, sir," Andrew said. His head was hanging.

Mitch Evers wasn't easily intimidated, but neither was he insubordinate. So when the big boss, Hollis Collingsworth, summoned him, Mitch went, if in his own good time. But he didn't go in fear, as others had. He'd survived eight months of infantry combat in Korea, winning a battlefield commission and the Silver Star; now no one without a rifle or a hand grenade was capable of frightening him very much. He'd earned a political-science degree at State, evening division, while working as a copyboy on the *Bulletin-News;* after mustering out of the army at Ord, cityside had taken him on as a cub reporter. He'd taken over the political beat within a year. He was no Reston, but he wasn't a hack, either, although he usually wrote what they told him to write. Now he was ushered into Hollis Collingsworth's regal presence. He'd heard about the cannon; by hell, it was there, all right. Hollis shook his hand and waved him to a chair. It was not the electric chair so notorious around the sheet. He was offered a cigar.

"No, thanks, I'm hooked on these," Mitch said, shaking a crooked Camel from a pack.

Hollis laughed, his cheeks pink. He was as handsome as a gray fox. "Want a drink? I have some twenty-year-old bourbon in the house."

"I'll pass. My coach, the editor downstairs, tells me if I persist in drinking, I will find myself warming a bench."

"I liked our coverage of the convention," Hollis said. "Did you coordinate that?"

"Working with the managing editor, yes." Mitch had tightened his tie before coming up. Now he found himself loosening it, an act he usually performed before sitting down at his typewriter. His nerves crawled tightly. The lead for his overnight story had just come to him and he itched to get back to the newsroom and bat it out. Lighting another Camel from the heat of the expiring one, he said: "It was a newsy convention. It wrote itself."

The graying fox sat down behind his rolltop desk. He studied papers for a long time, squinting under half-lens reading glasses, while Mitch fidgeted. It was quid pro quo;

he hadn't responded immediately to the Fox's summons and now the Fox was making him squirm. Finally Hollis looked at him.

"What would you answer if I asked you to describe the mood of the country today?"

"The mood?" Mitch fumbled for a Camel, stalling. Then he said: "Fear, I guess. We're not over the threat of the bomb. We don't trust the Russians. We're not sure we should have fought in Korea."

Hollis stood up. "No, I think there was justification for Korea. That's about the only thing that bastard Truman did that I agree with."

"I left something out. I also think we're on the edge of a racial revolution."

"Oh, they come and go," Hollis said, waving an unlit cigar. "Tell me. We all want something in life. What is it that you want?"

"Something that's impossible," Mitch responded.

"And what is that?"

"To be happy."

Hollis laughed. "We have a philosopher in our midst." He began to pace. "I want to create a president," he said. "You know Senator Demming, of course. What do you think of him?"

"His strong suit is world affairs. His weak suit is that he often appears to be more concerned about himself than the country. In other words, he's more of a politician than a statesman."

"We'll make him into a statesman, or at least appear to be one." Hollis drew up a chair and pushed his face close to Mitch's. "I've come to the conclusion that if I don't step in and help put this country back on the right track again, somebody else who's dead wrong will try it, like that Kennedy clan. Now where do you fit in? Why have I brought you up here? Because I want to expand your function around here. I want you in charge of all political coverage, news and editorials, for both my papers. You report to me." He paused, then added, "And something else."

"What?"

"I understand you were on the boxing team in college."

"I played at it, yes."

"More than played. I hear you were pretty good. I say this because I want you to teach my son to defend himself."

Later, at the Westwood apartment of his girlfriend, a UCLA journalism student named Jane Raymond, Mitch told a story. It was about Al, the freight-elevator operator at the *Bulletin-News*. The freight elevator was gone now—the whole wing had disappeared in a modernization—but it had been there, run by Al, when Mitch worked in the stockroom before becoming a copyboy. One of his duties had been to descend in the elevator to the bowels of the subbasement to fetch the foul-smelling acetic acid for use in stereotype. It was a slow, jerking descent. Al usually had a pint of Old Taylor in his pocket. He kept his left hand on the elevator control switch and his right hand was always in his pocket. The joke was that Al played pocket pool; the truth was that his hand had been severed years earlier in a mailing-room accident. He was ashamed to show his stump.

Al accepted his lot. When asked how he was, he usually repeated an old joke, "Well, life's got its ups and downs, you know." And he'd grin, revealing broken teeth. He could roll a cigarette with one hand, and as he smoked he warned the boys from the stockroom not to get hooked on the habit. One day, with Mitch aboard toting his acetic acid pail, Al picked up a pressman on sub-2 and stopped the elevator between floors.

"Number two horse in the sixth," the pressman said.

"I dunno," Al said. "That horse is big odds and I have to lay it off at the newsstand. I may not have time on my break."

"You get it laid off," the pressman snapped.

Mitch was then a green kid from Wisconsin. Now his respect for Al, whom he'd regarded as sort of a wet-brained fool, increased immeasurably. The man was a real, live book-ie. His respect increased even more the next day. Mitch was the checkers champ of the building, a game he'd played thousands of times on cold Wisconsin nights. He was so good, in fact, that no one challenged him in the recreation room anymore. One lunch hour he sat by the board, playing against himself, when he looked up to see Al, hand in his pocket, standing above him.

"Line 'em up," Al said. "I'll try you a game."

Al didn't sit down. He stood up the whole game, his hand

in his pocket, moving rapidly. Mitch got a double jump on the third move. Al smiled. "I move fast," he said, pushing a checker. He didn't mind sacrificing one for one, even though Mitch was one up. Soon the board was almost clear. Al pushed a king. Mitch jumped. He saw his last three kings disappear in retaliation. "You play a good game," Al said, walking out. The game had taken less than five minutes.

Mitch made his first bet with Al a week later, a precious two dollars on the nose of a Hollywood Park filly named Maureen Grey. She came in at 4 to 1 and Al paid immediately, doling out dirty dollar bills on an elevator stopped between sub-2 and sub-3. "First bet?" he asked and when Mitch nodded yes, Al said, "Well, don't do it no more," and moved the elevator up.

But Mitch was hooked; he'd won a half-day's pay in a few minutes. He invested in the *Racing Form* and picked a long shot, a stretch runner called Sporty Jack, in the fifth the next day. He gave Al two dollars on the nose and two dollars to place. Al cautioned him that the bet was valid only if he laid it off. The next day Mitch went to the racing results Teletype in editorial, getting there just in time to see the keys punch out, "Sporty Jack: $24 win, $12.40 place." He lost no time getting to the freight elevator. But Al wasn't there. His substitute, Rita, said he'd called in sick.

"Probably sick at the track," Rita snorted. She ran one of the passenger elevators and didn't like demotion to the subbasement freight. "Or sick in a bar."

Mitch glared at her, hating her. Al didn't return for three days; when he did come back, he had some bad news for Mitch.

"I couldn't get your bet on Sporty Jack laid off," he said. "I came down with this cold and couldn't get it laid off."

"B-b-but you owe me!"

"Don't owe you, son. I couldn't get it laid off."

There was nothing Mitch could say. He suspected he'd been cheated—Al had probably laid it off and collected it for himself—but there was no court of appeals on bookie welches. For days he brooded and finally he forgot it. Then one day Mr. Newsome, the former stock boy who'd worked his way up to the amazing level of a ten-thousand-dollar-a-year job as manager of purchasing and building maintenance, summoned Mitch to his office. Mr. Newsome, not one for stalling around, came right to the point.

"We suspect," he said, "that there is gambling on that freight elevator."

Mr. Newsome sat crouched behind his big desk, his fingertips together, his eyes blazing like an inquisitor's. Mitch was amazed. He thought everybody in the building knew. He shrugged his shoulders. He looked Mr. Newsome square in the eye. The inquisition continued.

"Yesterday at approximately noon you stopped the freight elevator. You had a small white envelope in your hand. There was a substitute operator on the elevator. You asked for the regular operator. You were informed he was on his lunch break. The substitute operator asked if you wished to leave the envelope with her. You said no. Is all of what I've just related correct?"

"Yes."

"What is your ambition with this newspaper?"

"When I finish school I want to transfer to editorial."

Mr. Newsome leaned forward. "We suspect there is gambling on that elevator. Is there gambling on that elevator?"

Mitch turned away. He was thinking about Sporty Jack. He was thinking about his ambitions in life. Finally he said: "Yes. There is gambling on that elevator."

He never saw Al again.

"It's a good story, Damon Runyon," Jane said, "but the point escapes me."

They were cuddled on her couch, a digestive phase after dinner that he hoped was a prelude to sex. He called Jane his girl, but he was never sure; she had a way of reminding him of their age gap. He'd been hooked after their first date, following a lecture he'd given to her class. After their third date, they had sex at her place, and he realized he was in love for the first time in his life. But they didn't talk about love. She had much too much to do to get seriously involved, and Mitch, although he knew now he was capable of feeling love, found he was unable to express it.

"There are several points," he said, reaching for a Camel. "I thought about Al again today because something happened to me."

"What happened?"

"First let's talk about Al. He loses his hand and the company expects him to be grateful because he's kept on, running the freight elevator. He takes a few bets. Now the green kid from Wisconsin thought at first he'd been set up for a sting—I no longer do—but what most certainly is true is that I did betray Al."

"But he cheated you."

"No. He had made it clear that if he couldn't lay off high-odds bets, the bets were off. His customers understood that. So they dangled a little ambition in front of me and I sold Al out. And today they dangled a little more ambition in front of me. Maybe this time around I'll sell myself out."

"What did they dangle today?"

"Complete charge of political coverage for both papers. I report right to the top."

"Do you mean right to Hollis Collingsworth?"

Mitch nodded, blowing out smoke. "Exactly."

"Honey! Do you realize what an opportunity that is?"

"Well, I almost didn't take it."

"Be serious," Jane said.

"I am serious."

"Do you know how many people would give their eye teeth for a job like that? And you say you almost didn't take it."

"Oh, I suppose the truth of it is that I knew I'd end up taking it as soon as he offered it."

"What is Hollis Collingsworth like in person?"

"I'm not even sure he is a person, not in the conventional sense. You get the impression he was the same as he is today on the first day of his life. He's cunning and he's instinctive. He knows how to read people and he knows he's in control. But there may be something in him that in the long run he'll be unable to control."

"He sounds fascinating. I hope you'll introduce him to me someday."

"I'll do it if you promise not to run off with him."

"Cross my heart," she said, smiling.

Mitch's throat was raw from smoking, yet he reached for another Camel. "Well, maybe I'll get a book out of the experience," he said.

"You should do a book. You're a great writer."

"Talk to me. Flattery will get you far."

"It's not flattery. I mean it."

"I think I'm in a trap. What's worse is that I like it."

"You really *are* concerned about it, aren't you?"

"I'm a storyteller today, so here's another. There's this

Persian tale. A fox wakes up, sees his long shadow, and says, 'I'm going to get a camel for breakfast.' He hunts and hunts, but there is no camel to be found. In the afternoon, seeing his small shadow, he says, 'Perhaps a mouse will do.' Moral? Time blunts our appetites and makes us see things as they really are."

"But you're still young."

"I'll say this. His offer took years off me." He snapped his fingers. "Oh! Forgot. The fox also wants me to teach his kid to box."

She smiled. "Really? Mitch, I think you're now in the in group."

"Probably true."

"What is it you really want to do? I mean, the future?"

"He asked me that. I blew it. I said I wanted to be happy. But what I really want to do is observe and record the nature of the human animal."

"Will that make you happy?"

"Perhaps sad," he said, reaching for a Camel.

When he was ready, Andrew Collingsworth went to school bursting with an almost fiendish delight. He faced Bo-Bo Yardley at the playground, surrounded by a circle of boys.

"Give you a free shot, queer," Andrew said.

Bo-Bo lashed out, but he hit nothing but air, for Andrew had sidestepped, dancing the way Mitch Evers had taught him, hearing him now: "There are boxers who make it on speed and those who make it on punch. Maybe you think you have only one arm, but that's not true. You can use the other one for defense. And you haven't got a shrunken leg, have you? And remember that your good arm, because you use it so often, might have as much strength as someone has with both arms. You get in a good punch, what you punch is going to fall, unless it's a tank or a Mack truck. And you have a brain, too, remember that. A boxer fights with his brain as much as with his fists. Now show me that stance again."

Again Bo-Bo struck thin air. The boys were cheering Andrew. Bo-Bo rushed at him, snorting and kicking. Andrew stepped aside and hit him hard between the ribs. Bo-Bo stopped, gasping for breath and holding his stomach, spittle trickling to his chin. Andrew threw a short hook at his mouth, hitting him flush, a wet smacking sound that seemed to echo.

Bo-Bo collapsed like a slashed windbag, blood squirting between his teeth, falling to his knees and then toppling onto his back, his fat blood-specked throat like the white flesh of a stoned frog.

PART 4

Peter Russell

1.

HE DID NOT know who he was, where he had come from, or why he was here. He was told that his name was Peter Russell, that he was an American, and that he would go to America for his education. He was also told that both his mother and father were dead; an American friend of his parents had agreed to provide for him. He did not understand why, if he was indeed an American, he was not now there. He was told that the answer to this question would come later, if he still thought it important. He lived at a boy's home on the Rue Gay Lussac between Rue Street and Boulevard St. Michel, where long-haired university students debated existentialism at sidewalk cafés. The boys were not orphans. They went home to their well-to-do parents on weekends and holidays; on weekdays, wearing white uniforms like the dress of sailors, they participated in group games, some sports, and took lessons from outside tutors.

But Madame Colombier's, as the home was called, was not a school, not principally a school, at least. It was a convenient place to deposit offspring of the upper middle class and the true upper class while their parents traveled or worked. Some of the boys, ranging in age from four to twelve, took tutoring credits that could earn them direct entrance into preuniversity schools. Others merely played or fought or sulked. The home was a huge, two-wing marble structure with a large courtyard, ripe with the scent of chestnut-tree flowers in the spring and filled with red-orange leaves in the autumn. From his window Peter could see the Panthéon and the Jardins du Luxembourg, and at night, the silver lights along the Boulevard St. Germain.

The help was composed totally of women—cleaning maids, play instructors, nursemaids. The headmistress, a stocky woman with a bun of white hair, said she had lost her husband and three children in a concentration camp during the Nazi occupation. She said she had no bitterness; she said she understood the madness of war. She wore a ring on every finger and bead necklaces. Peter did not leave on weekends, as many of the other boys did, so often Madame Colombier took him with her on shopping and walking trips. Occasionally they went to Notre Dame, which he loved, or the nearby Panthéon, whose chilliness frightened him. Peter had a good allowance—so good, in fact, the other boys were constantly in debt to him, but he kept a balance sheet and always collected—so sometimes he treated Madame Colombier to an ice cream or sweets from a sidewalk vendor, or to a ride on the *Bateau Mouche* at sunset down the Seine. Several times they ascended the Eiffel Tower and looked out over the city. After the outings he always thanked her politely.

"And I thank you, Mr. Peter Russell, for the Métro fare and the flowers. You are a gentleman escort," she said. "If you continue to extend your charities, next I'll work you up to taking me to Laperouse."

"All right. I will do it."

"My husband and I went there—once." A mist came to her eyes, no doubt reflecting sad memories flooding her mind, but then she smiled. "Usually we settled for Chope St. Germain. Or bread and wine at home."

"Madame Colombier, do you know how long I'll be here?"

"If I only had an American penny for every time you have asked that question, I would be a rich person."

"It's not that I don't like it here. I do. It's just that . . ."

"Yes?"

"I'd like to find out more about myself."

"I can tell you only that you are a lucky boy. You have a generous benefactor in America."

"Do you know who it is?"

"As I have said many times—no, I do not."

"I would like to find out."

"Perhaps it would be better if you never found out," Madame Colombier said.

They spoke French. French was his first language, but he also spoke perfect English, tutored by a former Oxford professor who said he'd "chopped his way out of the rat race" after World War II to paint and write on the Left Bank and play chess in alleys of the Jardin des Plantes. He often won at chess, but he'd yet to sell his writings or even a single painting. He gave one of the paintings to Peter, who did not admire it but nevertheless, in deference to a man who'd had the courage to escape into a life he enjoyed, he hung it in his room. It was a small canvas of floodlit fountains on the Place de la Concorde.

He got along with the other boys at the home, but he made no real friends. They seemed to regard him as different, as an orphan, if an orphan of means. They did not invite him to their homes on weekends. It was known to them that he was an American who someday would go to America and it was also known to them that he was not a Catholic. Because of his skill at soccer, which he'd mastered after long practice sessions on weekends, he was admired by some of the boys, especially those younger than he, but he knew he'd never be truly initiated as a member of the group. He did not really care. He knew that indeed he was different from them. He learned with ease, he could beat everyone at games, and he was a favorite of Madame Colombier's. He was lonely and puzzled and sometimes moped in despair, yet he had a feeling of excitement to come.

On the treks with Madame Colombier, his senses opened fully to absorb the sights and smells and movement of Paris. In the spring the city burst in a shower of scents, so heady they were as much tastes as scents—fresh fruits and vegetables at the Marché des Ternes street market, the Métro smelling like an indoor public bath, the sweet scents of perfumes and the acid odor of auto exhaust, the aroma of the flower markets, strong smoke from the huge pipes of bearded men expounding on Sartre and de Beauvoir at boulevard cafés. He marveled at the steeple of Notre Dame, the perfection of the Arc de Triomphe. Tugboats on the Seine were beautiful to him. Madame Colombier had a name for him—the "native tourist." It was true. Each time he came out he embraced the city with the awe of a first-time visitor to it. Except for occasional walking tours taken by groups from the school, he was kept almost like a prisoner, forced to obey strict rules. Getting out was an escape into delightful experiences.

One Sunday while Madame Colombier was at mass and Peter was hemmed in under the watchful eye of her assistant, the former nursemaid Denise Vanner, the gate bell rang and Denise responded, returning to him a minute later with great excitement in her eyes.

"You have a visitor," she said. "There must be some mistake, but she's asking for you."

"Why must there be some mistake?"

"Comb your hair. Did you wash up?"

The visitor was a dark-haired woman wearing a white raincoat and sunglasses with gold rims. Denise Vanner ushered her in and stood gaping and fawning, rubbing her hands together. The woman took off her sunglasses and looked at Peter for a long time. Her eyes seemed misty. Peter fumbled, embarrassed.

"Isn't there anyone else here?" the woman asked.

"Usually there aren't many here on Sundays," Peter said in French. Then, realizing his visitor didn't understand, he repeated it in English. "Most of them go home," he added.

"I see. Then aren't you lonely?"

"Sometimes. I don't mind it."

The woman smiled. She was the most beautiful woman Peter had ever seen. She said, "You're wondering why I'm here. You see, I was a friend of your father's."

"Oh."

"Is there a place where we can talk?"

"We can go into the courtyard outside."

"Then lead the way, and we will talk."

They went past the still-gaping Denise Vanner into the courtyard. It was early spring and there had been a light rain around dawn, a rain that had awakened him full with a lonely despair, but now, the air warm and clear and ripe with the scent of flowers, a beautiful, dark mystery woman beside him, he felt his mood lighten and some inner sense he could not explain told him everything in his future would be all right. He felt comfortable in the presence of the woman, a comfort as complete, if in a different way, as that he felt in the presence of Madame Colombier. He even decided he would try to be a host.

"Would you like some tea or coffee?" he asked.

"What I really would like to do is take you to a café and then maybe we could go to the cinema."

"I couldn't go out without Madame Colombier's permission."

"Maybe I could sneak you out."

"Oh, I couldn't do that. She would worry."

"Well, we'll leave her a note."

"No, I couldn't do that. Besides, Madame Colombier and I are going to the Louvre when she returns from mass."

"Oh, I see."

They were seated on the metal chairs that Madame Colombier had imported from Germany—to illustrate, she'd once said, the German propensity for stiff discomfort—and now, as the mystery woman gazed at him with a look he could not interpret, Peter began to feel slight mental discomfort. Turning away, he saw Denise Vanner snooping at them from an upstairs window. When she realized she'd been spotted, Denise darted away. The mystery lady removed a small package from her purse and handed it to Peter.

"It's a little gift," she said. "You can open it after I leave."

"Thank you," he said, taking it.

"Do you like it here?"

"I suppose I do. I'm anxious to find out things, however."

"Find out what?"

"About the future, I guess. Professor Carmichael says I'll soon be going to America."

"Where in America?"

"Boston, he says."

"Do you like Professor Carmichael?"

"Yes. Very much."

"Will you live with him in Boston?"

"I'll be going to school in Boston."

She leaned forward, smiling. "Does Professor Carmichael come to see you very often?"

"Quite often, yes. He says he is my official guardian."

"If that is so, I'm sure you are in very good hands."

They paused. He sat stiffly, holding her gift. A slight wind had come up and the sky was clouding. Questions pressed in his mind but he dared not ask them, fearing they might drive the beautiful lady away. He did not want her to go. And he *did* want to attend the cinema with her. Yet he had promised Madame Colombier that they would go to the Louvre. Finally he got up enough nerve to ask one question, concerning his father. The woman stirred.

"What kind of man was he? Well, he was a strong man, busy, intelligent."

"Did you know my mother?"

She hesitated. Then she said: "No."

"How did they die?"

"In an accident."

"Did they die together?"

He had gone too far. The woman stood up. "We had better get in," she said. "Before the rain."

It took Denise Vanner about twenty seconds to descend upon Peter after the woman left, vanishing like a white-robed ghost into the rain. "Do you mean to say you know *her*?" Denise pried, her large brown eyes nearly popping from their sockets.

He was puzzled. "I don't know her," he explained politely. "She said she had known my father."

"Then you don't know who she is?"

"No. Is she somebody famous?"

"Famous? I should say so. That was Deborah Reading, the American cinema star."

Peter was not impressed. He seldom went to the cinema; the only motion pictures he saw were Walt Disneys and educational films shown occasionally at the home. His visitor had impressed him on a different level, as a genuine human being who had seemed somehow concerned about him. In the privacy of his room, he opened her present. It was a plain gold ring. He looked at it for a long time, thinking of the woman, and then he put it on his middle finger. It fit perfectly.

Professor Carmichael arrived for one of his periodic visits a week later. Peter looked forward to visits from the professor with eager anticipation, not only because they gave him an opportunity to escape from the boundaries and rules of the home for a whole day, but also because each visit provided him with a little more information about his heritage and the plans his American benefactor had for his future. The professor usually wore tweeds or dark three-piece suits. He always wore a hat and he carried an umbrella if there was even the slightest hint of rain. At first Peter had regarded the professor as stiff and formal, a diminutive figure with a gold watch chain and thick-lensed horn-rim glasses, but soon after the start of their first trip out, as the awaiting taxi launched them on a marvelous adventure, he began to feel warm and comfortable in the man's presence. The professor was the only grown man with whom Peter had had contact. He regarded him with affection and awe, as a model to follow. Professor Carmichael taught American law, but that certainly was not the limit of his interests or knowledge. He was a student of philosophy, confessing a love for Spinoza in particular; he knew the scientific names of flora and fauna; he spoke French,

Spanish, Italian, and German. But he was not just a man of knowledge. He was also a man of wisdom.

"You will attend schools and learn," he said in the taxi, "but you must remember that there is a great difference between degrees from universities and an education. Perhaps you will have to unlearn much that you learned to find wisdom."

"When will I go to America?"

"Soon."

"But when?"

"Soon enough."

He knew it was useless to ask the professor the name of his American sponsor, for he would not get an answer, but he thought it appropriate to mention that he'd had a visit from Deborah Reading. When he did so, the professor withdrew his pipe, stuffed the bowl with sweet-smelling tobacco, and slowly lit it.

"I haven't met her," he said. "I've seen her on the screen—and just last year on the stage in New York—but I've never met her in person."

"She knows about you."

The professor smiled and tried to make a joke, something he rarely did, at least with success. "Did she then say she would blackmail me, Peter?"

"I mean—well, you know—that she knows you know me. She also said she'd known my father. She gave me this ring."

"That is a very nice gift," the professor said.

He would say no more, at least about those matters Peter was eager to discover. His refusal to discuss them was his sole annoying aspect. It was almost as if the matter were some deep and disgusting secret. Madame Colombier, world-wise and instinctive, had told him he'd perhaps be better off not knowing. Maybe that was so. But he knew he'd get to the bottom of it no matter how long that took.

On this trip they went down Avenue de la Grande Armée from the Arc de Triomphe to Parte Maileat and there took the miniature train to Le Jardin d'Acclimation. It was a marvelous park, and lost in it alongside the professor, a man whom he realized now he'd learned to love, Peter closed all the nagging questions from his mind and enjoyed every second of a day dazzling with full sun. They sailed in small boats on a mystery cruise through forests and tiny islands. They looked at fat goldfish swimming an inch below the surface in shimmering pools. They had lunch on the grass, attended a Punch and Judy show, spent an hour watching the antics of the bears and monkeys at the zoo. As Peter watched the sun go down, he knew he did not want to go home. Never again. He wanted to call home that place where Professor Carmichael lived.

"When will I go to America?" he asked, again, at the gate of Madame Colombier's.

"I think you are ready," the professor said.

Nathan Carmichael was not exactly a romantic, but Paris often aroused feelings in him that before had been dormant. After the death of his son, the period of his life he now called the dark years, he'd thought about settling in the city, perhaps to study art as a form of catharsis for his grief. He had not consciously abandoned the idea; it had merely slipped from his mind. Now, visiting regularly, he found the city a tonic for his soul. It was a constant process of discovery and rediscovery. He loved the night floodlights at the Louvre, the promenade along the Champs-Élysées, the *le canard presse* at Tour d'Argent, customers at outdoor cafés singing to the strains of an accordionist, and the blue and red colors in the rose window at the north transept of Notre Dame. He found himself a willing ambassador of Hollis Collingsworth, enjoying the unlimited expenses, enjoying also the large brown inquiring eyes of Peter Russell.

One morning, coming from his rooms at the Relais Bisson where he usually stayed, he recognized Deborah Reading in the lobby. Her disguise of glasses and a floppy yellow hat was not working, at least not enough to foil a group of girl students from America who had followed her into the hotel to demand her autograph. They formed a captive circle around her, giggling and squealing. Their noises drew the attention of others, resulting in a commotion inappropriate to the area. Soon the desk clerk, assisted by bellmen, went to her rescue, gently shooing her admirers to the sidewalk. She stood alone, looking weary and disheveled. Carmichael went to her and introduced himself. Her eyes widened with genuine joy and surprise.

"You have no idea of the number of times I've started to call you, only to hang up halfway through the dialing," she said.

"I would have been happy to speak with you at any time."

"Let's talk now. Find a place where not even the pope would be recognized." In the taxi she removed the glasses and smiled. "I complain, but don't let me fool you. I want attention. I love it."

They went to a café on Rue St. Jacques, on the Seine in view of Notre Dame. She ordered Burgundy wine and cheese; he ordered espresso. The proprietor turned away, polishing glasses.

"I've seen Peter," she said. "But you know that."

"Yes."

"What will happen with him now?"

"He will go to school in America."

Slowly she cut the cheese into thin slices. "Why are you doing this? For Peter?"

He tapped his pipe on the table. "Well, there is a stipend, of course." Then the words rushed out. "But I do care for the boy. He is a delight to be around. He has an extraordinarily nimble mind. I see a brilliant future for him."

"Not if Hollis Collingsworth gets his hooks in him," Deborah Reading said, her eyes beginning to flare. "And I suspect there already is some manipulation, if from a distance." She removed her hat; hair tumbled down over her shoulders. "Professor Carmichael, I will not let him get Peter. I warn you of that."

He did not respond. They sat silently. Through the window he gazed absently at the Seine. White bubbles popping on the brown surface seemed to entrance him. She ran her finger around the edge of her glass, making it sing a soft, vibrating tune. Finally Carmichael said:

"I think he is honestly trying to provide for the boy."

"No. Hollis does nothing without a private motive in mind."

"It's my nature to be trusting. I trust until I see reasons not to trust."

"I thank you for what you are doing. I think Peter might have a chance with you around. But—believe me, wise professor—the time will come when the devil is paid his due. Since you are Peter's guardian, may I enter into a conspiracy with you? I want to see him again."

"I'm afraid I cannot permit that, Miss Reading."

She put a cigarette into a holder and he snapped open a lighter for her. "Then will you promise to write me about

him, tell me how he is doing? Will you do that much? I want
to learn to love that boy."

"I believe that you love him now. I will write, of course."

She sighed. Smoke trickled from her nostrils. "There's a
problem with being an actress. You play the lives of others so
often that you forget your own. I said that I love it and I
suppose I do, but I threw away a lot of things to get here."

"A wise man once said that the only thing worse than not
getting what you want is getting what you want."

"What is it that you want?"

"My wants now are simple. I want peace. I want to train
some minds. I want to leave this world in some small
measure a better place than when I entered it."

"Right now, my want is also simple. Another glass of wine."

Carmichael signaled the proprietor. *"Les plus sages ne le
sont pas toujours."*

"I see clearly now that we are all a part of an experiment
he is conducting with human lives," she said after the wine
came. "He offers what we think we want and we take it, only
to find we are in his web. No one tempted by him is ever
free."

"I am free."

"No. You are inhibited by your emotions. You play his
game because you believe, or you tell yourself, that it will
help Peter. But you will see, if you don't already, that it is he
who controls." She raised her glass and laughed. The wine
had reddened her cheeks. *"Le roi le veut,"* she said.

Madame Colombier gave Peter a party the day before he
left for the United States. A white-robed glee club sang "God
Bless America," bringing tears to Peter's eyes. There were
cakes and cheeses. The older boys were allowed to sip wine.
Peter got gifts of silver charms of the Eiffel Tower and Notre
Dame, de Gaulle political buttons, and parchment maps of
Paris. Madame Colombier started to make a speech, but
choked halfway through and was unable to finish it. Even
Denise Vanner, when she hugged him and kissed his cheeks,
could not control her tears. Boys his age shook his hand and
looked deeply into his eyes. They swore they would see each
other again, like soldiers once companioned in combat parting
at a train station. Peter found himself choked with emotion.
He was leaving this place where he'd felt he did not quite

belong for a new adventure across the Atlantic, and now that he was to go he felt he truly had belonged. He wondered, in fact, if he would belong as much in the United States.

2.

PROFESSOR CARMICHAEL DID not drive, so he hired a chauffeured Citroën to take Peter on the first leg of his journey to discovery. It was a five-hour trip through the countryside from Paris through Rouen to the port of Le Havre. The professor did not talk very much on the trip; he sat with his beaked nose deep in a lawbook. Peter drank in the landscape—vineyards, bright villages, horses prancing freely in green fields, a dazzling sky filled with enormous clouds. His heart raced excitedly. It was a new phase for him, a giant step toward knowing. Already memories of Madame Colombier's were fading. The driver sat silently and morosely behind the wheel, cursing loudly when cattle or sheep blocked his path. At the pier in Le Havre, under soaring gulls etched like paint dabs against a red sunset, they boarded the liner *Victor Hugo*, bound for New York City.

They had first-class accommodations. The professor knew many of the officers, including the captain. The Atlantic was rough the first two days out and Peter spent most of his time in bed, beset with wrenching dry heaves. On the third day he emerged with a ravenous appetite. Professor Carmichael smiled and put his thin hand on Peter's shoulder.

"You will become a sailor yet," he said. "What do you want to eat?"

"A steak. The biggest steak on the ship."

"You shall have it."

The trip was uneventful, at times even boring. Peter looked forward only to the meals, which were extraordinary. Professor Carmichael played shuffleboard with him every morning, always losing by a substantial margin. After lunch Peter usually went to the top deck to gaze at the ocean, a tranquil, smooth green expanse on which he drifted lost and alone. Sunsets often found him astern, watching the ship's wake. He rubbed the ring given to him by the mystery woman, the one they had called a famous American motion-picture star, and somehow he felt that he would see her again.

The professor deposited him in a woodsy prep school in Salem above Boston, telling him his allowance had been raised to two hundred dollars a month and assuring him he'd be all right if he followed the advice of his counselor and obeyed the headmaster's orders. Then Professor Carmichael smiled, shook Peter's hand, put on his hat, and went to the taxi that had taken them there. Peter sat hunched on his bed in the small room, fighting waves of loneliness and even fear. The door was flung open and a boy his age swaggered in, wearing a gray jacket and trousers, a white shirt, and a black tie. He went to the second bed in the room, fumbled under the covers, and drew out a package of Camels. He lit up. Finally he acknowledged Peter.

"A rook," he said.

"What?"

"You're a rookie here."

"Oh, yes. I guess I am."

The boy approached him. He had freckles and red hair. "Want a smoke?"

"I don't smoke." He added hesitatingly: "Do they allow smoking here?"

"They don't allow anything here. They tell you when to take a crap. But because they don't allow it doesn't mean I don't do it. What's your name?"

"Peter."

"Last name. We use last names here."

"Russell."

"Russell, I'm Crowell. Do you know Crowell Steel?"

"I've heard of it," Peter lied.

"You flunked your first test. There is no Crowell Steel. We lie around here, Russell, lie to the instructors, the bastard headmaster if we can, but we do not lie to each other."

"I'm sorry," Peter managed.

Crowell snapped the cigarette to his lips, drew deeply, and flopped down on his bed. "Where you from?" he asked after a pause.

"I'm—I'm from Paris, actually."

"Ch-*rist*! I thought you talked funny."

"You mean I have an accent?"

"You talk like an Englishman."

"Oh."

Crowell sat up. "It's okay. The head's English. Say, I don't often do this, but I was wondering if you could advance me a ten until the month's over."

"I suppose so. All right."

"What's your father do, Russell?"

"He's dead."

"Mine's in steel. That's what he wants me to do, steel. I suppose I will, but that doesn't mean I can't have some fun first. D'you suppose you could make it twenty?"

"I guess so."

"Good man. I'll get you laid one of these nights."

Peter's life became a regimented routine. He woke up at the same hour each morning and went to sleep at the same hour at night. It was not a military school, but it demanded rigid discipline; tardiness to class, or late papers were not tolerated. The instructors, all male, were old and humorless. Peter studied Latin, algebra, and English literature in the mornings, and physics, world history, and physical education in the afternoons. The students moved briskly from one red-brick building to another between classes, toting book bags. In their somber black uniforms like Puritan cloth, they seemed like a parade of cardboard figures. There was some joking and laughter, and occasional frolic at meals, but most of the time everyone seemed grimly concerned about the next class. Peter, as a "rook," had expected some hazing, at least subservience to boys in higher grades, but he quickly discovered all such nonsense was against the rules. It was a place to prepare for entrance into a university, an Ivy League university, not a place to play. The students, ranging in age from twelve to sixteen, accepted him as one of them. He made no particular friends, just as he had not at Madame Colombier's, but his classmates did respect him for he was always on the honor lists. He was known as a soft touch for a loan, for his willingness to help others in studies, and as the only boy in the school who'd made old Alexander—the Latin instructor with the chalk-marked gray suit and gray face to match—break into a wide smile of pleasure. Peter felt his mind stretching, absorbing knowledge like a sponge, as days fled into weeks and weeks into months. Professor Carmichael often came and took him away to Boston on weekends; they rowed on the Charles, toured Concord and Cape Cod, and lunched in Harvard Square. It was obvious the professor was pleased by Peter's grades. Peter no longer sought to solve the mystery of his past. He thought only of the future.

"And what is that future? Law?" the professor asked one afternoon. They were seated on benches on a long green lawn in front of Harvard. The crew was practicing on the Charles, a coordinated force of timing and rhythm, at once poetically free and authoritatively disciplined. It was a crisp day, with the smack of autumn in the air. The atmosphere rather mesmerized Peter, and when he did not respond, Professor Carmichael said, *"Qui tacet consentit?"*

Peter turned. He gazed into the professor's kind eyes. "Actually what interests me more than anything else is history."

"History is important, of course. But it could hardly be called a career."

"I find it fascinating."

"Remember that much of the history of men is the form of their laws."

"It is also their art, their customs, and their literature."

The professor smiled. "Well, you do have time to decide. But I shall argue as convincingly as possible that the law is a fine and satisfying career."

Peter hesitated, turning away. He turned back and said slowly: "I want to learn everything. That's what I really want."

"But you will find you must choose. Even you, despite your fine mind, cannot learn everything."

"Faust did."

"That is legend. You live in a real world."

"You say choose. Sometimes I wonder what choice one really does have. Look at the boys at my school. Everything is ordered for them. As a result, they seem like zombies."

"Don't you like the school?"

"It's a good school. Yet somehow I can't see the value of rote recitation of Latin verbs."

Again the professor smiled. *"Lucidus ordo,"* he said.

"Then you agree."

"I am enjoying that I see in you a small spark of revolt.

When I was your age, at a school not dissimilar to the one you now attend, I voiced exactly the same complaint."

"To find out later you were wrong?"

"To find out later that I was quite right, as a matter of fact."

It was the first near-adult to full-adult conversation they had ever had.

He measured the passage of time by the trees surrounding the school—leaf buds of spring, the full green of summer, the flush of red and orange in autumn, and the gnarled brown of winter. Peter spent the holidays at Professor Carmichael's house in Cambridge, enjoying the rap sessions with Harvard Law School students held after dinner and occasionally participating in political and philosophical discussions with Harvard professors. He was an inward person, but these periods brought him out. The wonder of life now burst fully upon him and all things seemed enchanting. The pines and elms in Harvard Yard, the great Widener Library, and the pink reflection from brick buildings on the snow in winter were poetic pictures in his mind. The stream of ducks in Jamaica Pond and the swan boats in Boston Public Garden thrilled him. All humans seemed lovely. The rich, proud boys at the school, before seeming like cardboard, took on flesh and blood, and some of them became his friends. His roomie, Crowell the steel heir, became his best friend. He began to live by a motto in Professor Carmichael's study: HOMO SUM: HUMANI NIHIL A ME ALIENUM PUTO. *I am a man; I count nothing that is human indifferent to me.* Madame Colombier and the home she ran now seemed distant to him, although he wrote her often and never waited more than a week for a long letter of reply. Yet, despite his awakening, when he skated at night on the frozen pond near the school, his blades flashed signals to him on the hard ice: *Who am I? Who am I? Who am I?*

As spring burst, Crowell's fancy turned to love. He slipped Peter a note in geometry class: "Tonight we'll go hunting." When he went to his room after his final class of the day, Peter found Crowell lying on his bed, reeking of shaving lotion. His uniform lay in a crumpled heap on the floor. He was wearing yellow corduroy pants and a green short-sleeved sports shirt, specked with yellow dots. He had his Weejun loafers on, but no socks. His hair was longer than school regulations permitted.

"C'mon, wash up," he said, springing from the bed. "We're going huntin'."

"Hunting? What do you mean?"

"We're gonna have meat for supper."

"I have to study."

But Crowell was an expert at persuasion, and an hour later Peter found himself breaking the rules for the first time since he'd enrolled in the school. They escaped at dusk, sneaking like fleeing felons through a woods heavy with the odors of spring. The ground was damp and spongy. Only haunched squirrels a nd frogs croaking on the edge of ponds witnessed their flight. A warm breeze tickled the back of Peter's neck, stirring blood in his loins. He felt guilt and apprehension, outweighed by the lure of excitement. He wasn't at all sure that Crowell's ruse—pillows under the covers to simulate sleeping boys—would fool the night bed checker. But Crowell was sure. He said it had worked before. Besides, he said, old Sherrill, the checker, was blind anyway.

They emerged out on a narrow paved road. The full moon was captured in a jagged circle of red-brown that gave way to a dark, smoky sky. There were no stars. Crowell hurried. Peter followed. Faint lights twinkled ahead.

"Almost there," Crowell said.

Peter had not been told their destination, but he'd guessed it—an off-limits girls' school called Kirkland. He found his excitement mounting as they hurried toward their target. There was an iron fence with a locked gate, but it presented no obstacle to the eager hunters. A minute after they had scaled the fence, dropping into the territory of females, Crowell told Peter to stay put and ventured alone toward a brick dormitory. Peter heard whispers. He heard pebbles glancing off windows. Soon Crowell returned. He slapped Peter's back painfully, a habit he'd lately developed.

"We got it made," he said. "Brother, we're in like Flynn."

Moving stealthily and suppressing giggles, two young members of the opposite sex materialized in the moonlight, perfumed nymphets in silk dresses so ethereal and enchanting it seemed as if they were dancers in a dream. Peter gulped. He stepped backward. Crowell mumbled introductions, arranged to meet Peter in an hour outside the gate, and slipped off into the night with one of the nymphets, leaving the other, whose name was Sue. Now the moon had slipped behind a dark cloud and Peter could not see the girl, not clearly at least, and he stood fumbling, sensing and scenting her.

"I didn't want to come out," she said. "I'd better go back."

"D-d-don't go," he managed.

"I didn't want to come out," she repeated.

He stood with his hands in his back pockets, his mouth dry. She was a blond girl in a yellow dress hemmed at her knees and she appeared before him in varying clarity relative to the movements of the capricious, scudding clouds. She was about fourteen, perhaps fifteen. He was aware in situations like this that the male was expected to take charge, yet he could hardly move or speak. For a second or two, he yearned to be of an age where he could solve a problem by seeking the protection of Madame Colombier's skirts.

"I'd better go back," Sue said. "I didn't want to come out. I've never been out. Like this, I mean."

Peter found his voice. "Neither have I."

"Well, I suppose I could stay out for a little while. But let's go over there. They could see me from here."

They moved in the moonlight, he slightly behind, hearing the faint swish of her dress. Perfume fragrance trailed her. Peter's senses heightened, the earth smells exaggerated in his nostrils, blood surging in his neck, his pulse suddenly perceptible. She stopped under the dark haven of an elm tree. An owl hooted. Sue turned. He could not see her. A faint light twinkled from the dorm.

"What do they do if they catch you out?" she asked.

"I—I don't know. Forty lashes, maybe."

She laughed. His hand brushed hers. He felt a stirring between his legs; his gentleman's training at Madame Colombier's fought his animal instincts. Sue, under the tree's protection, turned suddenly talkative.

"My mother sent me here. They teach you a little math and some history and stuff like that, but mostly they teach you social graces. Did you ever have to walk across a room with a book on your head? That's what they teach you here, how to walk with a book on your head. And then they have ballet classes. And hygiene. My mother sent me here."

He shut her up with a kiss. It was his first real kiss, and he'd had no intention of doing it until that very second, a second when the moon reappeared to outline her face. She broke away, uttered a tiny, "Oh!" and tried to escape, but he caught her and again pressed his lips to hers, hard. She relaxed, letting him explore her mouth with his tongue in the way some of the older boys at Madame Colombier's had said renders a girl helpless and ready. He sensed her resistance but only held her tighter, kissing harder, forcing her down to her knees and then on the ground. He was now all animal; the gentleman had been defeated. She struggled. He held her, feeling her small, immature breasts under the silk dress, holding the kiss. He tried to roll on top of her. But Sue proved to be too nimble; she maneuvered away, her hands little drumming fists, and rose to her knees. She screamed. She had a fantastically penetrating scream. She screamed again, a shriek that approached the level of a prison siren. Lights came on in the dorm. A dog barked. Peter scrambled up, running before he'd fully gained his balance. He stumbled and fell painfully. He reached the gate, imagining the hot pant of a hound on his heels, and clambered over it in one bound. He raced down the paved road, his body streaking sweat. He didn't stop running until he reached the boundaries of his school. His heart hammered. He gasped for breath. Stumbling into his room, he confronted the cold eyes of old Sherrill, standing with his arms folded and his chin jutting out.

There was a major investigation, during which Peter and Crowell were confined to quarters, and then a militarylike hearing judged by a triumvirate of officials, including the headmaster and two of the most merciless instructors. When Peter was called in to explain his actions, he saw that Professor Carmichael had been summoned. Shame overwhelmed him. The professor avoided his eyes. Peter stuttered through a recapitulation of the felony, his cheeks flaming with embarrassment. Finally, he was excused. The professor visited him two hours later.

"They've agreed to pardon you, Peter," he said, "with the warning that any similar such occurrence will result in expulsion."

Peter lay on his bed, his face hidden. He fought tears. Finally he managed to say, "I—I'm sorry."

The professor sat on the bed and touched Peter's shoulder. "I'll tell you a story," he said. "When I was your age, something remarkably similar happened to me. And they were even stricter, even more proper than they are now. I thought I'd be on bread and water for a year."

"What did you do?"

"I defended myself. I set up a mock court of law and argued for myself. I didn't try to pretend that I was without guilt, but I did, I think, argue rather effectively that it was an act not of carnality but one of revolt and self-expression. I pointed out that not so many years before at a point not too distant from here people were hanged on suspicions of witchhood. All you expressed, Peter, was a form of revolt. The incident is forgotten."

Again he fought tears, this time not of shame but of love.

He saw Crowell in their room. Crowell was packing.

"They expelled you?" Peter asked.

"It's not the first time, Laddie Buck," Crowell said, "nor do I think it will be the last. This old boy's got a mind of his own. I've decided, by the way, not to follow in the old man's footsteps."

Peter looked at him with admiration. He extended his hand. "I'll miss you."

"I'll miss you. You've been a good roomie. Although I *am* pissed about something."

"What?"

"Why you couldn't wait awhile longer before you set off the fireworks out there? I was five seconds away from a sure score."

3.

PROFESSOR CARMICHAEL TOOK Peter on a summertime cross-country train trip as a reward for his straight-A average at the school. It proved to be the most exciting three-week period of Peter's young life. The vastness and diversity of America stunned him. Plants in the big eastern industrial centers belched fire and smoke like gigantic steel dragons. Miles of grain and corn streamed to the horizon on the midwest flatlands. Peter had read widely about the nation when he'd lived in Paris, poring over atlases, memorizing state capitals, reading history books. He loved the nation before setting foot on her soil. Now it all materialized before him. He did not fail to notice the blight, however, often evident as the train entered and left stations. In most of the cities, rotting tenement buildings slumped along the tracks, their paint chipped, their shattered windows repaired with black tape, rows of laundry strung on lines like distress signals.

At dinner in a Denver hotel, the professor asked him what he thought of America. Peter paused, considering his answer. Hasty answers to the professor often resulted in a debate, a Socratic dialogue that led to defeat. What did he think of America? He really did not know, not yet at least. One could love a nation and still see its faults. He had heard politicians praise the states as the finest example of civilization in the history of the world, a strong and free society under God that was living proof of the merits of its economic and political system. Now he'd seen that strength. Yet he'd heard other politicians say millions of Americans go to bed hungry. He'd now also seen evidence of that.

"The contrasts strike me," he said. "Rich and poor."

"Don't other nations have contrasts?"

"Of course. But America is the richest nation. Therefore, it seems strange there is any poverty."

Professor Carmichael's eyes sparkled. "Ah, you are the idealist. But then you are also young."

"I wish I were older."

"That is a wish you will get."

Their next stop was Los Angeles.

Hollis Collingsworth was regarded as one of the leading media lords in the nation, but he was far from satisfied. He had assembled a competent management team and had long-term plans to buy more newspapers and television stations in key cities around the nation. The facilities were available; only his lack of heavy cash flow prevented him from moving rapidly. The *Light*, his morning paper, was losing money, a deficit that mounted month by month. Revenues and profits from the studio were down. Only the *Bulletin-News* and his television station in Los Angeles were showing strong profit growth.

But the slight financial pinch was not the main factor bothering him. He was now the age his father had been when he had been killed. He was acutely aware of his mortality, an awareness that disgusted him. He raged at time because it passed so rapidly.

He and Marion had made an unsigned pact. They were in conspiracy together. He judged her to be a good wife, competent and intelligent, excellent at social functions. She had found herself. She had become a first lady. She served on various important civic committees with distinction, concerned with improving cultural activities of the city. Her parties often had a purpose; all helped him. He was not completely faithful to her, especially when on trips, but he knew she was faithful to him. Their sex was most ritualistic, mechanical. They did not discuss it. Nor did they discuss much else, except social events. She did not pry into his business, although he had noticed of late she was becoming bolder about it. One evening, seated in his father's old chair, he casually mentioned his financial squeeze.

"Well, no wonder, with you supporting that studio," she said.

"That's just a gnat."

"I think you should sell it."

"The studio is doing all right."

She leaned forward, in the light, and he saw again how truly attractive she was. "Hollis, that's not the point. Motion pictures simply are not dignified enough for a man of your stature."

"Well, I'll think it over."

But he had no intention of selling the studio. It was his only plaything. Still, the next day, when a merger broker brought him a deal so wonderful he could hardly believe it, he found himself considering that very idea. It was a near steal of three Texas newspapers owned by a conglomerate whose other operations were dragging it down.

"Where do I get ten million?" he asked the broker.

"Borrow."

"Not at these rates."

"Sell something."

Again, he thought of the studio. But he didn't have time to

sell it; this was an accept now or lose out deal. Yet he *wanted* those Texas papers. He looked at the merger broker.

"How much time do I have?"

The broker shrugged. "For you, since you're a good customer, I can stretch a week, ten days."

Hollis reached for a cigar. He was buzzing the legal department. "I think I know how I can get my hands on that money and solve my biggest problem at the same time."

His biggest problem was the *Light,* which never really had gotten off the ground in competition with the powerful *Times*. He was losing over a million a year on the paper and there was absolutely no hope of improvement. It had only minor asset value, since it used the presses and composing room of the *Bulletin-News;* its only worth was its good will and circulation list, which had dropped to under 200,000. The Associated Press editor he'd met on the ship returning from France and hired as publisher of the *Light* was long out the door. He'd spent more of his time traveling around the world and writing silly page 1 columns with his photo attached than he'd spent selling ads and subscriptions. He was the last man Hollis would ever hire on a whim.

But now he saw a way to solve the problem. He arranged for a conference with Vernon Grant at the Jonathan Club. The Grant chain operated two papers in the city, a strong morning sheet and a weak afternoon one. Vernon Grant was the son of the founder. They were more than competitors. They were enemies who hated each other, as their fathers had. Yet they were cordial when they met at newspaper publisher conventions. Grant was a huge man with a shock of straight black hair combed down over his forehead to hide his bald spots. His great red face rolled in gobs of fatty flesh as he talked. He dressed casually and drove his own car, a three-year-old Chevy. Now he plumped on a leather couch in the private conference room Hollis had taken at the Jonathan, breathing heavily.

"Why didn't we meet at your office?" he asked, his pudgy hand drawing a fat cigar from his vest pocket. "I hear you got a cannon there. A war cannon. I'd like to see that, make sure for myself you got a war cannon."

"Well, I've had it removed now, since we have labor peace."

"I admire you one thing. I admire how you kept out them fucking goddamn fucking unions."

"I've found out that's easy. You hire a writer to write how great unions are, you hold an annual employee picnic and play catcher on the softball team that day, you pay two cents above union scale, and you get a personnel manager who knows which whorehouses the heads of the locals visit."

Grant threw back his head and issued a genuine laugh so mighty the light fixtures seemed to shake. "Collingsworth, in this town I'm not afraid of Chandler, although he might well come out on top, and I'm not afraid of Hearst either, but I'll tell you true, m'boy, I am afraid of you." His beady, hoggish eyes sought Hollis's. He was not one to underestimate, despite his casual air and appearance. Grant's father had taught him to mistrust most non-Grants and all non-Grants who operated newspapers. And he was a diligent worker. Each morning at eight, his footsteps were heard clomping up the stairs to his office, an alert warning to his staff; he appeared in sections—the face, torso, and massive legs—puffing and snorting, pawing like a bull, ready for the day. "I'm meeting you because you said if I did I'd walk away richer than I am." He lit the cigar and sat in a thick haze of smoke. "Show me how."

Hollis stood. The door was closed. "We're both busy, so I'll come to the point. I want to fold the *Light*."

"You'd better. Before we put you out of business."

"This isn't a time for gambits, Vernon. The *Light* is in your way and you know it. The *Bulletin-News* beats you in the P.M. field here. I'll kill the *Light*, merge it with the *Bulletin-News*, if you fold your P.M.*"

Grant snickered. "I've heard you're pinched for cash. If you're pinched for cash, I'll loan you some."

"No. My father once told me that taking a loan from a competitor is like naming your doctor in your will."

Again Grant laughed, ending in a spate of coughing. He rubbed his wet eyes with a giant red handkerchief. He waved his cigar, knocking off the ash in a shower on his pants. "I like my little P.M.," he said. "The women read it."

"But it has a red income statement that is getting redder. There are too many newspapers in this town. TV is coming on strongly. Papers are going to fold. I think I could hang in there more than most because I haven't got a union around to call a strike at the drop of a hat. Now I'm willing to kill a money loser if you kill your money loser. We both win."

Grant twisted his face into a smear of amorphous red flesh. "D'you realize this talk violates antitrust laws?"

"What antitrust laws? It's merger talk. A man can do as he likes with the businesses he owns."

"Well, I gotta salute you," Grant said, doing so with his cigar. "Like I said, I admire how you kept those goddamn fucking unions out."

Mitch Evers was in the city room of the *Light* when the rumors were confirmed. The rumor had started almost two weeks ago, rising in intensity each day. The *Light* was folding. Veteran copyreaders joked that no one had much time in this business if he hadn't been on a paper that folded. But the jokes were hollow bravado. No one really laughed. A strain hung in the air. Typewriter keys clicked less rapidly and the calls for copyboys were not excited roars but muffled requests. Pastepots were not refilled. Then, early in the afternoon, Hollis himself appeared. He announced that the *Light* would cease publication, effective immediately, and merge into the *Bulletin-News*. There were genuine tears in his eyes as he read the statement.

"The *Light* was my dream," he said. "Unfortunately it was a dream that did not come true."

A deep silence descended. Hollis went away, surrounded by aides from the business office. Reporters from other papers and the wire services who were there covering it were ushered out by guards. "Let them die in peace," one guard said, summing it up.

A long party, a wake, at the Red House bar across the street began almost immediately. Each participant chipped in forty dollars from his severance pay and the stake was turned over to the owner, who was instructed to cut off the drinks when the money ran out. The money ran out in seventy-two hours. Everybody got drunk, especially the editor, who never drank with his boys. Stories were swapped. About the photographer Shambliss who was sent out for a traffic picture and, when traffic was light, stalled his car on Broadway, causing a jam and getting his picture. About the rim rat Kelton who lived in the building for two years, shaving in the john and sleeping on the editor's couch, sometimes making the night cleaning maids on the couch. About the cannon and electric chair in Collingsworth's office. About reporter O'Neill who tipped over the phone booth on the user who wouldn't give up the line so O'Neill could relay his hot story.

For the most part, the *Light* had an older staff. Never again would most of them see what they loved so well—the nude photos on the walls at the city-hall beat, upright phones at the police beat, the cruiser car with its L.A.P.D. squawk box and two-way radio, the red fire phone on the city desk, and the indescribable excitement alive in the city room with the breaking of a big story. Malcomb B. Swearington, an imaginary personage whose impressions of the Rose Bowl were faithfully noted in the sheet every year, would give no more impressions. An obit appeared in the last edition of the paper ever to be printed: "Malcomb B. Swearington, who has attended every Rose Bowl parade since the inception of the annual spectacle, died quietly at his home in Pasadena today."

Jane was crying on Mitch's arm. "It's so *sad*."

"It's a lesson for you. Go into electronic journalism."

"But I want to *write*."

"So do these people," Mitch said.

Two weeks later, leaving the *Bulletin-News* after dark, Hollis saw a tall figure in a black raincoat standing by the building, between him and where Shelton waited in the Cadillac. The collar of the raincoat was turned up. A surge of alarm went through Hollis's body. He pushed at the glass door to reenter the building, but the door had locked automatically behind him. Slowly the tall figure advanced. The street was empty, lighted by a pale blue glow of a lamppost. Hollis froze, watching the man. He could not see his face. Shelton appeared to be sleeping behind the wheel. There were no sounds. Hollis stepped out on the sidewalk, slowly at first, then moving more rapidly, but the dark figure had cut him off, standing between him and the car. A chill seemed to descend. Wisps of fog clung to the curb. The man's arm moved, coming from a pocket of the raincoat, and Hollis saw the silver barrel of a small automatic pistol pointed at his chest. The night held him. He could not move. It must be a dream. Soon the dark figure would dissolve and he would awaken. He did not look at the man; he looked at the pistol. It pointed for what seemed like an endless time. Then it

clicked. It clicked once again. Hollis stirred; he was coming
out from his trance. He swung his briefcase at the man,
hitting his head, and raced past him, banging on the Cadillac's
door. Shelton stirred. The door flew open. "Move!" Hollis
screamed at Shelton, jumping into the backseat, feeling for
the weapons there. The Cadillac leaped from the curb, its
back door open. Hollis glanced out but he could see no sign
of the dark figure.

It didn't really hit him until he was home and on his third
brandy. Then his hands began to tremble and nausea engulfed
him. He sat in his study, his shoulders huddled. It seemed
true that a curse followed him. He waited for courage, for
anger that would give him courage. In the silent darkness of
the street, he had not seen the man's face. It had seemed as if
the dark figure had not really been a man, but a hooded
specter. But that was foolish. It had been a man, someone
who knew about him. Power creates enemies, his father had
told him. What would his father do if this had happened to
him? Now Hollis Collingsworth rolled his eyes toward the
ceiling and clenched his fists, calling upon the spirit of his
father for advice. At the same time, he realized something
that left him numb. This day was the anniversary of his
father's death. He stiffened, gulping brandy. Marion tapped
at his door; he sent her away. He must not leave this room, or
this house, perhaps for several days. Here he could summon
the ghost of his father, and that ghost would protect him.
Then the awareness hit him. It was not a ghost he summoned; it was a ghost within him. He *was* his father. And
then he knew what he would do, what he must do. He would
fight force with force.

Grant had saluted him for keeping the unions out—could
this would-be assassin have been sent by labor?—but Grant
did not really know the tactics that were sometimes necessary
to remain nonunion. Sure you pay better fringe benefits and
provide secure employment, but that sometimes was not
enough, particularly with tough pressmen and composing-
room locals always agitating to organize. His father had used
strongarm methods in breaking unions, sometimes calling on
his city-hall contacts to dispatch policemen with nightsticks,
but also on occasion using outside services. Hunter. He
hadn't spoken to Hunter for years; perhaps he was retired or
dead. He'd find out. He found the number in his file and

dialed it. The voice came on in a few minutes, sounding sleepy.

"Long time no hear from."

"Well, war smooths things on the home front."

"What can we do for you?"

"Some bastard tried to get me tonight."

"To hit you? All right, we'll look into it. Meanwhile, don't worry."

"I appreciate what you've done in the past."

"Well, I owed your father some favors. So I paid them to you. It's the same thing."

"It's worth a lot to me, peace of mind."

"Well, I don't need money. I may ask a favor in the future, but I don't need money."

"What kind of favor?"

"Like, some politician wants to make a name for himself pinning me to the wall, you call it off."

"I may not have that power."

"I think you do. Your old man, he did. You're as good a man as he was, I'm sure."

It was a phase of rapid growth. It was destiny. He had been elected to this, born for it. He worked, driven and unafraid. Naked before his mirror at night, peering into eyes that saw the future, he praised and worshiped his mythical godhead, his father within him, and he pondered a miracle and a mystery of the ages, how the genes of centuries united by chance to produce the current species in the mold of ancestors. He thanked spirits of eons past. They were his gods. From them he drew immortality.

Yet one factor served to remind him of his mortal being. He could not get Deborah Reading out of his mind. He would not admit to love—that was a trap—but privately he admitted to need. Marion was his partner, but Deborah was part of his spirit. He knew his times with her had been his times of happiness. It would be irresponsible to try to go back to that. But he was tempted. It was his sole concession to humanity.

When Nathan Carmichael called, saying he'd brought Peter Russell to Los Angeles, Deborah's vision again materialized before Hollis. He had not thought much about Peter. His concentration now was on Andrew. Yet telephone reports from Carmichael about the boy had pleased him; Peter obviously had potential. He was now about to enter Harvard, despite his tender years.

"I suppose there they will make a left-winger of him," Hollis snorted.

"Peter has a mind of his own," Carmichael said. "A fine mind of his own."

"I want to see him."

"Do you think that's wise?"

"I think the time has come for it. Bring him here. I want to look him over."

Andrew and Mary often came home from college on weekends and usually had dinner with their parents on Saturdays. When there were guests, such as this week, the meal was formal. Marion handled the details, working with Fairbanks, Trobridge's replacement, and Mrs. Reich, the cook. It was dinner for ten—Hollis and her, Andrew and Mary, Nathan Carmichael and his young protégé, Peter Russell, Senator Myron Demming and his wife, Sandra, and Marion's parents. Marion didn't like mixing her parents with nonfamily guests, but this time she'd had no choice; Clarence and Audrey had been invited two weeks ago for this Saturday and Hollis had announced at the last moment that he'd invited four additional guests.

"Couldn't you have told me earlier?" she asked.

"I didn't know until now. It will work out all right. Just make sure Fairbanks waters your father's drinks and tell your mother to hold down her chatter."

He was brusque about it, as he always seemed to be when it came to discussing her parents, but he was probably right. Clarence drank too much and Audrey talked too much. She had become a pest and a boor, her every move dominated by astrology; her sole achievement seemed to be that she possessed the longest and most jeweled cigarette holder in the Polo Lounge. Clarence, his hands withering with arthritis, had given up trapshooting and golf, slipping deeper each day into the oblivion of alcohol. Marion cared, but did little about it; perhaps it was best for him. She was far removed from her parents' world, above it in Hollis Collingsworth's world, and that of her own. On occasion she raged secretly, shedding lonely tears, for she knew she would never get to the soul of the complex, haunted man whose bed she shared. Yet he was the route to what she yearned to achieve, the instrument through which she would bring a full and permanent culture to a city she considered grotesquely bizarre in many respects. There would be a shrine in her name. She was content. She was growing. Her social life was satisfying. She was active on the museum board, the Philharmonic, a hospital, and the transit committee of the Chamber of Commerce.

The dinner was a disappointment. Hollis, Myron Demming, and Nathan Carmichael discussed politics. Andrew seemed self-conscious about his deformity. Mary picked at her meal, seated in a private reverie. She'd become aloof, a loner who dabbed in art and several times had dropped out of school to wander in Europe. Marion sighed. Suddenly her children were grown, and she had paid only cursory attention to them, trusting their development to tutors and servants. She'd simply been too busy. Yet they were turning out well, schooled in social graces, intelligent, and polite. Andrew was a good student and Mary at least hadn't caused a scandal. Perhaps it was best to raise children by keeping your distance from them.

Audrey waved her cigarette holder. "Honestly, I think Beverly Hills has become almost common," she declared to everyone, to no one. "Some of the shops even are dirty. And that *drugstore* on Canon."

Clarence nodded weakly. Marion felt a wave of pity for him, a once magnificent figure now dominated by a vastly inferior woman. He hadn't drunk much, but Marion could tell he'd had a couple before arriving.

Demming mouthed clichés. His compliments to the chef. It was always good to get home to the soil of the Golden State. The unrest in the South was a sign of the times; probably the Communists were behind it. His wife sat silently by his side. Marion noticed she'd been sneaking drinks.

Peter Russell interested her the most. There was something haunting in his dark brown eyes, a restlessness that made him appear to be far away in spirit. When Hollis asked him what he wanted to become, he answered with downcast eyes that he hadn't really decided.

"Well, come out here one summer and work at the paper," Hollis said. "Andrew is going to do that. Is that right, Andrew?"

"Yes, sir," Andrew agreed.

Peter glanced at the professor, who turned away. Hollis spoke no more to Peter, but Marion noticed that he cast occasional surreptitious glances at him. Marion's mind churned. She saw before her the spellbinding eyes of the alleged medium, Mrs. Sandborn, and again heard her words: "There is another one. A boy." Looking at Andrew and then at Peter, a flash of intuition went through her, but she dismissed it immediately, for she did not want to know the truth.

4.

THEY RETURNED TO Boston via Washington D.C. and New York City. It had been a glorious trip for Peter, one during which he'd gained new respect for Professor Carmichael. In a flaring of independence and intellectualism at the Salem school, he'd begun to regard the professor as old-fashioned and out of tune with the times. He no longer did. He'd come to see the truth of something Professor Carmichael had tried to teach him—learning begins with a confession of ignorance, leadership and ability are not self-bestowed but bestowed upon you by others. In every city where they had stopped, Professor Carmichael's advice and opinions had been sought by high-ranking officials and academics. He'd made several speeches, receiving enthusiastic applause.

Before the trip, Peter realized, he'd known very little about his country; the books he'd read showed him practically nothing. Now he had read the angry graffiti on the brick walls and smelled the garbage in Harlem. He'd seen the lost, red-eyed zombies who passed for men wondering on Main Street in Los Angeles, begging for dimes to buy a life-saving bottle of wine. He walked among the Chicanos on Brooklyn Avenue in east Los Angeles. By contrast, he had dined in the finest restaurants and most luxurious homes, had stayed in the best hotels, and had attended parties of the society elite. One thing he realized. The professor was pushing him, if gently, toward government and politics. In Washington Senator Demming had taken them to both houses of Congress and to the White House itself. In Los Angeles he'd thrilled to a political convention where delegates had selected one of

Massachusetts's own as their standard bearer. In Chicago Peter had spent two days with a red-faced advance man named O'Keene, visiting docks and factories, knocking on doors, attending tea parties. O'Keene said it all depended on television now; your man goofs on TV, he's an immediate fool to millions. Prior to TV, he said, you could get a mannequin elected. O'Keene was a marvelous impersonator; he was a dock worker, a truck driver, a butcher, and a gentleman at the tea parties. He had run for alderman once but said he'd lost when the other machine stuffed ballots more rapidly. He said he didn't have the puss for politics now, blaming TV. "Actors, they got the best chance," he said. "Your Jimmy Stewarts, your Spencer Tracys, they'd be naturals."

Peter's undergraduate years at Harvard were a breeze, easier than the prep school. After long consultations with Professor Carmichael, he'd decided to concentrate on political science and economics, managing to squeeze in history classes. He did not merely learn; he absorbed. He was the youngest student at his house, yet the first choice when study groups were assembled. Many of the students preached revolt yet down deep embraced conformity. It was a path hewn for them. Peter did not think about the path that apparently had been selected for him. He mingled as little as possible with his fellow students. They were bright, but they seemed insincere. When a minority leader spoke on campus, they took off their Gucci shoes and went sockless in cheap loafers to chant, "Fuck the feds, fuck the feds." They talked like liberals, some even like radicals, yet they acted like conservatives. They aspired to the Crystal, the "final club" on campus, wore tweed jackets with elbow patches, yet held coke parties with girls in their rooms. It was obvious that something was in the air. There were rumbles of a deepening commitment in Vietnam. Blacks were marching. Revolt and nonconformity swarmed in the summer humidity of Harvard Square, taking forms that were to Peter as grotesque as sideshows. He discussed it with Carol on Saturday, walking in the Public Garden.

"Of *course* there's a revolt," she said. "Where have you been?"

"Studying, I guess."

"I can see. When have we been on a date when you haven't brought a book?"

He called her his girl, and he guessed she was, although they had not gone beyond the good-night kiss. She was a junior at Boston College, majoring in sociology and education, and working in a hospital, whom he'd met when one of the more social men of his house had dragged him to a Saturday-night dance. Her name was Carol Kingsley and before the dance had ended Peter was in love with her. He had no experience with love and he could not define it, but he knew it was there. He dared not tell her, for fear it would make her vanish; he knew that first love, while the sweetest, is also the most precarious. Carol was a person of contrasts. She was serious and humorous, shy and bold, sincere and teasing, impatient and understanding. He found that he could talk to her. He'd told her of his past, of his guardian Professor Carmichael, of the stipend, and the mysterious influence that seemed to be shaping his life.

"Isn't that kind of eerie?" Carol asked.

He lay back on the grass of the Garden, smelling roses and drinking in the warm sun. "Well, I'll find out. In due time, I'll find out."

"Does Professor Carmichael know?"

"He refuses to discuss it. I'm beyond bringing it up anymore. But I'll find out."

"Let me get this one more time. You were raised in Paris. You were told that your parents, Americans, were dead. Why Paris if they were Americans?"

"I have no idea."

"But Carmichael does?"

"I've told you. He won't discuss it."

"And you have a benefactor—not Carmichael—who is taking care of your education? You've never met the benefactor?"

"Not that I know of."

"I should have such a benefactor," Carol said, sitting up. She looked at him, brushing back her long dark hair. Perhaps she was not beautiful to everyone, but she was beautiful to him. She smiled, causing a wave of warmth to surge in his body. "I wouldn't worry about it, if I were you. You said you'll find out someday."

"Yes."

"Then just accept it."

"I do. There isn't much else I can do, I suppose. It's just that..."

"It's just what, Peter?"

"That I feel I'm being maneuvered, manipulated."

"By Carmichael?"

"No. Carmichael—Professor Carmichael—is like a father to me. I love that man. He's been an influence on me, but he hasn't manipulated me."

"You're sure?"

"Sure I'm sure."

She jumped up. She was like that, snapping to action to implement a new inspiration. "It's almost *noon*," she said. "I have the whole day off from the hospital and I want to make the most of it."

"Would you like to go rowing?"

"If I can row."

"You can do all the rowing if you like."

"While you read."

"No. I'm going to throw this book into the Charles."

"When you throw a book away, that will be the day the world ends. Don't you do anything else? Don't you see movies?"

"Do you want to see a movie?"

"Yes. There's a new Deborah Reading movie I want to see."

"All right. Watch me impress you."

"Impress away."

"I know Deborah Reading. She visited me in Paris. She gave me this ring."

Carol squinted at him, her finger on her chin. "You're a man of mystery, Mr. Russell. Perhaps your parents were Russian spies sent to Paris on a mission. Perhaps the Russians are paying your way through Harvard. I may be getting in over my head here. Perhaps I should immediately run back to the hospital."

Her use of the words "getting in" thrilled Peter, for he interpreted it to mean that she was opening up, that she was coming to him. They scampered off, holding hands, heading for the subway, not knowing where they were going, nor caring. Now, for the first time, he felt from her a return of what he felt for her. She clung close to him as they walked on Broadway near Columbus Park. Before, she had been reserved, even aloof, someone who kept her distance and limited her affection. But now Peter felt she wanted his hugs, even his kisses; it was as if this day he had broken through to her, and that made it a good day indeed, perhaps the best in his life. In love, he loved all things. Peter had always had a deep awareness of nature, something Professor Carmichael had shown him, and today his senses were more alive than ever. The darkening sky was a poem, the bay a color-streaked painting, a cry of birds a song.

A shower struck and they raced for the shelter of a restaurant awning on the pier. Sailboats tacking in Boston Harbor swerved low against the rising squall. Gulls struggled shoreward. A couple ran by laughing, newspaper shields over their heads. They stood in the mist of the warm rain, encased and alone. He put his arm around her and she pressed against him. Their eyes met. For a long time he looked at her, the fair face with eyes the color of her hair, and he felt they no longer had to say words to know.

He really knew very little about Carol. She worked as a nurse's aide to help pay college tuition. Her parents lived at North Chatham on Cape Cod. Her father was a retired Coast Guard surfman, a sea lover who became agitated and morose if lured more than a few miles from the Cape. Carol also was addicted to the sea. She could sail with the best of them and had built model ships, not sewn doll clothes, when she'd been a girl. She also liked sports, teaching Peter about hit and run and run and hit at Fenway Park on Sundays. He had little interest in American sports. But he learned about them because she liked them. Despite the fact Carol enjoyed good times and recreation, she seemed much more aware of the dynamics of the era than he; on occasion, teasing, she called him a monkish bookworm shut-in. She talked of blacks on the march and warned of potential student unrest. She had participated in demonstrations and sit-ins; once, she proclaimed proudly, she'd been arrested.

"But I'm not a radical," she explained. "I'm a liberal. What are you?"

"A Kennedy man. I attended the convention in 1960."

"Oh! I've seen him at Hyannis, on the beach. Dad says he's a frustrated seaman. Let's drive out on the Cape this weekend. We can stay at my parents. I hear J.F.K. is going to be there and it would be fun to try to get a peek at him—if we can get through the Secret Service men."

Peter beamed. It was a milestone for him; she had never before invited him to meet her parents. On the other hand, he had never invited her to meet Professor Carmichael. He had not, in fact, even told the professor about her.

"I'd love to go," he said.

"Good. Pick you up Saturday morning."

She had a '54 Ford, a yellow convertible, which got her from hospital to school and out to the Cape every other weekend. Peter was embarrassed to admit he'd never learned to drive, a deficiency which seemed a low priority item to the professor. Just outside of the city, Carol asked him if he'd like to take the wheel. He stammered, flushed, and said:

"No. That's all right. I mean, if it's all right with you."

She smiled. "I'll teach you to drive," she said.

Carol was like that. She couldn't be fooled. He also suspected she realized something else, although they had never discussed it. Peter was a virgin. The closest he'd come to sex was that adolescent fumbling in the moonlight at the girls' school, Kirkland. He wondered what had become of that girl, the one in the yellow dress who said the school had taught her only how to walk with a book balanced on her head. He wondered, also, what had become of the expelled Crowell. Perhaps he was working at his father's steel company, his revolt over.

Peter took in a deep breath of air. It was an enchanting period that seemed to linger in precarious delight between the death of summer and the birth of autumn. First tentative streaks of red had begun to tint green leaves and cool winds skimmed the ponds with tiny undulating ripples. The taste of the sea hung in the air. Carol wore blue jeans and a sweatshirt. Her hair was swept to one side, contained by a silver ring. She provided him with a brief history of the towns as they turned the rotary to enter them. They stopped for clam chowder and fish and chips at Hyannis. The waitress said she'd once served J.F.K. She announced it as if it had been the highlight of her life.

"Little did she know," Carol said when they were back in the Ford, on the free road to escape," "today she might have served a future president."

"Me? You're teasing again. Just because I'm a poly-sci major?"

"I'll vote for you. Even if you are square."

"I'm not as square as you might think," he said.

And he was not. Something had been building in him for a long time, a spirit of revolt. His life to this point had been regimented by classrooms and force-fed books. He was being educated, but he was not being taught to think, to express his own opinions, whether they were right or wrong. In deference to Professor Carmichael, he had not expressed the revolt. But he felt it. It was smoldering within him. He didn't know quite what he wished to revolt against; perhaps it was authority itself. He had been passive, a nonfighter, accepting it. Now left-wing assistant professors in jeans and T-shirts had introduced him to Engels and Marcuse and had shown him that free enterprise was not really free, since you had to conform to reap its benefits. The ladder to success was strewn with the bloody bodies of the downtrodden, they said. Perhaps they were right; most assuredly, they were right. Peter wasn't free. He was in an iron cage, with Professor Carmichael his beneficent jailer. The booted men seeking hard-shelled quahogs in ponds and streams around them now were freer than he. Carol was freer. Now she was singing for him.

Cape Cod girls they have no combs,
Heave away! Heave away!
They comb their hair with codfish bones,
Heave away! Heave away!
For we're bound for South Australia.
Heave away, my bully, bully boys.

She smiled. Her eyes were bright. He was so much in love that the sight of her rendered him speechless, and he wondered how he could have counted any of his days before he'd met her as happy days.

Cape Cod boys they have no sleds . . .
They slide downhill on codfish heads . . .

Her parents lived in a two-story Cape Cod house on Old Wharf Road. It was built close to the ground, with a door in the middle and two windows on each side of the door. The afternoon sun accented the bluish-green hue where moss sprouted from the silver-gray walls. Peter stood before it, holding Carol's hand and drinking it in. It was a home. He had never had a home. It was a home with a green porch and white shutters and a big backyard with a view of an inlet that led to the Atlantic. A rubber-tire swing dangled from the limb of a maple tree. There were two boats in the garage.

The door opened and a man in boots and a plaid shirt rushed out, gave Carol a hug that took her breath away, and whirled her around. She laughed, her hands on his shoulders.

"Your mother's out shopping," he said. "We're going to have stuffed cod and clam cakes for supper and boiled eels for breakfast."

"Eels? Daddy, you know I hate eels."

"Who is your handsome young man?"

"Daddy" was Captain Jon Kingsley, who had worked his way up from surfman no. 9 to the commanding officer of a Coast Guard rescue and patrol station on the Cape, a hardy, proud man who looked much younger than his years. He insisted Peter call him by his first name. The sea smacked and rolled in his speech and bearing. From the first firm grasp of the captain's hand, Peter knew he'd met a friend—one he liked immediately and could learn to love. It seemed that the very elements of earth and sea formed his being. He had vitality and presence. Carol had warned Peter that her father was a storyteller, and he was, his voice rising like the roar of the sea to stress a dramatic moment and subsiding to the quiet of small waves lapping on the sands as the story ended. The captain was the opposite of Professor Carmichael; he existed in body and action, while the professor existed in mind and books. There were books in the Cape Cod house, too, mostly sea books with photographs of barks and frigates and old mariners, ocean conquerors sturdy as oak and defiant as dragons. The other books were Thoreau, Emerson, Hawthorne, Melville, and Whitman. Pushing Carol in the tire swing as the sun settled a crimson glow over the lawn, Peter felt a perfect peace.

Her mother also insisted on first names, although she said she didn't like hers, Amelia. She was a small, firm woman with strong hands and a face almost as ruddy as her husband's. Despite his rank as captain, it was obvious she ruled the house, at least before meals. After meals, the captain took the stage, lighting both pipe and fireplace and lounging in a rocker. He told of Cape Cod's people of the past—the pirate who wouldn't go into a room where there was a Bible, a witch who sold milk that would curse and sicken sailors, Old John who during a storm was chased by a monster that turned out to be a barrel howling in the wind behind him. Carol, seated cross-legged on the floor, a cup of coffee between her knees, swore that each time he told a story it was a new one to her.

"Well, they're not to me," Amelia said, knitting slowly. "But you never know how they're going to end because he'll change the ending on you."

"You should write a book, Captain Kingsley," Peter said.

"Jon," the captain corrected him.

"Sorry. I've been in garrison too long."

A dozen surfman stations had once dotted the elbow of the Cape, running from Monomoy Point to Race Point, with halfway huts in between. The stations had been connected by telephone. Duties were simple, even boring, during most of the year, but when the winter sleet or a powerful nor'easter came up, life became frenzied, excited, and dangerous. The job of the surfmen was to rescue sailors from floundering ships just off the coast. If they couldn't reach the ship from a line fired by a breeches buoy cannon, they launched long-boats and rowed out in the furious sea. As the captain described it, Peter could hear and see and smell it—the thunder of the surf from the moors and pitch pines, men in black oilers and canvas coats bent against the howling wind, the flicker of lanterns and flashlights and the red stream of Coston flares.

"I saw the sea split up ships like an ax will split a skull, crosswise and lengthwise," the captain said. "That sea'd toss ships on the beach like so many crabs—whalers, traders, schooners, freighters. And there were mooncussers, too, despite what they say that there never were."

"Mooncussers?" Peter questioned.

"Sure. They'd build driftwood fires on the beach at night, hoping to lure in a ship to break up on a bar so they could claim salvage. Then the moon would come out, showing the trap to the ship's captain, and those fire-lighting scoundrels would slink away, cussing the moon. And I'll tell you somethin' else. There's a creature walks those dunes. Whether a sea creature or land creature I don't know. But it's there."

"Oh, Daddy!" Carol said, laughing. "That's one you're not going to sell us."

"I've seen it."

"What did it look like? Like a cow with Christmas lights?"

"Had you faced it, I don't think you'd laugh."

Amelia stood up. "More coffee?" she asked. "In fact, how about some rum in your coffee?"

"No, thank you," Peter said. He felt warm and comfortable, at home. Night had come and a slight wind played against the eaves. They lounged in family love before the fire and Peter felt a part of it. He'd never felt so deliciously content before in his life. Gone were the austere professors, the pressure of finals, the riddle of his parenthood. He looked at Carol, a look he knew conveyed his feelings to her, and she smiled. "I still think you should write a book," he said to the captain.

"He's a talker, not a writer," Amelia said. She gave him a fond smile. "And I think I'd rather have a talker than a writer."

The captain knocked his pipe. "The surfmen had a saying. They'd much prefer to face a nor'easter than the sands. A simoon."

"Simoon?" Peter said. "That's an African sandstorm."

"Not only Africa, son. Here, too. I seen one or two and was in one. There isn't any reason why I should have gotten out alive. Give me a typhoon first." He paused, his eyes gray and steady. "Maybe that's the creature. The simoon."

Amelia put Peter up in a small, atticlike room that had no windows. She apologized for that, saying most Cape Cod houses had windows the height of the father, mother, children, and even dogs and cats. She left an oil lamp for him, in case he wished to read. About midnight Carol snuck in.

"I want my good-night kiss," she said. "Are you asleep?"

"I dozed off. That little wind on the roof will lull you to sleep like a rocker."

"What do you think of them?"

"I think they're great. I'm envious. I could listen to your father all night." He paused. Then he said: "They love you very much, you know."

"I'm an only child," Carol said. "Maybe I'm spoiled. Do you think I am?"

"Hardly."

She kneeled and kissed him lightly on the lips. She smelled of perfumed soap and cold cream and the taste of her mouth made his head swim. He pressed harder, holding her now, wanting to touch her in places but not daring. Finally she pulled away.

"I want more, but this isn't the place. Or the time. Yet."
She stroked his hair. "I'm happy."

"Then I am," Peter said.

They did have boiled eels for breakfast, something Amelia
said had once been a Cape Cod delicacy. They were skinned,
cut up, cooked eight minutes in butter and salt, then dipped
in corn meal and fried in bacon fat. Carol spurned them,
preferring traditional bacon and eggs, but Peter tried them,
saying he liked the taste.

"Did you really?" Carol asked later, walking with him on
the dunes by the sea.

"Sure."

"Honest?"

"Honest."

"Want to run?"

"No. I want to get a picture of you."

"Where's the camera?"

"In my mind's eye. One I can remember."

"Remember? Are you going away?"

He felt a surge of depression. "I—I don't know. That's part
of the problem. I don't know about *anything*. I'm being
pushed toward something. I can't *decide* anything."

"You should talk about this with that precious professor of
yours."

"You don't like him, do you? You haven't even met him and
you don't like him."

"I know what he stands for," Carol asserted. "The American flag, big business, the establishment, and ultraconservatism."

"He's a brilliant man. And a very good man."

"I believe that," she said.

They walked slowly, hand in hand, and when she tightened
her grip and smiled, his depression vanished. The surf was
high, rippled by a cool wind that smelled almost of winter.
He was entirely aware of the environment and felt free and
happy in it. She was there. Her shadow touched his. The
marshes and wind-bent brown hay fields, tangled like inrooted
tumbleweeds, glowed with a special beauty. The violet-tinged
sea played a symphony of sound on the beach—a roar and a
rumble, sharp cracks like gunshots, a rush forward and a
returning like birth and death. Courting ducks cried, a plover
played his flute, and gannets plunged like arrows into the

surf. A billion billion living things crawled and walked and grew around them—goldenrod and dusty miller, sandpipers and fox sparrows and shore larks, flies and spiders and grasshoppers and horseshoe crabs. Peter experienced total perception of the day, sensing that Carol felt it, too. He knew that the scene would not affect him so deeply if he were alone; and that no lover is lonelier than one who sees beauty by himself. When he stopped to kiss Carol, she lifted her chin as if she had planned it.

"Let's run," she said, breaking away. "Race you home."

The word home had a poetic ring for him. She won the race.

They left with reluctance, taking a dozen of Amelia's clam cakes, which she lovingly made by mixing chopped clams with beaten eggs, flour, salt, and pepper, and frying them until brown. Peter had lied about liking the eel, but he didn't lie when he said he loved the clam cakes.

"Then come again soon for some more," Amelia said.

The captain embraced his daughter, shook Peter's hand firmly, and ordered them to return in two weeks—or even sooner if they wanted.

"You were a hit," Carol said as they got into her Ford.

They took one more glance at the Atlantic, watching the blue waves splinter to white as they crashed on the shore. Again Peter felt surges of melancholy as the car headed toward Boston. She cheered him up, singing. He watched the water as it turned from orange to bronze to purple, and, in the final red sunset, to a crimson tide. Carol didn't make any pretense of taking him to Cambridge. She went directly to her apartment on Van Ness off the turnpike. They held each other going up the stairs.

"Lonely Peter Russell," she said, kissing him. "My lonely Peter Russell."

Later she came to him naked in her bedroom, caressing him and lying warmly next to him. "I wasn't ready for a romance, but I think I'm hooked," she said, running her fingertips over his chest. "All I wanted to do was to finish school and then howl over social injustice."

"I'll howl with you."

"Will you? Will you really?"

"I want to tell you something."

She put her hand over his mouth. "Don't tell me," she said. "I know what you're going to say and I can't say it back.

Not yet. But I think I will." She put her head on his chest
and he stroked her hair. His restless, uneasy feeling, his fear,
was gone, eased from his consciousness by her warmth.

When Peter finally told Professor Carmichael that he had a
girl, his guardian merely smiled and said, "Well, I should like
to meet her, of course."

"I'll warn you beforehand. She's a liberal."

Again the professor smiled. "Perhaps then we can show her
the error of her ways. I'm having dinner guests on Friday and
I think it would be appropriate for you and her to join us."

"I'll ask her."

Carol accepted the invitation immediately, in fact seemed
eager to go, which somewhat unnerved Peter. She said she
loved to debate conservatives.

"It's not a debate," he said. "It's a dinner."

She smiled slyly, her eyes twinkling. "Don't worry. I won't
embarrass you. I know how much you love and admire your
Professor Carmichael. I just want to show you that he lives in
the Hoover era."

The professor had four guests in addition to Carol and
Peter. There were two students from the law school, dressed
in gray and blue pinstripe Brooks Brothers suits, and Senator
and Mrs. Myron Demming. That brought some reaction from
Carol.

"Two peas in a pod, Demming and Carmichael," she
whispered. "This is going to be better than I thought."

Peter stirred uneasily, wishing he hadn't mentioned the
invitation to her. A powerful conflict raged within him. Politics most certainly would be discussed; Carol, who seemed
already to have fire in her eyes, would see to that. And Peter
no doubt would have to take sides. He knew now where he
stood. His views were akin to Carol's, even if that meant they
were antagonistic to those of the professor. In the drift of his
life, he now felt that he belonged. He had both a home and a
cause. He was on the threshold of open revolt.

Senator Demming looked much older than the last time
Peter had seen him, three years ago in Los Angeles. He'd
gained weight. His eyes were puffed. He looked tired, defeated.
Yet he remained on several important committees of the
Senate, including Appropriations, and remained a favorite of
the industrial establishment, especially the southern Califor-

nia aerospace industry. He was as strongly anti-Communist as ever. His name was still mentioned as possible presidential timber, at least as a running mate for the next Republican candidate. When, just before dessert, Carol eased the group into political discussion by asking him who he thought that candidate might be, the senator said it was too early to make an intelligent judgment. Carol plunged on. She asked about Richard Nixon.

"Well, he certainly remains active, as you know," Demming said. "He lost by a whisker. Perhaps, indeed, he really did not lose."

"Then you think the talk about Chicago was true?"

"I do, yes."

Professor Carmichael, spurning dessert, took out his pipe. "Whatever the truth, I think public exposure of the Chicago vote was harmful to the country. I would venture to say that Mr. Nixon agrees with that."

"He does, as a matter of fact," Demming said.

They went into the living room, Peter walking beside Carol with a nervous twitch in his throat. It was starting now. He had endured the dinner with rising anxiety; he couldn't recall what had been served. It had been a chit-chat dinner, with the anonymous law students expounding on esoteric precedents in contracts as if they were practicing for moot court and the professor gently yet persistently probing for information about Carol's past and parentage. She responded politely and Professor Carmichael seemed impressed.

"One thing I can say with authority and that is that this man in the rocking chair in the White House sold us a bill of goods on the missile gap," intoned the senator, seated with a brandy snifter, warming up to a discussion. "There is no missile gap."

"Would that there were no missiles," Carol said.

"Amen," Demming responded, raising his glass. "But the world is not ideal."

The professor, his face engulfed in a blue cloud of sweet-smelling smoke, asked what the Hill now thought of the administration.

"Not very much, if the truth is to be told," Demming said. "It is a popular and lively administration, but ineffective in the Congress. It is crisis after crisis. Bay of Pigs. Cuban missiles."

Carol could no longer restrain herself. "At least there is progress in civil rights."

"Some progress, perhaps. But even there we see vacillation."

Carol pushed on, while Peter sat stiffly, wincing. "I agree," she said. "Our Port Huron Statement said as much. But I am optimistic a commitment will be made."

"Continue," the professor said, waving his pipe. "I want to hear your views. I will moderate."

She smiled at him, a smile Peter interpreted as a tolerant one. "My views are fairly well summarized in the SDS Huron statement. We are uncomfortable about the world we will inherit."

"SDS?" Demming said, questioningly.

"Senator, you don't know what SDS stands for? Students for a Democratic Society." Little anger lines wrinkled Carol's forehead. "This is a rich nation, but it also is an impersonal one. We stand for peace, yet we buy for war."

"Defense," Demming corrected.

"All right, we'll use any term you want." She glanced at Professor Carmichael, as if to ask permission to use his home as a forum to advance views that challenged what he and Senator Demming represented. The professor nodded, granting the permission. His law students sat silently, like figures in wax. Peter, seated beside Carol, leaned forward, his shoulder brushing hers. He felt better. He felt proud of her. "I have been asked to give my views, so I will," Carol said. "Remember I am not alone. There are many of us who share these views. We're concerned over racial injustice. The caste system concerns us. We feel trapped by established authority."

The senator leaned back, sipping brandy, his little finger extended from the base of the snifter. "I am familiar with your SDS, of course. I also have read your manifesto. If I remember correctly, it terms anticommunism in America a mindless paranoia. It assumes that Russia does not want the world and therefore military preparedness is irrational. Such a document is irrational." He leaned forward, his cheeks twitching. "And dangerous." He smiled. "You are much too pretty and intelligent a young lady to embrace such ideas."

"I thank you for saying I'm pretty, Senator, but I don't see what being pretty has to do with it."

"Nevertheless, I shall stand by my statement."

"Your manifesto," the professor said, clearing his throat, "has a familiar ring to it. A C. Wright Mills ring."

She turned. "Yes, it's based on Mills. And others."

"Remember that Mills said the Soviets have their own power elite."

"If you think that I'm arguing here in support of the Russian system, you're one hundred percent wrong. As Mills himself said, the only difference is that the Soviets *know* they live under tyranny."

"Gentlemen?" Professor Carmichael said to the law students. "Any reaction?" They had none; one said that perhaps if the professor weren't such a tyrant in class, they would be permitted to research something besides law. The professor smiled and looked at Peter. "You've been remarkably quiet. What do you think? Surely our sole political-science major here must have an opinion."

Peter did. He'd read everything Mills had written. *The Power Elite* was this minute on the bed in his room, underlined and dog-eared. But he hedged. "I believe there is truth in much of what Mills wrote."

The professor said, "Then you don't accept it whole cloth, as they say?"

"No. It's too pessimistic. If I interpret Mills correctly, he is saying that we wander helplessly under the control of power groups and that change is beyond the power of the average man, who is trapped whether he is white or black. But I believe we can determine our own destiny and bring about reform."

"Hear, hear," Demming said. "Nathan, you've brought up this boy properly."

Carol scowled. She looked at her watch. "I have an exam tomorrow," she said.

She punished him for what she described as a wishy-washy position, claiming she had to study when he asked her for dates, but early one Saturday morning in November she called him and announced she'd be over to pick him up in fifteen minutes. She told him to bring weekend clothing. In her Ford, she kissed him warmly and said they were going upstate to the small college town of Hammond.

"A concert?" he asked.

"No, silly. It's political." She explained that the House Un-American Activities Committee was to hold hearings in Hammond, witch-hunting the professors of the liberal arts college. "It could be another San Francisco Black Friday."

"You mean we'll get hosed down? In the snow?"

Carol laughed. She was wearing a Santa Claus cap and a wool ski sweater. The top was up, but it had noticeable holes and the heater wasn't working properly. Their breath came out in a frost. He was happy. They were off to adventure again, both of them together. They would sleep together two nights in a row, something they'd never done before. He wondered if he would fumble when he registered at a motel.

"Come over here," she said, one hand on the wheel. "I'm cold. Let's snuggle."

"My pleasure."

"When am I going to teach you to drive?"

"You won't have to. I'm taking lessons. So is Professor Carmichael."

"*He* doesn't drive?"

"He says he wants to evolve into the modern world."

"I like him," Carol said. "He has possibilities."

"What about Myron Demming?"

She made a face. "If that man ever became president, I'd leave the country."

"He still thinks he can."

"Let's not talk about it. It gets me upset and I want to be happy now."

"What is that you're wearing? It smells good."

"I'm wearing goose pimples," she said. Big snowflakes fluttered down, dying as they struck the windshield. Carol made kissing sounds. She stopped the car on the sloshy side road and moved warmly into his arms. "Oh, God, it's a mess," she said.

"What's a mess?"

"The world."

"All right. It's a mess. We'll straighten it out."

"I *care* that it's a mess. Your professor and that Demming don't care. Or, worse yet, they think everything is neat and orderly, hunky-dory."

"The professor cares."

She moved back and peered deeply into his eyes. "I want to say something. I haven't been able to say it before, but I can now. I love you."

"Say it again. I don't believe it. Say it again."

"I love you. Peter Russell, I love you."

He flung his arms around her, consumed with a warm surge of joy. It was as if in that second he had found himself. He felt her tears on his neck. It was snowing harder, encasing them in a protective white blanket. At least for now, there was no one else on earth.

Then it was two days and nights of love. They did not discuss politics. They did not discuss the future. They made a snowman, had snowball fights, slid down a hill together on cardboard, walked finger-linked in an icy meadow, sang winter songs, bought hot chestnuts, and daringly dipped bare toes in a cold stream. They were young, they were healthy, they were free, they were in love.

Monday broke cold and gray.

Carol found a parking spot for the Ford three blocks from the courthouse in downtown Hammond. She took his hand. "Let's run," she said. "It'll keep you warm." They did, the freezing air cutting into their lungs, their overshoes slipping on the compacted snow. Peter heard his last name being called and he turned to view in a flood of warm delight the cold-reddened face of Crowell, his roomie from the Salem prep school. They embraced each other. Peter was almost in tears.

"What in the world are you doing here?" he asked.

"Revolting, just like you."

"Carol, this is Crowell. His family's in steel."

"Toilets, actually," Crowell said, and he laughed.

They moved ahead, three comrades going to battle. A half-dozen state-police cars lined the street by the courthouse, where perhaps fifty students had assembled. About twenty uniformed officers, holding long, thin sticks attached to their wrists with leather thongs, stood in a row by the cars. Peter felt a flash of danger. The scene froze in front of him—the students on the steps congealed like herded cattle, the row of square-jawed helmeted policemen tapping their clubs in their palms, a background of cold gray sky. Carol tugged him forward. They joined the students, arm-locked and swaying, chanting, "The Inquisition has returned, the Inquisition has returned." A whistle sounded, strident in Peter's ears. The policemen moved forward. One, a sergeant, collared the group's young leader. As if by signal, everyone sat down, still linked, and continued to chant. The policemen were all over them, snapping at their hands with their sticks.

Peter heard a distant siren. Carol was beside him. Crowell was on his other side. It was all right. He shouldn't worry. They would not be harmed.

But then it exploded. It exploded in shrieks and curses, in churning arms and legs, in sudden splotches of blood on the snow-covered steps, in shrill cries and even shriller whistle blasts. Several students were hurled down the steps; they tried to struggle back up, only to be driven down by policemen. A club banged Peter's shoulder, forcing him down. He glared at his attacker; the fat cop grinned. "Pig!" Peter shouted. The others took up the cry. "Pig, pig, pig, pig, *pig!*" Carol was on her back, trying to get up, flailing at overshoes and snowboots that trampled around her. Peter was powerless in the melee, held and shoved and buffeted. He lashed out with his fists and elbows. Everything began to whirl, churning dizzily; it was like watching grotesque shapes through undulating mirrors. He was down, first on his hands and knees and then on his stomach, and when he turned he saw Crowell beside him, blood gushing like bubbling ooze from a crack in his skull.

Professor Carmichael said: "Well, are your revolutionary spirits now quenched, or will you miss class again tomorrow to press on with your cause?"

"Where is Carol?"

"She's all right. They're questioning her."

"And Crowell?"

"I know of no one by that name."

"He's a friend of mine, from the prep school."

"Oh, yes," the professor said slowly. "It seems I *do* remember him. I see he is still getting into mischief."

"He was hurt."

"Then we shall try to find out about him."

"How did you find out about this, for that matter?"

"It so happened that I witnessed it on television."

They were outside the Hammond police station, standing in the chilly dusk. The professor turned away, obviously upset and disappointed. Peter's back ached and his head throbbed. He was concerned about Carol, even more so about Crowell. About thirty of the demonstrators had been arrested, the injured taken by ambulance to an emergency hospital.

The professor said: "Peter, this was staged, wasn't it? Staged for television coverage."

"It was *not* staged. The cops just moved in, that's all."

"Why did you go?"

"I went because Carol was going."

The professor's face showed deep irritation. "I want you to promise me you'll never get involved in something like this again."

"I'm sorry." Peter looked away. "I can't promise that. Not after what happened here. You simply do not understand."

"I do understand. But I do not condone demonstrations."

"How, then, would you make a point?"

"Through the courts."

"I'm afraid the courts are too slow," Peter replied. "And sometimes unjust."

Carol appeared by the station door, wearing her floppy cap. She waved. She came toward him, limping slightly.

"Please ride back with us," Peter said to the professor. "Maybe we can talk this out."

"No." Professor Carmichael thrust out his chin. His eyes could not hide his hurt. "I'll take the train. I have some thinking to do."

He walked away, his shoulders square. Peter watched him go. He looked at Carol, then back at the professor, afraid that he would have to choose between the two persons in his life he knew he loved.

They visited Crowell in the hospital. His face was pale, but he seemed in good spirits. A white bandage encircled his head like a turban. "Red badge of courage," he said, tapping it. "Ouch." Then he smiled.

"Are you going to go out again?" Carol asked.

"I have only begun to fight," Crowell said. "Did you bring any booze?"

5.

RELATIONS WITH the professor remained strained from that point on, although they were seemingly cordial. Peter sulked in a blue despair, haunted by visions of Nathan Carmichael's hurt eyes. He had disappointed a man who had done more for him than anyone else in his life, and he had disappointed a man whom he loved. Yet he could not—or would not—do anything about it. He had found a new love, a new commitment, and a new home. The professor adamantly resisted sharing any of them with him. He was showing his stubborn side. It hurt Peter to hurt him. He finally forced a confrontation in the professor's office at the law school. There was more than just Carol on his mind, but he opened the conversation with a discussion about her.

"I can understand your objection, of course," he said, gesturing with his palms up. "But I think the objection is based on a lack of knowledge."

The professor arranged the papers on his desk in a neat row of stacks. That defined him—order and precision. He said: "All right, Peter. Let's hear your defense."

"Is this a court and is she the accused?"

"We will call it moot court. I will be the judge."

"But it's not some game we are playing."

Professor Carmichael got up and went to the window. He stood with his hands linked behind his back, staring out. "I had hoped you would soon be in these classes." He turned. He was wearing his Phi Beta Kappa key, which he wore only on campus, once explaining that a display of academic accomplishment in social circles was as vainglorious as a soldier who came to your dinner wearing his medals. "Is that still your goal?"

"I—I really don't know."

"It was once your avowed goal. Now your head has been turned. May I inquire into the nature of your new goal?"

Peter looked away. Then he stood up and gazed into the professor's eyes. "I want to find out who I am," he said.

"Oh. It's back to that again."

"It's never left my mind. I may have put it aside for a while, but it's still there. You've told me my parents are dead. Did you tell me the truth?"

"I will not discuss it, Peter."

"Why? *Why?*"

"I can't tell you why. In time you may know."

"Professor Carmichael—"

The professor smiled. "Perhaps it *is* time for something. I wish you would use my first name. I rather like my first name."

It had been awhile since the professor—Nathan—had smiled at him, and the action warmed Peter. But he said: "I rather think you're throwing me off the track."

That brought a frown. "I cannot and will not answer your questions concerning the matter, as I've told you many times in the past. I understand your curiosity—"

"Anxiety would better describe it."

"You will simply have to put it aside."

Peter's voice rose. "I feel like . . . like some pawn in someone's game. Is it any wonder that I sympathize with people who want to revolt?"

"You are not a pawn. You have a mind of your own. It is a brilliant mind, and you have a brilliant future. I am very, very proud of you, for you have exceeded my most optimistic expectations." He paused. Then he said: "Until now."

"Until now. Until now that I demonstrate I have a mind of my own?"

Nathan Carmichael strolled across the office to the row of lawbooks that lined the wall. "You want to bring about reform. You want to be an instrument in purifying a system you believe is inherently imperfect and perhaps even tyrannous. I do not deny your right to challenge. It is the basis of our way of life. This nation was born in challenge, in revolution. But you do not accomplish that by risking your life at a student demonstration. You do it through knowledge, by invoking law—a law that admittedly is not flawless yet has a flexibility of interpretation that leads to justice. You accomplish it through *this!*" His knuckles rapped a book binding. He turned. The corners of his lips twitched and there were red spots in his cheeks. Peter had never seen him so animated. The professor returned to his desk, sat down, and took up his pipe. His voice softened as he continued. "I understand this spirit of revolt. I once felt it myself. There are times when I still do. Even an old stiff like the bald-pated antiquity you see here can feel outrage on occasion."

"You're not an old stiff."

"I also understand your feelings of kinship and affection for the young woman."

"It is more than kinship and affection. It is love."

"Then it is love." The professor's eyes fell, riveting on the pipe. "But I cannot condone nor sanctify it. I must ask you to end it, to enter law school as we planned, and to learn." He raised his head and peered over his thin glasses. "To *learn!*"

"I can't break it off. I won't."

"Then I fear we shall remain in conflict."

"Earlier you asked me to defend her. Now I will. She's a wonderful person. She has wonderful parents. She's intelligent, outgoing, a humanist who's in touch with nature."

"And beautiful," the professor said, tapping his pipe.

Peter used his last defense. "Professor, have you ever been in love?"

"I have been in love, yes. I don't want to sound like a cynic, but I fear it is an emotion that is ephemeral."

"I think that you're wrong."

"If you'll allow me a single conceit, I will tell you that I am a man who is not often wrong."

"I've seen that. And I know what you've done for me, Professor, and I'm not ungrateful."

A little smile. "Nathan."

"Nathan," Peter said. "Habits die hard."

"You are making a transition now and many habits will die. Law school is as different from undergraduate school as undergraduate is from high school. I forecast you will not have the time to demonstrate in behalf of the downtrodden. Instead, help them with knowledge."

Peter stood for a long moment, considering. "All right. I will enter law school. But I will not break it off with Carol."

"I will accept that," Nathan Carmichael said, "as a reasonable compromise for now at least."

They shook hands. Peter left, feeling better.

Carmichael called Hollis Collingsworth in Los Angeles. "Well, you keep after him," Hollis said. "I have a lot of training and money in that boy and I'm not going to give him away to the first broad that lifts her skirts for him."

"He's a little confused right now."

"Unconfuse him then."

"I have a suggestion. If he does go to the West Coast to work on your newspaper in the summer, perhaps it is time you tell him the truth."

"I'm not even going to see him when he's here, for Christ's sake!"

"He's going to find out, Hollis. He has a mind of his own and he's determined."

"It's that radical he's seeing. A man can control another man with money and the lure of power, but a woman can control a man merely by spreading her legs. I want you to do something about that, and soon. If you don't, I will. How about her parents? Do they need money?"

"I've never met her parents. But if they're like Peter describes them to be, they wouldn't take money to discourage it."

"Everybody has a price. Isn't that right, Professor?"

He winced. "Please understand something," he said. "I'm doing this out of affection for Peter, not for your money."

"Oh, sure, I understand."

"I'm not sure at all that you do."

"Then I'll cut off your stipend. And you'll go right on doing it for him."

"I would."

"Not as effectively, I suspect."

"I've asked you this before, but I have not received a satisfactory answer. What are your long-term plans for Peter?"

Hollis laughed. "My long-term plan is to see Andrew Collingsworth president in a decade and Peter Russell president within two decades."

"I want a serious answer."

"That was a serious answer."

"Do you plan to tell Peter who his parents really are?"

"I might, I might not."

"He asked me today if I'd ever been in love."

"Well, he's moonbeaming. If I'd married the first woman I ever felt up, I wouldn't be where I am now. Women have great pussy power, but only because men let themselves get trapped by it. You straighten that boy out. I don't want a doped-up flower child. I'd rather have him turn queer."

"He's hardly a flower child. He just might be the best student I've ever seen. He has a very fine mind."

"Of course he has. You keep him in line."

"You risked his discovery by putting him in contact with your family. Why did you do that?"

"Judge, sometimes I wonder about your perception. It was a test. It had to happen someday. And if he hasn't swallowed the story we gave him, but instead suspects he has a living father and mother who want to keep it secret, he'd figure the last thing in the world his anonymous old man would do is invite him to dinner."

"I see your logic."

"You straighten him out."

"I'm confident Peter will turn out just fine."

"If you don't straighten him out," Hollis said, "then I will."

Carmichael hung up, slightly disturbed. He knew more about the strength of love than his friends and certainly his students thought. He'd had it until his ambition had destroyed it; he now knew he'd been a fool. But he couldn't go back. His relationship had been shattered by grief and guilt and it was no more possible to rebuild it than it was to repair a broken mirror. Now he had his books, his students, and Peter. Again guilt assailed him. It was a dilemma that had no real solution. If Peter severed his relationship with Carol to please his mentor and guardian, he would do so with hostility and perhaps even hatred. It could result in a final break between them, something Carmichael knew he could not bear. He sat behind his desk, watching the lengthening shadows, punishing himself. *You, you old scheming, miserable man, are you jealous of the boy's time? Do you really do this for evil Collingsworth dollars? Who are you to rule and to control another's life? Because you are hardened by past pain, must you plot to destroy the happiness of others?*

There had been times in the past when he'd been on the verge of abandoning this experiment. Now he knew it was too late. Hollis Collingsworth, his power and control and confidence growing daily, apparently considered nothing out of his reach. There was a streak of dementia in him; he was, in fact, a dangerous man. His every action was calculated for personal gain. And Carmichael was in league with him. He realized, in a surge of helplessness, that he could not break his pact. He saw clearly for the first time how he had been used. One thing he knew. Peter had become a large part of his life. He

had to stop him from channeling energy into useless radical-
ism. That would be a total waste. And he saw now that it was
inevitable that sometime in the future a serious confrontation
would take place between him and Hollis Collingsworth.

Peter felt a rise in the tempo of revolt. Drop-out flower
children sprawled in communes, singing "Strawberry Fields
Forever." The Woolworth's sit-in had spawned dozens of
imitations. There were rumbles about acceleration in Vietnam.
The president had been murdered in Dallas and no area in a
stunned nation felt it as grievously as Boston and Cape Cod.
The weather that week had turned from mild prewinter into
an overnight chill and bleak, cold dawns, and then into a
wind that stung sleet into the ears and eyebrows. Kennedy's
Peace Corps gained recruits. Chapters of the Student Nonviolent
Coordinating Committee—called "Snick"—were formed on
almost every campus. Clark Kerr of Berkeley had anticipated
student unrest in his Godkin Lecture at Harvard. The term
lumpen proletariat became common—masses on campus herded
and regimented. Students paraded with IBM cards—do not
bend, fold, or mutilate—strung to their necks. Peter, Paul,
and Mary sang "Blowin' in the Wind" and Bob Dylan's words
for the song were a poem to Peter Russell:

How many roads must a man walk down
Before you can call him a man?
How many times must the cannon balls fly
Before they are forever banned?
The answer my friend, is blowin' in the wind
The answer is blowin' in the wind

He was seeing Carol as much as his studies permitted and
often they drove to her parents on the Cape. He was beginning to feel like a member of the family. It made him both
happy and guilty.

"Certainly I can understand why you feel that way," Carol
told him one afternoon. "But it's more Carmichael's fault than
yours. I'm not going to pretend in front of him that I'm
something I'm not. And if he can't see my side, I'm certain I
won't try to see his side."

"He can be stubborn."

"I don't like it, but I'm afraid it's cold war between him and me. You're always over there for dinner, but when has he invited me? I don't even think he wants me to come to your graduation."

"Oh, sure he does."

"Does he?" They were strolling in the twilight near her apartment. Now she stopped. "Peter, I love you, but I'm not going to change. Not now, at least. What I'm doing is simply too important. Maybe Carmichael is right about us." She looked away and when she turned back he saw that there was moisture in her eyes. "I don't want to hold you back. Perhaps I am."

"What are you suggesting?"

She moved into his arms and he felt her tears on his cheek. "I don't know, I just don't *know*! I love you, but I just don't know if it will work."

"Of course it will work. We love each other. If we love each other, we can work anything out."

"I have to tell you this. I'm going south this summer to work with a Snick chapter there. I've put off telling you. But I have to go."

"All right. I'll go with you."

"Oh, sure. Carmichael would tar and feather you."

"He doesn't control me."

"I think he controls you more than you think."

"If he controlled me, I wouldn't be here with you."

She broke away and stood with her back turned to him. "That's partly the point. You are here with me and that means you're defying him. That can't go on forever."

"Then let's go and have it out with him."

"It wouldn't do any good."

"Well, I'll have it out with him."

But he didn't. Instead he compromised, agreeing to accept the long-standing invitation to work as a summer intern on the Los Angeles *Bulletin-News*. He had graduated summa cum laude, a ceremony that Carol had witnessed from the back row and Nathan Carmichael from the front. The law school had accepted him. His life again seemed patterned, as if it had led to this despite his attempt at revolt, and that disturbed him. He was heartsick when he saw Carol off at the train station, the first leg of her sojourn to the racially torn South.

"I'm going to miss you terribly," he said.

"I'll miss you."

"Board!" shouted the black conductor. "All aboard!"

"I'll worry," Peter said.

"Now don't. You sound like my parents. I'll be all right. Write me."

He kissed her, long and hard, and when she backed away, he held her hand until only their fingertips touched. Several students boarded with her. Peter waited. The train began to move. He saw her in the window, waving at him. She forced the window up and stuck out her head.

"I love you!" she called.

He watched the train until it was out of sight, his hands crammed deeply in his pockets.

Although he missed Carol furiously, Peter found that he enjoyed the work on the newspaper. He got fifteen copies of his first bylined story, an interview with James Baldwin, and sent five to Carol and five to Nathan Carmichael, pasting the other five in his scrapbook. He liked his boss, Mitch Evers, despite the fact that Mitch was constantly encased in choking cigarette smoke. Mitch was properly cynical, tremendously well-informed, and had a wry sense of humor.

"See that rim rat? No, the one over there, Peter. Know what we call him? We call him the Pink Rabbit. The one beside him is Golden Dome. Now here comes the editor. He's called Lurch."

Peter laughed. "What do they call you?"

"The Human Torch," Mitch said, lighting up. "What else?"

Mitch could type faster than any human alive, and his copy came out clean. He never took notes at press conferences; he said he always could tell what the politicians were going to say before they opened their yaps. If a copy editor touched a word of his, he'd threaten to chop the man's finger off. He got into the habit of calling Peter "Harvard," which Peter discovered he liked. They said Mitch reported right to Collingsworth; that, Mitch said, didn't get him any brownie points with Lurch.

"Hollis Collingsworth?" Peter said. "I've met him. I had dinner with him and his family a few years ago."

"I rather thought you had connections, Harvard. Not many interns around here get an apartment near the sheet and a company car."

"Well, Mr. Collingsworth is a friend of a friend of mine, a professor at Harvard."

"I forecast you will go far if you want to stay on this paper. Although I don't know why you'd want to do that."

"Why do you say that?"

"Because the Gray Fox upstairs is to the right of Barry Goldwater and you do what he says or you look elsewhere."

"The Gray Fox? Mr. Collingsworth?"

"Who else?"

"Then you do what he tells you?"

"Yep."

"And you don't like it?"

"Not always."

"Then why don't you look elsewhere?"

"Harvard," Mitch said, blowing smoke, "let's just say I'm waiting around to see how the story comes out."

There were regular letters from Carol, describing what she termed the deplorable racial conditions in the south. He loved the letters, but they made him miss her and worry about her even more. He wrote her in care of a hotel in Montgomery. She said she'd been water hosed, spat and cursed at, and threatened with rape. One southern gentleman had expressed a desire to pin her down and shove a bottle up her Nigger-loving ass. Another accused her of loving watermelon, chicken, and Nigger cock. "Aside from that, it's very hospitable here," she wrote. "I love you." Her love was evident in all the letters, and it was clear to him that she missed him as much as he missed her. His shortest letter was four words: "Will you marry me?" She wrote back an even shorter one. "Yes!" Peter beamed. He couldn't wait for the summer to end. When it did, Mitch took him for a drink at the Red House.

"Harvard, despite your education, you're not a bad newspaperman."

"Thank you. I think I should say, instead, thanks *to* you."

"Coming back?"

"I don't know. I like the work. But there's law school."

"There's something else, too."

"What?"

"The way you've been panting to get out of here, especially the last couple weeks, it's not difficult to tell that a pretty skirt awaits you in Boston."

"Well, as a matter of fact, yes."

"Salúte," Mitch said. "Luck."

"Luck," Peter said.

*   *   *

Two days later he was in the same place at the rail station in Boston where he'd let her go, a time that seemed years ago. The train steamed in, passengers got off, and he could not see Carol. Despair and concern went through him. Then she was there, calling his name, running toward him, and when she was in his arms he felt a joy and contentment so complete that he knew he was the luckiest person on earth. He had brought her Ford. In the front seat, her luggage in the trunk, he kissed her again and took out her one-word letter.

"Is it still yes?"

"It is still yes. Yes, yes, yes. I've thought about it and I think we can work it out. I think we're mature enough to work it out."

Peter surged with exquisite joy. He had learned something. If he had vigorously protested her going, waving his hands and weeping, he might have lost her. Now she had returned, fulfilled, and she was his. When she warned him that her marching days were not over, he said his were not, either.

"Did you learn anything on that right-wing paper?" she asked as he eased into traffic.

"Yes. And I met Golden Dome, the Pink Rabbit, Lurch, and the Human Torch. But I didn't see the Gray Fox."

"You mentioned them in your letters, but not the Gray Fox. Who is he?"

"Hollis Collingsworth."

Carol made a face. But she was in a very good mood. She sat back and did a passable imitation of George Wallace. "I draw the line in the dust and toss the gauntlet before the feet of tyranny and I say segregation now, segregation tomorrow, segregation forever." She laughed. She wanted to know where she was being taken.

"The Cape," he said. "I have a question to ask your father. It concerns a young lady's yes letter."

"My, you turned out to be an old-fashioned one, didn't you? I think I like that."

"I'm nervous," Peter said.

There wasn't any reason to be nervous. When he looked at Captain Kingsley's rugged face, the pale blue eyes, and the goatee-type beard he'd grown, he knew the captain knew what was going to be asked. The captain shook his hand. Amelia hugged him. Then she stuffed him with clam cakes.

If he was nervous before facing the captain, he was four times as nervous about facing Nathan Carmichael. They went together to the professor's home in the evening. A maid showed them into the living room and soon he came downstairs, smoking his pipe and wearing a velvet robe. He offered sherry, which they both accepted.

"I can guess," the professor said, slumping into an easy chair, "what this is all about."

Peter didn't like sherry, but he downed his little glass in a gulp. He looked at Carol. "W-what d'you mean?"

"Even an ancient bird like me has the ability to judge the meaning of the looks you two have in your eyes. You want to get married."

"Y-y-yes," Peter said.

"Perhaps you should have more sherry, Peter. It might help you get your voice back."

"No t-t-thanks."

The professor puffed. He looked at them both. "You have my blessing," he said.

Carol ran to him and kissed his cheek. "I haven't reformed, Professor," she said. "Do you still feel the same way?"

"Young lady, I learned a long, long time ago that when two people your age want to get married, no force on the planet or in the universe can stop them. I could try, but I do not imagine myself in the role of villain. Have you set a date?"

"Yes," Peter said.

"No," Carol said.

"No," Peter agreed.

"Which is it?" the professor asked.

"Well, we haven't, not really," answered Peter.

The professor looked at Carol. "Perhaps *you* could be more specific than my sputtering protégé here."

"We had an argument about it," Carol said. "Well, not an argument, but a discussion. I have a year left as an undergraduate and I want to go on for a master's. He has three years of law school. I wanted to wait until we're both finished, but he doesn't."

"Peter?" the professor said.

Peter stood up. He went to Carol and touched her hand. "I want to get married now."

"Well, one can be a law student at Harvard and be married," the professor said slowly, "but it would be exceedingly difficult to be both an attentive husband and a good student. Have you thought that it might put a strain on a marriage?"

"No. I want to marry Carol as soon as it's humanly possible."

"And, I will assume, you have a good reason why you wish to do that?"

"Yes," he said, holding her hand. "I can't really explain why, but I have a terrible feeling that if we don't get married now we may never."

"A *feeling*? That seems an unsubstantial reason for making such a decision."

"Professor, we finally agree on something," Carol said.

The comment brought a slight smile to Carmichael's lips. He rose. "Well, I'm going to disqualify myself as an arbitrator in the matter. And, in fact, I am going to bed. Help yourself to more sherry."

Peter finally did accept a compromise, agreeing to wait until Carol graduated, and when he entered law school he quickly realized that she had been right. His days consisted of five hours in the classroom and ten of study; the rest of the time he slept. Again, he had a book or study notes in his hand whenever he saw Carol. She had the good sense not to say I told you so. One morning she woke him up on the telephone with concern in her voice.

"Daddy called just now," she began. "He said an anonymous caller had threatened him and mother. Peter?"

"Threatened? In what way?"

She had difficulty finding her voice. "It was about us, Peter. At first he offered money. Then he threatened."

"I don't understand."

"The man offered a hundred thousand dollars to my parents if they could stop our marriage plans."

"What!"

"And when Daddy said something like, 'You're joking,' the man said, 'When your house burns you won't think I am.'"

"A crank," Peter said.

"Peter, I don't think so."

"Why?"

"Well, I have no disgruntled ex-boyfriends and I haven't told many people about our plans. This person knew something. And then I got to thinking. A hundred thousand. Peter, you don't *know* your background. But don't you think it odd that you've been sent to the best schools, given almost whatever you've wanted? Where did all the money come from?"

A chill went through him. "You're saying I have a backer, working through Professor Carmichael, who isn't very anxious to see us get married. No. I still think it was a crank call."

But he wasn't sure. He went to Nathan Carmichael's office, where a prim secretary informed him that the professor was in New York addressing the bar association. She said it in a voice which conveyed to him that he should have known that without asking. Peter returned to his room. Again the questions of his past rang in his mind, as they had hundreds of times before. They were innumerable, but they boiled down to one. *Who am I?* He dialed Carol.

"Please don't worry," he said. "I'm certain it was a crank."

"I hope you're right."

"You're not getting cold feet, are you? About us?"

"No. But I was thinking about what you said about getting married right away. I mean, if we didn't we might never?"

"I think you might be getting cold feet. Just slightly?"

"No. I love you."

He went to class in a daze, forgetting his notebook, and when he was called upon he found he couldn't remember the case. The professor excused him, telling him to return when he was prepared. It was the only black mark he'd received since he had entered law school. Peter returned to his room, received no answer when he dialed Carol, and flung himself on his bed in despair. His hands were unsteady. His mouth was dry. He'd had a premonition, a fear that he could not explain to anyone, and now there was a sign he'd been right. It hadn't been a crank call. And something else would happen. The phone shrieked, startling him.

"Oh," Carol said. "You *are* there. I thought you might be in class but I decided I'd try anyway." Her voice seemed calmer. "I just wanted to tell you that I'm going to see my parents."

"When?"

"I'm leaving right now."

"I want to go with you."

"No. You have classes, honey."

"So have you."

"I can afford to miss a few. You can't. Did you reach Carmichael?"

"No. He's in New York."

"I'm all right," Carol said. "Believe me."

"I want to see you before you go."

"All right. Merlin's?"

"Half hour."

They met at Merlin's often. The owner knew they were lovers and always found a quiet table for them. It was a small Italian restaurant with oilclothed tables and red lamps. Often Mario, the waiter, sang opera. It was a blustery day with a hidden sun and a sky etched with a strange yellow haze. She was already there when he arrived, seated at a back table. They kissed and sat holding hands. The owner, Merlin Savio, brought coffee and left them alone.

"I think it might rain," he said. "Maybe you shouldn't go today."

"I'll be careful. I'm a good driver."

It was chit-chat, avoiding-the-subject chit-chat. Neither wanted to bring the matter up. Across the table, her face bathed in the lamp's pink glow, Carol seemed to him more beautiful than at any time in the past. Never had he loved her more. He told her that. She smiled radiantly and held his hand tighter.

"It was just a crank call," she said. "I've convinced myself of that now."

"Then why are you going?"

She stuck out her lower lip. "Because I want to get to the bottom of this."

"And how do you propose to do that?"

"If they get another call, I want to be there. And if they offer the hundred thousand again, I'll take it." She said it in mock seriousness. Then she smiled. "Don't look so downcast. I didn't know you were worth that much. I'll give it to the N-double-ACP and CORE."

"Be serious."

"I am serious. I may even try to jack it up, find out really how much you're worth."

"Have you ever been poked in the eye?"

"Recently. Down Montgomery way."

The banter, he knew, was like the chit-chat, to cover the issue. Peter felt a sinking sensation in the pit of his stomach. He was going to lose her. He knew that he was going to lose her. *Stop it. Stop it.* He'd had similar feelings when he saw her off at the Boston depot. But they hadn't been as strong at that time, though the reasons then had been even stronger. He didn't know. Perhaps he had thought all along that his relationship with Carol was too good to be true. She had been with him whenever she possibly could be, sometimes sacrificing other plans to do so, but she was a person with a commitment in her life, at least for now, and on some heart-sinking occasions he believed that if she was forced to make a choice the commitment would win out over him.

He said: "I want to marry you."

She responded: "I want to marry you."

"On the house, kids," Merlin said, filling their coffee cups.

Soon Carol started to get up. "I'd better go," she told Peter. "Beat that rain. You stay here. I'll walk out by myself." She looked at him. Her eyes seemed far off and misty. "God, how I love you."

Then she was gone. There was lipstick on her cup. Peter ran his fingertip over it.

"What's wrong, you kids have a spat?" Merlin asked.

"Oh, no. Carol is driving out to the Cape to see her parents."

"Now? It's blowin' up out there."

"Well, it's very important to her that she go now."

"Women." Merlin stood with his hairy hands folded over his fat stomach. "You'll find out what I mean."

"I will?" He added crossly: "What do you mean?"

"They're wonderful," Merlin said, breaking into a wide grin.

Carol hated tailgating cars, but a tailgater in a high wind was an insanity that turned the hate to fear. A Pontiac had been on her rear bumper for several miles now. When she sped up, the Pontiac sped up; when she slowed, it slowed. There were two big men in the front seat. The wind buffeted her Ford, lashing the doors and hood, cracking on the windshield. It whipped the trees into stiffly bent forms and drove the grass flat. The ponds were heavily rippled, strewn with broken pussy willow stems. Sand swept across the highway in wide sheets. But the visibility was fair, lighted by an eerie orange sun behind her, and she had made good time. Perhaps the foolish tailgater was using her as a windbreaker.

The Pontiac's chrome grill and headlights glistened ominously in her rearview mirror. Carol pushed her horn to protest, but no sound came out; the damn thing wasn't working. She thought about pulling over to let the Pontiac pass but quickly abandoned that idea. Perhaps that was what the men behind her wanted. The fear that had replaced the anger rose in her, pulsating in little waves. She pushed the Ford to fifty, fast as she dared drive in the high wind. The Pontiac, as it had done before, also accelerated. Carol switched lanes. The other car did likewise. The wind cracked on the Ford's convertible top, streaking in on her through the rips. *Are my doors locked?* They were, giving her some comfort. She thought: *Why did I come out today?* She thought: *Peter.* Her mouth was dry. Her hands were unsteady. She was now only a few miles from North Chatham and the warmth and safety of home. Traffic was sparse, almost nonexistent. Cape Codders respected a blow. Carol had anticipated winds, but not as severe as these.

The Pontiac was now right behind her, closing to inches; then it bumped her, a gentle bump followed by a harder one. She floored the accelerator, edging into the right lane. A powerful crosswind struck her and the Ford began to swerve. She twisted the wheel the other way, but the car was out of control, spinning and turning, caught in the wind. She was going around. That much she knew. She braked. She heard the howl of the wind and the squealing of her tires. Her head whirled. She clutched the wheel, aware of moving terrain around her, churning like a slow whirlpool. The Ford finally came to a stop in a ditch across the shoulder, facing the direction from which it had come. Carol sat with her hands over her face, trembling.

"Hey, you all right?" A man stood outside, tapping on her windshield. Carol looked up. She gasped. It was one of the men from the Pontiac. He had a huge red face and broken yellow teeth. A scar split his cheek. Thin strands of his hair blew in the wind. "You okay, I asked?"

Her hands had stopped trembling. Anger had replaced the fear. "I'm all right, but no thanks to you. What kind of a crazy fool *are* you? You drove me off the road."

The man grinned. "Aw, that was my partner. He likes to fool around, you know what I mean."

"Get away from me!"

"Naw, c'mon out. We'll take you into town. You need a tow

truck to get you outta here. We'll pay it. Figure we owe you. Sorry, but my partner's pretty crazy sometimes."

"No! Just go away!"

Again the man grinned. He wore a dark suit and a tie. Slowly he reached into his pocket and took out a jackknife. He opened the blade. "Well, we can't leave you here, so if you won't come out, I'll just have to cut you outta that heap." He jammed the blade into the Ford's canvas top and slashed downward. The canvas gave way. Then his hand was in, fumbling for the door button. She struck at it with her fists, but he pushed her away with the back of his hand, unlocked the door, and pulled it open. He bent down, hunched and grinning like an amused ape, and put his hairy hands on her shoulders. She moved away and tried to scream, but the scream was lost in the wind. He seized her arms and forced her out. She tried to struggle, but found her strength was gone, drained by the terror of the skidding car. The man supported her, half carrying her, moving toward the waiting Pontiac. A car went by, slowed, and sped away. Carol felt an absurd anxiety. She had left her purse in the Ford. She couldn't speak. She couldn't think. She was conscious of the wind, of a throbbing pain in her back, and of the man's hands and arms. He opened the Pontiac's back door, pushed her in, and got in beside her.

The man who drove did not speak. He crouched over the wheel like a robot whose destination had been programmed. The man beside her in the back kept apologizing, assuring her everything was all right now. Carol said nothing. She sat huddled in terror, listening to the scream of the wind, as the man calmly cut and cleaned his fingernails with his knife. They were driving through North Chatham, at the elbow of the Cape.

"Let me off here," she said, finding her voice. "My parents live here."

The man grinned and continued to clean his fingernails. Finally the Pontiac stopped. They were high in the dunes by the Atlantic, alone at the road's end. The driver did not turn. The other man put away his knife.

"Some wind," he said. "Eh, Tat?" There was no answer. "We ain't gonna hurt you," the man told Carol. "It's just that we come way out here to talk to you, and since you come along we thought maybe we'd just go ahead and do it now."

"W-w-what do you want?"

"Now don't be afraid. I said I just wanted to talk to you. I know you're a sensible girl, a college girl. I got a girl in college myself. Not all the students are sensible, you understand, but I'm one that believes most of the kids there on the campuses are sensible. Like you. And most of them—they ain't got enough money. Understand you're getting married."

"How do you know that? Who *are* you?"

"I'm the one that called your papa."

"But why? Why?"

"Well, there's reasons. Somebody's got plans for that boy you wanna marry and if you marry him the plans are off. It's simple as that. So you two, you don't get hooked up. We make it worth your while."

She was gathering her senses. Her head had cleared. Anger again flared in her, coming with a renewal of the pain in her back. She huddled against the door. The wind struck, increasing in fury.

"No!" she yelled. He reached out for her and she dug her fingernails in his hand. "Get away!"

"Tiger cat," he said, grinning. "Tell you what. Now, you're a shapely, pretty little thing, and since I ain't had any for a while, there's nothing I'd like better than to lay you down here and play awhile, listening to that wind. Tat wouldn't mind. Huh, Tat? He can go second."

She pushed back. Her elbow brushed the door handle. Quickly she reached out and shoved it down. She kicked the door open. At demonstrator schools in Montgomery she had learned how to escape punishing blows, which places on her body could absorb them with the least effect, and now she put the training to use, springing her legs up and sprawling out of the car barkward. She lost a shoe. She rolled on the dunes, sprang up, and ran. The other shoe came off. A voice rang out behind her, but she paid no attention. She didn't look back. The wind screamed around her, blinding her with sand. She put her hands over her eyes, lurching on. Now the wind seemed to be carrying her, blowing her northward along the dunes, caught in a pommeling rage of rolling weeds, rocks, and dirt clumps.

Her father had told her of the simoon, a sandstorm more dangerous than the worse tempest, usually preceded by a strange orange sun that deepened to carmine as it set. Like today. She tripped, falling painfully. She spat out sand. She thought she could hear crashing waves. She struggled up.

Again the wind took her, tearing her clothes, pushing her along in its force. All sense of direction was gone. She could not see. No longer could she hear. A gray uprising encased her, buffeting her at first forward and then backward. She tried to think. She must find some shelter. She must not panic. The shrieking sands caked her body, driving her to her knees. She flailed her arms, crawling forward. Blackness surrounded her. The wind hurled her down; her head smashed something hard. She fought waves of dizziness. She was in and out of consciousness. Visions fled before her—the eyes of her father, Peter holding her, the laughter of her mother, blood streaming from the temple of a black boy clubbed during a demonstration. It seemed better now. The wind and the whipping sand were fading, drifting away. She was slipping into a great hole of darkness, a haven of peace.

The Cape gave off a pungent after-rain odor, holding thick and heady in Peter's nostrils as he walked the dunes by the sea where Carol had died. Walking seemed to help. The dunes lay before him like a bleak, gray slate, swept barren and clean by the windstorm. The skeleton of a once-buried longboat lay half exposed in the sand. Dead birds littered the beach. He stood transfixed, staring at the green waves that rushed to the shore. Here they had frolicked like children, lost in their love. He turned and slowly retraced his steps. He could stand this self-imposed punishment no longer. He was dead inside. He'd wandered stunned since learning of her death. His mind did not function. He found it difficult to talk without stuttering. Her funeral this morning on the Cape had been a torture which he'd staggered blindly away from in its middle. He'd come here, to the dunes, and to more torture. Slowly he made his way back to her parents' house. He found the captain in the backyard, beside the maple tree with the swing.

"I don't know whether to cut the swing down or keep it up," the captain said.

Peter tried to say something, but he couldn't find his voice. Raindrops hung in a silver row on the drainpipes, losing hold and dropping several at a time, racing each other to the ground. They held Peter's attention. He had been like that the past few days, hypnotized by little things, tired but unable to sleep, eating and washing and wandering in a mechanical stupor. He could not even feel guilt; he felt only emptiness. Her car had been found at the edge of the dunes, where the road ended. Her death by suffocation had been ruled an accident. He was beyond questioning it, because he was beyond thinking. The captain put his hand on Peter's shoulder.

"I'll go in to Amelia now," he said. "I want you to know that you're welcome here at any time."

He peered into the captain's kind blue eyes. He could not speak. He could hardly move. He was dead with her and death had neither voice nor movement. It was a blind nothing. It had no dignity, no pride, and no pity.

He was packing in his room at the law school when a tap came on the door. Professor Carmichael appeared. "May I?" he asked, stepping forward.

"All right."

"Are you leaving?"

"Yes."

"To go where?"

"I don't know. Maybe back to Paris."

The professor sat down on the edge of the bed. He looked worn and tired. He looked old. He'd been to the funeral, but Peter had not spoken to him. Only a few words had passed between them since he'd learned of her death. Now he said slowly:

"I am so terribly sorry, Peter."

"Are you?"

"Of course I am."

He was coming out of it, at least slightly. "But you didn't like her. You didn't like her because she could stand up for what she believed."

"That isn't true."

"You opposed us every step of the way."

"No. I gave your union my sanction, you remember."

"Why did you do that?"

"Because I changed my mind. When I thought about it, I realized that I was wrong."

Peter felt his mind working; the hurt remained, but mitigated by anger and confusion. "Professor, I think you know something about this."

"About what? It was an accident."

"I'm not sure it was. Why would she drive her car out to the dunes, past her parents' house, in a storm?"

"Perhaps she was lost."

"No. She knows that area well." He paused, catching himself. "Knew," he said, and the emptiness returned, engulfing him. He was choked to speechlessness. Mechanically he resumed his packing.

"If you think there was foul play, why don't you try to find out exactly what did happen?" the professor asked.

"I might. I just might."

"Good."

Peter stood motionless, his fists clenched, his teeth tightly set. New surges of hurt undulated through his body in sharp waves. With them came complete exhaustion.

"Will you feel any better if you drop out of life?" the professor asked. "Do you suppose that is what she would have wanted you to do?"

"I don't know. I know only that if I had never known her she would be alive."

"So you feel guilt?"

"Yes."

"And you're going to run away from that, too."

"I—I don't know." For a long time Peter did not talk; he could not. A fly buzzing on the window caught his attention. His eyes felt tired, his mind was sluggish, and he was so weak it exhausted him to raise his arm. Black spots wavered before him. His mouth felt sore and dry. Finally he said: "All I know is that I'm dead inside. I can't stay here. There are too many memories."

His voice trailed off. He avoided Carmichael's eyes. Instead he saw Carol's eyes before him, the way they had looked when she had said, "God, how I love you." They had been her last words to him. Then all the days of their short life together ran before his vision like a kaleidoscopic succession of shifting pictures, vivid in color and smell and sound. They were watching a rainbow over Boston Harbor; they were wading in a Cape Cod pond, where fished jumped and booted men sought quahogs; they were lying together in the bedroom of her apartment, the scent of sex on his fingertips; they were walking in a winter woods, holding hands and spying on squirrels. "Let's run," she had said to him, and he heard her now and he was running with her. Then they were on the dunes of Chatham, smelling the sea and listening to the music of plovers. Goldenrod sprinkled yellow dots over the tangled vegetation of the marshes behind them. It was his most vivid memory of her; it was as if she seemed a part of that place where she had died. Dimly he heard Professor Carmichael's voice.

"I understand how you feel. I understand perfectly. And you should remember her. Remember her beauty, her unselfishness, her giving. But you must believe me when I say the pain will lessen. I understand that pain. I've felt it. And so have many, many others. Most adults have felt the hurt that comes after the death of someone they loved. And perhaps the guilt, too. But it is a mistake to carry it. The dead must go."

"She will never go," Peter said.

"But she has, you see. Peter, she has. You have the memories—and do treasure the memories—but she *has* gone. Don't make the mistake I made when I lost my son."

Peter glanced at him. He hadn't known Professor Carmichael had lost a son, and now he realized the professor had never really spoken of his personal life. It had always seemed to Peter as if he'd merely been there when needed, a benevolent man in a three-piece suit who peered over the rims of his glasses and smoked a pipe, a well-adjusted and competent man, a father figure sprung whole and mature with no past and no personal attachments except books and blackboards and class lecterns. For the first time, Peter saw him as fully human, able to feel and understand human emotion.

"What mistake?" he asked.

"The grief nearly drove me out of my mind. The grief and guilt. For years I wandered around like some ghost. I felt like you. Empty. Until I realized something. I was feeling sorry for myself. And I wouldn't let anyone replace that dead boy. Not, at least, until I met you." Peter looked at him. Faint tears misted the professor's eyes. "You helped me come back to life. Now should I allow you to throw yours away?"

Then Peter broke. He went to Professor Carmichael and put his arms around him, letting it out, the hurt and the pain and the lost feeling, sobbing in great helpless convulsive heaves.

Part 5

Andrew

1.

THE PRESIDENT OF the United States attended the
event that announced to the city, the state, and the nation
that the Collingsworths were now officially the proprietors of
Green Manor in upper Beverly Hills, California. Hollis had
mounted stubborn resistance to moving, but Marion had
won. She'd known she would win when she had first taken
him to the estate, for he had immediately commented favorably on the twin stone eagles perched over hanging lamps on
concrete posts that flanked the iron-gate entrance. The name,
Green Manor, was his. She had argued that the word *manor*
to describe an American estate was obsolete, referring to
feudal mansions of English lords. Yet he'd insisted, and she
had let him win the point. *Green* certainly described it, from
the massive yard off the back terrace with a view of Beverly
Hills, beyond to the palms, oaks, and peppertrees backgrounding the sixty-foot swimming pool with its terraced pool house,
dressing rooms, three gazebos, and large cabana room with a
kitchen. The purchase, which Marion described as a steal for
five million, was somewhat of a personal triumph for Hollis.
It had been previously owned by Major Victorson, a leading
producer for a rival studio who had put fifteen million dollars
into a Technicolor spectacular that had flopped. It was a crisis
sale. It had a large velvet screening room with two projectors.
With a chuckle of satisfaction and victory, Hollis had personally
addressed an invitation to the premiere of Green Manor to
Major Victorson. The R.S.V.P. came back explaining that Mr.
Victorson would be in Italy that evening.

It was much more than a party. Parties were for lower
Beverly Hills. And it most certainly was much more than a
housewarming; such events were for West Covina and the
San Fernando Valley. It was a ceremony. It was a coronation
and an inauguration. It was a display of a King. A maverick
mayor was trying to erode Collingsworth's power base in the
city and Sacramento balked on occasion, but Hollis's role as a

national kingmaker had expanded. He was the man to see now not only in California but also in several other major states. Texas called him a carpetbagger, but acknowledged his power; Pennsylvania, where he'd bought two dailies and three television stations, accepted him with only minimal resistance. His ambassadors lobbied Washington and sought to satisfy him at political conventions. He was nearing his goal of becoming the undisputed media king of the nation, eclipsing the Chandlers, the Hearsts and the Luces. Green Manor was one symbol of that power.

He had renewed respect for Marion; she understood those symbols. They had spent weeks in consultation, in conspiracy, over the guest list. It was a series of compromises, with his rejections compensated evenly by hers. He insisted some major motion-picture stars of dignity and poise be invited; after hours of discussion, she agreed upon Wayne, Peck, and Hepburn. Hollis argued for Deborah Reading, saying it would be good for business. He won only by allowing Marion to invite her parents. Exactly one hundred guests were invited, meaning that with spouses and dates, about two hundred would come.

It was a major logistical event. Marion had temporarily recruited the services of Thomas Featherington, Hollis's aide at the office, to help coordinate the undertaking, hoping she could convince him to become a permanent employee of the Manor. He was incredibly efficient, if prissy, and she needed a helper who could oversee the domestics without totally alienating them. And Featherington, most certainly, would not bother the maids.

Four accordionists and twenty waiters and waitresses were hired; three guides, briefed on the home, were assigned to show it to interested groups. It would move with the precision of a military exercise. Cocktails and tours were from five to six, dinner was served in the swim area and lawn starting at six-thirty, after-dinner drinks and mingling continued until eight-thirty. Marion, flanked by Featherington and the head butler, Fairbanks, briefed the temporary help each morning for a week before the party. The president was to pay a brief visit about six; Secret Service agents had inspected the Manor, marveling as they left.

There was much to marvel about. The home, on a ten-acre lot, had thirty-five rooms and a fifteen-car garage with a private service station. Guests entered the foyer through huge double doors, where their invitations were checked by two men in formal dress. The Collingsworths—Hollis, Marion, Andrew, and Mary—greeted them individually with hand-shakes in the marble-floored receiving room. Cocktails were served in the living room, the bar room, and the morning room; all of the servants had directions to the ladies' and gentlemen's lounges. The living room had built-in bookcases, chinois ceramic mantel and fireplace, and a stereo system. French doors led to a terrace. Doors also led to a terrace off the morning room, which had a black and white marble floor and mirrored panels. Off-limits to the guests were the two butler's pantries and the servants' quarters. A circular stair-case with a wrought-iron banister and a crystal chandelier overhead led upstairs; guests who wished to take tours, however, were asked to use the elevator. Off the upstairs center hall was the master suite and dressing room with glass bureaus, closets, and barber's chair. Hollis's bedroom was separated from Marion's by a sitting room. Upstairs also were four guest suites, all with full baths and fireplaces. There were five bedrooms in the children's wing. Under the main floor was a recreation room with a bar and bath, Hollis's private gun room, a temperature-controlled wine cellar, a playroom, and a furnace room. The real-estate broker listed it as a single-family home.

The decorations, with the exception of Hollis's upstairs study and downstairs gun room and the projection room, were coordinated by Marion. She'd insisted on the colors, reds and blues. Only the morning room remained pale. Two brass lion sculptures, gold-plated, crouched on a marble table to greet guests in the entry foyer. A marble elephant, its trunk raised, was on the table made of walnut. Marion had bought them for Hollis; they pleased him.

"Gol-*ly!*" whispered Jane Raymond as she entered the living room on the arm of Mitch Evers. "It's not real. Pinch me. I'm dreaming. Pinch me."

"I would be improper to pinch you here. I'll pinch you later."

"I refuse to believe this."

"Gin, easy on the ice," Mitch told a waiter in black.

"I'm impressed," Jane said. "You really are in, aren't you?"

She was even more impressed when the president singled Mitch out and shook his hand. Mitch introduced her to him.

"I think I'm in love," she said later.

"With him?"

"No. You."

Senator Myron Demming was all smiles and mixed expertly, but he was inwardly worried. He and Sandra were staying over at Green Manor tonight and Hollis had said he wanted to discuss Demming's political future. That could be good or it could be bad. Hollis had seemed cool to him in recent months, and Demming was concerned that he'd lost favor to a certain other national figure from California, a man with growing credentials. And he was tired. God knows, he had worked; the kids were growing up, but they hardly knew him. And Sandra had turned morose.

"Lay off that stuff," he told her.

"I've only had two."

"That's your limit."

"You're always putting limits on me."

"Ah, Governor!" Demming exclaimed, beaming. "You look in the pink. How is the state of the state?"

"In the pink," the governor said, winking.

Deborah Reading could still turn heads, even in a group that included Peck and Hepburn. She entered in a glow, escorted by Victor Levin, now a gray-haired presence with a rank of senior statesman in The Industry. But no one was much of a presence in the company of Deborah Reading; she had learned to walk with a floating motion and she smoked cigarettes through a golden holder. She handled the reception line well, shaking Marion's hand tightly and looking her in the eye.

"Count me as an admirer," Marion said. "I shall have to visit that studio of my husband's someday."

"Tell him to have it painted," Deborah said.

Levin kicked her ankle. "Don't be smartass with her," he said, pushing Deborah into the sunlight-sprinkled morning room for a cocktail. "They can still kill you, these people."

She looked at him. "We don't have any secrets, do we? We can talk, can't we?"

"No secrets, doll. We can talk."

"He's showing off that son of his—Andrew?—but I came here to see his other son."

"Oh, Christ, not that again."

"I know Peter has been in Los Angeles. Professor Carmichael writes me all the time."

"Forget it," Levin said. "Roll with it."

"I can't forget it, and you know that." Deborah's wide brown eyes, a heart melter in close-ups, were filled with anxiety, a longing he'd seldom seen in them. "Sometimes I want to see Peter so badly, to see how he's turned out, that I find myself bawling like a hurt child."

"So take the work cure."

"I'm going to take Peter someday," she said. "Wait and see."

Andrew was amazed by the attention paid to him. His father introduced him to everyone, including the president. Andrew glowed. His confidence had improved remarkably from the moment he'd looked down in triumph to see Bo-Bo groaning on the ground. His withered arm no longer rendered him self-conscious and ashamed. Mitch Evers brushed by him, asking about his left hook, and he felt a wave of affection and gratitude toward the man. He felt, in fact, the same for almost everyone there. When he was home on weekends from Stanford, his father often took him riding in the valley. They were becoming friends. He was taking graduate courses in communications and planned to continue on to his Ph.D. He worked summers in various departments of the *Bulletin-News*.

"It's almost like I'm guest of honor here," he said to his sister, Mary.

"Maybe you are."

"I wonder why."

"I think he has plans for you. Watch out."

"Why watch out?"

She sipped her martini. "Oh, I don't know. Maybe I'm jealous. You may have the best brain of the Collingsworths, but you're a little naive, too. Watch your flank."

"I like what's happening," he said. "Stop punching at me."

When the guests began to line up for food, Hollis went to his study to take care of some business. The president had left, thanking him politely for the invitation, asking him to visit at the White House the next time he was in Washington.

He sat down at his desk and dialed Hunter's number. "You went too far," he said. "I didn't want her killed."

"It was an accident. Believe me."

"Well, we're not going to do business anymore."

"We're not? Maybe we don't have a choice about that," Hunter paused, his breath labored. "We've been together off and on a long time, but now we're involved, friend. In deep."

"You son of a bitch."

"Words don't hurt me, friend. I'm too old for that."

"You bastard."

"Listen to me, friend. I saved your bacon years ago after the union hit your paper, but I didn't get too much gratitude for that. So I forgot it. Then it started to get at me, gnaw at my gut, so to speak. So I sent a friend to spook you outside the paper that night, figuring you'd be on the horn to me right off, asking for advice."

"I don't believe you."

"Then don't. But think about it. You needed me in the past and I needed you. It's been mutual. And it's not over. We'll do more business. I'm not as young as I was, but I'm still ready and able." Again, the pause; again, heavy breathing. "You're not as young as you were, either, friend. And sometimes I wonder if you'll ever be the man your father was."

Hollis slammed the receiver down, anger surging through his body. The intimidating bastard, the blackmailing son of a bitch. To hell with him; he was a nobody, a throwback. Not the man his father had been? He'd surpassed his father. He'd made the Collingsworth power grow, extending it beyond the state into the reaches of the nation. He fought for calm. He must control his temper. Anger was an enemy that drove him to impetuous acts he later regretted. It was like fear, which also addled his senses; fear had caused him to renew contact with Hunter earlier. He must be calm. He must be unafraid. Perhaps he would use Hunter again, but it would be his use of Hunter, not Hunter's of him. And Hunter was old. Soon he'd die. It would all be forgotten, lost in history.

He looked at his desk. That very act seemed to calm him. It had been his father's desk; now it was Hollis's and it was a comfort, like a friend in secret conspiracy. He kept a diary within its hidden compartments, with entries in a code he'd devised. He felt compelled to write down his triumphs and setbacks, his fears and desires. He would even write about Hunter. It was a form of confession, of catharsis. And he needed to tell his story for posterity, just as his father's papers, kept in the secure innards of the old desk and occasionally reread, had satisfied similar needs in him. Looking at the desk now, Hollis gloated in his secret knowledge.

Soon he would have to return to the party. He was stalling, and he knew why. It had been a mistake to invite Deborah Reading. The sight of her had again stirred memories. She was the enemy of the ghost that held him, guiding and inspiring him, perhaps the only person who could exorcise it forever. So he had fled here to conduct business he could have conducted at any time. Perhaps the ghost, to protect itself, had driven him here.

The phone jangled. He let the answering service pick it up; then, a few minutes later, he called for the message. It was Nathan Carmichael, whom he'd been avoiding. He decided to call him. It would expend more time and perhaps Deborah would be gone when he returned downstairs. He dialed the professor at him. Carmichael, as Hollis had expected, was very agitated.

"I'm sorry," Hollis said. And he had been, genuinely, when he'd read of Carol Kingsley's death in a Boston newspaper—sorry and disturbed. "Is Peter all right?"

"He's agreed to continue law school, but he most certainly is not all right. Someday, that young man is going to get to the bottom of this."

"To the bottom of what? It was an accident."

"I'm not so sure it was an accident."

"Of course it was."

There was a long pause. Then Carmichael said: "I want to know the truth."

"You have the truth. You told me Peter was thick with a radical student. I told you to break it up. Then you call to say you failed. They're going to get married."

"And you said, your exact words, 'I will handle it.' "

"Yes. And I tried. I had one of my lawyers contact her parents and offer a sum of money to discourage the relationship."

"You say one of your lawyers? What sort of lawyers do you have? The way her parents described it to me, it was much more like a threat than an offer. Besides, I told you they were not the kind of people who'd react favorably to bribes."

"And I reminded you, Professor, that everyone has a price."

"What happened after her parents refused the money?"

"You know what happened. The girl was killed in a storm."

"Do you expect me to believe there was no relationship?"

"I do. Because there wasn't any. I'm not foolish enough, Professor, to arrange for the murder of those who stand in my way. If you believe that I am that foolish, I wish you would resign my employ now."

"I am not in your employ."

"But you are. I'm told you cash the checks sent to you from the Swiss account. Am I misinformed?" There was no immediate response, so Hollis continued. He lowered his voice almosts to a whisper. "I want you to try and forget what has happened and make the best of it with Peter. You've done an extraordinary job with that boy and I appreciate it. He may turn out to be the best of us all."

He hung up. Standing before the mirror, he brushed his jacket and straightened his tie, preparing to rejoin the party.

Marion judged this event to be the most successful she had ever staged. She circulated gracefully, receiving innumerable compliments on her gown, her taste in decoration, and on the house, which was awesome even to the rich. They said it was magnificent, not tastelessly ostentatious as it had been, some said, when owned by the producer. Marion was pleased and she moved among her guests like the queen she had become. She ignored only Deborah Reading, who, if one was to judge by the circle that constantly surrounded her, seemed not to need the attention of the hostess. When Hollis joined her, she smiled and took his arm and they moved together.

Later, when asked to do so by a police lieutenant, she would not be able to describe in detail what occurred in the next few minutes. Much of it would be blanked from her mind. As they entered the morning room to greet guests sipping after-dinner drinks, the terrace doors opened and a dark, gaunt figure came in, a man in black. He looked at them; then he moved toward them. She couldn't remember, later, whether he'd been wearing a tailcoat or a cape. She remembered his eyes, bloodshot and fiercely sunken. He was a very old man with a gray face streaked with deep creases. She recalled that as he approached, the tinkling of glasses and the laughter seemed to fade, like the receding background in a play when the spotlight shines on the face of a lone performer, dominant and arresting.

Marion found herself recoiling, aghast. Her hand tightened on Hollis's arm. The shrunken old man stopped before them. He smiled, revealing a toothless hollow. His hands moved and Marion saw he held something that at first seemed to her like a small black iron pipe. But as he moved it up, slowly, holding it in both hands, she realized it was a pistol. She gasped. The pistol continued to come up, leveled at Hollis as he stood frozen, his face expressionless, and then the old man twisted the barrel quickly, thrust it into his own mouth, held that position for what seemed like minutes, and pulled the trigger. It didn't sound like a shot; it sounded more like a sharp pop. Yes, a sharp pop, she would tell the lieutenant, struggling to keep her voice from trembling. The man's head snapped back, spraying blood, and he sprawled on the white marble where he lay twitching, his jaws a crimson yawn, his arms outstretched. Marion heard screams and gasps, cries of disbelief, and then it seemed dark and quiet in the room. Hollis stood in front of her, shielding her from it.

2.

SANDRA DEMMING CAME awake in the darkness, aware of a headache and hands that stroked her breasts. "Don't, not now," she said, pushing away the hands.

"Come on," Myron Demming said. "I need some now."

"After what happened down there tonight?"

"Come on."

"What time is it?"

"About four o'clock."

"In the morning?"

"Yes. What else?"

He had his hands on her again, feeling under her night-gown; finally, with a sigh, she submitted. He took her on her stomach, lying on top of her back, his favorite position and her least favorite. She did not move. She lay waiting for him to finish, feeling nothing. When he did, climaxing with a small groan, Sandra pushed away from him and lay huddled on her side of the big bed.

They had been on the terrace drinking brandy when the man had pushed through their circle and entered the morning room through the French doors. A moment later, they had heard the shot. Sandra hadn't gone in. She'd stood in shock, listening to the shrieks and sounds of confusion within, trembling and watching with fixation as the setting sun spread red streaks across the sky. Later, she'd gone to their guest room, put on her nightgown, and consumed almost a pint of Bombay gin before falling on the bed. She was out until his hands had awakened her.

"Who was the man?" she asked. "The man who shot himself."

"Just some old drifter."

"What was his name?"

"Lowenfelt," he said, yawning. "Used to work for Collingsworth. Some sort of bookkeeper."

He began to snore. Sandra lay in a tight ball, stroking her throbbing temples. She felt alone and insecure and afraid. She hadn't wanted to come to this party to be again exposed to the cool, patient greetings of Hollis Collingsworth and the proud, superior airs of his wife. She was far beyond enjoying any of the affairs Myron was compelled to attend; there had been too many—many too many—over the years. She hated the campaign trail, her life as a political wife. She was always smiling and waving, struggling to keep her weight down, addressing ladies' clubs and judging 4-H contests, expressing his political views and positions on the issues whether they were hers or not. He had reduced his intake of liquor, slimming down for the next campaign, while she had increased hers. She had become a daytime and a secret drinker, an alcohol dependent, and it terrified her. Yet she could do nothing about it. He suspected but did not know, for Sandra, like most alcoholics, was very clever. He suggested all of her problems could be solved if she'd go to a month-long beauty clinic in San Diego, where forty-year-old women were subject to torturous mud plasters, diets, and exercises to emerge thirty-year-old women without worry or stress. Myron also had suggested a plastic surgeon; there *were* wrinkles, he told her. She fired back at him, telling him he could use some clinic work himself. But Myron went into training only before elections. When he did, he displayed remarkable restraint.

Yet she no longer believed in him. Once, she had thought, as he had thought, that he'd be president of the United States. She no longer believed that. She had once admired him. She now merely put up with him. Sex with him was a bore, a duty; his parties, even last night's, were excessive and mechanical. He'd become a puppet of the wealthy.

"Oh, Christ," she whispered, her head alive with pain.

Her life had become a nightmare, a hell culminated now by being a near witness to a horrible suicide. She should go back to Washington, take the kids out of school, and return home to her mother in Ohio. Perhaps there she could find some peace, some purpose to her life. But she knew she wouldn't. She didn't have the courage.

Senator Myron Demming turned on his side, snoring like a pig.

The incident had not so much unnerved Marion as it had humiliated and outraged her. A stranger had infiltrated into their midst and ruined and cursed her celebration. Marion told herself she was not a superstitious woman—not certainly anywhere like her mother—yet she could not completely rid herself of a feeling that a suicide taking place at the unveiling of their new home might at least be an evil symbol. She'd been horrified when the maids had told her they could not fully scrub out the man's blood, which had seeped into the floor where he had died. When she suggested this symbolism to Hollis, he laughed.

"I know it wasn't pleasant, but try to forget it," he said. "It's all over. The ambulance is gone, the police are gone, it's a new day. There is nothing now that can be done."

"But *why*?" she asked. "Why did he do it?"

"Some people are nuts, that's all."

But Hollis wasn't at all sure that Lowenfelt had been insane at the time of his death, although his brain certainly had been rotted by liquor. He'd been drunk, in fact, when he'd crashed the party. Hollis thought he understood it. He'd had Lowenfelt's life since leaving the paper checked out. The man, a family man, had lost three sons in the war. Then his wife had died.

His other children had grown up and left. Lowenfelt had wandered, jobless, his pride prohibiting him from asking for anything on the paper again. Undoubtedly he had begun to nurse a grudge as he saw Hollis's wealth and power grow. If you get grudges out of the way by decisive action they disappear, but if you nurse them for years they magnify. Lowenfelt also carried a guilt, a foolish guilt (as all guilts were); he'd aided and abetted two generations of a family that down deep he considered evil. After his wife died, he'd fallen as low as a Main Street wino, only to crawl out by working as a fund raiser and accountant for poverty groups—again paying for his guilt. He'd begun to drink again. His Collingsworth obsession haunting him, he'd reasoned with a liquor-soaked brain that killing himself before an elite group would drive home a point that they lived by exploitation of the downtrodden. It had been foolish. Lowenfelt had accomplished nothing. As the English gentry would say, it was bloody bad form. The incident wasn't even mentioned at lunch with Myron Demming in the morning room.

"I'd like you to consider," Hollis said, "not running for the Senate next election."

Demming's mouth fell. "But *why?*"

"Because I think it's high time you—and the party—start making the big move. And I don't think it matters where you are if you're ready for the nomination. I don't think another term will help you qualify any more. You should travel. Meet heads of state. I can arrange it and I can finance it."

"Well, I don't know, Hollis."

"I think I do. You go on the campaign trail for America. You'll come back stronger and wiser. It could lead to at least the running mate the next time around."

"*Running* mate?"

"I said at least."

Demming gestured, his face pale. "I've said before that I don't want the fucking spit pail they call vice-president."

"Somehow I don't quite believe you. Think it over. Now there's something else, something you can do for me when you return to Washington."

"Name it."

"It's in Justice there, antitrust. I merged a couple of papers a while back and they're looking into it. See if you can stop it."

"I'm not sure, Hollis. That sounds—"

"You have friends there, do you not?"

"Of course."

"I'm thinking there must be someone in antitrust who owes you a favor. There is nothing like personal contact to get a point across."

"I'll see what I can do."

"I'm sure you can do much. Cigar?"

"Thank you. Lunch was delicious."

They were ten feet from the site of Lowenfelt's suicide.

Victor Levin called the next day to submit his resignation.

"Well, send me a letter," Hollis said dispassionately.

"I've worked for cold ones before—this business, you know—but never for a colder one than you, dear ex-boss."

"Get it out of your system, Levin, if you think that helps you. You have two seconds to do so."

"Lowenfelt didn't kill himself. You murdered him."

"If you say so, Levin."

"You are a pure son of a bitch."

"Yet I kept you in lettuce for quite a while."

"You are an absolute son of a bitch."

"Levin, if you had shown enough spunk to talk to me like this when you ran the studio, maybe I would have given you a freer rein."

"I doubt it."

"Lowenfelt is dead, Levin. Roll with it."

He hung up and reached for a cigar.

3.

HE PLUNGED INTO everything he tried with a fervor that approached religious conviction. He was determined to learn by himself, from study and practice. His father had taught him to ride and something about shooting, but, he learned later, he had been taught imperfectly. So Andrew studied, learning the equipment before he tacked up his horse. He knew a curb bit, a running martingale, Weymouth bridle, bridoon, and cavesson; he learned to ride for show as well as for speed and pleasure. The accoutrements of a rugged male outdoors life began to fascinate him—spinning and saltwater reels, a Winchester Model 1400 auto shotgun, a .222 Remington magnum rifle. His father's gun room became alluring and he went there often. Since his friends knew that Hollis Collingsworth collected guns, they sent him rare items, often including literature on the models. There was a .36 Beaumont-Adams revolver, a German wheel-lock carbine, flintlock pistols, Star and Rogers & Spencer .44 revolvers, blunderbuss handguns, and various derringers. Most of the weapons were operational, or could be made so with very little work. Andrew delighted in them, spending much of his spare time classifying and tagging them. He had a dozen well-thumbed books on firearms.

He did not have enough spare time. This he regretted, for fishing and riding and hunting were accomplishments that proved to him he was as able or even better than men with two good arms. He had earned his Ph.D in communications and now he had an office close to his father's at the *Bulletin-News*. His initial duties were to listen and observe. He did that, taking notes at executive meetings. His father conducted them in his shirt sleeves, always in command.

Andrew admired his father, yet wondered if his feelings were not as much fear and awe as admiration. His father was firm, usually insistent, yet never raised his voice, never raged. If he could not discuss or demonstrate love, he could be compassionate and understanding. Andrew had almost everything he could want. He was an inch taller than his father, broad-shouldered and athletic, a high hurdles and 440 man on the track team as an undergraduate; he was handsome and intelligent, an honor student attractive to women despite his deformed arm—which, in fact, seemed to intrigue some women. He limited his sexual adventures, knowing he was a Collingsworth and therefore suspicious of womenly motivations. He conformed. He could not disappoint his father. He had been born to accomplish, to follow, and to increase; that was his duty. He had carefully read his grandfather's journal several times. It was given to him by his father, and although it puzzled him that such a document seemed an object of pride, he understood Hollis's intention that he be made to more fully comprehend his heritage in order to perceive where that heritage would lead.

He was discovering what it was like to be a Collingsworth

Some students spurned him because of his name; others, including the professors, treated him with respect. He made few friends; he suspected most students cozied up to him to gain future favors. He became, in fact, somewhat of a loner. He knew his future—to replace his father. And here was his father: a towering gray figure, a thunderclap on a steed, mighty as Zeus; a white-shirted, animated presence in the boardroom, directing and getting; a practical conversationalist in a tuxedo after dinner, mingling and driving home his views.

And his mother: A lovely woman who looked much younger than her years with blond hair and blue eyes, her gift to him, assured and confident, proud with a lifted chin and white neck, a behind-the-scenes leader in the development of community culture, who could be attentive to her offspring but let them know that there were other matters equally as important, or perhaps even more so, than them. Andrew considered her to have the grace and poise of a queen. She was not one who showered affection, who hugged or kissed, but she was one to inspire and lead. And so of course was his father—even more so. If he had not hugged his son, he *had* given him his blood. They had talked about that, but Andrew did not really begin to understand it until an incident occurred concerning the modernization program.

The newspaper was in transition from hot lead type to cold type, a photographic process that rendered several trades obsolete, including Linotype operators, stereotype workers, and some composing-room makeup workers. Although capital expenditures for the computerized equipment were high, it eliminated several steps in production and in the long run would save millions, primarily from tradesmen labor costs. Early one morning in June, Andrew was called into his father's office and introduced to an old man who walked with a cane. The man's name was F. Montrose Lukens. Andrew had heard of him. He was a maverick union organizer who, some said, still had a formidable power despite a decline due to his years. He had a creased face and hard eyes and a habit of clearing his throat before he spoke. Andrew sat down. He had been called in, he knew, to listen. His father was pacing. Now he stopped. He gazed at Lukens.

"Every time we start to make progress, you show up," he said. "You show up to spew your garbage at my men, to organize them against me, to sell them a bill of goods. And now you're here trying to organize again. But it's only for one reason. It's to make a personal comeback by tramping on my body."

"No. It is to save jobs."

"Like hell it is. It can't save jobs because there will be no layoffs. Only by attrition."

"Is that your word?"

"It's my word."

The old man cleared his throat. "I have observed in the past that your word is not very meaningful."

Andrew winced, but his father waved him to silence. "You were the one who got your way—need I remind you?—after that fire here. You wanted them to plead guilty to keep unionism dirt out of the papers. Do I recall that correctly?"

"Labor has changed over the years."

"Has it? I doubt that. If anything, it's gotten dirtier as it's grown more powerful. Look what it's done for that paper in Cleveland. I could give you a dozen other examples. No. You will not get in. You've been unable to get in and now this has become a personal goal, a vendetta for you."

"Then I have your oath that no one will be laid off?"

"You have my oath that I will handle my business as I see fit."

"You leave me little choice but to argue for unionism."

Hollis Collingsworth strolled to Lukens and bent down, his face two inches from the old man with the cane. "Go trouble someone else, old man. Know that a newspaper, yes, is a business, but know also that it is a part of the community, and your attempt to cripple it therefore cripples the community."

Lukens stood up. He tapped his cane. He cleared his throat. "The best thing you can do for the community of Los Angeles," he said, "is to sell the *Bulletin-News*." Nodding at Andrew, he left the office, walking with a dignified limp.

"He'll make trouble," Hollis said. "He wants me in a corner."

"But if there are no layoffs, how could he gain the power to organize?"

"Well, there will be layoffs."

"I don't understand. You told him there won't be any."

"Never tell anyone from labor what you're planning."

"How many will be laid off?"

"A number," Hollis said. "A number."

Andrew suspected he knew some of them, hardworking

men with families to support, using skills developed over many years. He'd met them during his own apprenticeship in the shops. Although he had realized that because of his name he could never become friends with them, he'd found that he'd liked and admired many of them. And Andrew had gained confidence during those summers in the pressroom and composing room; he'd discovered his handicap was not a deterrent to doing the work of men.

"Can't jobs be found someplace for them?" he asked.

His father was not looking at him. He was behind his desk, looking at papers. "I'm afraid not," he said after a pause. "Most of them simply are too set in their ways. I'm even afraid some of them might try to throw a monkey wrench into the computers, especially with a rabble-rouser like Lukens around. They have to go."

"But that's not *fair*! They've been loyal."

Hollis smiled tolerantly and looked at his son. "There are two sides and you can only be on one. You're on this side. It's where you were born. It's your blood. If you don't see that completely now, you will later." His voice was low and he spoke slowly, yet with a force and effectiveness that seemed to drive home his point better than if he had chosen to shout and wave his arms. "If I could employ everyone in the world, I would. But I cannot. Now those professors you've had probably told you, you have choices—and that's true. But one choice you do not have is blood. You're one of the lucky ones."

And he was lucky; well he knew it. Secretly he cursed his shrunken arm, wishing it whole, but he gave equally secret thanks for his heritage, that blood of his father. He had a quick mind, great strength, and he knew his future. It disturbed him somewhat that it all seemed planned for him, but he refused to give that much thought. He would conform. What had been given to him, and what he would become, was tempting, a head-spinning panorama without a horizon. He gladly and gratefully accepted it. But his sister, Mary, did not.

"I've been studying a new thing," she said at lunch near the paper. "It's called cloning. Something identical to yourself is formed from yourself."

"I think I detect a message coming."

Mary lighted a cigarette, a mentholated Kool, and sipped her martini. She had yet to find herself, living periodically at home, taking classes that she seldom finished. She was a dilettante, perhaps even a potential revolutionary. Today she wore blue jeans and a leather jacket with thongs. Andrew felt both pity and affection for her, a pale presence with scarlet lips and nibbled fingernails. No, it was beyond affection; it was love. He remembered her support of him when he'd been a cowering mouse on the school grounds. It also made him think fondly of Mitch Evers, who had taught him to box, and of his father, who had arranged it. Yet there was a missing element. He spoke to Mary about it.

"Sometimes I think I'd give up all he's given me for just one expression of affection."

"I'm not sure you would. Although I know what you mean."

"It's just not his way, I guess."

"You could leave all this," she said. "Go on your own."

"The truth is I like my life, what's happening to me."

"He's cloned you," Mary said. "Next he'll suffocate you."

"Lukens?" Hunter said on the phone. "Isn't he harmless?"

"Far from it. Not when it comes to me."

"How strong shall we go?"

"I just want him out of town, that's all."

"How far out of town?"

"I want him off my back," Hollis said. "I don't remember the day when he hasn't been on my back."

"All right, friend. I owe you that much."

Hollis suggested the event be held at the Ambassador Hotel, but he gave in to Marion's insistence that the staid Beverly Wilshire, which had been remodeled, would be more appropriate. He started the event while the group was still on dessert. From the podium he told about a poor boy who had arrived in Los Angeles from New Jersey, living in a flophouse and working in the rail yards. The boy's name was Thomas Collingsworth. Working with that great pioneer, Colonel William C. Dickerson, Thomas Collingsworth had nourished a small newspaper into a great one, proclaiming

"Liberty and Industrial Freedom" on a masthead with an eagle. Hollis told of their vision for the city, how their efforts had attracted millions of immigrants to southern California, helping to create new industries and the finest employment opportunities in the nation. Then he spoke of the formation of Collingsworth Communications, of its growth and expansion and diversification. And then he got to the point.

"I have spoken of the past," he said. "Now I will speak of the present and the future. We have now arrived at the main event." He looked at Andrew. Then he turned again to his audience. "I want to introduce you to the new publisher of the Los Angeles *Bulletin-News*. Ladies and gentlemen, Mr. Andrew Collingsworth."

The room trembled with a thunder of applause. Andrew stood up, slightly embarrassed, but when he looked over and met his father's eyes he knew that he was where he should be.

The edition of the *Bulletin-News* that carried the story of Andrew's appointment as publisher also carried one stating that Marion Jordan Collingsworth had been elected as vice-president for community relations of Collingsworth Communications, which Hollis Collingsworth headed as chairman, president, and chief executive officer. Another story, on page 15, said a labor leader named F. Montrose Lukens, described as a once powerful figure in organized labor, had been reported missing by his wife. Lukens had gone to dinner with associates and had never reappeared. An anonymous phone call to Mrs. Lukens informed her he was dead.

4.

A NIPPY WIND blew off the Potomac, hinting of an early winter. The trees were tinted with autumn colors. To Myron Demming, standing there alone in the presence only of God, it seemed somewhat symbolic. The nation had a chill. Atomic disaster loomed. Everywhere there was unrest. Terrorism and anarchy threatened. Looking at the gray sky, he thought of Yeats:

> *Things fall apart; the centre cannot hold;*
> *Mere anarchy is loosed upon the world,*
> *The blood-dimmed tide is loosed, and everywhere*
> *The ceremony of innocence is drowned;*
> *The best lack all conviction, while the worst*
> *Are full of passionate intensity.*

He had been raised a strict Baptist, but he'd abandoned his faith under the influence of agnostic college professors. But now it returned. It was as if he'd been born again, as if he'd had an epiphany. He knew his role, he knew his future. He was the political messiah; he was the candidate of God. He saw the patterns of the times in the visions of Revelation. He read to Sandra at night:

> And he *was* clothed with a vesture dipped in blood: and his name is called The Word of God.
> And the armies *which were* in heaven followed him upon white horses, clothed in fine linen, white and clean.
> And out of his mouth goeth a sharp sword, that with it he should smite the nations, and he shall rule them with a rod of iron: and he treadeth the winepress of the fierceness and wrath of Almighty God.

Sandra's brow wrinkled. "That's the Bible? Some bloody old book, isn't it?"

"Don't you see? Strength. We must have *strength*."

"If I didn't know you, I'd think you've flipped."

He kicked off his reelection campaign with his first wrath of God speech at an aerospace convention in Philadelphia. He lashed out with familiar themes, but delivered them with colorful allusions and metaphors that dramatized the immediacy of an impending crisis. Might is right. Nonpreparedness is suicide. The Russians understood only one thing—strength. He brought a Bible as a prop and read from it. The audience listened in a reverent hush and when he was finished the hall exploded with a standing ovation. Demming bowed before them. There were tears in his eyes.

The newspapers picked up the theme. Editorials labeled

him as a reborn William Jennings Bryan; Senator "Myron," they said, was now Senator "Bryan." Demming found his campaign contributions picking up, particularly from industrialized centers. That was the support he wanted. He was not the farmer's candidate. He was the candidate of the mighty, the producers of arms that would assure safe shores and, if necessary, obliterate the internal and external forces that loomed so threateningly. Before he had vacillated; now he had found his theme. He felt free of the forces that had guided him before, free of the Collingsworths of the world. He could now grow on his own. He was undefeated and he was unconquerable. Yet when Hollis called to ask for a progress report on that "small antitrust favor" Demming had promised, he agreed to try to help. He invited David Stumbo, head of the antitrust division, over to dinner at his Aurora Heights home. He warned Sandra to limit her drinks to two; she defied him, having four plus wine, and deliberately embarrassed him at one point during the meal.

"Myron is beginning to rule with a rod of iron," she said, following the comment with a giggle.

Mrs. Stumbo flushed and turned away. Her husband said: "I have noticed fire in his eyes, yes."

After dinner the men went to the terrace for brandy and cigars, while the women made forced conversation over crème de menthes in the living room. Demming, feeling his new force, came right to the point.

"Grapevine has it you're going to launch an antitrust investigation into West Coast newspapers," he said.

Stumbo was a little man, hardly five feet tall, and the cigar looked absurdly large in his mouth. But he had an able brain and he was a decisive trustbuster; on the Hill, they called him the Knife. One gained nothing by stalling around with him, leading up to a point and introducing it through the back door.

Puffing smoke, he asked: "Are you an ambassador for Mr. Collingsworth, Myron?"

"No."

"But he did support you, did he not? And doesn't he still?"

"He was a help. But I feel now that I really don't need him anymore. I'm launched on my own."

The little man tapped ashes into a glass ashtray. He put down his cigar and folded his arms. "Well, you can tell him that he's home free. We looked into it, yes, and there was some evidence of collusion there, but we're going to drop it."

Demming beamed. He quickly brought the evening to a close and five minutes after his guests had left he was talking to Hollis on the telephone. He had decided to play a dangerous game. His new personality called for some chance taking.

"It doesn't look good on the antitrust front," he said. "I think they're getting ready for a major investigation."

"Then stop it."

"Hollis, these things take time. You can't take a meat ax approach on them. I don't like to be the messenger who bears bad news, but those are the facts. I'll work on it."

"You do that," Hollis said.

When Sandra came into the bedroom, swaying slightly, he put his hands firmly on her shoulders and squeezed. "I want you to straighten out," he instructed. "I don't want any more smartass comments before important people at dinners, I don't want you drinking anymore, and I don't want any defiance from you in public. We're going to go up."

She glared at him. "Let go of me, you bastard! Let go!"

He telephoned Collingsworth a week later. His voice had the sound of urgency and elation. "Hollis," he said, "you're home free. Justice dropped that investigation."

"You did it?"

"I did."

"I owe you one."

"Something else. I'm going all out for the White House."

"God be with you," Hollis said.

The messiah stumped the country with his message of military power. He added new issues to his main theme, calling for tougher law enforcement and firmer judges. He backed capital punishment. His staff increased; volunteers came out. There never seemed to be enough money, yet he pressed on. He mortgaged his house, dipped into savings, borrowed from a Washington banker who owed him a favor. It was time to collect on favors. Demming also went into training. He gave up liquor; he gave up sex. He became a vitamin and health-food addict, he did sit-ups and push-ups every morning. Before major speeches, he stood on his head for ten minutes, flooding his brain with fresh blood.

He did not travel with the California delegation to the Miami convention. He went alone. Sandra said she'd join him the second day. At the airport the lurking television crews ignored him. But perhaps that was all right. He was playing this one low profile. And he'd decided something. He'd go for the spit job if he couldn't get number one; after all, such names as Theodore Roosevelt, Calvin Coolidge, Harry S Truman, Lyndon Johnson, and Richard Nixon had been veeps.

He kept the low profile, even turning down interviews, which aroused the curiosity of the press corps. He readied himself for his Tuesday address. He had caught the imagination of the people; now he would catch the imagination of the delegates. He would call for peace with honor in Vietnam, a society free of government encroachment, and military preparedness. It would be a speech of strength. He watched the descending GOP stars and mingled unobtrusively among them—Reagan, shrugging his shoulders and grinning boyishly; Nixon, a quiet party, relaxed and confident; Percy, small in stature but not in voice; Rockefeller, the big spender with his network of portable radios; handsome Lindsay and staid Goldwater and pragmatic Romney; and, yes, the inevitable Harold Stassen.

On Monday Demming went over his speech with his principal adviser, Lewis Davis, a convention strategist as expensive as he was fat. He spoke in rapid staccato, earning him the nickname of Windy. He knew how to flatter and how to persuade. He knew the delegates. And he knew the mood of the country.

"No," he said, "there's not enough for the south in what you have to say. And those boys at the Barcelona, those Texans, they are going to decide this thing."

"But we're not going to try for the top spot."

"No," Windy said, "of course not. But we're going to act like it, worry them a little. What they're not going to tolerate out there is a liberal. The glamour boys are dead in the water. Reagan's a little more than a dark horse, with Tobin behind him, but I think you'll see Nixon steal Tobin's thunder. You see, Nixon studied how Tobin did it for Goldwater in '64. No. Nixon lost California but I think he's going to win the nation. Rocky's already desperate. Did you see those pregnant women carrying NIXON'S THE ONE signs? Rocky's behind that. Jeeze! Conventions are silly enough without that kind of shit. And that ad today. Nixon and Reagan are unacceptable to black America. The one signed by all the blacks? Well, I hear Rocky paid for it. The man's finished before he starts, no matter how much money he has."

Sandra arrived in the morning, looking fresh and young in a blue silk dress. Demming had been in a tight, worried mood, but now his spirits picked up. She had apparently returned to her role as a political wife and that pleased him. From his planning room with Windy at the Fontainebleau, Myron Demming struck out, attending lavish parties, yachting with delegates, chatting with the contenders. Windy was by his side and Sandra was on his arm. His speech was a success, carried on national television, and, to the country, he was beginning to look like a candidate. Using biblical allusions, standing erect and confident, he lashed out at the rebels, the terrorists, the rioters. He spoke with force and conviction on the issues—Vietnam, communism, crime—interweaving his theme of military preparedness. An ovation followed his final sentence, which he uttered like a prayer, and he thought he could hear chants of "Demming, Demming, Demming" from areas of western state delegations. That afternoon and evening, he was swamped with requests for television and newspaper interviews. He granted them all. It was time, Windy said, to open up.

"I think," he told Sandra that evening, "we're going to have an office in the White House."

"And I think," she responded, "that I've heard that before."

"But this time it's for real. I can feel it."

She was painting her nails, preparing for a Rockefeller extravaganza. "Is that why we're followed by shadowy men?"

"Secret Service," Demming said. "It's a status symbol here. When they peel off, you've had it."

"Myron . . . ?"

"Yes?"

"Oh, never mind," she said. "Not now."

The worst day in Demming's life was Thursday, August 8. The faceless Secret Service man seemed to disappear from his sight, to fade into invisibility; with that fading also faded Demming's hope. He reacted with anger, venting his disappointment on Windy.

"What happened?" he demanded. "Where did your grand strategy go wrong?"

"No," Windy said, "it wasn't me. I thought you had a friend at a newspaper in California. Such friends the devil should have."

"What do you mean?"

"I just read it. Here. The wires picked it up."

He handed Demming a Miami paper. A front-page story rang out: "Private Millionaires' Fund Backs Demming." Demming read it in a blaze of rising anger. It credited Mitchell Evers of the Los Angeles *Bulletin-News*. The story told of a massive political fund put up by West Coast aerospace companies to support Demming. It accused him of being a mouthpiece for vested interests, advocating a continuation of the war and increased defense expenditures so the companies could sell more military wares.

"Shades of Dickie, way back," Windy said, reaching into his vest for a cigar. "And you haven't got a dog named Checkers to defend yourself."

"Get out," Demming said.

"Sure. I'll go. I think we fought a good fight. But we can't fight *that*."

"Get *out*!"

Windy left, shrugging. Demming read the story again and then he crumpled up the paper and flung it to the floor. The phone jangled, a shrill ring that cut into his forehead like a knife thrust. It was the Associated Press.

"I have no knowledge of such a fund," he said, trying to keep his voice calm. "That is all I have to say right now."

The phone rang again as soon as he put the receiver down. Someone was knocking on the door. Sandra came quietly into the room, looking pale and puzzled. When she moved to answer the door, he seized her arm.

"I'll handle it," he said. "Go back to the bedroom."

"What's wrong?"

"Nothing is wrong. Now do as I say—now."

A few electric seconds passed between them, as the telephone began to ring again and the persistent knocking grew louder, and he thought she would defy him, his final defeat. But she did obey, retreating with a frown. He answered the phone, telling United Press exactly what he had told A.P., and then went to the door. The hallway was crammed with television crews. Demming exhibited his best political smile.

"Not right now," he said.

"When?" asked CBS.

"Pretty soon. I have some calls to make."

One was to Hollis Collingsworth, and, somewhat to Demming's surprise, the powerful man answered himself.

"Of course I saw the story before it went in," he said. "I printed it because it's the truth."

"You neglected to state that you yourself contributed to the fund."

"You didn't read the story very closely."

"I read the A.P. version of it."

"Our story noted that I had once contributed and had once supported you. But I have withdrawn my contributions."

Small stabs of pain danced in Demming's stomach. It seemed as if a gray, hazy shade were being drawn down in front of him. "I'm not going to let you get away with this, Hollis. I'm going to tear you up on national television. In just a few minutes."

"I'd think twice about that if I were you."

The anger was returning. He must control the anger. "Why?" he questioned. "Why did you do this to me? For the sake of Christ, *why?*"

"Because I don't like the way you've been acting lately. You got to thinking you could get along without me. Hell, for a while you wouldn't even return my calls. I don't like a person who doesn't return my calls. You forgot that I created you and therefore I could destroy you. And you lied. You said you'd fixed that antitrust investigation, when in fact you did nothing. By the time I heard from you on it, I'd already fixed it, with one phone call to a man in an office not five blocks from yours. I don't like people who lie to me, just like I don't like those who refuse to return my calls. And I also don't like people who take credit for something they had nothing to do with. I have to hang up now. There's another paper to put out. You're our lead story."

Demming's hands were trembling. He needed a drink. He needed a pill. He fought anger and waves of encroaching panic. The impatient news seekers (he had a pretty good relationship with the press, but privately he thought they twisted news and sought sensation) were again banging on the door. He went into the bedroom.

"Come with me," he told Sandra.

"What is it?"

"I want you by my side in this. All you have to do is give the impression, with me, that we have been wrongly treated."

"But what is it all about?"

"You'll see. I need you."

The reporters descended like a pack of hungry wolves. Demming, in the beam of lights, acted coolly and confidently. He had learned to handle media. He denied any knowledge of a secret fund; he said all contributions to him were legal and recorded. When asked about the irony of this having once happened to the person who had won the nomination at the convention, Demming smiled and said: "Unfortunately, I have no doggie named Checkers." The crews switched off their lights, packed up their gear, and left. They had their pithy quote, and they were satisfied.

Demming faced his wife. His act was over.

"That son of a bitch," he said. "That stinking son of a bitch. I'm going to get his ass if it's the last thing I do."

"What son of a bitch?"

"Hollis Collingsworth."

"I thought he was your friend."

"Sandra, you are a stupid woman."

"All right. Take it out on me."

"Do you realize this could *ruin* me?"

Waving her red fingernails, she plagiarized a famous line: "Frankly, my dear, I do not give a damn."

"Did you ever?"

"Yes. I did once. But you took it out of me. No. Don't talk. You *listen* for once! I've followed you around the country, campaigned for you, raised money for you, met your political bosses and advisers who smell of gin and cigars. Once I thought you were right. Once I even thought you were a great man. But I no longer do."

He stood up. He began to pace. "Sure. Turn on me. Everybody else has, so why not you? Everybody loves a winner but they give the finger to a loser. Well, remember I am still a U.S. senator."

"Myron, I would have done this even if you had been selected for vice-president."

He stopped pacing. He looked at her. "Done what?"

"I'm leaving you." Sandra sat still, her fingers intermeshed, and met his gaze. "I'm leaving now."

Demming found himself stuttering, something he never did. "B-b-but why?"

"I won't lie to you. I have a lover."

He sneered. "A *lover*? You? Little plain Jane, she has a *lover*?"

"All right. Keep it up. Do your best."

He walked to the window. He must remain calm. It had been raining but now it had cleared and billowing clouds filled a bright blue sky. But not all was peace. There had been riots the past few days and in the distance Demming thought he could see rising smoke drifting toward him. The riots on television, juxtaposed with the free-spirited, horn-blowing delegates—the representatives of the people who had rejected a millionaire and the glamour boys to pick a two-time loser as their standard bearer—seemed symbolic, an omen to Demming. And this day had been a thunderous turning point in his life and career, a turning for the worse. He looked at Sandra.

"I won't take you back, you know," he said slowly. "When this . . . this lover dumps you."

"I will not want to come back."

"You picked a fine day to tell me."

"I didn't want to tell you now, but you started it. And I had to tell you sometime." She paused. She looked away and then stood firmly, facing him. "I've become me, Myron. I am no longer the adoring, dressed-up doll who does what she is told. I have my own mind. And I have a man I love who loves me."

She squared her shoulders. Her eyes were bright, confident. Now that he was accepting the fact he was losing her, he saw an attractiveness and value in her he'd overlooked, taking her for granted, a possession to be used in his upward flight. The blackest day of his life was ending on its blackest note yet. Just minutes ago, he'd been on top, expecting a call asking him to be running mate with a man who, despite his losing record, very likely would become the next president of the United States. Now, betrayed and abandoned, he had plunged to the bottom. The anger and frustration returned, burning painfully in his brain and flicking in his bloodstream like tiny needle thrusts. His cheek twitched. He glared at her.

"Get out of here," he said. "I don't want to look at you anymore."

Sandra met his glare with a darker one than his own. "The feeling," she said, "is mutual."

Then she was gone, disappearing with the bellman's click of the door, and Myron Demming stood alone. He clenched his fists and gritted his teeth; then he went wild, upsetting chairs, breaking the television set on the floor, hurling the phone across the room. Finally he calmed, and slumped to his knees. His head fell into his hands and he began to sob bitterly, the stinging tears of a defeated and lonely man who

had once been a contender for the most powerful position in
the world.

5.

ALTHOUGH EXECUTIVES MUCH older and more experienced than he reported to Andrew, he was not intimidated by the biggest challenge of his life. Sometimes he took
their advice and sometimes he did not. He was the youngest
publisher of a metropolitan newspaper in the nation, and he
knew he must prove the position was not merely a gift from
his father but something which he deserved. He found
himself working twelve-hour days and bringing home a briefcase at night. He had very little time for a social life, except
the mandatory dinners a publisher must attend. He joined
everything, from the Chamber of Commerce to the Rotary;
he usually accepted invitations to speak. He found himself in
endless rounds of meetings with advertising and promotion
executives, production foremen, and circulation. Andrew had
ascended to the publisher's suite in times difficult for newspapers in general, and particularly, it seemed, for afternoon
papers. Sometimes he wondered if his father shouldn't have
folded the *Bulletin-News* instead of the *Light*. Television was
making rapid inroads, newsprint costs were soaring, and the
new cold-type production system developed bugs. A composi-
tor once pushed the wrong button on yet-to-be-printed classi-
fied ads, expunging three million dollars' worth. And the
unions were a constant harassment. They told their members
not to buy the *Bulletin-News*. Pickets occasionally marched
outside its door and strikers threw rocks at its trucks. Orga-
nizers were constantly holding meetings with *Bulletin-News*
pressmen and other production workers. Recently the pressmen
had turned down union organization by a scant twenty votes.
Andrew responded by raising salaries and fringe benefits,
which squeezed budgets and cut into profits. His father, busy
running the company at the corporate level, interfered very
little, which frankly surprised Andrew. Once when he
complained to his father about the pressures he was under,
Hollis Collingsworth grinned and said:
  "What d'you want, an easy job?"

He enjoyed working with all departments, but none so much as editorial. Everything else was fairly mechanical, routine procedures repeated each day, but editorial was diverse and creative, the paper's heart and soul. A newspaper was not merely newsprint and ink and photographs; it was like a human being. And the *Bulletin-News* was a human Andrew loved. But that didn't mean he thought it perfect. The editorial policy was far too conservative—to the right of John Birch, one of Andrew's college acquaintances had told him on a recent visit—espousing Republicanism and free enterprise, views on antilabor and anti-big government, with such a fervor that it seemed sanctimonious and self-serving. It was not modern and this was no doubt a factor in a declining circulation. Andrew planned to change it, and also the graphics of the *Bulletin-News*. Its eight-column format with 7 1/2-point type was gray and unattractive. He made major changes in editorial policies, and the city and the state noticed that for the first time in history the *Bulletin-News* was presenting both sides of political disputes. He implemented all changes without his father's approval. But the biggest shock was yet to come. The eagle came off the masthead.

Marion noticed that her husband was beginning to relax. He took weekends off. He joined the Balboa Bay Club and bought a yacht, a magnificent eighty-foot craft that slept twelve and had a full-time crew of four. Hollis called it a tax write-off and a lure to advertisers; besides, he said, it was about time an old man like him began to enjoy life.

"Oh, you're not old," she said.

"Well, Hearst had his castle. I can have my boat."

He took to boating, even fishing on some weekends; he had a marlin trophy mounted in his den, where Marion seldom ventured. She went out on the Pacific with him a few times, but she was prone to seasickness, so she usually declined to go. Besides, she was busy. Funding was in for the arts center and construction had begun; Hollis's friends, tapped for contributions, called her the best arm twister in the city's history, a description that pleased her immensely. She was reaching her goal, a woman behind an important man and a contributor to the city's culture. Hollis had mellowed. Marion wasn't always positive she was right in that assessment, but she made herself believe it.

In truth, however, she lived in a slightly discomforting atmosphere of apprehension. One could even call it fear. She was not sure that her role of queen would hold sway against his as king should a confrontation develop. And she feared such a confrontation, even now; it was as if he were settling into a quiet planning period, leading later to an explosion of his wants. Despite her own growth, she was not sure she could cope with him if he returned to his old mode of possessiveness, of manipulation, of forming the lives of others. Something lurked in the darkness of his brain, she suspected, but its course and effect were mysteries to her. And she had other reasons to be fearful, more physical ones. She had been unable to shake the unnerving effects of the gruesome suicide by the man Lowenfelt that had spoiled her party. She had read that the labor organizer, F. Montrose Lukens, had disappeared and was presumed dead; Lukens, she knew, had been a bitter enemy of her husband's. Once, she had received a threatening letter, saying Hollis would die in violence after causing violence to be perpetrated upon his sons—"sons," not "son"—and when she showed it to Hollis he read it calmly and said he'd turn it over to the company's security department.

"When you're well-known and have money," he said, "there always will be a crank or two pestering you."

She could do nothing but accept that, but it didn't lessen her apprehensions. She could not escape a feeling that something was slowly building up to an explosion, or a series of explosions. Another matter bothered her. He was healthy and strong, not yet sixty, but he seemed to have no sexual appetite, at least with her. She suspected an affair. Perhaps he was again sleeping with Deborah Reading, now the nation's leading female star and a woman who seemed to grow more beautiful every year. Hollis talked constantly about selling the studio, which he owned outright, not a part of Collingsworth Communications, but he did nothing about it. If it was not Deborah Reading, then Marion was almost certain it was someone else. Perhaps several women. Hollis was a powerful man, growing even more handsome as he grew older, and very attractive to women. Marion was as concerned about his exposure in a love nest—that would be an unbearable embarrassment before her peers—as she was about her own agony and sense of inferiority over being the wife of an unfaithful man. Yet she did not confront him with her suspicions.

Just as she knew she had been good for him, she knew he had been good for her. She was a leader. The *Times* had honored her as a Woman of the Year. Hollis showed her no real affection, but he showed her respect. He remembered their wedding anniversaries and her birthdays. He'd named the yacht *Jordan I*, her maiden name. Clarence had died, a quick and merciful heart attack, and Audrey was in a rest home, an old woman with sunken eyes and gray skin who cackled like a witch and attacked visitors, including Marion, with accurate thrusts of her cane. When Marion suffered a visit to her, Audrey warned her of coming disaster. Looking at her mother, Marion felt gratitude to Hollis for marrying her and taking her away from home. She was now, she knew, as was Hollis, at the peak of her power. Yet some of her fears remained and she considered herself, at least to a degree, a failure as a mother.

"I'm going to ask Mary to dinner," she said to Hollis. "If she accepts, I want you to talk with her."

Hollis shrugged it off. "She's going through a defiant phase, that's all. I guess everybody does. Even I did. And look what Andrew is doing."

"Andrew?"

"Have you read any of his editorials lately?"

"I haven't, no."

"Then read them."

"Why don't you put a stop to it if you don't like it?"

He leaned forward, fumbling for a cigar in his vest. "Understand something. When you're trying to shape someone, you can't be too obvious. I know what I want for Andrew, but if he thinks I'm pushing, he might really revolt."

"What do you see for him?"

"Politics. Things are opening up. There's real scandal brewing in Washington."

"Politics seems . . . well, rather *grubby* to me."

"Only when you have to beg for a handout."

"Speaking of politics, Myron Demming has been calling."

Hollis's eyes twinkled. "I backed him, as you know, but when I found out he'd lied about helping me out on an antitrust matter, I stopped his clock. It helps clear the road for Andrew."

"I don't understand why you supported Demming at all."

"Tell me why you say that."

"He has that weak chin, and his eyes twitch."

"And his ass is adding lard."

"Don't be vulgar. You know I detest vulgarity."

"Now I have an eye on another one," Hollis said, blowing smoke rings. "The young man Carmichael brought here, Peter Russell. I like his style. I'm going to bring him out here for a while, look him over."

"In case Andrew does revolt?"

"He won't. He's a Collingsworth."

"And Mary?"

"Mary? Who knows? Maybe Mary is a Jordan."

About midnight Marion left her bedroom and walked down the hallway toward her study. Clara, in a nightgown, appeared before her.

"What is it, ma'am?" she asked.

"Nothing," Marion said, smiling. "I was unable to sleep so I decided I would do some work. You go back to bed."

Clara retreated. Marion went into the study, turned on a lamp over her desk, and took out a sheet of lemon stationery monogrammed with her name and address. She sat down and wrote:

Dear Pamela:

    Would it be possible for you and your daughter, Edith, to join us here

She crumbled up the sheet and cast it into the wastepaper basket. She began anew:

Dear Pamela:

    It was delightful seeing you and your lovely daughter, Edith, once again. I cannot thank you enough for the generous contribution made by you and your husband to the arts center.

    Would it be possible for you and Edith to join us here at Green Manor for a tea the afternoon of the 25th? I plan to begin about two P.M. It is just an informal group for chit-chat, and I do hope that I can count upon you and Edith.

                 Sincerely, and gratefully,
                 Marion Jordan Collingsworth

She sealed the note in a matching lemon envelope and wrote a name and address on it, first checking her address book. Pamela was the wife of a local savings and loan association founder, Richard Whitefield, who was one of the richest men in the state. He had donated almost one million dollars; a wing at the center would bear his name. Marion had talked with their daughter, Edith, only twice, but that had been enough. She would be a perfect match for Andrew. Marion had checked her background. Edith's college grades had been good, majoring in art history at Radcliffe, and there was no evidence of any deviations. She was motivated, independent, conservative politically; she was a good conversationalist with a pleasant personality. It was time Andrew got serious about a girl. Today Hollis had shown that he had not abandoned his obsessive need to manipulate; if that were so, then she, Marion, was permitted some countermanipulation.

She found herself shivering. A breeze seemed to be coming from the hallway. She looked around, disturbed, again afraid.

The arts center opened on schedule, and it was Marion's day. A giant yellow ribbon swept from colonnade to colonnade at the top of the wide marble stairs. A band played in the bright sun. Marion, flanked by the mayor and the center's director, whom she had personally selected, was the target of television cameramen and newspaper photographers as she cut the ribbon with a huge scissors. The crowd cheered. There were no speeches, except a welcoming from the mayor and a thank you from Marion. Then it was open, her dream was open. The crowd was huge, since she and the director had arranged for a first-time-ever exhibit of seven artists—Monet, van Gogh, Cézanne, Renoir, Degas, Toulouse-Lautrec, Gauguin. It was a stunning debut, although Marion considered the advertising for it somewhat gaudy. Well, she couldn't control everything; not yet, at least. She accepted congratulations from the city's power brokers as they filed past, honoring her. On the lawn, now coming up the stairs, she saw Andrew and Edith Whitefield. They were holding hands. Marion smiled, pleased.

Peter Russell was an admirer of many persons, but none quite so much as the legendary trial lawyer, Timothy S.

Lockwood, who now lived in semiretirement at an East Sixty-third Street apartment in Manhattan. Once—a day Peter never forgot—Lockwood had judged moot court at Harvard Law School. At first, to Peter's disappointment, Lockwood appeared old and sleepy. Then, in the middle of a presentation, he'd jumped up and roamed like a bear, driving home his points. It had been a marvelous performance, a tour de force; Peter found himself humbled before a master. Lockwood had disappeared before Peter could introduce himself, something he'd always regretted. He had graduated with honors and then had spent a few years as an associate in a Boston law firm, trying to sort matters out. He wanted to strike out to find his destiny and identity, yet he stalled. One day he approached Nathan Carmichael concerning Lockwood.

"I'll make an appointment for you to see him," Nathan said. "I'll warn you, however, that Lockwood isn't exactly a believer in school-educated lawyers."

"What other kind are there?"

"Ask him," Nathan said, smiling.

Peter did, seated two feet from the great-faced god two days later, a god with a lion's eyes and hair like a lion's mane. Lockwood's only concession to age was to admit he was often chilled. He wore a topcoat into late spring and donned it again in late summer, at the slightest streak of autumnal red in tree leaves. Now he wore a woolen shawl, knitted by his wife, who had died a year ago. The apartment smelled of books. Peter had come to believe that lawbooks had a peculiar smell of their own, the only book smell he'd sniffed for three years, but he detected no such odors here. These books had different, and well-used, smells. They were on philosophy and psychology, penology and sociology, history and education. The Harvard Classics filled one shelf with gray eminence. There were two biographies of Lockwood and his own autobiography.

"Oh, I suppose you could get it studying on your own today, like that fellow from New Jersey just last month," Lockwood said. His voice was still strong, although certain syllables betrayed him, showing the strain of age. "But that's rare. Today it's law school. It was different in my day. I began really to learn in preparing for cases and in the courtroom." He lifted his hands. "And—oh, I'll admit it—some of it was histrionics."

"That hasn't changed."

"What's your leaning? Criminal?"

"I'm not sure yet, sir."

"I have a name, young man, and it's not *sir*. It is Timothy." The old lion cleared his throat. "Are you going to take the New York bar?"

"Not at first. I'm going to California."

Lockwood issued a little chuckle. "I had only one case there, and it never came to trial. People still think I got whomped in that one."

"You did not get whomped. You might have saved the labor movement."

"I appreciate the comment, lad, but you've exaggerated."

"I've met that man who owns that newspaper. Collingsworth?"

"I assumed that. Nathan Carmichael was to be the judge on that bombing case. You were lucky to have him as a professor."

"Actually, I wasn't in any of his classes. I disqualified myself, since he's my guardian. But I think he was more of a help to me than any professor I had."

"He's a great man," Lockwood said.

"His description of you. And mine."

"I have not always been modest. But perhaps one of the fallacies of our culture is to associate modesty with greatness."

"Nathan Carmichael is modest."

"Ah, don't let him fool you. He has an ego like the rest of us."

Peter leaned forward. He was so awed to be seated before this giant, drinking his tea, that his words came out hushed. "The views you've expressed before, especially on criminology— do you still hold them today?"

"Absolutely."

"That the criminal, excepting crimes of passion, is born to his lot?"

"Statistics bear that out."

"It seems too pat. It seems to say that a person's fate is determined before birth."

"And, to a large extent, that is true. A man born rich doesn't choose that path. It is his luck, or his curse. A man born poor has likewise no choice in it. They cannot choose the color of their skins nor the shape of their ears. One born poor can try to lift his way up, but if he is born both poor and brainless, he has little chance. He is a prime candidate for criminal acts. You cannot hate him, because he has not had a choice. Now one born rich may on occasion opt for the priesthood or social work, repudiating his legacy, but that is very rare, because by the time he is three he has been taught that he is superior. He is already on his superior path, just as the poor is on his inferior path."

"It still seems too pat. I think people have more control."

"Your skepticism pleases me. I fully realize that I deal in generalizations. Perhaps you yourself will be influential in bringing about reforms that will invalidate my theory. I see that you indeed have a mind of your own."

"Everyone has a mind of his own."

"Oh?" Lockwood said, peering over his glasses.

"Harvard!" Mitch Evers screamed into the phone. "Good to hear you. You're in L.A.?"

"I'm little boy lost, searching for his roots."

"From your tone, I think you're serious."

"I am."

"Meet you at the Red House," Mitch said. Seated with a martini in a back booth, Peter Russell with a Coke across from him, he asked: "Why are you looking here?"

"I may have mentioned this to you when I worked on the paper that summer. I think my parents were from Los Angeles."

"Why?"

"Well, Nathan Carmichael once lived here, and, of course, he knew them."

"He also lived in New York. And Boston."

"But there's something else. Deborah Reading once visited me in Paris. She said she'd known them. And she's lived here all of her adult life."

Mitch whistled. "Deborah Reading, eh? Harvard, you have friends in high places."

"Well, I really don't know her. I've seen her only once."

"But she knows you."

"My parents, as I said."

"Did Carmichael ever tell you what your father did for a living? What his first name was? *Where* he died?"

"No. Only that both my parents were dead—died together, he said, in an accident—and that he had been appointed my guardian, drawing from a trust fund established by a benefactor. That's all he'd say. I gave up asking questions after a while."

"But now you're asking again."

"Mitch, as far back as I can remember I've had my nose in books. There always was another test scheduled, two hundred pages to study on *Carson* vs. *Mitchell,* or something like that. But now I'm free of that—well, at least after I pass the bar here."

"Why the California bar first?"

Peter shrugged. "Carmichael suggested it."

Mitch shook a Camel from a battered pack, lit it, and sipped his martini. "Harvard, why is all of this so important to you?"

"I've never told you this. I had a girl—"

"I remember. You couldn't wait to get back to Boston."

"She died," Peter said, looking away.

"I'm sorry."

"She was killed in a severe windstorm on Cape Cod. Her parents live there." Peter's eyes grew misty and his voice fell almost to a whisper, and the pain of memory that crept over his features became in part Mitch's pain. Because Mitch had been there, suffering the hurt of others. In his police beat and cruiser-car days, he'd seen the stunned faces of the sons and daughters and wives and mothers of accident and murder victims; he'd taken their pain into him, suffering it with them, writhing sleepless at night brooding about it, the gore and the anguish and the hurt of living with the wounds of the city. The police-beat reporters, cynical and alcoholic, hardened like veteran cops, told him that if it gets to you you're dead on this beat. It got to Mitch. He'd solved the problem by transferring to the political beat, where his cynicism had developed on a different level. Peter said slowly: "We were going to get married."

Mitch waved at Sally, the waitress, and after the martini came he sat silently, waiting for Peter to talk. Words could not assuage hurt, he knew. Only time did that. And, with some, that time could be long.

"I don't believe that Carol's death was an accident," Peter said, his head snapping up. "I think she was murdered."

"What evidence do you have?"

"None. But she wouldn't have just walked out into that storm. Even if she was lost, she would have stayed in the car. Somebody was trying to break us up. Her parents received a threatening call. Whatever happened, I know it's related to this riddle of my parentage. And I'm going to find out. I don't care how long it takes, I'm going to find out."

"Well, you've taken your good time about it so far."

"I really can't explain it. I was drifting. I couldn't get things sorted out."

"Do you want my help?"

"Yes, I do."

"Well, we can run some checks at the Hall of Records. If your parents did live here, there may be something on file." He snubbed the fire off his Camel into the ashtray and lit another. "It might take a long time. And it just might be impossible, since we don't know your parents' first names. And Russell. There'll be hundreds of documents under that name, maybe thousands. Why weren't you named Yturriaga?"

Peter smiled faintly. "I'm not even sure Russell is my real name."

"I don't know how I can start checking it without more information. Why don't you go after Carmichael for more?"

"I could try, but I think he'd continue to stonewall me. It's almost as if something... malevolent happened, something he's trying to shield me from."

"I'd go at him again, tell him you're old enough to face up to anything." Mitch stood up. "I've got a deadline. Call me tomorrow and we'll put our heads together on it again."

"I will. And thanks."

"Luck," Mitch said.

"Luck."

And Mitch did have some luck when he got back to the city room. In fact, he hit what he considered a jackpot. He asked Paula in the library to check the clippings under the "Russell" heading and among those brought to him was a small item with an eighteen-point, three-line head dated June 15, 1946.

Mitch read it twice, frowning. He reached for the phone. But, damnit, he'd neglected to ask Peter where he was staying. Mitch paused. He read the little article again. Somehow, it just didn't seem to ring right, but he really didn't know why. His phone jangled. He snatched it off the hook. It was Andrew Collingsworth's senatorial headquarters; the flack there was breathless with excitement. Former senator Myron Demming, trailing badly in the polls, had dropped out of the race, leaving the field open to Andrew. Mitch verified it with Demming's headquarters, alerted the city desk he'd have a story for the last edition, and cranked a copybook into his L.

C. Smith. Five cigarettes later, he wrote "30" on the last page of a six-hundred-word story, backgrounding every step of the race. A copyboy rushed the story to the city desk, almost paragraph by paragraph. Later, the slot man who tubed it to cold type said he'd caught two typos; he told Mitch he must be getting old, but he said it with respect in his eyes. In his rush to get his story out, Mitch had forgotten the Russell clipping. Now he searched through the piles of papers and reports on his desk and finally located it. He slipped it into his wallet.

Jane called at six to say she had to fill in as coanchor on the eleven P.M. news. The regular anchor had called in sick. It meant she would have to break their dinner date.

"I'm sorry, honey," she said.

"Don't be. I have a long overnighter to do on Demming."

"I *saw* that. We're crediting you on the early news. He was going to have a press conference tomorrow, presumably to announce it. How did you get it?"

"Well, we have some connections around here in the Andrew camp, you know."

"What do you think will happen now?"

"A flea could read that," he said. "Andrew Collingsworth is a shoo-in to become a senator."

When Peter called the next day, Mitch took the clipping from his wallet and read it to him.

L.A. Couple
Take Lives
In Paris Hotel

Warren and Esther Russell of Los Angeles were found shot to death in a Paris hotel room yesterday, in what police described as a murder-suicide.

Russell, 30, served in the European theater during the war. The couple is survived by an infant son, Peter.

"Does that solve your mystery?" Mitch asked.

"Some of it, I suppose. What I can't understand is why Nathan didn't tell me this."

"Maybe he doesn't know it. Or maybe he wanted to shield you from the knowledge that your parents committed suicide."

"I'm still not satisfied."

"All right. You're not satisfied. But, if you're willing to take some advice from an old guy, I'd say the best thing for you is to get on with your life and forget about the past."

"I can't forget," Peter said.

Mitch sat pondering. No. The little story didn't ring true. No city editor, no matter how soused, would have let it pass. Who were Warren and Esther Russell? Why Paris? Where was the "infant son" born? To make the paper, even a backyard suicide would have to be someone famous or an unusual caper, such as a twenty-story leaper. Even double suicides were too common to make type. So, here's a nobody in Paris who makes the paper. Something was wrong. It looked fake, as if it had been planted to sucker prying eyes. Yet he decided to let it go, at least for now. He had an overnight to bang out. Again, the phone rang.

"Mitch?" Jane said. "I'm off, after all. Did you ever go grunion hunting?"

He blazed out the story in a silver blur of typewriter keys, flipped it into the night city editor's basket, and dashed for the elevator. A March wind was blowing and the moon was fat and high. Jane was waiting in her top-down MG. She gave him a warm, open-mouthed kiss.

"That's for the story I picked up from you."

"I think the story is worth more than that."

"Later," Jane said. "And you know you're welcome, tip or not. I don't give my apartment keys to everyone, you know."

They were off, streaking down Wilshire under the moon, work thoughts behind them, carefree as children and free as the birds. Jane was animated and flushed, in a full-spirited mood for adventure. Wind played around her dark curls and her eyes were filled with excitement. They did not talk about their offices. Everything seemed attractive and humorous to them. The traffic increased on the Coast Highway and fires sparked on the beach. The Pacific rolled in a great silver wave. Jane parked and they went to the sands, their arms linked. He had a gunnysack with cooking oil and an army mess kit inside. If it was chilly, he did not feel it.

They lit their beach-wood fire and lay cuddled, watching the moon. They did not speak. Mitch felt he'd never been this close to her before. She held him tightly, her breath a tickle on his neck. In the midst of many, he felt that they were alone; all the cynicism and anger and frustration dissolved from him and he felt peace.

"I hear the spell of the moon catches the grunion," she said.

He nodded. "So they say."

"And they come in in pairs, like lovers, the female to deposit and fertilize her eggs, while the male protects her and draws attention away from her. Then they dart back into the ocean, those lovers fleeing away. Are we evil, waiting for them to catch them?"

"It may be evil, but I am hungry."

She sighed. "I suppose many people are like that, dashing in herds, risking their lives to perpetuate their species."

"Are you like that?"

"Hardly."

"But you are in a soft, romantic mood tonight."

"I want you to know I love you, Mitch. I always will. No matter what happens."

"What d'you mean, no matter what happens?"

"I just want you to know that I'll always love you."

The beach began to stir with activity. A man shouted, "They're comin'!" Mitch stood up. The man ran barefooted to the water, a sack over his shoulder, and jumped up and down in the surf. Then everyone ran. Mitch and Jane found themselves swept along. They held hands, laughing. And then he saw them, hundreds of writhing, ghostly streaks, riding the moonlit waves to the beach, squirming forms a half-foot long; not hundreds now, but thousands, mad attacking battalions of slippery, quicksilver darts. They bent down, trying to catch them with their hands, but the grunion skidded between their fingers like scurrying eels. It seemed almost as if they could slip out of their skins, or change shape from bloated to thin. Everyone was shouting and squealing; it was like a mad revel urged on by the full moon. Mitch tried everything—stepping on them, anticipating their movements by snapping his hand down inches to their right and left—but they seemed to be able to anticipate his moves with the instincts of a fly. Then, finally, he got one; he held it up by its tail in triumph. Jane laughed. She was caught up in the spirit, in the madness. She got one, then another. When the hour-long run was over, they had about thirty in his gunnysack. Mitch relit the fire, greased the mess kit pan, and filled it with their captives. The pan popped and smoked; the little fish turned brown. He handed one to her on a fork.

"Eat it all, head and everything."

"The *head*? Ugh! I won't."

"It's the way you do it. Watch."

"Ugh! Mitch, you're a savage."

"No harm. Like the goldfish in college."

They ate their fill, then lay back. The sea had calmed. The revel had died. Again there was peace.

"Where will it be tonight?" he asked. "Your place or mine?"

She was silent for fully a minute. "Mitch, look, I'm sorry but I feel I'd better get home to bed very soon."

"Oh-oh. Headache."

"No. You know I never have a headache. It's just that Mr. Collingsworth is coming to the station tomorrow and I want to be bright eyed and bushy tailed."

"Which Mr. Collingsworth?"

"Hollis Collingsworth."

"Oh," Mitch said. "I see."

6.

IN AN ERA when public trust of elected officials fell to the lowest point in American history, Andrew Collingsworth seemed a natural for quick recognition, and that he received after his first few speeches. He was testing the waters, and he found its warmth to his liking. The state and the nation, reeling in the upheavals of Kent State and Vietnam and Watergate, were searching for new faces, for new purpose—"to bind up its wounds," as the unelected president had phrased it. They were looking for innocence. That Andrew had. He could not be sullied because he'd never been to Washington. And his other qualifications were manifold. He'd proven his administrative ability, keeping the *Bulletin-News* profitable and even with the *Herald-Examiner* in circulation, if behind the powerful *Times*. The political coverage of the paper was balanced, even if the editorials did favor the conservative view. His biggest obstacle was labor, a tarnish that had been passed on to him, but he was nimble enough to sidestep severe damage, pointing to the contentment of the nonunion *Bulletin-News* "family" of employees. His education in communications had taught him how to use the media. He had money and he had connections, helping his acceptability to the party. But his greatest asset was something that could not be bought or learned. It was his manner, a sincerity and straightforwardness that appealed to audiences, especially younger people, who identified with him. When his detractors accused him of being a puppet for a powerful man, backed by a nationwide string of media outlets, he merely smiled and said:

"I'm a captive of no one. I'm not even sure the *Bulletin-News* is going to back me. There is a political editor there who is cantankerous and independent—read him, you'll see—and he doesn't like everything I say."

Andrew turned his handicap into an asset, even making jokes about it. He said it took only one hand to carry a big stick. He pointed out that many congressmen were handicapped in less obvious ways, such as a lack of brains or a sense of morals. When a would-be rival displayed his desperation by referring to him as a "one-armed bandit," Andrew said he preferred a handicap of the limb to one of the mouth. Yet, privately, the below-the-belt taunts, either expressed or suggested, hurt him deeply.

Edith Whitefield, who met him in some of the cities where he spoke, said that was foolish. She touched the shrunken arm, stroked and kissed it. Andrew guessed that he was in love with her. Marion had chosen well. Edith was a redhead with freckles, full hips and breasts; she was intelligent, dressed well, and had good instincts about people. She was spoiled, but not as much as most of the rich girls he had met. He was thankful to his mother for this gift to him. They had made love on their third date and she'd proved to be the most uninhibited sexual partner he'd ever been with. Now, coupled with her in a Sacramento hotel bed, he slowed his motion as he approached climax.

"Don't hold back," Edith said. "I'm IUD'd, remember?"

Later, stroking her naked hip, he said: "I won't have children. You know that. My father isn't exactly happy about that, but I won't chance producing another shrimp arm."

"Well, you know I'm not exactly your little-mother type," Edith said. "If I had kids, I'd worry too much about them."

"Sometimes, I really don't think he wants me to have one."

"You talk too much about your father."

"Well, he does sort of stand out."

"Andrew, what do you think your chances are?"

"For senator? Cinch."

"Aha. Overconfidence."

"I'll make it," he said. "I'm certain of it."

"You love it, don't you?"

"I've never experienced anything like it before in my life. Did you *hear* that crowd today?"

"They loved you," Edith said, tickling his chest.

They were married at the Methodist church where his father and grandfather had been married. Hollis, back in the publisher's suite while Andrew campaigned, gave them what he considered a generous wedding gift, a two-week cruise on the *Jordan I*. They had planned a simpler honeymoon at Niagara Falls, but took the cruise instead.

"To my son, the president," Hollis toasted, raising his wine glass to Nathan Carmichael. They were having lunch in the dining room at Green Manor, where Carmichael usually stayed when he visited Los Angeles. "Long may he rule."

"You're rather rushing it, aren't you? Andrew has yet to win the Senate."

Hollis winked. "Who says I'm talking about Andrew?"

"Do you mean Peter? You must be joking."

Hollis put down the glass. "Am I joking? Perhaps I am not joking at all. Perhaps it was Peter all along. Andrew, yes, but he has a drawback, a handicap. Peter is almost perfect. You have said so yourself." Hollis began to get agitated, moving his hands. White spittle ran from the corners of his mouth. "I've been thinking about it. It is a possibility, a distinct possibility. I was sincere about Andrew, but when I put him in charge at the paper, he turned against me. Did you see what he changed that paper into? Some people around here call it a pinko sheet. So it might be Peter. I think Peter can be formed. I took Andrew off the paper and let him fool around in politics, let him think he's going somewhere, just like when he was wasting time at school."

Carmichael leaned back in amazement, staring at his host. Hollis had not changed in physical appearance since he'd last seen him, over a year ago; his handsome face had a healthy flush under a brushed crop of gray hair and his eyes retained their indomitable twinkle. But apparently his mind was getting addled. Now he grinned. Then he laughed, his head back.

"Professor, I should like a photograph of your expression just now."

"Then you were joking?"

"I want you to know something." He peered at Carmichael. "I'm no longer the single-minded bastard I once was. I'm even taking some days off. You must join me one day on a cruise. And I'll admit something. I need your help. You helped me before, and I'm grateful for it. I'm convinced Andrew does have the equipment to make it to the White House, but I can't do it alone. Someone like you could help open doors for him. I'd like you to take a sabbatical from Harvard and work on establishing a national organization for Andrew. You can't get started too early on those matters."

"I'm not sure I am the person to do that."

"Well, you consider it. Bring Peter Russell into it. It would be good experience for him."

"Do you know that Peter is in Los Angeles?"

"Of course I know that. He stalled around a long time but now he's here snooping."

"He is not convinced that Carol Kingsley's death was an accident. Nor am I."

"And that bothers you?"

"Of course it bothers me."

Hollis's eyes narrowed. "I had nothing to do with that matter. It was an accident. I didn't approve of her, of course, but I had nothing to do with her death. If you don't believe that, get out now."

"It is quite too late. I think far too much of Peter to leave him to your wiles."

"My wiles? Judge, you've grown more brazen." Hollis broke into a laugh. He was feeling good; things were breaking his way. He'd just heard that old Hunter had died, a natural death in his sleep. Hunter had been the last human aspect of Hollis's legacy, a man never seen but well-known, perhaps the only person he'd contacted whom he'd been unable to control. He looked at Carmichael. "Sometimes it doesn't help to plan. All you have to do is wait it out."

"I don't think you were joking just now. You do want Peter."

"Of course I want him. He's my son. My blood."

"Your blood," Carmichael said, "but my son."

* * *

Shelton had retired as the Collingsworth chauffeur a few months after the attack on Hollis outside the newspaper. Marion, who now had a major say in hiring servants, had found Evans, a stern middle-aged man in black who was even more silent than Shelton. On a blustery day in March, he drove Hollis to Collingsworth Productions for the last time. Hollis was not recognized at the gate. The old lot brought back memories. Levin and Lowenfelt. Premieres, contract talks, deals, agents and studio flacks, emotional directors and pressing fans. Hedda and Walter and Ed. And, of course, Deborah Reading in her first hit. Had he grown old since? It was best not to think about that. Now he had sold his plaything, to a real-estate developer from Denver, for over fifty million dollars net. It probably would be torn down, rows of identical condos taking its place. But that hardly mattered; the offer had been too tempting. Marion had been urging him to sell it for years, and she had been right. The studio-contracted star system was dead, television was the rage, and the unions were murdering bottom-line profits. Let the Denver developer tear it down. He left the car and walked on the back lot unrecognized, feeling the gusts of wind. Ahead were the converted mobile homes that served as quarters for stars filming on the lot. He stopped a grip who was carrying two potted plants.

"Which one is Deborah Reading's?" he asked.

"Deborah Reading? She still around? I dunno, mister."

He went to the first mobile home and tapped on the door. No answer. Now he was determined to try every one until he found her. Perhaps she wasn't here; perhaps she wasn't making a picture. No. Someone had told him she was here; she had to be here. He hurried along in the wind, his heart hammering. It was foolish, childish. But he felt he *must* see her. Then the door to number four opened and she stood looking at him, frowning.

"I play a schoolteacher in this one," she said, seated before him inside her tidy quarters. "Second lead, but then we can't always be fussy, can we? I've never played a schoolteacher before. They'll call it the mature Reading."

She offered him a drink, which he refused. He had not seen nor talked to her since the opening of Green Manor, yet now she had received him as if his dropping in were an everyday occurrence. He never saw her movies; he never read her publicity. She had added the years well, gracefully and beautifully. He knew that he still wanted her. She still had that power over him. He closed his eyes and for a few fleeting seconds he went back, seeing them together, laughing and almost carefree. He had been closer to her than any woman he'd known and he knew he would never have that closeness again. He stood up, conscious of a pain in his back. It was not good to relive the past, however briefly.

"I hear you've sold the studio," Deborah said.

"Yes. It will be announced today."

"What will you do in your playtime now?"

"This was not play. It was business."

"And I was not a plaything?"

"You were not," he said. "You know that."

He turned away. He wished he had not come. Her words were tinged with sarcasm and slight vindictiveness, and perhaps she could not be blamed. He had thrown her away—breaking his promises to her—to live the life his good sense told him was right. It was his life's sacrifice to the dictates of his legacy. Looking at her, he did not regret what he had done, but he knew fully what he had lost.

"Have you seen Peter?" she asked.

"I have. He is a lawyer now and will be an extremely good one."

"Do you see him much?"

"When I can."

"I think he would be better off if you stayed away from him completely."

"What I do with Peter is no concern of yours. I seem to remember that you elected to make movies and leave the boy to me."

"Well, I most certainly haven't forgotten him."

"My advice is that you do forget him."

"But I won't. I can't."

He changed the subject. "How is Sarah?"

"Sarah has gone home. She never liked it here, as you know."

"Nor did she like me."

Deborah looked at him, a small frown on her lovely features. He felt a surge of sexual excitement. "Sometimes I think I never liked you either, Hollis. I was in love with you, but I'm not sure I liked you."

"You liked something about me, I'll tell you that. When is your cue? Do we have time for a little fun?"

"Get out," she said. "Don't come back here."

He dialed his television station from the Cadillac, asking for Jane Raymond. "Meet you about seven tonight?" he asked. "Yes, the same place."

Mitch Evers had a way of finding things out, and when he began to suspect Jane was having an affair, he went after the truth with the fervor of a tracking bloodhound. A number of incidents aroused his suspicions—dates canceled at the last moment, excuses for not having sex, flares of anger over small matters, her criticism of his clothing or table manners (both of which, admittedly, were not the best). He did not confront her with his suspicions; instead, he investigated. He became neurotic about it. Once he even searched her apartment for evidence while she was on television. He found nothing. Yet his emotions raced. His productivity at the office declined. He was drinking more. Only now, when he suspected he might be losing her, did he realize how much she meant to him. When he discovered the truth, he sat stunned in disbelief. A buddy in the public-relations department at the telephone company told him several of her outgoing calls were to a private line in Hollis Collingsworth's Beverly Hills home.

Mitch, his emotions drained, decided it was confrontation time. He had three doubles at the Red House and drove to her apartment. He let himself in with a key she had yet to ask him to return, and he waited. The door opened about nine P.M. Jane gasped.

"Mitch! You scared me half to death. In the future I wish you'd call me before you come over."

"There won't be any future," he said.

"What do you mean by that?"

"I'm not very good at sharing."

"You are also drunk."

"I am not drunk. I will be drunk tonight, but I'm not drunk now. I know you've been seeing Hollis Collingsworth."

"Oh? How do you know? From a peephole?"

"Is it true?"

She walked slowly across the room, her head high, not

looking at him. She put away her coat, closed the closet door, and stood with her hands behind her back.

"Yes," she said, her eyes meeting his. "It's true."

"How long has it been going on?"

"A few months." She gestured, palms up. "I was going to tell you, but I just couldn't get it out."

"You're a fool, do you know that? When he tires of you, you'll find yourself thrown in a dung heap. You're in way, way over your head."

Her eyes glared. "What I do is my own business. Just because we've gone together doesn't mean you own me. Mitch, sometimes I think you're the most possessive man I've known."

"No. You're going to bed with the most possessive."

They stood staring at each other. Her jaw trembled and her lips began to twitch. "I don't know how it happened," she said. "God, how I wish that it hadn't happened."

"Then get out of it. Break it off."

"Mitch, I'm not sure I can!"

"Sure you can. Just call him. Call him on his dirty little private line."

"So that's how you found out? Does anyone else know?"

"No. It was my personal business to find out."

"I've told you before, Mitch. I am not your private possession."

"Are you his?"

"No. I belong to nobody."

His voice softened. The anger he'd felt, building up in him as he'd waited for her in the dark, not knowing what he'd do, seemed suddenly to leave him. "I loved you," he said. "I still love you and I always will."

"And I love you. You know that."

"Then *why*?"

"I don't know. I really can't explain it. There is something about him that draws you to him like a magnet. He is absolutely the most awesome man I've ever known."

"You're a pawn," Mitch said. "We all are. All his pawns."

"I won't be able to explain it to you, Mitch, because I can't explain it to myself."

"Don't try. I'm going to get a drink."

"Wait. Stay with me. Just a little while." She clutched her hands to stop the trembling, and Mitch felt a wave of pity for her. "I'm so strung out!" Jane said. She looked at him, her eyes seeming to plead. "Mitch? Come here? Hold me."

He did, tightly, and soon he realized that she was crying. He had never seen Jane cry before; he had thought her incapable of showing emotion. She trembled in his arms, her chin on his neck. He found himself beginning to choke. The phone rang and she broke away from him with a small gasp of astonishment, almost as if she were afraid. Then she answered it. The call, from the office, was for Mitch.

"Oh, Christ," Mitch said. "When?" He cupped the receiver and said to Jane. "Any coffee? I need some coffee." Then he listened. Finally he hung up.

"What is it?" Jane asked. "Mitch?"

"Collingsworth," Mitch said. "Somebody got him."

7.

LABOR TROUBLES HAD developed at the newspaper almost immediately after Andrew began his campaign for the Senate and Hollis reassumed the post of publisher. The pressmen, on their third vote, had agreed to unionize. Hollis, feeling betrayed, angered because he'd granted concession after concession to keep out unions, countered by ordering an immediate cost-of-living raise for all employees who were not covered by union contract. The pressmen found themselves earning less than cold-type punchers and makeup personnel. There was unrest, strike rumbles, written protests, and, one morning, the pickets again appeared. Hollis feared labor unrest more than any other single occurrence; vivid in his memory was the holocaust of the bombing. He sent his representative down to talk with the union organizer, authorizing retroactive pay increases if the pressmen would reconsider their union vote. The organizer had no choice except to present the proposal to the rank and file. He did; they voted the union down. Hollis chuckled in private and in public. He had defeated labor again.

The ploy went largely unnoticed. But one person most certainly observed it, a man with a twenty-five-year prison record, a leaky eye from a beating by a guard, a single suit that was tattered and stained, and an old body racked with arthritic pain. Donald Sheehan had gone to prison an idealist who advocated violence only for a cause, but he'd left it a hardened cynic monomaniacally bent on revenge. He had submitted to the outrage of homosexual assault, had suffered verbal and physical torture from sadistic cellmates, and had held the pathetic, skin-and-bones body of his brother in his arms as he died of pneumonia. Each day and week and month and year, the name Collingsworth was burned more deeply into his smoldering consciousness. Sheehan had lived, had suffered to live, for one purpose only. Vengeance. His body was dead, but his mind was alive. He could plan. He operated out of a roach-infested hotel room on Main Street, a dirty room permeated by gag-stench odors from absorbed vomit and urine and perhaps even feces of past inhabitants, but he did not consider it as dehumanizing as his cell. Even to the lost men who wandered on Main, he was a particularly menacing figure, limping like a disembodied apparition with a crooked eye and an age-splotched face. When he visited Mickey Ryerson, a union fire starter in the old days who was now living at a rooming house near Hill Street, Mickey gasped and closed the door in his face.

"It's me—Don," Sheehan said. "Sheehan."

Mickey opened the door a crack. "Don? You out?"

"Been out awhile."

"What'd they *do* to you?"

"Tried their best to kill me, that's what they did."

"What d'you need?"

"Let me in, I'll tell you." When Mickey did admit him, Sheehan came to the point quickly. "I need a vial of acid. Strongest stuff you can get your hands on. Stuff that'd blind a man."

"What'cha got in mind?"

"You'll read about it."

"I don't read. You know that."

"Then you might hear about it." Sheehan paused, rubbing his oozing eye. "Wal, I'll tell you. Collingsworth. Who do you suppose put Mr. Lukens in cement? Collingsworth, it was. Oh, I keep up. Even up in the can, I kept up."

"I'd take another think before I went after Collingsworth. He's got an army of guards, Christ sake."

"I'm going after his blood. Get his blood, get him."

*   *   *

Andrew was invited to speak before the Young Republicans Organization at Roger Young Auditorium, a signal honor, for it was clear the party was searching for new leadership. He had planned his usual address, words that had given him the reputation as a liberal Republican—calling for a balance between government regulation and free enterprise, outlining a program calling for budget cuts yet continued entitlements, advocating price controls as a weapon against inflation—but he detected a resistance in his audience as he started, so he quickly switched his course. It was his first act of political duplicity; he did not, at least not yet, fully believe in what he would here advocate. He said it nevertheless. And, as he spoke, he felt himself changing, growing. It was a delicious, mind-stretching experience. He told himself that it was a return to truth. He had resisted parental teachings, his heritage, when he had balanced political coverage at the newspaper and afterward when he was trying for the Senate. But always an inescapable voice had whispered within him, pulling him back to the path that he knew had been set for him. His ambition, growing daily, was defeating his rebellion. So he told the Republicans what they wanted to hear. He said business should be free, the marketplace should regulate prices; he called for union restraint in wage demands and outlined a program to reduce government waste. Ripples of applause followed each time he drove home a point; and when he finished, the audience was on its feet, cheering. Andrew found that his eyes were moist. Hollis Collingsworth, inconspicuously crouched beside Nathan Carmichael in the third row, led the applause.

Andrew preceded the question-and-answer session with a joke about the Nobel Prize-winning professor on the lecture circuit whose chauffeur said he'd listened to the lecture so many times he judged that he could flawlessly deliver it himself. The professor thought that a capital idea. So they switched uniforms, the professor-chauffeur at the back of the hall, the chauffeur-professor at the lectern. He delivered the address perfectly, received a thundering applause, and then was asked to answer questions. The first was not a question, but more of a lengthy challenge, putting the fake professor on the spot. But the wily chauffeur was up to it. "That is the most stupid question I've ever been asked," he said. "It is so stupid, in fact, that I'm going to ask my chauffeur in the back there to answer it."

Andrew's audience—his captives—roared.

His spirits were high. He felt absolutely confident. He had been accepted; it was as if he'd returned after confused wanderings. He launched into the question-answer session with vigor, parrying challenges, driving quickly to his point. Then Andrew detected a strange difference in the atmosphere; his audience had hushed, and a murmur slowly rose. A man in front stood up, pointing to the stage. Andrew had been so caught up in the give and take, in the spotlight, that he failed to see the figure entering the stage through a side curtain until the man was only a few feet from him. Until it was too late. He turned, facing the intruder. He froze. It was an old man with a pale, creased face and one eye hanging crookedly below the other, his lips curled over his black, rotting teeth in an animal snarl. His hand snaked forward, dashing liquid into Andrew's eyes. Blinding pain struck him and he sank slowly to his knees, his elbow over his forehead. He was conscious of a rumble from the crowd, intermixed shouts that seemed to rise and echo off the ceiling and the walls. He heard a loud trample of shoes. He heard a woman's scream. He was slipping away in darkness, and amid the horrible pain, he thought he could hear laughter, strident and cackling, as if the demons of hell were calling to him.

Fairbanks drove Marion to the hospital, where she pushed past a group of reporters and television camera crews, and into a white-walled private waiting room. She had wanted to hear Andrew's speech, but it conflicted with a charity ball from which she'd been unable to escape. Now she was privately thankful that she had not gone to hear Andrew; it would have been too much to bear. Blinded. The radio had said blinded. It had not hit Marion yet, not the full force of it; she walked in a numbed daze, her body cold. Hollis and Professor Carmichael were in the waiting room, seated at opposite ends of the couch. They stood up when she entered. Hollis took her arm and led her to a chair. It was only then that she felt it. Her hands were unsteady, a queasiness undulated in her stomach, pain pulsated in her forehead. Tiredness overwhelmed her. She was too weak to move.

Mary, whom she had not noticed, rose from a chair and took her hand. Marion looked up at Hollis.

"H-h-how did it happen?" she managed.

"Some labor agitator, some crazy bastard from the past," Hollis said. "He was behind the bombing."

"Do you want to lie down?" Mary asked.

"No. No, I think I'm all right."

"The doctor will be in soon," Hollis said. "There's some hope it's not as bad as we first thought."

Marion tried to talk, but her mouth was so dry no words came out. She closed her eyes, avoiding a light so dazzling that it hurt. Labor agitator. From the past. From the bombing. She opened her eyes and slowly raised her head.

"You did it," she told Hollis.

He said nothing. He turned away.

"You!" Marion screamed.

Hollis said calmly to Nathan Carmichael, "Would you excuse us, please?" and after Carmichael had left, he kneeled beside Marion and put his hand over hers. She pulled away. "You're emotionally drained. You don't know what you're saying."

"I think that she does," Mary said.

Hollis whirled. "Stay out of this. Stay out of it."

"Why should I? I'm a part of this family, I am sorry to say. I have its curse, too."

He stepped to her, drew back his hand, and slapped her sharply on the cheek. Mary gasped, her eyes flaring, and tried to strike back, but he had her hands and held them tightly together. Their eyes met, a mutual blaze of anger, perhaps even of hate, and then he let go. He turned away, sighing.

"You did it," Marion repeated. "You did it with your pushing and your manipulation. That person was only an instrument."

"All right, Marion. Do your best."

She tried to get up, to lash out at him, to strike him down as he stood there, a dark form wavering above her, reacting dispassionately and calmly to this horror. But she did not have the strength to rise.

A doctor in blue entered, his face grim.

Andrew had a dream. He dreamed he was addressing an audience of the blind. His own eyesight was impaired, but he could make out tones of light and flickers of color in the crowd. He spoke of courage in overcoming a handicap; he was an evangelist of optimism, and a healer. Applause interrupted him. The blind cheered him, their champion. His eyes filled with tears. He was a leader, and he was loved.

PART 6

The Grand Design

1.

THE STERN SERVANT, a tall, thin man with enormous bushy eyebrows, gestured Peter Russell into the foyer of Green Manor. Peter stood in a hushed and almost reverent amazement, knowing he'd been admitted to a world the likes of which he'd never before seen nor even thought existed. "If you will follow me," the servant said, "Mr. Collingsworth will see you now." Peter followed—past the circular staircase, under the giant chandelier, across the marble floor of the morning room, to a living room that seemed to have limitless space. A fire crackled blue flame in the hearth. The strains of Tchaikovsky's *1812 Overture* rose from the stereo, so quiet they seemed to come from another room. Hollis Collingsworth sat deep in a leather-bound chair, encased in cigar smoke. He rose, dismissed the servant, and shook Peter's hand.

"Hope you don't mind the music," he said.

"No. Of course not. It's one of my favorites."

"It's my *absolute* favorite. I can't wait for those fucking cannons to explode. Can we get you anything? Sherry? Brandy? How about a cigar?"

"No, thank you."

"Never forget when my father gave me my first cigar. I got sick as a dog." He eyed Peter, his eyes sunken but bright under a shining thatch of gray hair. "Well, enough chit-chat. Sit down. Let's talk. Let me look at you."

Peter sat down obediently in a big chair across from Hollis. The chair seemed to absorb him. Everything in the room, in fact, seemed larger than normal life. The Tchaikovsky overture grew louder, falling and rising in a growing crescendo. Hollis listened, his fingertips joined and his thumbs under his chin. Then the music quieted.

"I haven't had much time to get acquainted with you over the years, but believe me, I've kept a distant eye on you," he said slowly, tapping a long ash off his cigar. "You've turned out to be a fine specimen. The judge has done his job well."

"The judge?"

349

Hollis grinned, revealing even, tobacco-stained teeth in a strong ironlike jaw. "I've always thought of Carmichael as a judge. I suppose, to you, he's a professor."

"I regard him more as a father," Peter said.

"I suppose that you would. He is your official guardian, of course. You see, your parents were very special people to me. So is the judge. So I asked him to look out for you. I'm sorry I haven't paid more personal attention to you. That was my mistake."

Again, the pounding strains of the overture rose in the room, permeating it for a moment. Something in the man's face caught and held Peter, almost in a hypnotized spell. He did not know what it was. Perhaps the eyes. Hollis Collingsworth was, then, his benefactor, something he'd long suspected but only lately began to realize for certain, and he felt a wave of gratitude that such a busy and powerful man would have taken such an interest in him. Yet there was much he wanted to know, unanswered questions that had haunted him since childhood. This man, he suspected, had many of the answers.

"Can you tell me about my parents?" he asked.

"I will, later," Hollis responded, snapping the words out. "Right now, there are more important matters. There is you. What are your plans for the future? What do you want to do?"

"I've been thinking about criminal law."

Hollis snubbed out his cigar in a huge ashtray, producing a shower of red coals. "Criminal law is for bleeding hearts or those who get their satisfaction through persecution. I rather think corporate law would be best suited for you. At least as a start. Does politics interest you?"

"Somewhat, yes."

"I suspect you're a flaming liberal."

"I'm afraid so, Mr. Collingsworth."

"Well, you're young. Ideas change." Again he smiled and his eyes caught Peter's, holding him. "I'd like you to move in here, take a room upstairs. Carmichael is staying here for the summer. Maybe we can put our heads together and scheme out something for you. Would you like that?"

"I—I think I would. Thank you."

"If you've never been riding, I'll take you. We have a ranch in the valley. And we all just might be going off on a yacht trip soon. You'd like that."

Peter left. The meeting had not answered his questions; it

had merely posed more. Well, he would move in here, seeking the answers, the truth. But, walking through the house behind the obedient and silent servant, he wondered if the magnificence of the place would not addle his mind and sway his purpose. It also seemed strange to him that Hollis Collingsworth had not mentioned Andrew. Perhaps it was too painful; of course, that must be the reason. Peter felt a wave of pity for him. And he felt, for himself, that he was entering a new life.

It *was* painful for Hollis Collingsworth. Something he had created and nourished had been stricken down, in effect destroyed, and it was as if a part of him had been destroyed. A dark force from his past had risen up, smiting the son to smite the father. But he would not blame himself. That would be foolish. His plan, his grand design, had been interrupted, but he would not surrender it. Now, Tchaikovsky's music rising around him, he sat in his big chair and chuckled. Peter was the one; perhaps, as he'd said to Carmichael, Peter had always been the one.

Andrew had come home, spending most of his time in his room, sometimes roaming below in the gun chamber. He did not speak. A male nurse had first accompanied him, but Hollis quickly fired him as incompetent. The best ophthalmologists had examined Andrew; all had dismissed his case as hopeless, beyond even the powers of laser surgery. Beyond Collingsworth's power. Hollis accepted it. Marion blamed him, of course, and he didn't defend himself. They lived in cool aloofness of each other. She had an office at the *Bulletin-News*, but she seldom went to it. He did not know what she did with her time, nor did he care.

He remained active, resuming his duties as publisher. Never before had he felt more strength or purpose. His health was excellent and his sexual appetite so massive that it amazed even him. When he'd been young, his sexual drive had been fumbling and experimental. He had sought some form of affection. Now he sought only satisfaction; he wanted only to conquer. It did not matter that Marion no longer would accommodate him. Others would. They, in fact, sought him. He took only those who were discreet, those who would not demand. He kept women in apartments around the city. Sometimes he took taxis to their places and other times his chauffeur, the taciturn and faceless Evans, waited for him in the Cadillac while he was being serviced.

He was still writing it down, compulsive words that flowed smoothly from his pen, his journal like his father's, which he had presented to Andrew long before the blinding. Andrew had not commented about it. Hollis could not explain why he kept his own journal—it was, in fact, incriminating—yet he knew he was compelled to do it. He knew it was safe, locked in secret compartments of his desk, itself behind the locked door of his study—where no one, including servants, dared to venture. That night he wrote about his plans for Peter Russell; and, as he wrote it, the plan, the grand design, became even clearer to Hollis Collingsworth.

Nathan Carmichael, who had now moved into Green Manor, confronted him one afternoon about those plans. "That's my secret," Hollis said. "Your job with Peter is over. You did it well. I'm proud of that boy."

"Since he's been here, I've already seen changes in him."

"Good."

"I'm not so sure it is good. I think, in fact, he's being manipulated, just as you manipulated Andrew."

Hollis scowled. "All right, Nathan, you're a guest in my house but that doesn't mean we can't talk frankly. We always were able to be open with each other. What's on your mind?"

"I want you to let Peter go."

"All right. I'll let him go."

Carmichael fidgeted, raising and lowering his glasses, clearing his throat, brushing the sleeve of his coat. Hollis suppressed a chuckle. The professor had become a dark-suited old man who walked with a cane, a white-haired shadow whose voice sometimes cracked and whose eyes often assumed a far-off expression. They were on the terrace near the morning room, overlooking the vast green lawn. It was a day full of sun, warming Hollis and reminding him of his strength.

"Well," he said, "at least perhaps you'll allow me to take the boy on a cruise we're planning later this month. You come, too. Even Myron Demming is going to come. That old bastard is after me again."

"I can't stop Peter from doing as he wishes," Carmichael said.

Hollis sprang up. He paced. Then he stopped. "No. You

have said the exact truth. You cannot stop him. Nor can you now offer him much more. What can you offer him?"

"Perhaps his soul," Carmichael said after a pause.

"His *soul*?" Hollis threw back his head and laughed. "*Soul*? Can you define that? I believe you cannot." Again he paced, stopping only to gesture as he made a point. "What else besides this mystic soul can you give him? Can you give him money, position, importance?"

"If I told him who you are, I believe he would listen to me."

"Then why haven't you told him?"

"I—I haven't had the opportunity."

"You haven't had the *opportunity*? My dear old judge, you've had nothing but opportunity. May I tell you why you've kept your mouth shut? It's because if you tell him now, he'll think less of you."

"No. That's not the reason."

"Besides," Hollis said quietly, "he would come to me anyway. You see, I've already explained it. It's blood. Between environment and blood, I believe in blood." He continued to pace, more rapidly than before. "I don't think you can stand in my way, Judge. Say anything you want to Peter, I still think he'll be mine. And that, you must admit, is not a bad position to be in."

"He has a choice—"

"Not much of a choice," Hollis said.

Edith had also moved into the Manor, to be with her husband, but she didn't show much of a propensity to do so. She spent most of her time in the pool. One day Marion found her packing.

"You're leaving?" she asked.

Edith looked away. "Well, it's just that there is so much to *see* in the world." She caught herself. "I'm sorry."

"Just about everyone else has deserted him. You might as well, too." Marion motioned. "Please get out. I'll admit I made a mistake about you. Will you leave right now?"

"Sure, if that's the way you feel about it," Edith said.

Marion decided to confront her son. Her own life had once changed on advice from her father, but Andrew no longer had a father to give advice. So Marion took it on herself. She tapped on Andrew's door late one afternoon and quietly entered his room. He sat near the window, in a robe and dark glasses. He didn't move.

"I wish you would eat dinner with us," she said.

He was silent.

"Andrew, I really would like to talk with you," she said.

"Why did you send Edith away?" he asked without turning.

"I didn't send her away. She wanted to leave. I don't know what she told you, but it was probably a lie." Marion advanced cautiously. "Andrew, I don't think you'll like what I'm going to tell you, but I'm going to say it nevertheless. You have a simple choice. You can mope around and feel sorry for yourself or you can get up on your hind legs and yell. Do you want to yell?"

"No."

"I think you do. Let it out. Yell your head off. I think it will make you feel better. Then get off your backside and join humanity again. We will welcome you."

She left quietly, wondering if she had done the right thing.

With the master and the mistress of the Manor in a silent feud that promised no armistice, Featherington took full command of the servants, and the rituals of the place became almost militaristic. When lesser servants complained of the new discipline to Marion, she refused to take sides; she'd always considered servants somewhat childish, and she was happy to let Featherington handle them. He was thin as a scarecrow and walked with an awkward, ostrichlike stride, but he most certainly got things done. Also, he never tried to pry into Manor business. Nothing aroused Marion's ire more than a snooping servant. She was sure the rest disliked Featherington, regarding him as a privileged snob, but they did what he told them to do. Dinners were served precisely at seven; even the master received a scornful gaze if he arrived late.

There were now two guests, Peter Russell and Nathan Carmichael, and Mary Collingsworth had appeared at the Manor several weeks ago, asking not for her parents but for Andrew. With the master and the mistress, Featherington knew he could expect five for dinner. Andrew never appeared; he took dinner in his room. The meals often were passed in silence, sometimes tense silence. It was more of a ritual than a meal, people who seemed unwilling to reveal themselves to each other; it was enlivened only when Hollis Collingsworth was served a dish he didn't like, which could result in a tantrum.

One Saturday just before dessert was to be served, the French doors opened and Andrew appeared, wearing white slacks and a blue turtleneck sweater. Thick dark glasses covered his eyes. He stood there, gazing. Featherington fumbled in consternation. Mary rose, went to her brother, and led him to the table.

"Bring him a setting," she told Featherington.

"No, I'm not eating," Andrew said. "Who do we have here? Mother? Father? Professor Carmichael? Is Peter Russell here?"

"Yes, he's here," Hollis responded.

"I understand you're planning some extensive yachting," Andrew said. "Does one need a written invitation?"

There was a short silence. Then Marion said: "Of course not, dear."

"Will you go, Mother?"

"Well, I hadn't planned to go." She reached out to touch his hand, but Andrew pulled away. "I will go if you wish, dear."

"I've heard it will rain tonight," Andrew said. "Isn't that exciting news?"

"Andrew . . ." Marion began. Her voice trailed off.

Andrew touched Mary's hand. "I'll bet I still can outswim you. I'll bet I can outswim Peter Russell, too."

"No doubt of it," Peter said.

"Featherington, we'll take coffee in the living room," Marion said.

2.

LIKE MANY WHO try to use others for advancement, Jane Raymond found herself being used. It had started innocently enough; it was thrilling to her that Hollis Collingsworth himself singled her out, calling her "my discovery." Then there had been a few dinners at the Bistro, always with the station manager present, and, inevitably, the dinner between the two of them. It was at an inconspicuous Italian restaurant on Melrose Avenue. The waiter had recognized her, but not him.

"That's the way I want it," he explained. "I am not a star. I don't want to be. I create stars."

"So I hear, Mr. Collingsworth."

"Hollis. Around the office, use my last name, but not here." He peered at her, an extraordinarily handsome man with silver-gray hair and piercing eyes, a man with such vitality and magnetism that it seemed to sparkle around him like electricity. Here she was, the little eastsider who averaged three fights a day going to and coming from grade school, with a German mother pregnant with gloom and an Irish father who always had whiskey on his breath and seldom bathed, seated at a clandestine dinner with one of the city's and perhaps the state's most powerful figures. Hollis asked: "What is it that you want? More than anything?"

"Network anchor," she said without hesitation.

"What people do you admire?"

"Here? Connie Chung. Nationally, Barbara Walters."

"No men?"

"The network anchormen seem to be wearing out. We all admire Walter Cronkite, of course, but you have to consider him somewhat of a fuddy-duddy."

"How about the ancient bird you see before you now? A fuddy-duddy?"

She smiled. Her smile, she knew, was her greatest asset, and she practiced it before mirrors, perfecting it. "Hardly," she said.

"I don't have time to beat about the bush. I'm interested in you. I want to warn you that I am very married, however."

"Are you hitting on me, Mr. Collingsworth?"

"Hitting on you? Is that how they say it now?"

"Yes."

"Then I am hitting on you."

"I don't sleep with people I work with, especially those I work for."

"A good rule. But break it."

She felt flattered, yet slightly nervous. "I do have a boyfriend, you know."

"Mitch Evers."

"Yes."

"Are you going to marry him?"

"I have more respect for him than anyone I've known. He's been very considerate and helpful. But, no, we'll never be married. I'm not sure he has all that many good years left in him. But I love him. I love him like a—"

"Like a father?"

"No. Not like a father, nor like an older brother. I love him as a man. But I don't think it would work over the long run. He lives his life in . . . well, too much heat and fury, and I think he'll burn out. I don't want to become a nursemaid again. I ended up being a nursemaid to my father after my mother died."

She paused. Perhaps she was revealing too much of herself. This man before her was, actually, a stranger to her. Yet she found she could talk to him. Again, looking into his eyes, she felt his drawing power. It was not totally physical. There was something about him that was almost boyish, a haunting loneliness that attracted her. Her father had told her, his deathbed wisdom, to use everything that she had; men had done that, he said, throughout the years and perhaps now the age of women was dawning.

"I want your answer now," he said.

"I—I simply don't know, Mr. Collingsworth."

"Hollis."

"Hollis."

"No one will know. It's between us."

She squared her shoulders. Her nipples tightened in an arousal she had never felt merely seated across from a man. She said: "All right. I guess it's true. You only go around once in this life."

So it began, that night in a Pacific Coast Highway motel room overlooking the ocean. It was to become their point of assignation, meeting at least one night a week. Hollis proved to be extraordinary, and, unlike most men she had been with, including Mitch, he left her drained and relaxed. He was so big that at first she feared she couldn't accommodate him, but when he rolled on top of her, his hard smooth body heavy with a viril man's smell, she opened up to take him with ease, climaxing immediately and again five minutes later.

"God," she said, lying beside him listening to the ocean. "Oh, God."

"We're a good fit," he said.

"And, from the looks of things, you're not through yet."

"Turn over on your stomach. Right now. *Now!*"

She had his private numbers, both at the office and home, and did not hesitate to accept his invitation to use them. Within a month, Jane felt herself gripped by an anxiety that approached fear. She wanted to see him more than the time he had available. Her nerves crawled, wondering where he was, causing her to flub some lines on television. It was now an affair, full-blown, and she worried about discovery. She felt concern when he did not answer his telephone. She snapped at coworkers and began to take tranquilizers. Her drinking increased; now she needed wine to sleep. Thoughts of him crowded her mind by day, and at night she dreamed of him, his body covering her like a warm blanket that both comforted and trapped her, those steel eyes she could not avoid, his voice whispering, "Come to me. Come." It was almost with terror that Jane realized she probably was falling in love with him. It wasn't because he was much older and married; it was because she regarded love as a trap, perhaps a pleasant one but at this point in her life she was ill prepared for it. She wanted to tell Mitch, because she could talk with him, but she didn't dare. His discovery of the affair, in fact, somewhat relieved her, for she hated deception and lies. She had not seen Mitch after their confrontation the evening Andrew Collingsworth had been attacked; he hadn't called her and when she called him he was terse and impolite. Obviously he was licking his wounds, hurt and disappointed, his respect for her gone, and in one cry session late at night Jane cursed herself and the name Collingsworth. She was ready to run. Mitch, as if he had powers to divine matters, called her the next day.

"Can I see you?"

"When?"

"Tonight."

"I—I suppose so. What is it about?"

He called at eight, just after she got home, saying a late-breaking story had delayed him, and he appeared just after nine, rumpled and needing a shave, looking exhausted. "I did it," he said. "I finally quit the bastards."

"You didn't!"

"Do you want to see a copy of the resignation letter? It's a masterpiece, if I do say so myself. When the editor saw it, he went into a rage, tearing it into pieces. Later I saw him in there Scotch-taping it back together."

"What set this off?"

"Do you have a drink?"

"Sure. You know where it is."

Relaxed with a martini, he began to talk, and as he did, Jane felt her old respect and love for him returning, feelings she had brushed aside, overwhelmed by Hollis. She had been a fool, she realized, but, looking back at it, she also realized there was nothing she could have done about it. It was something that in retrospect she knew had to happen. How had Mitch put it? A pawn. She had become a pawn of Hollis Collingsworth. And, in so doing, she'd risked something much more than the love of a man like Mitch Evers. She'd risked his respect and friendship. He spoke as if he could read her mind.

"I think I've gotten away, once and for all," he said, his eyes avoiding hers. "I kept staying there because I thought it would get better. It didn't. Sure, under Andrew it got better, but, I think, even had he remained there, he would have reverted to the old pattern. And as soon as the Fox came back, the pattern started again. He promises, but he doesn't deliver. We're back to the same one-sided coverage. I don't see it getting any better. So I quit. Once and for all."

"What will you do?"

"Well, I don't want the *Times*. A security blanket over a velvet coffin doesn't appeal to me. I might apply at Hearst. They got a new editor over there—Bellows?—and that paper is showing signs of life again."

"Mitch, are you sure you've gotten away?"

"I'm positive."

"I'd like to shake your hand."

"Sure," he said. "Shake."

"I believe you."

Now he looked at her. "How about you?"

"If you can do it, so can I."

"Then prove it."

"How shall I prove it?"

He drew out an airline ticket and flipped it on her coffee table. "I'm going to La Paz in Baja California tomorrow morning. Go with me. Meet me at the airport."

"Mitch, I *can't*! I have a commitment to the station."

"Tell them you know Collingsworth. They'll let you go for a week or so."

"That was below the belt."

"Well, I'll be at the airport," he said, draining his martini.

He stood up, straightened his tie, and went to the door. He turned. "I'd like you to be there. But it's your choice." He paused. "Everyone has choices, Jane. Yet if you let things go on too long, you lose your options. I almost did. Don't you."

Knowing Jane's devotion to career, Mitch assigned odds of about one in twenty that she'd show up, and as he waited by the gate watching the last passengers file to the jet, he realized with a small, sad shrug of his humped shoulders that he had been right. And he couldn't blame her. What the hell, most girls her age considered career the dominant factor in their lives, a happy alternative to diapers and ironing boards, to Tillie the Toiler or Blondie. And, considering the crop of egotistical, pampered young men around today, Mitch couldn't blame them. It was the Now Generation. On-the-make, one-night-stands, me-first, the joy of sex. Well, what the hell, that was the way it stood. Handing his ticket to the attendant, he felt a weight of age and rejection. Then he heard his name being called and he turned to see Jane running toward him, laden with luggage, smiling, her face flushed and her eyes bright. Suddenly he was feeling much younger.

Their headquarters was the Hotel Los Cocos, under a coconut grove by the beach. From there they spread out, boating to the Isla Espiritu Santo, crossing the Sea of Cortez by ferry to Mazatlán, walking the palm-lined Malecon Drive by the waterfront, dashing into the warm ocean each morning and afternoon. It was lazy and there was no time. Saint's day fiestas burst around them and the sounds of love songs drifted from rooftops. They explored tide pools, watched the brown pelicans dive for fish, skipped stones in tranquil bays. He felt like painting. He felt like writing poetry. He did not need liquor; the air and the sun inebriated him. A beach boy conned him into buying one of the dried stingrays that hung from lines like grotesque shrunken human forms. When Jane saw it, she shrieked and made him throw it away. But she laughed. They both laughed. The beaches in the mornings and evenings were as red as Mars. One could reach down between rocks and catch a lobster. Butter clams filled the lagoons. The sea and the sky were bright blue and at night in their room they could hear the crash of the surf on the sand, lulling them to sleep. They gained weight, their cheeks turned red, and their noses peeled; they seemed to have the energy of ten year olds, sleeping like babies and eating like teenagers.

One day, exploring alone in their bathing suits, they found a peaceful bay surrounded by cactus-dotted volcanic rock cliffs. The water was bright blue, still and warm, and the beach sand was white as chalk. It was as if they had stumbled onto a landscape of dark beauty where no one had previously been. He looked at her, tall and lithe in her blue, two-piece suit, her sunburned face now innocent and girlish.

"What are you thinking?" she asked.

"The same thing you're thinking."

"Will anyone see us?"

"I don't care."

She kissed him, hard, her hands on the back of his neck, her hips pressing tightly to his thighs. His heart thumped and his breath exploded from his nostrils. Jane pulled away and began to remove his trunks. She dropped to her knees.

"Love me," she said, looking up. "Mitch? Love me?"

They were alone, at an unearthly place they had discovered and considered theirs. They had no responsibilities. Gone were all worldly weights. They had all that they needed, for now, and that was each other. He fell on top of her and climaxed almost immediately after entering her, sensing her climax at the same time. She opened her eyes and smiled.

"We have a witness," she said.

He looked around. "Where?"

"Just that little old crab."

They held hands as they walked back toward the hotel, moving into an area populated with natives and tourists, and Mitch felt a pang of dismay, almost depression, for he knew they must soon return to reality. He brought the subject up.

"When do you have to be back?"

"Pretty soon, I'm afraid."

"When?"

"Monday. How about you?"

"Never," he said.

"Then you really have quit?"

"Yep."

"Good." She squeezed his hand. "Let's not talk about it. Let's not even think about it. I'm going to test you again. Ready? What is that plant?"

"Simple. Sour pitahaya."

"Good. You're learning. You have possibilities. Quick. Name that bird."

"That's a bobbie bird."

"No. You fail miserably. It's a cormorant, dummy."

He felt a little better. It was not over. Not yet. They had some time. Jane's awareness of nature was a side of her he'd been unaware of; here in the warm spring sun, she was a different person than the one bound by time and duty at work. She was more open, unafraid to express her need for love, more human and aware and caring. And so was he. His cynicism dissolved. He saw beauty in the face of a withered old Indian woman in a shawl and the fat lady making tortillas. He enjoyed bargaining with souvenir hawkers. And the sea hypnotized him, its lazy undulations casting a warm softness over him. Now that this ephemeral dream was coming to an end, he wanted it to last forever.

Jane pulled his arm and they raced to the water.

The chubby man had a pleasant, suntanned face, blue-eyed and smiling. He was dressed in nautical blue, his shoes shined and his trousers sharply creased. Despite his initial diffidence, there seemed to be an aura of command about him. He came up to Mitch and Jane as they sat on the hotel's terrace watching the sun go down.

"Miss Raymond?" he asked.

"Yes."

"I'm Captain Thomas Keane, of the yacht *Jordan I*. Mr. Collingsworth and his party would like to invite you aboard."

A sinking feeling went through Mitch, as if a thrust to his solar plexus had knocked out his wind. "We expected you," he said. "But I had rather thought you would be wearing black."

"Sir?" the captain queried.

"Pay no attention to him," Jane said. "It's his sense of humor getting loose again."

"I think I'll take my sense of humor to the bar," Mitch said, standing up. He nodded at the captain. "You two settle this by yourselves."

He stamped away without looking back, knowing the dream was shattered. The end had to come soon. Might as well get it over with. Forget it. Forget everything. Get smashed. He was on his second double martini, feeling very sorry for himself, when Jane found him.

"Crying in your beer?" she asked.

"No, in my gin."

"I'll have one. I need one."

He ordered it. "When do you leave?" Through the window over her shoulder, he could see the sky, red as blood. "And how do you suppose he found you? Did you drop pumpkin seeds?"

"Mitch, I *had* to tell my station manager, or he would never have let me go on such short notice."

"Why didn't you just tell him you planned to go on a sail with the big boss?"

"Now stop that!" Her eyes lit up. "Listen to me. Will you, damn it, *listen* to me?" The waiter brought her martini. She sipped it slowly and then looked at Mitch. "I told him I wouldn't go," she said.

"That doesn't sound like the Jane Raymond I know."

"All right. Fire away. Have at me while you can."

"You told him you wouldn't go. But you want to go, don't you?"

"Frankly, yes. I do. But not without you."

"No. I've quit him."

"Then quit. Become a beachcomber."

"I might. I just might."

"Mitch, before you have six more martinis and get so drunk you won't be able to understand me, let me try to tell you something. I'm ambitious, yes. I want to get ahead. I *must* get ahead, to prove something to myself. I'm not exactly the kind of person who goes around with the smell of bleach on her hands. I had too much of that when I was a kid. I don't ask you to understand me or even to respect me, although I do want your respect. Now I made a dumb mistake. I went to bed with Hollis Collingsworth. I tried to explain to you why, that it wasn't for ambition, or at least totally for ambition, but whatever the reasons it was a dumb thing to do. I may live to regret it. I'm beginning to think the main reason I did it was because his attention flattered me. All we career bitches are basically insecure, you know."

He touched her hand. "I didn't mean it. That 'the Jane Raymond I know' crack, I mean."

"I know you didn't."

"If I were you, I'd go aboard that yacht."

"I turned it down already, remember?"

"Oh, he'll try again, probably in person. You can wager rent money on that. He isn't one who likes to be turned down."

"Well, if he does come back and ask me, I'll go only if you go with me."

Mitch scoffed. "Somehow I have difficulty in believing that."

"I don't want to go alone. But I do want to go. He's taken a personal interest in me and I'm not going to ignore that. But I'm not going to bed down with him again, either."

"He will ask you to."

"But I won't compound a felony. I'll quit first."

"What if he doesn't want me to go with you?"

"Then I won't go."

"All right," Mitch said, shrugging his shoulders. "I'll go with you. I have nothing to win, or lose. I'm finished with him."

"Are you?"

"Why do I get this feeling you don't believe me?"

Jane smiled. "Because I don't think we're very much different when it comes to career."

3.

THEY WENT UP the Sea of Cortez, hugging the east coast of Baja, from La Paz past Loreto and Mulege. The water was calm as glass, green-yellow by day, red and orange at sunset, and like black marble at night. The traffic was American sails, power cruisers, and native fishing boats. Gulls and pelicans swooped around them. Mitch, amused that he was here on a cruise with the Big Boss after he'd quit the paper, found himself lazily enjoying it. Three days up the Cortez, they came to an area dotted by islands.

"Ah," said Captain Keane. "Here we are a million years old, or more. It is a shame to disturb it."

"Are we going to disturb it?" Mitch asked.

"We will not go in. Over there, Canal El Infierillo. The

little hell. And Canyon El Diablo, the devil canyon. The water there can split you in half."

"So let's go in," said Hollis, appearing behind them.

They did not go in, with Hollis acceding to the experience of his captain, but later that afternoon they did witness some excitement. "Pileup! Pileup!" exclaimed a deckhand. The passengers rushed to the deck. Mitch saw a huge silver sheet form just under the surface a hundred yards off the bow. It was a giant school of small fish, herring and sardines, and into its midst now came much larger fish—yellowtails, sea bass, sharks. Then it exploded. The bigger fish moved with powerful strokes, sleek juggernauts, devouring the smaller, leaping and tearing and ripping. Screaming pelicans and terns appeared, diving and wheeling. Sea lions bellowed, echoing on the rocks. It became a churning roar, a massacre and carnage. The sea turned deep red with blood. Parts of fish floated on the oily surface. It lasted about fifteen minutes and then was gone.

"Christ, what I'd give to have a film of that!" Hollis said. His eyes flashed. "That's what it's all about."

There were nine passengers, not including Captain Keane's crew of four. Jane seemed at ease, spending most of her time sunning on deck. Hollis said hardly a word to her. Myron Demming was the most garrulous; Marion Collingsworth and her daughter, Mary, seemed reserved and unsure in a hostile and unfamiliar environment. Andrew Collingsworth said hardly a word. Nathan Carmichael was even more silent. He was often seen seated in a deck chair under a shawl, drawing on his pipe and reading.

"How has the old boy been?" Mitch asked Peter one evening. "He seems bored to death."

"He is not an old boy."

"Oh. Sorry. I see." Mitch fumbled for a Camel. "Well, one reason why I joined this party is to find out what you've been up to."

"I hardly know. They've certainly treated me well, however."

"And you like it, don't you?"

"I'll have to admit it," Peter said. "I do."

And it was a good world, Mitch reflected, this first-class travel. The *Jordan I*, a sleek knife painted cream with red trimmings, moved on the glassy sea like a skilled skater. Crew members showered and changed uniforms to serve as dinner waiters. The chow was good, the wines excellent. The beds were a little cramped and the showers small, yet it was a luxury world, timeless and tempting.

The fifth day out from La Paz, Hollis took his first kill, using light tackle with a nine-thread and a body belt with reel socket. It was an albacore, showing at first color to be about forty pounds. Near the boat the fish made a dash away and down, taking five hundred feet of line. Hollis began to reel in again, bending the rod almost double. The gaffer stood by; a deckhand shouted, "Color!" The gaff slashed down.

"Fresh tuna for dinner," Hollis announced, wiping his sweat-streaked brow.

Mumm's was broken out early and everyone cavorted in almost a reveling atmosphere. They lay at anchor in still waters off Cabo San Lucas, under a full moon that cast a yellow light over the sea. Marion remained grave, but Andrew's spirits seemed to improve. Demming led the party with vigor. Even Carmichael had a second glass of Mumm's.

The *Jordan I* had an excellent chef, a fat Frenchman named Reni who boasted he'd once bossed the cooks at the Waldorf. The tuna, transformed into a garnished feast, was consumed with white wine in a meal that proceeded like a hedonistic revel. Hollis chewed with his mouth open and belched loudly, ignoring his wife's scowl and his daughter's embarrassment. He fired up a big cigar.

"It was a fighter, that fish, and now that I ate him, I salute him," he said. "My arms feel like lead."

"Was that your biggest fish?" Demming asked.

"The biggest yet, but not the biggest I will ever take."

"My compliments to the chef."

Hollis's eyes danced. "Now I have something to say. This may seem a strange place to say it, but I want to talk about our nation." He paused. The silence was absolute. "I have a plan, something I like to call a grand design. There is something very wrong in this nation, a pernicious force eating away at its fabric. Those in Washington are only making it worse."

"Hear, hear," Demming said, drumming the table.

Hollis glared. He continued: "I intend to do what I can about it, to attack it in editorials, to use what media I have to get across a message. Perhaps it has become an obsession with me, but, if so, it is a good obsession. We must restore freedom in America. My full support will go to the candidates for all offices who will campaign on that simple message." He glanced at Peter Russell. "Why did the students revolt? Because they were not *free*! Their parents paid out good money to send them to prisons. They emerged with degrees, but without educations. They revolted from the system, as well they should have. If their methods were wrong, their hearts were in the right place."

He paused, tapping his ash; all eyes were on him. "We're family here, even if we aren't all one blood. We have a force here, a beginning team. I have the financial resources. Judge Carmichael, despite his modest front, is a leading authority on political contests. We have an ex-senator here who knows the ropes. We have another who would have been a senator, and beyond, except that he cannot function now due to the very perniciousness of the system I have just mentioned. And we have a potential candidate, a lawyer and a thinker, who is as naturally qualified for high office as anyone I have met. Ladies and gentlemen, I want to introduce to you my new protégé. His name is Peter Russell."

Demming lay squirming, fighting incursions of anger. His head throbbed. His back was hurting. He was cramped and hot and totally uncomfortable. He felt tricked and insulted. Hollis had lured him aboard the *Jordan I* on false pretenses, hinting that he might back Demming in a comeback, at least on a state level. Yet now it was apparent that Hollis only wanted to use him, to pick his brains, backing instead a green kid from Harvard who seemed so weak that the first political bout surely would send him sprawling. Demming's hands turned to fists that drummed his thighs. The sea slapped gently against the side of the boat. Demming groaned. He thought, *I was at the top, the near-top*. He relived the applause, the TV interviews, the admiring eyes of volunteer workers. He had fought good fights and he desperately wanted to fight again. Only now did he fully realize that it was over. Hollis had hurled his final insult at him. He had raised Demming to the near-pinnacle only to cut off his legs; now he was trying to assign him to the ignominious position of fund raiser and advance man for a boy in whom he saw star potential. Demming realized that he had never really been

free. He was not now free. He would not be free until Hollis
Collingsworth was dead.

Peter found himself both surprised and thrilled. He had
agreed to take the yacht trip only because Nathan had
asked him, but now he found himself the guest of honor.
He had thought about entering politics before, although
not seriously; now, in an action Peter suspected Nathan had
introduced and nurtured, he had the apparent support of
one of the nation's leading political backers. It could bring
him back, end the drift of his life that still gripped him, a
dark philosophy of the meaninglessness of life that had set
in with Carol's death.

He was too excited to sleep, so he went topside about
midnight, emerging from the hatch into a warm night, silver
with starlight and moonbeams. He was now again thinking of
Carol. He stood by the port side rail, looking at the stars, and
a great loneliness swept through him. Her memory had
faded, driven away as he strove to finish school and then
plunged himself into work. Now it came back. He heard her
laughter and he saw her running.

"Hey," a voice said, "if it isn't the birthday boy."

He turned. Mary Collingsworth, a glass in her hand, stood
behind him. She clicked the ice and drank.

"I'm sorry," Peter said. "I didn't see you."

"You look like your best friend just jumped overboard."

"I was just thinking about something, that's all."

"About the White House over there in Washington,
D.C.?"

"No. Of course not."

"You must be something, if he elects you. Cheers."

"Cheers."

"I'm half-high, so I can be honest. When this boat docks, if
I were you I'd get off and run away. Run fast. Don't stop."

"Why do you say that?"

"Because I've had experience. I'm female, so I don't count
with him, which might mean I'm lucky."

"I don't understand."

"Christ, didn't they teach you any common sense at Harvard,
how to read people?"

He smiled. "No. Only contract law and liberalism."

"Well," she said, drinking, "welcome to the club. Welcome to the club of Karamazov baseness."

Someone tapping on his shoulder awakened Peter before dawn. "Come on," said Andrew. "I want to see what you've got in you. Did you ever wet-suit dive?"

"Once or twice," Peter said sleepily.

"Then you'd have no problem beating out a blind man."

In the water on the *Jordan I*'s port side was a skiff with a Johnson outboard motor. One of the deckhands, a Mexican named Lopez, was in it. Dawn painted the sky in red smears, reflecting on the water like fire. Peter followed Andrew into the boat and Lopez shoved off. They moved slowly over the red water toward an island now taking shape in the sunrise ahead. Peter heard the barking of seals. Soon the island revealed itself, alive with scurrying seals and whitened with the droppings of hundreds of chattering birds. Lopez cut the motor.

"Scare birds, bad omen," he said.

Andrew already was in a wet suit and goggles. He handed a suit to Peter. "I move well in water," he said, tapping his deformed arm. "Automatic flipper, you know. And don't worry about the sight. It's all dark down there."

Lopez beached the skiff and went poking among the rocks with a stick. The sun had now appeared, a red ball that fringed the clouds with pink, and the water lapped calmly on a rocky beach. Peter put on the wet suit and followed Andrew into the water. It deepened quickly. Andrew dove in, disappearing, and Peter followed him; he went down, far down, into the forest of the sea. It seemed a long ways up. He rose in a beam of shimmering sun, his bubbles trailing the assent; he burst to the surface fifty yards from shore, his chest hurting. He dog-paddled, looking for Andrew. It seemed a long time. He could see Lopez on shore, hunting through rocks. The birds had returned to their perch and the seals had quieted. Where was Andrew? Just as Peter was beginning to feel real concern, Andrew burst to the surface six feet in front of him, grinning.

Lopez shouted to them, motioning, and they joined him among the rocks. The Mexican had a small bottle of vinegar in his back pocket. He stood smiling, poking the stick deep into a rocky hole. He uncapped the vinegar, sniffed it, and dashed the liquid into the hole. His grin was wider. The tentacles of an octopus appeared from its den.

"I vinegar-stung him," Lopez said. "He come fast."

He did, a dark blubbery ejecting mass, squirting a black inky cloud over Lopez's legs; he was fast, but Lopez was faster, grabbing the creature and letting its tentacles wrap around his arm. Lopez merely grinned. He buried his head into the squirming bubble and bit its neck with the ferocity of a Doberman pinscher snapping at a jugular vein. The octopus went limp.

"I fix," he said. He uncoiled his prey and began to dash it against the rocks. "You swim."

"What's he doing?" Peter asked as they went to the sea.

"Tenderizing," Andrew said.

They went down through kelp to a cave Peter had spotted earlier. One moment it was light, the next it was dark. He lost sight of Andrew, who had been swimming by his side. There was a warm current. It was almost time to go up. His lungs were beginning to hurt. Perhaps Andrew had already started up. Peter kicked his flippers, rising. The kelp seemed thicker than that he'd passed going down. It entwined his neck and legs, slowing him. He thrashed, only to become more entwined. The kelp fronds seemed living things, reaching out for him; it seemed as if he were going down instead of rising. *Easy. No panic.* His breath came out in a rush. Then he felt someone by his side, fighting the kelp. Andrew. He kicked his flippers. They were moving up. In a few minutes they lay exhausted on the beach, breathing heavily.

"Thanks," Peter said. "You saved my hide."

"Oh, you would have made it up."

"How did you find me?"

"Well, you were making enough noise, you know."

Lopez had the octopus cooking in a tin of water that was ruddy brown, colored by the excretions of his kill. He'd brought all the fixings, pepper and lemon and sauce, and when he skinned it and handed a piece to Peter, Peter figured he'd better not ignore an offering from a man with a bite like Lopez's. It tasted somewhat like lobster.

"Was there a reason for this swim?" he asked Andrew later, when they were stretched out on the rocks like sunning seals, their bellies full of octopus meat.

"Maybe I wanted to show you that you have some able competition yet. I'm not finished."

"I never considered you finished."

"I think you did."

"All right. Have it your way."

"I've decided I'm not dead."

"Why did you show me your grandfather's papers?"

"So you would know."

"To discourage me?"

"Maybe."

"I found it fascinating."

"We Collingsworths feel compelled to write it down. Perhaps that will end us."

"I feel just slightly out of place in this."

"You're caught up in it, aren't you?"

"I think I am."

"It's easy. Just close your eyes and let it happen."

"I'm grateful for the attention. I never had attention like this. Not really."

"Well," Andrew said, "watch your ass."

4.

IT SPRINKLED DURING the early morning hours but the dawn broke red and clear. At nine o'clock precisely, Hollis Collingsworth emerged on deck, wearing a T-shirt, jeans, ankle-high boots, and a faded denim jacket. He strolled to the fishing cockpit, where a deckhand handed him a three-six hickory rod equipped with an old-fashioned Coxe reel. The drag spring had been removed; it was a free spool. A butt socket harness lay on the deck. Hollis got into the right fighting seat and surveyed the ocean. Keane had moved the *Jordan I* about halfway off the coast of Baja between Todos Santos and Santo Domingo. Now he was working down sea at about six hundred R.P.M. in a depth of some two hundred feet, five miles offshore. He said the *Jordan I* was a good boat for raising marlin, particularly as she ran down sea; she hummed to the fish, he said, like the sirens of Ulysses.

Hollis breathed deeply, taking the sea air into his lungs. He held his breath as long as he could, expelling the air in a protracted whoosh. He felt good. He had never felt better, stronger, in his life. The sun was warm and the ocean was calm, a bright blue interrupted only by small streaks of white until it merged with a lighter blue on the horizon. He sensed a kill for this day. A big kill.

Keane called to him from the bridge. He was pointing. "Out there," said the deckhand, almost a whisper. He too was pointing, off the port beam. Then Hollis saw it, a giant broadbill swordfish, swimming on the surface, sunning itself. Hollis felt a surge of anticipation and excitement as the deckhand baited his hook with barracuda. The *Jordan I* swung in a tight circle. Marion had come on deck, followed by Nathan Carmichael. Hollis let out leader and line. Immediately the swordfish went toward the bait, moving slowly, so slowly. Hollis felt his pulse pick up. His heart was beating rapidly.

"I think he gonna hit," whispered the brown-faced deckhand.

The fish did hit, and hard, taking the barracuda in its bill and running fifty feet of line off the Coxe reel in the first three seconds. "Four, five, six," Hollis chanted. At ten, he'd snap up the rod, jamming the hook into his prey. "Seven, eight." His hands tightened on the rod. He felt a renewed racing in his heart. "Nine." One more second, one more long second. But, just as "ten" was on his lips, the fish spat out the bait, cut sharply to the right, and went down. Hollis reeled in the empty line. It was almost as if the broadbill had been playing with him.

They sighted two more swordfish in the next hour, but neither took the bait. Hollis had a light lunch and immediately returned to the fighting seat. Again it was Keane who spotted the fish, a broadbill bigger than the other, swimming in a school of surfacing mackerel, both fins showing, its tail proudly up. This was the one; somehow he knew this was the one. Every nerve in his body was alive and he felt his blood surge in a feeling slightly akin to sexual excitement. He let out line as Keane again circled. The fish snubbed both barracuda and mackerel bait. The deckhand suggested a mackerel spinner and Hollis reeled; out again went the hook, baited with a squirming mackerel. *Out to you, fish; take it now, fish.* He waited. He heard the purr of the *Jordan I's* engines. A slight breeze rippled the surface, turning the blue to a greenish hue. Hollis watched as the thrashing mackerel bait moved in front of the swordfish. His fingers tensed.

"Hit!" said the deckhand. "Strike!"

It was. The fish flashed its tail and snapped at the mackerel, seized it, and ran. Hollis began to count. He was tempted to snap up the line now, but that could break it; he waited patiently, counting, "Six, seven, eight." On ran the great fish, now perhaps two hundred feet away. "Nine." He now could see only the tail of the fish, and its wake. "Ten." He pulled up the rod. The line tightened; the rod bent. He could feel the hook jab deeply into the fish's mouth. He had it. There was no mechanical drag on the reel, his concession to sportsmanship and an expression of the confidence he had in himself. He had to apply drag by putting both of his gloved thumbs on the line as it unwound from the reel. He did this, alternately reeling in, for the first hour. His hands were tired and his legs ached. Sweat covered him. The fish ran on the surface, taking out more line, then sounded and jumped. Just about every passenger and crew member was now on deck watching the fight. They cheered and applauded as the big fish broke water, moving its fins and jerking its tail. Each time it jumped, Hollis took in line. He sat firmly in the chair, still refusing to use the harness. Twice he brought the broadbill within fifty feet of the boat, only to let it out again as it turned away or dove below. It was not with strength that you caught a great fish; it was with skill, letting it have enough line so that it would not break, signaling the boat to move just right. He felt the fish. And he talked in his mind to a ghost.

Call to me, speak to me, Father. Speak to me and tell me that I can have this fish. Call to me now. I want this fish, I want to defeat this fish. Call to me and hear me and let me have the skill and the strength to conquer this fish.

The fish sounded again, diving deeply and silently, and Hollis let it have the line, relieved to gain a moment's rest. The line had burned through the canvas gloves and his thumbs were bloody and blistered. Hollis signaled the deckhand, who brought another pair. The deckhand held the reel, looking concerned and frightened with his temporary custody of the sounding monster, while Hollis donned the gloves. Then he returned the rod.

Keane was there. "I'd guess you got maybe two-fifty, maybe three hundred pounds of fish down there," he said. "Maybe more. And this one's gonna fight a lot, lot longer. Sure you don't want me to tie you in the harness?"

"No. Not yet."

"Awright, Mr. Collingsworth," Keane said, grinning admiringly. "Bring it up."

Hollis did, not once but twice, but each time he got the fish up to the edge of the boat, so close Keane could almost grasp the leader and the deckhand was two feet from applying the gaff, it summoned the strength to sound again, going down deeper each time. The second time, the great fish stayed down. Hollis gripped the rod, his hands hurting, his arms like lead weights; he reeled in slowly, but he hadn't the strength to budge the fish. The fight had now lasted more than two hours and his back and legs were so strained they had little feeling remaining in them. His heart rammed against his ribs. The sky seemed to be whirling around. He shook his head vigorously.

"Hit me with some water," he told the deckhand. "Cold."

The deckhand dashed him with a bucketful that stung like ice. Hollis grinned, his teeth and jaw set, his eyes popping, his fingers, now encased in the third pair of gloves, bleeding openly on the reel and line and deck. He would have this fish.

Father, hear me, call to me, give me this fish.

He looked up and saw Marion on the bridge and his eyes caught hers.

"Christ, look at him," Mitch said to Jane. "I've got to give it to that old bastard. How long has it been?"

"Three hours. Over three hours."

"I've heard these things can go on all day."

"It's brutal, but it *is* exciting."

"Well, I got to give it to the old s.o.b. He's got guts."

"Or foolishness," she said.

He let the fish stay down and rest; he rested himself, letting the line go out further than before. He waited a long time, feeling the slack, and then slowly began to reel in. When he felt no pressure, he reeled faster, fearful for a moment that his prey had somehow slipped its hook, escaping into the black deep. But then he felt a tug. He smiled. He took in line; the rod bent almost double, and slowly, once again, Hollis dragged the great fish up. Keane was there. Again the deckhand stood with the gaff. Just when Hollis was certain he hadn't the strength to make a single more turn of the reel, the fish came to the surface, its long flat sword trembling, its front fins swollen and erect. A parasitic white remora clung to its belly just below the fins. Sensing victory, Hollis tugged the rod upward. It was a mistake. The huge fish churned, its tail kicking, and rushed away, taking line from under Hollis's burning thumbs. He let it go. He knew now that he had been right in removing the drag spring; had he been under drag, this mighty rush by the fish could have snapped the line. He sat exhausted as the line spewed out.

At the end of the fourth hour, he decided to accept the harness. It would not do much to relieve the pain in his arms, but it would certainly help with the back and leg strain. He felt now a form of second wind, a pounding of his blood, a renewed strength that had sprung from some unknown reserve. He was ready again.

"Let me have this fish," he said between clenched teeth. "Let me have this fish."

He began the final battle, drawing in two hundred yards of line a quarter turn at a time. Now fully he felt the weight and the struggle of his quarry, a tiring but desperate fish giving up ground only inches at a time. The strap tightened on Hollis's stomach and shoulders. He felt his heartbeat pick up. *Come, fish; come, fish.* He gained slowly, then more rapidly, as if the fish had given up. He could for the first time make full turns of the reel. Again, Keane; again, the deckhand with the gaff. Then, five feet from the boat, he saw the huge broadbill, his broadbill, his conquered and defeated broadbill. And he made his second mistake. He pulled the rod up so hard that, combined with the fish's last desperate effort to escape, a strap in the harness broke. Hollis felt the rod breaking from his hands; he reached out for it, grasping it just before it went overboard. Again the line went out as the great fish streaked away.

But now it was only a matter of time. The harness repaired, Hollis began reeling in again—again a quarter turn at a time. The exhaustion returned, deeper than before, and he toiled in what periodically seemed blackness. His eyes burned and his mouth was so dry he could not speak. His arms had barely the strength to hold the rod and his bloody hands were so weak he could not feel his fingers. Another turn of the reel. Another and another. Foot by foot the creature of the deep was dragged to its fate. No mistakes this time. It must be this time, for he knew that he could not pull in the fish again. Slowly Hollis swung the rod in Keane's direction. Keane had it.

"Now!" he told the deckhand.

The gaff slashed down, piercing the flesh of the great fish. It lay on the surface, defeated. Hollis dropped the rod and turned. Through what seemed a dense fog bank, he could see figures lining the deck. It was his audience; they were cheering loudly. But their voices seemed to fade from him, to recede into a shadowy darkness that came from somewhere, enveloping him.

The fight had lasted four hours and fifty-one minutes.

Just before dinner was served, Captain Keane aroused Marion from a light nap by pounding sharply on her door and telling her of an emergency. "I put him up in my quarters, since—quite frankly—he was so exhausted he couldn't walk another step," he said as they moved down the narrow corridor. "He fell to sleep immediately. Now he's awake, but he's very ill all of a sudden."

The compartment stank of stale air and vomit. Hollis lay retching on the bed, soaked with sweat, his hands clutching his chest. His mouth was open. His eyes rolled.

"Get Nathan Carmichael," Marion said. "I think he's had a heart attack."

She was very calm. She touched his hand. He tried to speak, but no words came out. Spittle ran down his chin; his tongue flapped helplessly. She looked at him, feeling superior to him for the first time since they had met.

5.

THE DOMINANT COLOR of the scenes that fled through Hollis Collingsworth's semiconsciousness as he fought for his life was blue. He recalled that when he awakened, becoming slowly aware of his surroundings, as if he were recovering from anesthesia. Even now, the room seemed tinged in blue. The fog cleared at an almost imperceptible pace, revealing a bottle above him dripping fluid into a tube connected to his arm, wires on his chest and ankles, the silly white gown he wore, an antiseptic odor. The silence was absolute. He tried to move his head but could not. With a great effort, he raised one and then two of the fingers on his left hand. It took an even greater effort to do the same on his right side. Finally managing it, he lay back, satisfied. He was alive. He had returned from the dead. He knew that he would eventually recover.

The color of death was blue, in varying shades, but mostly pale blue, a static fluorescence that glowed on the hills and mountains and spread a veil over the sea. And, in his death, he'd gone to both the mountains and the sea, gone on heroic missions to prove to the dark judges of eternity that he deserved to have life. And now he remembered. His first memory was of a doctor in blue, his face full before him like a motion-picture close-up, his lips moving, his voice coming to Hollis through the blue fog bank. Then the blue fog took over; Hollis moved in it, breathing it, tasting its iodine taste; he was enshrouded by it. He was going up a mountain. That much he knew. It was cold. The blue ran like a trail, casting off an irradiant glow, and he struggled upward, following it, sweating in the cold. From the darkness ahead came woeful cries and moans, at once individual and merged, a babble of human sounds that became louder as he moved. The cold cut into his lungs. He fought for breath. His legs throbbed with pain. His heart hammered. A wind had come up, stirring the strange blue snow and obliterating the path. He fell to his hands and knees, trying to find his way, the wind bitter in his face. He crawled, too exhausted to walk. The shrieks of despair and pain, now even louder, urged him on. He had been sent on a rescue mission. This was no dream. Now the path became a ledge, about three feet wide, jutting from the side of the mountain. On his left was a cliff that had no bottom. It seemed as if he had ascended to the clouds; they too were tinged with blue. Then he was off the path, on a flat meadow dotted with dead, gnarled trees whose trunks hosted wisps of diaphanous fog that sizzled like electric sparks, illuminating the place ahead where a broken and severed airplane lay, its wings sheared off, its fuselage split. Human forms writhed around it, groaning and sobbing. Hollis was up on his feet, stumbling toward the crash, waving and trying to shout. When he got there, no one seemed to notice him.

"There is a way out," he told a hooded figure.

The figure turned. Hollis gasped. It was a man with a hideously smashed face. He had no nose. His eyeball hung down on his cheek.

"There is no way," he said. Blood bubbled from his mouth as he spoke. "There is no way."

Hollis went from person to person, trying to tell them they could get out, but none would believe him. One man sat near the plane's tail section, trying to push back his bloody innards into a yawning cavity that had split his stomach. Beside him, another man was gnawing on a woman's severed arm. Body parts lay everywhere, heads and limbs and torsos. A man in an airline uniform came toward Hollis.

"There is a path out," Hollis said. "I came up the path."

The man said nothing. He appeared to be uninjured and his uniform was spotless. He put his hand on Hollis's shoulder, smiled, and went past, walking into the blue smoke that surrounded them. It had begun to snow—a normal, white fluffy snow—and the place grew immediately colder. Everyone was forming a line and walking slowly toward the airplane's cabin, which had been severed from the rest of the fuselage by the force of the crash. From within the cabin came a call, "Next," and a person went in. Soon the call came again; another went in. Immediately ahead of Hollis was a pretty young girl in a blue dress. She heard the "next," turned to him and smiled, and went inside. Hollis waited. He shivered in the snow. It seemed a very long time, but finally he heard it. "Next." He went up the short stairway and through the door. He peered inside, and then recoiled with horror, a scream caught in his throat. The man in the uniform stood smiling at him, beckoning. In his hands was a huge bloody sword. Headless bodies lay scattered like butchered animals. The heads had been neatly arranged in the cockpit. Hollis found his voice. He screamed loudly and turned to flee, but the door had been closed behind him.

"Easy," said a voice. "It's all right."

He was awake in darkness. He was lying down, and hands held him fast. His legs had feeling. He was alive, aware. He

did not know where he was nor did he have memory of the
past. He felt a rubbery mask on his face and he breathed
deeply. He was away again, floating in total darkness.

It was impossible to know how much time had passed
between the mountain and the sea—perhaps seconds, perhaps weeks—but he did know he was now in deep blue
water, swimming swiftly, a fish that did not need air. He was
not tired nor did he have to move his arms and legs; it was as
if he were being sucked down this blue shaft, moving in
water that grew warmer with depth. Swarms of small fish
swam ahead of him and behind him. He had no fear. He
found himself thinking, *If this is a dream, I must remember
it*. Yet he knew that this was not really a dream, at least not
his dream, for he experienced it without actually participating
in it. His actual self lay on a white bed in a white room,
observing the underwater figure that was a ghost or a spirit of
himself. Yet that did not seem strange. It seemed normal. If
it was not normal for all men, at least it was for him. At the
end of the blue shaft was a wall of white water; through that,
he found himself on the deck of a sunken ship, an old
three-masted schooner. It seemed in remarkable shape, as if
the sea had guided it to a special place where the ravages of
time had no effect. That did not seem exceptional to him, nor
did it seem unusual that the open hatch toward which he now
moved took in no water. He went down a rope ladder, into
the ship's belly. The light was blue. In the hold a group sat
around a large table, about to begin a meal. A chair at the
head of the table was empty. He sat down. All of the diners
were black except for one white man. The men had beards
and the women were all bare breasted. The bill of fare was a
giant swordfish, whose open eyes fixed upon Hollis.

I killed that fish, he thought. *It is their victory meal for
me*. And, although the diners seemed to look alike, almost-
faceless statuettes who moved with mechanical jerks and did
not speak, he began to recognize them individually as persons he knew. Andrew was there, an eyeless figure. To his
right was Nathan Carmichael; to his left, Myron Demming.
Marion was facing him at the opposite end. She was flanked
by Deborah Reading and Peter Russell. Mary also was there.
Jane Raymond and Mitch Evers were in the center, across
from each other. Marion rose, a large fork and carving knife

in her hands. Each of the diners, as if by signal, opened napkins. Marion approached the fish, plunged the fork into it, and began to slit it with the knife. A black ooze squirted from the fish's belly, following the cut of the knife. The cut widened as she slashed along and when she reached the tail, the great fish popped open, revealing a large form like a man inside. The form lay on its back, covered with the black liquid. Marion wiped the face of the dark form with her hands. A red substance trickled between her fingers. Hollis looked down at the face and saw that it was his father, blood squirting from a hole in his forehead; he looked again, his stomach churning and bile filling his mouth, and realized that in fact it was not his father's face but instead his own.

His eyes snapped open. "Uh!" he said, feeling pain in his chest and stomach. He lay quietly, waiting for the blue mist to clear. Someone touched his hand. From out of the mist came a human face. He was back. He had returned. This time, he knew, he was back to stay.

6.

MARION HADN'T BEEN to the Polo Lounge in over a year, but the captain recognized her immediately. "Mrs. Collingsworth," he said, bowing. "Right this way. Miss Reading has already arrived."

Deborah Reading sat inconspicuously at a back table, wearing a wide-brimmed yellow hat and an Elizabethan dress with a ruffled collar. Marion was more Victorian in appearance, in a jewel-encrusted blouse with frilly shoulder ruffles and a wide navy-blue skirt. She took Deborah's outstretched hand. They didn't speak until the waiter brought martinis. Then Deborah said:

"How is he?"

"He'll recover fully. He'll be coming home soon."

"All the worse," Deborah responded.

"I beg your pardon?"

Deborah looked up. "We won't spar. I didn't ask you to come here to spar. We're going to talk something out."

"All right. Let's talk."

"You are a proud woman."

"And you are a vain woman."

"Well," Deborah said, smiling, "that's out of the way, then." There were lines around her eyes and mouth, but she retained much of the beauty that had enraptured millions on the screen for decades. Marion found herself wondering if Deborah had had a face lift; she stopped herself, thinking, *Petty. You're getting petty.*

"I'm going to tell you something I think you might already know, Marion. Peter Russell is my son. Hollis is his father."

"I see."

"You don't look too surprised."

"I had suspected it, of course."

"But you preferred to put it out of your mind?"

"Peter is his, son or not," Marion said, sipping her martini. "I believe that they think alike."

"I'm going to make a short speech, a Polo Lounge soliloquy," Deborah said. "I wanted to go to the top and I did, with his help, but I do have a sentimental streak. I wore a hat like the silly one I have on today in my first lead role. This business can cut your heart out if you let it, but I said that wouldn't happen to me. It hasn't. I used to have a boss who always said, 'Roll with it,' and I learned to do that. I'm not a bitch. I'm not pushy. I can be at the top and still be human. What is this leading up to? Just this. I don't want anything bad to happen to my son. And now I'm afraid for him. Am I dramatizing?"

Marion lowered her eyes. She was thinking of Andrew. "No," she said. "I don't think you're dramatizing."

"God knows I don't deserve Peter. I gave him away. People make horrible mistakes in their lives." Deborah looked up. "You believe me, don't you?"

"I have no reason not to believe you."

"Ask him. He'll lie, but watch his eyes when you ask him. And I'm sure it's written down. He wrote everything down. Just like his father."

"I think I'd better go now," Marion said.

"But I think you'll stay. I don't think you want to run away from the truth anymore. I don't. And, since we are now being frank, I'll tell you this. I always thought Hollis would come back to me, even after he married you. I loved him. You never did."

"Would you have taken him back?"

"Up until a few years ago, yes." She leaned forward, a glint in her eyes. "You see, he and I are alike. Selfish and scheming. The difference is that I have changed. He has not."

The waiter brought second martinis. They sat in silence, avoiding each other's eyes, both lost in private thought. Marion found herself slightly amused. The wife and the mistress, having it out. She couldn't honestly challenge Deborah Reading's assertion about love. She couldn't remember ever having loved Hollis Collingsworth; it had not been a marriage, but a business partnership. A very successful business partnership and perhaps a successful marriage. But not one of love. She stopped herself. It did no good to reassess. She could not go back. And, if she could, she would have changed nothing. One could not divine the movements of fate.

"What is it you want me to do?" she asked.

Deborah Reading's eyes flashed an almost mischievous smile. "I want to form an alliance with you," she said slowly.

Fairbanks favored the master, Featherington the mistress, so Marion got the key from the latter—who shouldn't have had it but appeared to have access to everything. Marion paused before the door of Hollis's study, last minute doubts staying her hand. Then she turned the knob and pushed it. The door opened. It was dark inside. She could barely make out the outlines of a desk and chair. It was the old rolltop desk that had belonged to Hollis's father. Marion snapped on the light. The room was plain enough, small and white walled, with the desk and chair, a cot, and a row of steel files. It was unclean and stuffy. She sat down at the desk and rolled up the top. A series of drawers inside contained nothing but paper clips, coins, thumbtacks. But she knew in old desks there often were compartments behind compartments. She removed the drawers and felt inside. Her fingers brushed a latch. Unhooking it, she discovered a compartment behind it. She drew out two thick bundles of papers, bound with string and rubber bands. She paused, listening for sounds. Did she hear footsteps in the hallway? Her head snapped around. She felt like a thief, a spy. Her heart thumped. Her breathing was rapid. She waited. No sounds came. Carefully she replaced the compartments and drawers. Then, taking the papers, she went to her bedroom, walking stealthily, almost on tiptoe. She had intended to get a sound night's sleep, perhaps even take a pill, but her discovery kept her up almost until dawn. The first person she sought out was Nathan Carmichael.

The professor finished reading the papers by noon. "I think you should replace them," he said.

"No. I would like you to take them and get them copied. Bring the originals back to me. Then I'll replace them."

"Are you sure?"

"Of course I'm sure."

"There is evidence here that could involve Hollis in a criminal conspiracy. What is your intention, Marion?"

"Nothing. I just want them copied."

"Do you plan to turn the papers over to the authorities?"

"Of course not. Do you think I want to bring scandal to this household?"

"All right, Marion. I'll have the papers copied and return the originals to you."

"Please hurry."

"I will."

"Nathan?"

"Yes?"

"I'm afraid of him," she said. "I'm very much afraid."

That same day Hollis came charging back to Green Manor in a powered wheelchair, giving no warning. Two young nurses flanked him. He rolled to the elevator, a nurse on each side, and went to the master bedroom. Marion tapped diffidently on his door. He was seated in a Queen Anne chair by a leopard skin rug, squinting at legal briefs through bifocals. He'd lost weight and deep circles ran under his eyes, yet there was color in his cheeks and a snap in his voice.

"Have Fairbanks find rooms for the nurses," he said. "They'll be here a couple of weeks. They're not necessary, but the doctors made me bring them as a condition of getting out. I'll be taking breakfast and lunch upstairs, but we'll be dining downstairs. Is Carmichael still here?"

"Yes."

"Still the ancient leech, eh? Where is Peter Russell?"

"He has a temporary job at a law office. He's taken an apartment."

"Well, let's get him back. This is his home. We have work to do."

"But you should rest."

"Christ, Marion, I've been resting for two *months*! Over two months. I see you had the fish mounted."

"Captain Keane arranged for it. I wanted to have it up for you when you came home."

He chuckled. "I killed that fish, but he damn near killed me, too. I was down so far I could smell cinders, but I beat it. Now I'm not sure I can be killed."

"You certainly look well."

"I'm going to my study. When is dinner?"

Marion hid a gasp. Carmichael had not returned with the papers. He was hours late. She said calmly: "Wouldn't you rather rest on the terrace for a while? It's a very nice day."

"No, I have some writing to do."

"Very well. But you must not strain yourself."

"Actually, what I want more than anything is a cigar." He winked at her. "Or a roll in the sack."

"The only rolling you're going to do for a while is in that wheelchair. And, right now, I'll roll you down to the terrace."

He was dozing in the wheelchair when Carmichael returned with the papers. Marion heaved a great sigh of relief. She felt as guilty replacing them as she had taking them.

A stiff and proper Fairbanks came to Hollis in the library a week after he'd left the hospital and handed him a card. "Demming?" Hollis said. "All right. Send him to me." He sat before the fire in a robe and slippers, pretending to be reading as Demming entered. He didn't look up until he heard Demming clear his throat. Demming took a seat opposite Hollis and accepted Fairbanks's offer of a brandy. He began to talk about old times. He said Hollis looked great. Hollis said Demming looked great. Demming agreed with that.

"I'm ready to come back," he said. "Pound the beat again."

"And you want my support?"

"Frankly, yes. We're a good team."

"That was before," Hollis said. "I'm going for youth now. The world wants youth."

"Is it still Peter Russell?"

"He has a stamp on him. I can see it in his eyes."

"He's green. They'll kill him."

"Not with me there."

Demming got up. His hands were shaking. "I saved you. Did they tell you that I saved you?"

"When did you save me?"

"On that boat. Everybody else stood around, waiting for you to die. I arranged for the chopper. It was my connections that got it there on time. Ask Carmichael. Ask your wife. Ask Peter Russell."

"Good," Hollis said. He looked up. "So I owe you?"

"You owe me."

"Well, I thank you but I'll also remind you that I do not die easily. I would have made it anyway."

Between chattering teeth, Demming hissed: "What does it take to kill you?"

"More than someone like you. It would take someone much bigger."

Now Demming was trembling all over. "I'll see you dead," he said slowly, fighting for composure.

"Will you? Very well. Wait here."

Taking the elevator, he went to his bedroom, consumed with amusement. From his nightstand he removed the pearl-handled revolver, slipped it into the pocket of his robe, and returned to the library, descending by the staircase. Demming stood by the fireplace, still trembling.

"You want me dead?" Hollis asked. "Here's your chance."

He handed the revolver to Demming, who took it and held it awkwardly in a shaking hand, holding it as if it were a danger to him. Hollis stepped in front of him.

"Go on," he said. "That little jewel is loaded, I assure you. The safety is off."

"You're mad," Demming said, staring at him. He flipped the revolver on the divan. "You're mad," he said again, backing away.

Hollis laughed, his head back.

Peter Russell returned to Green Manor the following week-end and Carmichael often observed him and Hollis Collingsworth talking in the library, sometimes until late at night, as if they shared secrets. It disturbed him, but he did nothing about it. He tried to explain his inaction to Marion.

"I think he sees a real potential for the boy. It may be honest this time. Perhaps Hollis has changed."

"I don't think you really believe that."

"I've never before thought of you as cynical, Marion."

"Maybe I'm changing. Maybe I am getting more cynical."
They were standing by the cabana near the pool; across the
lawn, Hollis sat in the gazebo, talking intently with Peter.
"Hollis *has* changed in a way. I think he's afraid of temper
tantrums now, so he's turned to gentle persuasion. Look at
him. It's almost like the devil wooing a soul."

"It's hardly that, Marion."

She looked at him urgently. "You haven't talked to Peter.
You're procrastinating. Why?"

"Perhaps I'm just an old man who cannot make up his
mind," Carmichael said, tapping his cane.

He felt he should leave Green Manor. It was possible, as
Hollis had said, that he had done all he could for Peter. And if
Peter knew everything, would that help? No longer was he a
boy; he was a man with his own mind. Yet he hesitated; he
vacillated weakly. *You ancient Hamlet, decide*. He confronted
Hollis with the matter one evening, after a full meal and two
brandies.

"Sure, tell Peter anything you want," Hollis said. "Ruin it
for yourself with him, ruin it for yourself at Harvard. Ruin
your possible shot at the high court. You still have a shot, you
know. Go ruin it. You've known, or suspected, a lot of things
and you've shut up so far. If you spill it now, remember
you're a part of it. So go ruin it all."

"Peter has become an obsession with you."

"Well, trust me, he's in good hands."

"Why do you want him?"

"Why do I want him?" Hollis looked up, his eyes bright. "I
want him because he is the world to me."

Andrew, taking lessons at the Braille Institute and living in
an apartment nearby on Vermont, often came to Green
Manor on Sundays, usually for a swim. "I'm learning to
read," he told Carmichael. "I'm a Ph.D and I'm just learning
to read."

"I like your spirit."

"Where is the old monkey? Fishing for marlin again?"

"Not quite yet. But I suspect he will be. The doctors have
just pronounced him fitter than ever."

"Let's have a talk with him."

It had turned to autumn; the air emitted a moist tang thick
with the smell of peppertrees. Carmichael moved slowly, pain
from the lumbago he'd recently developed nipping at him.
He had lingered too long at Xanadu; the milk of Paradise was

turning sour. Yet Andrew's sprightly gait and sunny attitude cheered him. There was a man truly indomitable; perhaps, indeed, the Collingsworth gene was unconquerable and inextinguishable.

They found Hollis in the library, feeding fish in a large aquarium he'd recently acquired. He'd never been a church goer, but he usually dressed on Sundays, if only to nap outside on a chaise longue. Now he wore a charcoal suit and a white shirt. He looked years younger, a trim, gray, handsome figure. Andrew, in his bathing suit with a towel around his neck, seemed out of place. Hollis didn't let that pass.

"You should have changed in the cabana," he said.

"I'm sorry. I wanted to talk with you about something."

Hollis didn't respond. He shook a powdery substance into his aquarium and watched as the fish rose to absorb it. Then he turned.

"I'm going out soon," he said. "Can this wait?"

"I'd rather talk now, Father."

Carmichael, beginning to feel uneasy, found an excuse to leave, but Hollis held him. "No, stay here. Let's hear what he has to say."

It was a request, almost a plea. Andrew said he had adjusted well enough to return to the political front; he wanted to declare for the next Senate race, or at least the House. Hollis listened, seated in his chair, his hand on his chin. Carmichael felt like an intruder, as if he didn't belong; he knew now that soon he would leave, return to Harvard. A little wind tapped at the window, stirring the curtains. Hollis rose, speaking as he paced.

"I like your spunk, I always have," he told Andrew. "But now I think you're being unrealistic. I think you'd get out and find it pretty damn cold. Television puts people into office these days."

"And you're saying I wouldn't do well on television?" Andrew questioned. "Perform well, that is?"

"I'm saying that, yes. What I'm also saying is that I think, down deep, you still have a liberal streak in you. I really wasn't able to make you see it any differently. I'm not going to go for a candidate who'll give away the store in handouts." His voice softened. "But the main thing is that we have to face facts. You're no longer equipped to do what you once did. I'm sorry if that hurts, but it is the truth and we must face facts."

"Hollis—" Carmichael said tentatively.

Hollis whirled on him, his brow wrinkled. "Don't butt in. This is family. It's not your affair."

"You invited me to stay."

"Then I now invite you to leave. As a matter of fact, I've been meaning to tell you this: I think it's time you considered going home."

"I've been considering that for a long time."

"Then do it."

Andrew slumped, defeated. Hollis went to him and put his hand on his shoulder. "You go to Rome or some place like that. Rest up. You're out of it now, and lucky to be out of it. Go with the old judge here, the wise old judge. I'll pay. You both deserve it. The judge will take care of you. He's good at taking care of people."

"Of cripples?" Andrew asked.

"Of anybody," Hollis said, winking at Carmichael.

It was too much. He no longer could stand for it. He had wavered too long, mired in indecision, lulled by an extravagant and hedonistic atmosphere that had numbed his brain. It was time to act. Andrew had been cast loose like an unwanted plaything, scarred and abandoned; he had been replaced by Peter Russell. Carmichael saw Hollis for what he was, and he considered it extraordinary that he had been so long blinded. Perhaps he had wanted the blinders. But now they were off his eyes; his vision was clear. It was as if a weight had been lifted from him. He searched the Manor for Peter, intending to tell him everything, but Peter apparently had left. A light rain had begun, trickling from a gray sky. From the window of his room, Carmichael could see Andrew in the pool, swimming furiously from end to end. Fairbanks tapped on his door and offered him a letter on a silver tray. Carmichael read it slowly.

Dear Nathan:

I have sad news. Captain Kingsley has had a stroke, his second, and his condition is critical. I must go to Cape Cod and see if I can be of some comfort to Amelia.

They—just as you—have been like parents to me. I am sure that you understand.

I hope that you will be there when I return to Green

*Manor. I am very excited about the opportunities that
have apparently come my way in these past few months.*

> *With my respect and love,*
> *Peter*

Carmichael slumped down on the bed, his eyes moist.
Again he felt his resolve weakening. He had fumbled and
erred and now he thought of himself as a very old man,
vulnerable in flesh and mind. No matter what he did, he
would probably lose Peter. Fairbanks was tapping again, with
another message. This time it was from Deborah Reading.

Marion went with him, Deborah Reading's request, and in
the taxi he wondered which of the women had really planned
this meeting. Or perhaps it would be more of a confrontation
than a meeting. It was raining harder, heavy sheets that
formed small rapid rivers along the curbs. He felt somehow
elated, as if his long vacillation were coming to an end. His
mind was churning. He had an idea that was maturing into a
plan, perhaps a preposterous one. It made him chuckle,
aloud.

"What is it?" Marion asked.

"Nothing. I've been thinking."

"Are you all right?"

"I'm quite all right. Yes, quite all right."

Deborah Reading had not gone in for Hollywood living; she
hadn't moved for almost thirty years. It was a modest Beverly
Hills home with a rosebush-lined cobblestone path. The only
modern thing about the house were the bars on its windows.
Marion thought it necessary to help him up the path. The
door was open.

"Nathan Carmichael, it's been far too long," Deborah said,
coming toward him, her hands extended. He took both her
hands. She had aged well; in fact, had become even more
radiant. He'd heard she was not out of pictures. "Would you
like some coffee? Tea? How about a brandy? Marion?"

"No, thank you, nothing," Marion said.

"I came through it all pretty well," Deborah said when
they were seated. "No major scandals, I don't snort cocaine
or swallow 'ludes, and I've never been suicidal." She laughed;
her eyes drifted, as if in memory. "I learned to roll with it. I
have an Oscar in the closet and Sarah—dear Sarah, who is

gone now—kept the scrapbooks. Now I'm a little old lady with memories. Oh. And some warm letters about my son."

"You're hardly a little old lady," Carmichael said.

"Well, I don't regret too much. But there were times when I zagged when I should have zigged."

"We have all had times like that."

"Yes," Deborah said, her features thoughtful. "I guess that's why we're here tonight. I'm sorry to drag you out in the rain. But I had a sense of urgency. I don't really know why."

"Intuition?" Marion asked, smiling.

"Perhaps, yes."

Carmichael rose. "Perhaps it no longer is a man's world we live in, but I wish to assert a man's ego here and tell you I do have a plan. I want to discuss it with both of you tonight. I want to warn you that it will seem absurd, at least at first blush. Perhaps it is absurd. But I think, indeed, we must ram a stake through a vampire's heart."

"Nathan, isn't that a little extreme?" Marion responded.

"Is it?" he asked, turning. "Perhaps it is. But will you listen to an elderly personage as he deals in absurdity? I am sure you would both agree that we are challenging powerful forces. And perhaps you also would agree that we are not all without sin. If you agree to go ahead with my idea, much will be revealed of us all to each other."

"This man intrigues me," Deborah said.

"The judges will be judged," Carmichael continued, now pacing. He listened to the rain, white froth on the window panes; then he faced the seated women, his shoulders square. "I know where I can find Peter and I'm going to Boston tomorrow. What I want to do cannot be done without his permission. Or the permission of everyone. We cannot do it until we are certain of it. And, once it is started, we cannot back down. It must then go to its conclusion."

"What is it, Nathan?" Marion asked.

"Listen to me," Carmichael said. "Perhaps the time has come for the pawns to rise up."

7.

SADNESS AND LONGING tugged at Peter as he turned the rotary at Chatham. He didn't go first to Amelia. Instead, he went to the dunes where Carol had died. Marsh grass made a bid for existence on the barren sands; wading gulls pecked for food in the surf. He stood lonely in the wind, facing the dunes, an austere, foreboding wasteland he'd once considered hauntingly beautiful. Emptiness chilled him.

Amelia sat in her rocker, a shawl over her shoulders. "He died this morning," she said.

"I'm sorry. I'm so sorry."

"Well, me and his other cronies will miss him like the dickens." She looked at him, restraining her emotion. She was like the Cape, a part of it; she would endure. "Now I have two souls frolicking on those dunes."

"I loved them both."

"Aye, and they you, too. And me as well. It doesn't always turn out the way the books do." Slight moisture tinged her eyelids, but there was acceptance in her aging defiant face. "He knew you'd be here. But he couldn't stay long enough to see you."

Later, he lingered before the crimson tide of the Atlantic, hearing ghosts in the wind. He wanted to go to the ghosts, to join their gamboling and laughter. He had forgotten his vow to investigate Carol's death, lost in the crush to finish school and lulled by the promise of sponsorship from an important man. But here again on the Cape, he renewed his vow. He turned away from the beckoning ghosts.

After Nathan Carmichael told him, Peter walked for miles on Boston streets, moving down Boylston from the Public Garden, past Clarendon and Exeter and Massachusetts, to the Back Bay Fens, his collar turned up and his shoulders hunched, ignoring a hesitant sprinkle that drove away the sun. A rainbow arched beyond the Charles, beyond Cambridge. He looked at it, slumped on a bench. He had read the diary of Hollis Collingsworth which Nathan had brought to him. He now knew who he was; he now knew why Carol had died. Knowing, he wondered if perhaps he would be better off not knowing; once Madame Colombier had told him that, in fact more than once. He felt no anger, only confusion, despair, and bitter disappointment.

"Again," he said later, keeping his promise to meet Nathan at a restaurant on Scotia near the Prudential Center. "The part about Carol, I mean."

"I will tell you what I told you before. When you said you wished to marry, I informed Hollis."

"What exactly did you tell him about her? That she was a radical, a revolutionary?"

"Of course not. But he did not favor your marrying. And obviously he set about to find out what he could about Carol." Nathan tapped his pipe on the table. He was dressed impeccably in a gray three-piece suit, but he looked strained and tired. His face was ashen. "When he attempted to enlist my aid in discouraging the marriage, I refused. Then he said, his exact words were, 'I will handle it.'"

"You neglected to tell me that this morning."

"Peter, I'm not trying to hide my guilt. I've hidden it quite too long already."

Peter looked out the window at the rain, a mistlike patter that turned to steam on the sidewalk. He saw Nathan in a different light, a weak man who had served as a strong man's pawn. He knew the truth after an uncertain search that had lasted decades, but he also knew the pain of discovering that truth.

Turning back, he said: "This man named Hunter is mentioned several times in the papers you gave me. Is there enough evidence to start a grand-jury investigation?"

"There might be. But the chances of getting an indictment are slim."

"Why?"

"The evidence is stolen. The defense would accuse us of having unclean hands. Besides, much of the material is vague, perhaps deliberately so."

Peter's hands became fists. "So I've been manipulated and lied to. The truth is I never even suspected that he was my father. That makes me think of myself all the more as a fool.

He's a good actor. So are you. Even when there was murder, you did nothing. How much did you get out of it?"

"I did it to be near you and watch you grow."

"I don't quite believe that."

"If you will look back on it, you will see that I never lied to you."

"No. You merely kept the truth from me."

"I had no choice."

"It appears none of us had much of a choice." Peter's fists tapped the table. "But I know this. I will find a way to bring him down, to make him see the truth of himself."

"Or we the truth of ourselves," Nathan said.

"What do you mean by that?"

Nathan did not answer. They were interrupted by a great presence lurching up to them, smelling of rain. Timothy Lockwood pushed his way between them, vigorously rubbed his hands, and bellowed at the waitress to bring him a pot of coffee.

8.

HOLLIS COLLINGSWORTH AWOKE in a heavy sweat, an instinctive fear crawling within him. He sat up in the darkness, sniffing the air. He reached for the light. But he didn't touch it. Two figures burst on him, at least two, seizing him and dragging him from the bed. They held him fast. He tried to cry out, but his mouth was too dry. Was this a dream? They took him, blindfolded, down what seemed an interminable succession of stairways, holding his arms. It *was* a dream. When would he awaken? He heard a door opening. He was pushed ahead. The blindfold came off. He was in the gun room. To his right was Peter Russell; to his left was Andrew. Still he could not find his voice, but he knew now this was no dream. Other forms came into focus. A man was seated behind a desk at the front. Hollis squinted. It was Nathan Carmichael, dressed in a dark suit. Carmichael spoke.

"Will the prosecuting attorney please identify himself?"

"I am here," said a voice from the darkness. "Myron Demming, for the prosecution."

"And the defense?" Carmichael asked.

"Present," came a voice to Hollis's right, and a stooped old man with a great thatch of dry white hair streaming down his forehead appeared. He wore a gray suit and he carried a briefcase. He said: "Timothy S. Lockwood, your honor."

"Thank you," Carmichael said. Now he looked at Hollis. "You are charged, sir, with several felony crimes, but they are subordinate to the principal charge, which is conspiracy to commit murder and the commission of murder in the first degree. How do you plead?"

"My client pleads not guilty," Lockwood said.

"To all charges?"

"To all charges."

"Please be seated, gentlemen," Carmichael said. "The jury will enter."

Hollis was stunned to silence. He found himself meekly obeying as Lockwood took his arm and led him to a chair. It was a large, high-backed chair, similar to the one he used to excoriate subordinates in his office. The gray-suited man by his side, the one called Lockwood, opened his briefcase. It was indeed, Hollis realized, *the* Timothy S. Lockwood, the legendary defense lawyer with whom he'd dealt briefly after the *Bulletin-News* had been bombed. He'd sent the man home to New York, defeated. How long ago had that been? Thirty years? Forty?

"Just what in the world is this about?" he asked.

"Don't speak," Lockwood said. "Unless I ask you a direct question or put you on the stand, my advice to you is that you do not say a word."

He sat back stiffly. They had not even allowed him the dignity of dressing, dragging him down here in his robe and slippers. Lockwood was studying papers through thick bifocals. He looked very serious. Normally an outrage like this would have caused Hollis to storm with anger, yet he remained very calm; if they thought they could excite him to the point of heart spasms, they were wrong. He would fool them. He found himself chuckling inwardly. Of course he could leave at any time, but he chose not to leave. His curiosity kept him. He glanced around. Behind him was his magnificent collection of weapons, which, he now realized, he'd sadly neglected. He was back at the office, working ten hours a day, and there simply was not time for hobbies. In front of him, arranged on both sides of the desk occupied by Carmichael, were seven chairs. There was another chair, facing front, to the left of the desk. A group of people came single file from the rear, into the light, and occupied the seven chairs.

Hollis scowled. What *was* this? Just what in the hell *was* it? Could it be serious?

Leading the single-file group was Marion Jordan Collingsworth, her proud chin high, her shoulders square, her walk regal. Deborah Reading followed her and then came Peter Russell, Mary Collingsworth, Jane Raymond, and Mitch Evers. They moved slowly. Last came Andrew Collingsworth, walking unassisted, feeling his way to a chair beside Mitch Evers.

"This court," said Nathan Carmichael, "is now in session."

Court? Hollis scoffed. He'd had just about enough of this nonsense. Did they actually take this grotesque charade seriously? Was he indeed on trial? Why was he allowing this absurdity to continue? And, even if it were real, how could he expect a fair verdict from a jury of his enemies? Surely, all those seated before him were indeed his enemies, once his friends, companions, progeny, and lovers. But now they were his enemies. He had tried to help them to make something of themselves; thankless, they had turned against him.

Demming was into his opening statement. "We will prove, beyond doubt, the guilt of the defendant. We will show this court that he has a remorseless soul, a devious mind capable of evil machinations, and a heart incapable of showing the slightest pangs of conscience."

He went on for ten minutes, waving his hands and pacing, speaking rapidly in the manner of a Bible-pounding evangelist, his voice rising and echoing. He read the law, cited precedents, and then entered into the record certain pages of a document with which Hollis had absolute familiarity.

He was on his feet. "Wait! Where did you get that?"

"Counselor, please restrain your client," Carmichael said.

Lockwood took Hollis's elbow, but Hollis shook him away. "I refuse to put up with this nonsense," he said. "I will not sit through a witch-hunt in my own home."

"Please restrain yourself, Mr. Collingsworth," Lockwood said.

Hollis looked at him. Their eyes met briefly. In the lawyer's eyes was a spark of something, a glimmer that seemed to be almost mischievous, and his manner was calm, reassuring. Hollis sat down. Demming continued with his opening statement, finishing it in about five minutes. Hollis sat squirming. Soon he would terminate this nonsense. He would

order them out. Lockwood rose and said he had no opening
statement. Demming began to call witnesses. He called Peter
Russell first.

"Tell me, Peter, do you now know who your natural father
is?"

"It is Hollis Collingsworth."

"And your mother?"

"Deborah Reading."

So, Peter knew. Of course he knew. No doubt he'd read the
diary. He'd also no doubt read Thomas Collingsworth's journal; it was certain that Andrew had given it to Peter. But that
was all right. Peter was a Collingsworth, a Collingsworth by
blood. Hollis squinted. He looked at them. They would pay
for this. But not Peter. He was still the one. They couldn't
fool him, take him away from the opportunities still open to
him. It was all right that he knew. Perhaps he'd known all
along; perhaps he'd played a game, pretending not to know.
Hollis chuckled. Blood showed. Blood always showed.

Demming droned on, questioning Peter. "About August of
1964 did you inform your guardian, Professor Carmichael,
that you planned to marry a young lady named Carol Kingsley?"

"Yes."

"What was Professor Carmichael's reaction?"

"He said that he sanctioned the marriage."

"What happened to Miss Kingsley?"

"She was killed in a windstorm on Cape Cod," Peter said,
his voice barely a whisper. "Or, so the record showed."

"Then you do not believe her death was an accident?"

"I think she was murdered," Peter said.

Lockwood jumped up, his eyes alive. "Objection! The
question was leading and there is no evidence for the
conclusion."

"Sustained," Carmichael intoned dryly.

Demming excused Peter and called Nathan Carmichael to
the witness stand. Witness stand? Hollis scoffed inwardly. He
must not allow himself to think of this preposterous, shadowy
exercise in childish lunacy as real. Yet it had taken on the
atmosphere and nomenclature of reality; that concerned him
slightly. But he was still certain he could stop it when he
wished. He twisted in his seat. Sweat stung his eyes, obscur-
ing his vision. He would allow this farce to continue only a
little longer.

"You were Peter Russell's guardian," Demming said to Carmichael. "Was it at Hollis Collingsworth's request?"

"Yes."

"You were, in effect, in his employ?"

"I was paid by him, yes."

"Were you aware that Mr. Hunter once appeared as a hostile witness before a Senate subcommittee investigating crime?"

"Yes."

Now it was enough—more than enough. Hollis's eyes rolled. He licked his lips, tasting his sweat. He knew what it was all about. They were trying to undermine him before Peter. They were trying to take Peter away from him, filling his head with lies. He would stop it. But he did not. He seemed powerless to rise. He listened.

"When you heard of Miss Kingsley's death, did you suspect it was not an accident?" Demming asked.

"Yes," Carmichael said.

"Did you suspect that Mr. Collingsworth had something to do with her death?"

"Yes."

Demming turned to Lockwood. "Your witness, sir."

Lockwood approached Carmichael with his fingers in the front pockets of his trousers, his thumbs in his belt loops. His hair fell over his forehead. "You have just said, Professor Carmichael, that you suspected Hollis Collingsworth had something to do with Carol Kingsley's death. Later, when he denied he'd been involved, did you remain suspicious?"

"Yes, I did."

"Then why, Professor Carmichael, didn't you do something about it?"

Carmichael hesitated. His face, sweating in the bright lights, was almost as white as his hair. "There was nothing I could do about it. I had no evidence."

"You could have resigned Mr. Collingsworth's employ."

"I couldn't do that. Because of Peter."

"You had grown to love Peter?"

"He was like a son to me."

"And, by covering up your suspicions, you thought you were doing him a service?"

"Yes."

Lockwood turned away. He looked at Hollis. He looked at the mock jury. He said to no one, to everyone:

"I agreed to take this assignment only because each of you promised me you would not shirk the truth. I will hold you to that promise. If any of you breaks it, I will terminate my function in this matter, recommending you also terminate yours. We are here to discover the truth. The man I am representing, if he is to be accorded his rights, deserves that truth." Lockwood turned back to Carmichael; he resumed his pose, thumbs in his trouser belt loops, fingers in his pockets. "I will ask you now, Professor Carmichael, whether or not part of your reason for not telling Peter Russell of your suspicions and not turning the information over to authorities for investigation was to protect yourself from possible scandal. Is that true?"

"Yes," Carmichael said, his head falling on his chest.

"And during the time you served as Mr. Russell's guardian did you not make numerous trips and bill the costs to Mr. Collingsworth?"

"Yes."

"Did you enjoy the trips?"

"Yes. I did enjoy them."

"And you received a rather liberal compensation for your task, did you not? Some forty thousand dollars a year?"

"Yes."

"Are you sure, Professor Carmichael, that you merely did not want to end a good thing?"

"I wanted to protect Peter."

"But you are a professor of law. Like the wife of Caesar, you are above reproach."

"I fear I shall be a professor of law no more."

"Can you, in fact, honestly sit in judgment of this matter before us?"

"That I can do, and that I will do."

"Thank you," Lockwood said, and strolled to his client.

Hollis had watched the performance in awe. Truly, he now believed, he was on trial, no matter how absurd this mock court; and truly, also, he did have a lawyer, an old man once his antagonist, with views no doubt still diametrically opposite to his, but one devoted to truth and justice. Hollis admired the man and most certainly was happy to have him. If he wasn't exactly enjoying this travesty, he found that it was bearable. He would stay, see it to its end. Then he would talk with Peter, his cards on the table. They would not win Peter from him. That he knew for sure.

Demming called Deborah Reading. She sat primly, an actress to the end, describing her long relationship with Hollis Collingsworth. He listened with alternate disdain and amusement as she told of the promises he'd broken, the indignities he'd inflicted upon her, and his final rejection of her. Hollis snorted. Here he'd put the cunt where she was, trusting her as he'd trusted few others, and she was belittling him before Peter. She'd been nothing to him, he knew now, nothing but a lay, a piece of ass when he was lonely.

"During these times did you feel concern for Peter Russell?" Demming asked, adding: "Your son?"

"Of course I did."

"Was the concern particularly acute at any point?"

"Yes. After the attack on Andrew Collingsworth."

"You assumed Hollis Collingsworth would then turn to Peter Russell, becoming his patron?"

"I think he was waiting all along for Peter," she said. "Waiting to pounce on him."

Lockwood rose to cross-examine, but first he turned to speak to everyone. "If anyone here, including the defendant, wishes to terminate this session, please speak up now. If we agree to go on, and your silence will indicate to me that we do agree, then we must also agree to pursue this undertaking to its end." He waited. Silence. Lockwood said: "Mr. Collingsworth, you may leave if you wish. But I don't think you will, for you are not a man who runs. You'll stay?" Again he paused; again there was silence. "All right. It is done. As you know, I have taken statements from each of you here, with the exception of the defendant, so I have much information about you in my possession. I am an outsider, but that does not disqualify me from understanding. On the contrary, it qualifies me eminently, because I can view this matter objectively, without emotional impediments. Now, Miss Reading, you said you were concerned about Peter Russell, your son Peter Russell. Then you loved him?"

"Why, yes, of course."

"Why then didn't you attempt to claim him earlier?"

"I wanted to see him get a good education."

"But you could have provided him with that, surely."

"Well, I . . . I considered him to be in excellent hands, with Professor Carmichael guiding him. And the professor kept me informed about him, by letter."

"When did you make your last picture, Miss Reading?"

"Why, it was several years ago."

"So now, a woman of leisure, you felt you had time for Peter?"

"No. It isn't that. I felt Hollis was claiming him."

"And you considered that harmful to him?"

"Yes."

"Why?"

"Because I know Hollis Collingsworth?"

"How often did you see Peter when he was growing up?"

"I saw him only once. In Paris."

"Only once?"

"I was instructed not to see him."

"By whom?"

"Professor Carmichael."

"Come now, Miss Reading," Lockwood said. "You're a spirited woman. If you had wanted to see Peter Russell, you would have found a way to do it."

"That's not true. I did want to see him."

"Yet you made very little effort to do so. You made no effort to claim custody. Miss Reading, is it not possible you ignored your son because he would have been an impediment to your career?"

Deborah's chin firmed. "No. That's not true. And I didn't ignore him."

"All right. You pined for him, felt concern for him, from a distance. You could have taken custody action, but you did not. Were you afraid of scandal?"

"I don't think I want to answer any more of your questions."

"Miss Reading, I have said this should not be done if we fear to carry it to the end. You agreed. Did you not?"

"Yes, I agreed."

"Was it Hollis Collingsworth who ended your relationship?"

"Yes."

"Are you a jealous woman?"

"There is no woman with any feelings who is not a jealous person, Mr. Lockwood."

"I have no more questions of this witness," Lockwood said.

He paused, looking around. His large head jutted from his shoulders as if he had no neck. Hollis was now caught up in it. His eyes searched for Peter but could not find him. No. They would not have Peter. Deborah Reading had been debased, as had Carmichael. Now, perhaps, it was Marion's turn. She was taking the stand.

"At any time during your marriage, Mrs. Collingsworth,

were you afraid of your husband?" Demming asked, pacing.

"I have been, yes. Particularly in the past few months."

"Did he ever physically assault you?"

"No."

"Did he threaten you?"

"There were underlying threats."

"Did he ever embarrass you in public?"

"He was too calculating to do that."

"Calculating?"

"He sought the impression we were harmonious. It was good for business."

"But your marriage is not harmonious?"

"Certainly not in recent years."

"When did you first realize you were afraid of him?"

"I really don't know. It wasn't as if it just happened. He grew progressively more domineering and manipulative. After Andrew was attacked, he showed no remorse, only anger because his plans for Andrew had been ruined."

Hollis scowled. How could she have known his anguish? If he had chosen to grieve in private, was that not his right? This bitch would pay for that remark. What grief did he see in her? There she sat, hurling insults at him, dressed appropriately for the occasion—a black two-piece suit, a thin orange scarf, a single string of pearls—exactly as she would no doubt have dressed if she were testifying in an actual trial. She spoke in a low voice, that of a woman unjustly victimized who had borne outrage for years, without complaint. She had gone too far. She would pay.

"Did you ever fear for your life?" Demming asked.

"I don't really know. But I think he is capable of murder."

"Objection!" Lockwood screamed, leaping up. "That is unsubstantiated opinion."

Demming faced Carmichael. Everyone was so caught up in the proceedings that they used court protocol. It sent a shiver down Hollis's spine. Demming said slowly:

"Your honor, I maintain this witness has knowledge and the court has evidence to show that the statement is not unsubstantiated opinion."

"I overrule the objection," Carmichael said.

"Why do you believe your husband is capable of murder?" Demming asked.

"May I amend my statement slightly?"

"You may."

"He might not be capable of putting a gun to someone's head and pulling the trigger, for that does take some intestinal fortitude. But I believe he is capable of arranging murder."

Lockwood jumped up again. "Your honor, I object! This line of interrogation must *stop*! This is a trial, not a forum for the discharging of personal animosities."

"I rule that the questioning is proper," Carmichael said.

Lockwood went forward. Color had crept into his cheeks and his jaw trembled as he spoke. "We are here to seek justice, not to air vendettas. I object strenuously to this attempt to prejudice the jury by character assassination from a disgruntled woman."

"Your objection has been noted," Carmichael said. "I refuse to sustain it."

Lockwood clumped back to Hollis's side, fuming, genuinely angry. Hollis smiled. The old lawyer was giving his all to his last case. This was one man he should have hired years ago.

"Why do you say he is capable of arranging murder?" Demming asked Marion.

"There is proof, in his diary, in his own handwriting, that he called this man Hunter after he discovered Peter was going to marry Carol Kingsley. That call resulted in her death."

"What else?"

"He talked with Hunter about the union executive, Mr. Lukens, who later disappeared."

Lockwood advanced, gesturing, his bulldog's brow wrinkled. "I wish to correct her last statement," he told Carmichael. "The diary shows Hollis Collingsworth discussed Mr. Lukens with Hunter *after* Mr. Lukens disappeared."

Carmichael noted the error. "Thank you," he said. "Proceed."

Lockwood whirled. "The diary, Mrs. Collingsworth. Where did you get it?"

"I found it in his desk."

"While he was away?"

"He was in the hospital."

"Shall we then say you purloined this material? Filched it?"

"I suppose that's correct, Mr. Lockwood."

"You've said your husband is capable of arranging murder. Does his diary suggest he asked Hunter to go that far?"

"There is innuendo to that effect."

"Innuendo is not fact, Mrs. Collingsworth."

"Then we will leave it at innuendo."

Lockwood hovered above her, a hawk ready to pounce. "In the many years of your marriage, did you help your husband?"

"I most certainly did."

"In what ways?"

"Many ways. He was unmannered when we met. Crude."

"So you influenced him in social graces?"

"I influenced him in many ways."

"Were you always faithful to him?"

"Yes."

"Yet he was not faithful to you."

"Oh, his affairs were trifling, like that Raymond woman."

"Did you consider Miss Reading a threat to your marriage?"

"No."

"Indeed, did she not become your friend?"

"She asked me to help her. She was concerned about Peter."

"So you conspired, using stolen documents, to bring down Hollis Collingsworth? Are you sure of your motivation? Didn't just a part of you seek to punish your husband, perhaps for years of infidelity?"

"We conspired, as you phrase it, only to save Peter."

"If you were so concerned about Peter, why were you not concerned earlier about saving your own son from him?"

"I—I didn't realize what he was doing."

"Come now, Mrs. Collingsworth, you're a very perceptive woman. Isn't it true that you were too busy with your social life to pay much attention to Peter? Or your own children, for that matter?"

"No. That is not true."

"And these documents. Didn't you withhold them from public scrutiny for fear of a scandal, one that could involve you because it involved your husband?"

She looked up. "I didn't want scandal. That's true."

"I have no more questions, Mrs. Collingsworth."

Lockwood said he'd call only two witnesses for the defense. The first was Peter Russell. Looking at him, Hollis thought again, *Yes. He is the one*. He felt stimulated, exhilarated. He hadn't felt so young, or so strong, in years.

"Peter, whose idea was this trial?" Lockwood asked.

"It started with Nathan Carmichael."

"And you all sort of seized upon it?"

"Yes."

"Is it going as you thought it would?"

"Not exactly. You are a very good man with a curve ball."

"So perhaps you are learning more than you thought you would learn."

"I see matters in a slightly different light, yes."

"Now, Peter, when Professor Carmichael brought you Hollis Collingsworth's diary, and you read it, what were your thoughts?"

"It was overwhelming. Suddenly, all the answers were there."

"Did it make you feel anger toward Hollis Collingsworth?"

"Some anger, yes. I also felt pity."

"And disappointment? After all, this man was your sponsor, your supporter."

"I think I was just a little too amazed to think about that."

"What do you think of him now?"

Peter said slowly, "I haven't quite made up my mind about him."

"Why didn't you take the information to law-enforcement officers?"

"Because Professor Carmichael and I thought the evidence insufficient."

"Insufficient or inadmissible?"

"Both. There were inconsistencies and ambiguities in the documents that left it vague concerning exactly what actions Mr. Collingsworth had taken."

"Now you are being vague, Peter. What were the inconsistencies in the documents pertinent to his trial?"

Peter drew some papers from a manila file folder. He said: "Here is one entry: 'Investigation shows Carol K. to be a student revolutionary. *Must* prevent Peter's marriage to her. Carmichael too soft, incompetent. Will phone Hunter.' And here, a later entry: 'Matter handled. Accidental death. Am not pleased. Told Hunter no violence. Will sever all relationships with him. I am satisfied the death was an accident, however, and the matter is closed.'"

"Rather than inconsistent, Peter, is that not instead incriminating?" Lockwood questioned.

"But even with this evidence, which a court might not accept, the matter would have taken months to investigate."

"So you decided to hurry it along, set up your own court?"

"Yes."

Lockwood stood solidly, his arms tightly crossed. "Of course you realize, Peter, since you are a lawyer, that this session is far from a court. The procedure is improper. An actual court would disqualify all of the jurors. If it is a court, it certainly is nothing more than a kangaroo court. Do you agree?"

"It is not a court," Peter said. "But it is a trial."

"What do you hope to accomplish by it?"

"To find the truth."

"And do you think we will find the truth?"

"We've already found much truth."

"What do you want to accomplish in your life, Peter?"

"In terms of career?"

"Yes."

"I want to specialize in criminal law. Defense."

Hollis's hands tightened into fists. Defense? He had put this boy through law school so that he could defend criminals? What did defense attorneys do besides freeing criminals, scum like Donald Sheehan, so they could strike again? He must talk to Peter, show him how foolish the idea was. Perhaps he had made a mistake, stayed too far in the background as Peter grew up. But a man couldn't do everything at once. He would rectify that—as soon as this foolishness ended.

Lockwood continued: "At one time you were interested in a political career, were you not?"

"Yes," Peter said.

"How deeply were you interested in politics?"

"Very deeply, once."

"No longer?"

"I'm still interested."

"You said you wanted to discover truths, Peter. Let's probe for some truths. When Hollis Collingsworth offered you a convenient shortcut to political success, wasn't your head turned? Wasn't your ego swelled?"

"I'll admit that was true."

"You had some goals. To solve the riddle of your parentage was one. Another was to find out what really caused the death of a young woman you loved. True?"

"Yes. Of course."

"Isn't it also true that Hollis Collingsworth took your mind off these goals? That you closed your eyes to them?"

"Somewhat, yes."

"I suggest—almost completely. All your life you'd been lonely, confused. Now you had attention. Couldn't you see yourself getting the attention of the masses? Rising rapidly?"

"He said I could."

"And you believed him?"

"He is a very persuasive man."

"Could he persuade you now? After what you know? I want the truth, Peter, the absolute truth."

"I—I just don't know."

"You may step down," Lockwood said. "I call Hollis Collingsworth to the stand."

He didn't have to go. He could turn and walk out. Yet he did go, moving slowly, his head high, and seated himself in the uncomfortable chair next to Carmichael.

"Mr. Collingsworth," Lockwood asked, "is Peter Russell your son?"

He hesitated, then answered: "Yes."

"Yet you went to elaborate lengths to shield the knowledge from him, even putting a false story in your paper about the death of his parents, in case he investigated. Why?"

"Because I didn't know how he'd turn out. Offspring you can't guide directly can turn out bad, embarrass you."

"Your father kept a journal. You kept a diary. An entry suggests you asked a man named Hunter to look into a matter concerning Carol Kingsley."

"I don't know a Carol Kingsley. Or a Hunter."

"It is in your diary."

"You keep talking about a diary. I don't know anything about a diary. What you have is fake."

"Why do you think this session was called?"

"To frame me. That's pretty apparent." His fists drummed his legs. He would end this interrogation, but not before he'd had his say. "They're trying to prove I'm incompetent. They want to lock me up. They want Peter to think I'm a son of a bitch who controls and ruins people. They want my money. They want my power. But they won't get it. They've got to earn it."

"Have you earned it, Mr. Collingsworth?"

"Of course I earned it. I worked. I built it." He rammed his fingers together defiantly and crouched forward, his thumbs under his chin. His eyes bulged. "It's mine. It goes to no one who doesn't earn it. These people aren't friends. They're enemies." He began to speak rapidly, his hands gesturing, defying interruption. A rage was building in him, swelling the blood vessels in his neck and forehead. "Anybody who has accomplished something big is going to have enemies. There are few he can trust, men or women. I found that out early. Trust somebody, they turn on you. I built something for gain and there's no law against that, just as there's no law against trying to create somebody who's capable of carrying it on. That's a man's duty." He paused, wiping foam from his lips and spittle from his chin. He fought waves of tiredness. "Some of them said tonight they were afraid of me. Well, I was afraid, too, maybe of them and certainly of others. My father made it, so he had enemies that might turn on me. I made it bigger and that meant more enemies. A man has to protect himself. You can't go around feeling sorry for people who can't look out for themselves. I must protect what I made. If it goes to the wrong people, they'd give it away. Maybe they'd let in the labor unions, do even that. Labor tried to bomb me out of business. Now they say they've reformed. Have they? No. Certainly not. They've only changed. Changed from bombers to acid throwers. What do these people know? My own wife invades my privacy when I'm flat on my back. I give a career to Demming and he crosses me and lies to me. I create a movie star, make a hick famous and spill out words to her I've never told anyone, and even she never understood I acted not as I wanted to do but as I had to. Everybody is out to get what they can. If you teach your offspring anything but that, you're doing them a disservice." He was breathing hard. His mouth was dry. Exhaustion closed in around him. "I'll tell you this," he said, gasping. "You can't take me. I'm too big for you. I'm too big for all of you together. Get out of here. Out of my house."

He stopped. A long silence ensued. Then Lockwood said: "You may step down, Mr. Collingsworth. I have no more questions."

Demming waved cross-examination and immediately began to sum up for the prosecution, pacing in front of Carmichael and the seven-person mock jury. Hollis Collingsworth, he said, was a consummate manipulator of lives, twisting and forming others for his own benefit. He called Andrew's misfortune a perfect example of the sins of the father visited upon the son. He said there was a murderer in their midst— the accused—and he must not go unpunished. Demming spoke for ten minutes, an oration evangelically styled, and ended with a flourish.

"Ladies and gentlemen, you have not until now had the courage to resist or repudiate this man. None of us have. Perhaps we have not had the will. But we must now. You must see that he is guilty. You must be unafraid to judge him. Thank you."

When Lockwood rose for the defense summation, he drew an object from his briefcase and showed it to the jurors. "It is a chess pawn, as you see," he said. "A small wooden figure who looks quite dejected. And why should he be cheerful? He is the soldier who will be sacrificed for a greater cause. He is defenseless and manipulated. You here no doubt think of yourselves as pawns, used in another's drive for control and accomplishment. Are you? Perhaps so. But why?" He paused, holding the pawn up before them, between his thumb and forefinger. "I suspect strongly it was because you came willingly to it and did nothing to escape it. You see, ladies and gentlemen, you are not made of wood. You have brains and bodies and wills of your own. But you looked down the easy road, accepting it, and now in unison like so many ants in attack, you turn against him, the man who directed you. You ask for what you call justice and truth, when in actuality what you want is vengeance, forgetting that in vengeance we take on the characteristics of those upon whom we inflict our rage."

He turned away and then whirled toward the jury, startling its members. "All of you stand accused. Before you judge, look to your mirrors. You have already betrayed yourselves and each other here tonight, some of you revealing inner motivations that were far from truthful and hardly noble." Lockwood was warming to his act. His hands began to wave. "In cross-examination I have shown Nathan Carmichael's actions and inactions to be at least in part self-motivated. And Deborah Reading, admire her as we do, accepted the defendant's sponsorship willingly, and only after achieving her personal goals did her heart begin to respond as a mother. Marion Jordan Collingsworth has accused her husband of machinations, yet she has shown us she is also capable of machinations. And Peter Russell has admitted that a powerful man's attention and flattery swayed him from his goal of discovering the truth behind the death of a woman he loved.

"Am I too harsh? Do I exaggerate? We here are a court that judges. We cannot disparage a man whose hands are dirty if ours also are unclean. And there are others here who sit in judgment. Mary Collingsworth, weeping and drinking, blames the inattention of her father. Yet she cashes her father's checks. And Andrew Collingsworth, we feel for you as a victim of your father's sins, yet we must remind you that in the final analysis you abandoned your resistance to his ways.

And you did not resist his support. Mitchell Evers. Jane Raymond. You served with little objection. You forgot that compromising a moral principle to fulfill petty aspirations leads not to happiness but to despair."

Lockwood's cheeks were glowing. Beads of perspiration ran down his face. He took an enormous red handkerchief from his pocket and wiped his forehead. Slowly he walked across the room to where Myron Demming sat.

"I have very little to say to you or about you, sir, except you are very likely the most ignoble example of all. I decided not to question you before the bench because I concluded you have no respect for the truth and therefore your testimony would be meaningless. It would have been time wasted."

Now Lockwood moved to center stage, full in the spotlight. "I am not saying I am defending a man I consider to be a good man, but perhaps he is a man who cannot help himself. He is a throwback. He has been unable to adapt to the times. He professes to be the strongest, but perhaps he is the weakest, for he could not break the mold set for him by his father. So in reality *he* is the pawn. In awe of his father, he did not have the courage to escape control, even after his father's death. Perhaps it is not too late for this man to change. Does he deserve another chance? Will he, if spared, revert to his original state? When you judge that, ask yourselves if you deserve another chance. Because this man, I submit, will revert to his old ways only if you let him.

"I ask, if not mercy, then at least understanding. This man who controlled was himself controlled. And was he in control of the crime we are judging today? I submit that he set into motion a chain reaction over which he had absolutely no control." Lockwood paused, again striking his pose, an old actor in his final role. "Who is to judge how another person lives his life when that life was predetermined from birth? And who himself is not guilty—that person alone shall declare another guilty. The case for the defense rests."

The mock jury rose and filed out, as if to consider a verdict. Nathan Carmichael sat unmoving at the desk that had become a bench of law; Lockwood stored away documents in his briefcase; Demming began to pace, very slowly. Hollis squirmed in thick sweat. Had they locked the door behind him? What time was it? He closed his eyes. Perhaps he slept. He opened his eyes when he heard Carmichael speak.

"Have you reached a verdict?"

"We have," answered Marion Collingsworth.

"Will the defendant rise," Carmichael said.

Rise? All right, he would rise, rise and walk away, hurling back at them the insults they had inflicted on him. Yet when he did rise, assisted by Lockwood, he did not walk away. He stood there, facing his inquisitors, his hands now beginning to tremble. The shadowy group wavered in front of him; again it seemed a dream sequence, unbound by time and undefined by dimension.

"What is your verdict?" Carmichael asked.

Marion's eyes were downcast. She seemed to fade into the background, with only her face showing. "We find the defendant," she said slowly, "to be not guilty."

He stayed in the gun room after they had all left, waiting for Peter to return. They had tried to end him, resorting to child's play, trickery and charades, but they had failed. They had not shattered his grand design, his dream. He had won. They had not shown him his guilt; instead, they had been shown their own. They knew now they were willing pawns, eager to be led. Hollis sat unafraid in the semidarkness amid his weapons, rubbing his hands and chuckling, waiting for Peter. They would take a trip together, plan together. He would open vistas the boy never thought possible. Behind him, he heard a door opening; he stood and turned to see light entering from the corridor outside. Peter Russell came in. He hesitated and then walked slowly toward Hollis. It seemed that the light followed him.

"I knew you'd come," Hollis said, holding out his hands.

Peter stopped. "I was looking for Timothy Lockwood. Has he left?"

"Lockwood? Of course he's left. They've all left. It's only you and me now. That's all we need."

"I think you should go upstairs and get some sleep. I know it's been an ordeal for you."

His words rushed out. "Yes, and no thanks to you. The others, I could see how they would dream up a stupid act like this. But you? I don't understand that. I guess you just wanted them to be shown up for what they are."

"I wanted truth," Peter said. "I've not had much of that in my life."

Hollis gestured. "But you didn't get truth just now. You got lies. All *lies!*" His eyes were moist, smarting with sweat. He spoke rapidly. "They tried to railroad me, using fake documents, making things up. They want my money. They want to see me dead."

"I don't think so. I know I don't want your money—or anything else to do with you."

"I won't listen to talk like that. You can't run out now."

"But I will," Peter said. "I'm not coming back. What I do in the future I will do on my own."

"You *can't* go! We're just starting! Do you realize what I'm offering you?" His body trembled. His throat was dry. Pain burned his brain. "I paid for you. I took care of you. You do realize that you were the one, don't you? All along, you were the one. I was just playing with Demming. I was never serious about Andrew. I am about you. Come here now. Peter?"

Their eyes met in a long look. Peter was a mirror in time, taking Hollis back to his own youth; he was every Collingsworth, his father and his father's father. His bearing and voice, his eyes and manner of walk: he was Collingsworth in body and in mind and in blood.

"Don't be a fool and throw it away," Hollis said slowly. "Only a fool would walk out now. And you're no fool." He flashed a wet-mouthed smile. He wiped his chin with the back of his hand. "You're from strong stock. You have the blood."

"I'm not a horse bred for racing," Peter said, meeting Hollis's stare. "I know exactly who I am now. I am not you."

He strolled away. Hollis stood alone, peering around. His vision was blurred. He choked, fighting anger; bile filled his mouth, foul and bitter. He spat it out. He stormed down the rows of weapons, kicking over tables and strewing pistols and rifles and shotguns all about. He scooped up the weapons and dashed them to the floor. Then his rage subsided. Before him was his portrait and that of his father. He moved forward, his heartbeat slowing, and touched the texture of the paintings. Collingsworth eyes gazed down at him. He was on his knees. A sense of peace and well-being calmed him. It would be all right. Peter would return. He knew it. A man could repudiate another individual, but a man could not repudiate his blood. Hollis turned and surveyed the wreckage of his gun room, his arms raised and his fists tight, feeling the strength of generations surge through his veins like a flame.

EPILOGUE

MITCH EVERS EMERGED from the gun room into the pool and cabana area of Green Manor, fumbling for a Camel. The first burst of dawn broke the black sky with pink streaks. He heard the shrill cry of birds. Peter Russell came up to him, a large package in his hands.

"For you," he said, handing it to Mitch.

"What is it?"

"It's something I got from Andrew. You'll see."

Mitch looked at him. "Well," he said, puffing. "You have your answers. How do you feel now?"

"I feel just slightly undressed."

"We all do. What's the next step?"

"Right now? I'm going to find Professor Carmichael. And, after that, I'm going to find Lockwood."

"So long, Harvard."

"Good-bye, Mitch." They shook hands. Mitch grasped the package. "Do what you must with it," Peter Russell said.

Marion walked with Timothy Lockwood, listening to the song of the mockingbirds. Their cries had often awakened her in disgust, but now she thought their tones beautiful. "Mr. Lockwood," she said, "you are not a lawyer. You are a therapist."

"As your doctor, then, I should like to ask you to get your husband back to bed."

"I will. He'll rage like a lion, but I will."

She went first to Deborah Reading by the pool. Deborah looked up. Her face was radiant. They didn't speak; somehow, there was nothing to say. Marion looked up at Green Manor, her head high.

*   *   *

Myron Demming stomped into the gazebo, interrupting Peter and Nathan Carmichael. "I want you to know that Lockwood's attack on me was a filthy lie," he snapped.

"If you say so, we believe you," Nathan said, "for you are an acknowledged authority on lying."

Demming winced. He snorted and clumped away.

Peter looked into Nathan's eyes. "My next stop is the Cape. I'm going to tell Amelia everything."

"Will we see each other again?"

"That's certain," Peter said.

"I'll be at Harvard, back preaching the law."

"Then we'll see each other soon."

Nathan rose and walked slowly away, slump shouldered. Peter waited until he no longer heard the professor's footfalls. Then he walked out into the gold-fringed light. He heard his name called and turned to face Deborah Reading.

"I couldn't go until I explained something," she said. "Regardless of what was said in there, I did want to see you. Desperately, at times."

"I believe that."

"I'd like you to come home with me."

"I can't do that." He glanced at her, a stranger who was his mother, and he knew she would always be a stranger. Amelia was more a part of him than Deborah Reading, just as Nathan was more of him than Hollis Collingsworth. "You see, I have confidence now that I can make it on my own."

"With no one close to you?"

"I didn't say that. I want to be close to someone, but never totally dependent. I'm free now."

"He won't give you up, you know."

"He has no choice." Peter smiled. He held out his hand to her. "I still have the ring you gave me that day."

"Yes," she said, kissing his fingers.

"I'll always keep it."

Her lovely face was full with concern. "We won't ever see each other again, will we?"

"Of course we will."

"I know you have to go now. Let me go first. I don't want to watch you walking away."

He circled the block twice before he found Lockwood on a bus-stop bench. Peter stopped his rented Ford. "C'mon," he said, motioning. "I'll take you to the airport."

Lockwood peered at him. "Airport, nothing. You wouldn't find me there dead. The train gives you time to read."

"Then it's the train station. Get in."

Lockwood did. He sat silently for a while. Then he asked: "Were you serious about that? Criminal law?"

"Yep."

"Take the train with me. I'll teach you some tricks."

"I'm way ahead of you. It just so happens that I already have our tickets."

"A real manipulator, aren't you?" Lockwood flashed a full-faced grin. "Chip off the old block."

Andrew walked by, on Mary's arm, as Mitch Evers took Jane to her car. It was difficult to tell who was leading whom, but they were both smiling.

"Hi, champ," Mitch said. "How's the left hook?"

"Better than the right flipper," Andrew said, laughing.

They went away, skipping like children. Mitch opened the car door for Jane. When she was inside, fumbling in her purse for her key, he asked: "Do you know what day this is?"

"Sunday."

"More than that. It's Palm Sunday."

"What does that have to do with the price of rice in China?"

"Palm Sunday. Easter. The resurrection." He looked at her, half loving her. "Thanks for coming. It took guts."

"I'll be frank. I have a network offer and I don't think I would have done this without that offer in back of me."

"Still all career, is it?"

"Not totally. In fact, I want you to come home with me. Right now."

"I have work to do."

"On Sunday? Palm Sunday?" Her eyes fell. "I don't want to lose you, Mitch."

"Well, I'll be around," he said. "Face in the crowd."

He watched her car until it was gone, then found his battered VW and chugged it home. He went to his apartment, a plastic briefcase under his arm. The place smelled like an elephant cage; stale cigarette and gin smells. He pushed up the window. It was home and would be for a long time to come. Mitch opened the briefcase and took out the package Peter had given him. Thomas Collingsworth's journal, Hollis Collingsworth's diary. He grinned. Harvard. A great kid with a great future. On his own. He fired up a Camel, sat down at his desk, and cranked paper into his ancient L. C. Smith. He wrote:

THE KINGMAKERS
A Novel
By Mitchell Evers

ABOUT THE AUTHOR

ARELO SEDERBERG, who lives and works in Los Angeles, is currently managing editor of television's Financial News Network. From 1962–70 he was on the financial news staff of the *Los Angeles Times*, and from 1970–78 he worked as a public relations representative for financier Howard Hughes. Arelo Sederberg's earlier novel, THE POWER PLAYERS, was published by Bantam in 1981.

DON'T MISS
THESE CURRENT
Bantam Bestsellers

SPECIAL
MONEY SAVING
OFFER

Now you can have an up-to-date listing of Bantam's hundreds of titles plus take advantage of our unique and exciting bonus book offer. A special offer which gives you the opportunity to purchase a Bantam book for only 50¢. Here's how!

By ordering any five books at the regular price per order, you can also choose any other single book listed (up to a $4.95 value) for just 50¢. Some restrictions do apply, but for further details why not send for Bantam's listing of titles today!

Just send us your name and address plus 50¢ to defray the postage and handling costs.

RELAX!

SIT DOWN

and Catch Up On Your Reading!

☐	24607	**LINES AND SHADOWS** by Joseph Wambaugh	$4.50
☐	23845	**THE DELTA STAR** by Joseph Wambaugh	$3.95
☐	20822	**GLITTER DOME** by Joseph Wambaugh	$3.95
☐	22750	**THE KINGMAKERS** by Arelo Sederberg	$3.95
☐	24493	**DENNISON'S WAR** by Adam Lassiter	$3.50
☐	24172	**NATHANIEL** by John Saul	$3.95
☐	23336	**GOD PROJECT** by John Saul	$3.95
☐	24234	**MAY DAY IN MAGADAN** by Anthony Olcott	$3.50
☐	24116	**A CONSPIRACY OF EAGLES** by Bart Davis	$3.50
☐	23792	**THE COP WHO WOULDN'T QUIT** by Rick Nelson	$3.95
☐	22753	**THE GUNS OF HEAVEN** by Pete Hamill	$2.95
☐	23709	**OMEGA DECEPTION** by Charles Robertson	$3.50
☐	24646	**THE LITTLE DRUMMER GIRL** by John Le Carre	$4.50
☐	23987	**THE TAKERS** by Wm. Flanagan	$2.95
☐	23577	**THE SEEDING** by David Shobin	$2.95
☐	23678	**WOLFSBANE** by Craig Thomas	$3.95
☐	23420	**THE CIRCLE** by Steve Shagan	$3.95
☐	22746	**RED DRAGON** by Thomas Harris	$3.95
☐	23838	**SEA LEOPARD** by Craig Thomas	$3.95
☐	20353	**MURDER AT THE RED OCTOBER** by Anthony Olcott	$2.95
☐	24606	**THE SWITCH** by Elmore Leonard	$2.95
☐	24609	**THE TENTH CRUSADE** by Christopher Hyde	$3.25

Prices and availability subject to change without notice.

Buy them at your local bookstore or use this handy coupon for ordering: